Freda Lightfoot

Freda Lightfoot was born in Lancashire but lived in the Lake District for many years where she was a teacher, a bookseller and a smallholder. She is married with two grown-up daughters and still visits the Lakes as often as she can. Her first two Lakeland sagas, *Luckpenny Land* and *Wishing Water*, are also available from Coronet.

Polly's War

Freda Lightfoot

CORONET BOOKS

Hodder & Stoughton

To the memory of my beloved Anna
Wherever I am there's always you

Copyright © 2000 by Freda Lightfoot

First published in 2000
by Hodder and Stoughton
First published in paperback in 2000
by Hodder and Stoughton
A division of Hodder Headline
A Coronet Paperback

The right of Freda Lightfoot to be identified as the Author of
the Work has been asserted by her in accordance with the
Copyright, Designs and Patents Act 1988.

10 9 8 7 6 5 4

British Library Cataloguing in Publication Data
Lightfoot, Freda M.
  Polly's war
  1. Manchester (England) – Fiction   2. Domestic fiction
  I. Title
  823.9'14[F]

ISBN 0 340 71535 9

Typeset by Avocet Typeset, Brill, Aylesbury, Bucks
Printed and bound in Great Britain by
Mackays of Chatham PLC, Chatham, Kent

Hodder and Stoughton
A division of Hodder Headline
338 Euston Road
London NW1 3BH

Chapter One

1945

Polly Pride stared at her boss open-mouthed. 'Laying me off? I'm thinking that's a mean-minded, low-spirited thing to be doing to a body, particularly since you know I'm the family breadwinner just now.'

'Your Charlie no better then?' Jack Lawson had the grace to look uncomfortable, as well he might faced with the blistering Irish temper which now confronted him.

Standing with her fists bunched against her slim waist, Polly Pride was an awesome sight even in a crossover pinny. She was a handsome woman, her dark shining hair with its glint of red catching the light as she shook her head at him, greeny-grey eyes flashing dangerously. The fact that she was still known as Polly Pride for all she'd been wed to Charlie Stockton, her second husband, for near a decade spoke volumes. 'Indeed you know full well he's been off work these three weeks past. So how are we to manage without a wage coming in, will ye tell me that?'

Lawson's solemn face did not soften the slightest degree. 'Same as everyone else, Poll. By doing the best you can. Anyroad, your Benny'll be home from the front soon, and your Lucy's chap. That's why we have to let all you women go, to make way for our boys.' He raised his voice a little, glancing about him as if appealing to their better nature, but more than one woman in the workshop shook a clenched fist and told him where he could stick the cards he was giving them all.

'Put 'em where the sun don't shine,' yelled one, not known for her finesse.

'Aye, and then take a long jump off th'end of Irwell Street Bridge.'

Many of the women no longer had husbands, brothers or fathers to come home, and those men who had survived in one piece weren't necessarily coming home to them. Jack Lawson turned away, almost at a run, so eager was he to evade their accusations and sharp wit. The workers in this warehouse close by Potato Wharf weren't the only ones to get the chop, not by a long chalk. The building had served as a store for many things during the long war: cotton, timber, packing cases, even food. Now it was returning to its original purpose – a print works. There'd be no employment there for women like these.

The waters of the canal basin looked as black as ever,

thick with oil and clogged with rubbish, seeming to mirror the women's dour mood as Polly and her friends made their way home at the end of their morning shift. For all they'd dreamed of this day for years, happily planned the celebrations for weeks, yet there was precious little laughter as they walked up Medlock Street and past Liverpool Road Goods Station, the taste of coal dust in their mouths and the whistling and shunting of trains loud in their ears so they had to raise their voices to shout to each other.

It had been the most exciting summer anyone could remember. They'd already enjoyed VE Day with jubilant street parties as well as the usual May Day Parades, with Shire horses bedecked in ribbons and rosettes and the coronations of the various district May Queens. Now, with the surrender of Japan, hostilities really were at an end and red, white and blue bunting flapped joyously in the breeze, criss-crossing every street the women passed through, hung from bedroom windows more accustomed to blackout curtains during the long days of war. A Union Jack was painted on a back yard wall, the hammer and sickle also displayed side by side with the stars and stripes; bright, brave flags heralding a day the likes of which had never before been seen, not even in Manchester where they knew how to have a good laugh. They'd soldiered on and 'med do' for nigh on six years, and they were only too ready for a good knees-up.

Bright-eyed children were everywhere in threadbare

jerseys with holes in the sleeves. Boys in sleeveless pullovers and trousers they would 'grow into', hung on elastic braces, sparked their clogs on the setts as they kicked a ball about; girls were skipping in skimpy cotton frocks, dirty bare feet thrust into scuffed sandals, not a hair ribbon among them to hold back shining bobbed hair recently washed and trimmed for the celebration. But their singsong voices rang out with youthful joy and confidence in the future, one their mothers were now beginning to fear.

'Ta ra,' the women called as one by one they peeled off and went home to make dinner for their children, trying not to worry about what the next week, the next day, might bring.

By the time the remaining stragglers turned the corner into Pansy Street, a long string of a street which jostled with many another around the canal basin, they'd almost convinced themselves that they were performing a public service by allowing themselves to be sacked. Even so there was much bitter talk about how eager the bosses had been to take them on at the start of hostilities when men were scarce on the ground.

'It's all right for you,' Maisie Wright said, as she and Polly broke their linked arms for a moment to dodge a young lad wheeling a barrow load of coal to one of the barges moored on the canal. 'You can start up your precious carpet business again. It's the likes of me who are up the Swanee. What am I supposed to do? I'm too old to go on the streets. I'd have to pay them to take me on,' she joked.

'Nay, lass, you do yourself a disservice,' Maggie Stubbs told her. 'It's experience what counts every time.' And, chuckling at her own droll wit, was already yelling to her brood to 'get t'kettle on' even as she strode in through her open front door.

Perhaps, Polly thought, ready as always to look on the bright side, Maisie was right. Could this be an omen? Someone up above giving her a kick up the backside and telling her to do something different with her life? ' 'Tis mebbe true,' she agreed. 'I could take over the carrier's warehouse and fill it with carpets, so I could.'

'Aye, that'd be grand,' Maisie agreed, happy to go along with the fantasy. 'You could have the swanky manager's office and I'd be foreman and have the pleasure of giving po-faced Jack Lawson the boot.' Both women enjoyed a good laugh at the prospect, but the chuckles soon faded as they neared their own doorsteps.

'Well, me darlin', the war might be over but we still have a fight on our hands,' Polly said, 'if only to earn a decent living. But then, we're expert at looking after ourselves, so we are.'

Even so, as she gently closed her own front door behind her, some of the bright laughter slipped from her face to be replaced by pain and worry.

*

In no time at all, it seemed, the women were back on their doorsteps doing a bit of 'camping', revelling in the undercurrent of building excitement, arms folded over their pinnies, as excited as the children at the prospect of the street party that afternoon to celebrate VJ Day. Others sat on their window sills, the sash windows pulled down to their knees to hold them secure while they vigorously polished already gleaming glass. Today was a day when spit and polish was important, for a husband, son or father could walk in at any minute.

At the far end of Pansy Street a young woman knelt scrubbing a doorstep, her neat figure moving rhythmically with the effort, nose pert and mouth tight with concentration. A lock of soft brown hair fell across her brow. Lucy Shackleton pushed it away tiredly with her hand then sat back on her heels to survey the length of the street.

' 'Ave you not finished yon steps yet? You want to shape thissen, I haven't got all day.'

Lucy didn't even need to glance up to picture the pale screwed up face and blackcurrant eyes watching her through the window. It was a favourite occupation of Minnie Hopkins, owner of this fine double doorstep which, as she was so often at pains to remind Lucy, should be kept clean enough to eat your dinner off, if you'd a mind. Lucy tried to imagine the old woman pulling up her rocking chair, which she rarely left, to eat her pie and pickles off the whitened steps. It almost

made her laugh out loud but Lucy smothered the giggles
with the flat of her hand just in time.

'Rightio, Mrs Hopkins. I've nearly done, then I'll get
you a nice cuppa,' she called, as cheerfully as she could, and
slid the donkey-stone with a final flourish along the edge
of each step, to add an artistic touch.

'You said that an hour back.'

Lucy did not respond, merely surveyed the two steps
she'd just spent the best part of an hour cleaning. She'd
scrubbed them with a solution of washing soda so strong
her hands were red raw, then whitened them with a
donkey-stone got from the rag-and-bone man. They must
be the cleanest steps in all of Pansy Street and that was
saying something. But then nobody in this part of
Castlefield would be seen dead with a dirty doorstep,
despite all the muck dropped on to them from the movement of coal from barge to warehouse and back again, not
to mention factory chimneys constantly belching smoke.

Manchester's chief claim to fame was that although its
rows of back-to-back houses might be black, its cotton was
the whitest and finest in the north, if not the world, its men
the most inventive and skilful, and its women the hardest
working and most good-humoured. Give or take one or two
notable exceptions, Lucy thought as she rubbed at an itch
and deposited a smear of dirt on one round pink cheek.

'I suppose you're pushin' to get off to that party? I'll
have no slacking 'ere, nor any work skimped.'

Biting her lip, Lucy managed to hold her silence, which was ever the best armour against Minnie Hopkins's razor-sharp tongue. Lucy began wringing out her cloth and swilling the dirty water down the gutter. Today she didn't care about a moithering old woman who picked fights for no good reason. Today aprons and shawls were to be abandoned in favour of summer frocks and flower-decked hats in honour of the occasion. Eager hands spread margarine and potted meat on thick slices of bread, set out cakes, decanted jellies and wobbly pink blancmanges with a recklessness that denied the self-sacrifice it had taken to save sufficient coupons to purchase such treats. There was laughter in the air, a voice singing *Take Me Back to Dear Old Blighty*, and Lucy could almost smell the very real scent of freedom along with the tar bubbles and sunshine.

Today she refused to fret about the fact that she was bone weary yet had to do every job twice over in this house, though she'd no complaints from the others in which she worked as a cleaner in order to earn an honest living to feed her two children. What did it matter if here at number 179 she was considered to be the lowest of the low, barely fit to polish the mahogany dresser that took up the whole of one wall in the front parlour? She'd cheerfully dusted the many ornaments, the glass lamps with their crystal droplets around the rim, the gloomy pictures — mainly of highland cattle or young girls in smock dresses — without complaint for today was a special day. Today marked the end of the war.

Lucy lifted her gaze to examine the clear blue sky, cherishing the warmth of the sun on her face and the blissful surge of happiness that swelled in her heart at the thought that soon, very soon, her Tom would be home.

She'd worried about him quite a lot lately, what with there being no word for a while – a long while actually. But that'd happened before, she told herself. She'd hear nothing for months then get a bunch of letters all at once. War seemed to be funny that way. Oh, but she would welcome him home, just see if she didn't.

The women were covering the food with cloths now, keeping a weather eye out for marauders and enjoying a brew of tea and a chin-wag before facing the onslaught of the afternoon's festivities. Down at the corner shop, Lucy could see Gladys Benson leaning over her counter to have a natter with her friend Lily Gantry. No doubt swapping tales about the failings and misdemeanours of their respective husbands, both of whom had already returned from the war to a less than jubilant welcome from their wives.

In her mind's eye Lucy could see Tom striding up the street, kit-bag resting on one broad shoulder, a wide grin on his handsome face, fair hair shining. He'd swing Sarah Jane up into his arms and give her a big smacking kiss. Young Sean would be next. Then he'd look teasingly into Lucy's eyes, give her a big wink, and she'd know that her man was home at last and that he still wanted her. Later, when the children were tucked up in bed, perhaps hugging presents from a father they'd hardly ever set eyes on before, Lucy would slip into bed with this handsome stranger who was her own husband and they'd start to get to know each other all over again.

If she was honest Lucy was a bit nervous about this part of her fantasy. Would he still fancy her? Would she still fancy him? She wasn't the giddy young girl she'd been when he went away. She'd become a responsible mother to her two children, though her mother Polly would mind them sometimes so she could enjoy a bit of fun, like going to a dance or the Gaumont with her pals, shouting 'Put a penny in' at the projectionist whenever the film broke down, which was a frequent occurrence.

She'd held down several different jobs during the long war, had money in her purse, run her own life exactly as she pleased. Lucy knew that she'd changed. Perhaps Tom had too. He'd once seemed so strong, so forceful, sweeping her off her feet and arranging for them to be married in a hurry at the local register office, for all he had known that Lucy had longed for a white wedding in the Catholic church. They'd been hard up and far too young, had two children far too quickly, each following one of Tom's leaves home. Only this time he would be home for good. Filled suddenly with a mixture of apprehension and longing, Lucy didn't at first hear the door slam behind her.

'What the hangment are thee up to, dilly-dallying in the

gutter? I don't pay thee for day dreaming.' Startled by the sound of the sharp voice so close to her ear, Lucy dropped the bucket, which rolled noisily away.

Minnie Hopkins stood arms akimbo, brows beetled, small mouth sucked into empty gums. Her false teeth, kept largely for best, would be reposing in a glass on the bamboo table by her high brass bedstead. She'd slip them in later, when she deigned to put in an appearance at the street party, for all she'd stick chiefly to the jellies. In honour of the occasion she was wearing her best brown chenille frock with a marcasite clasp at the vee of the collar. Above this was tucked a lace front that hid her scrawny neck as high as the chin. She looked like a miniature Victorian schoolmistress, holding a broom handle in lieu of a cane. Minnie Hopkins was famous for battling with her yard brush. It was said she'd chased away every likely suitor with it, which was why, at well into her sixties, she was still unwed.

You don't pay me at all, your nephew does, you bad-tempered old goat, Lucy longed to say as she gave chase to the bucket which seemed set on rolling all the way to the bottom of Pansy Street. Moments later, marching down the narrow lobby into the back kitchen, she deposited brushes, bucket and cleaning materials under the brown slopstone, wondering, not for the first time, how the old bat's nephew could tolerate her as well as he did. He must be hard up to have to stop on with an aunt as mad as this one. Or else he had a patience born either of long practice or budding sainthood.

'I've done now, anyroad. How about that cuppa?'

'I don't pay thee for idling over pots of tea neither.'

'I thought it was you what wanted one?' Cut her own nose off to spite her face, Lucy thought. Aloud she said, 'I've plenty other jobs waiting for me when I get done here, so if you don't want anything more, I'm off.'

'Meaning tha's doin' me a favour by findin' time to come at all, is that it?'

'It's always good to be appreciated,' Lucy dryly remarked, smiling politely and not quite meeting that sour gaze in case the old woman should interpret the merry glint in her hazel eyes as insolence and sack her on the spot. This had been threatened so often that there were moments when Lucy almost wished she'd carry out the threat.

Coming twice a week to clean this big draughty house with its seven high-ceilinged bedrooms and heavy Victorian furniture was certainly no joy, with more criticism than thanks at the end of it. But then Lucy would think of Sarah Jane and Sean, the rent and gas and other bills that had to be paid, war or no war, and, as now, she'd bite her lip, placate and calm the quick-tempered old woman, and go home at least with a sense of pride that she was doing her bit without complaint.

She'd made more money when she was working in

munitions with Sal, an old friend who became her sister-in-law when Lucy married her brother, but that had meant leaving the children on their own too much. With cleaning, Lucy could always take them with her if they were a bit off colour. And though it was hard work, she'd done all right, got a bit put by for a rainy day. Even so, she'd be glad enough for Tom to come home and take over this bread-winning lark, so she could tell Minnie Hopkins to stick her job and settle down to enjoying her children. What a treat that would be.

'So where did tha find money to pay for a party, eh?' Minnie pulled out the bucket and cleaning materials that Lucy had just stowed away, and put them all back again in a different order. 'Or asti a fancy man wi' deep pockets tucked away some place?'

'Oh, you badmouthed old . . .' Lucy stopped, seeing the glint of satisfaction in her persecutor's eyes. There was nothing Minnie Hopkins liked better than to stir up trouble but unlike many, Lucy had remained faithful to her husband throughout the duration so she refused to defend herself before this nasty-minded old woman. 'We've all put in coupons. *Which is more than you have, you mean old bat,*' she finished under her breath.

'Go on, what am I?'

'Nothing.' Drat the woman for only being deaf when it suited her. Lucy yanked the curtain across the sink, nearly breaking the wire that held it. Her colour was high, though not nearly so high as her temper as she strode away, spine rigid.

Minnie Hopkins, not one to be outdone or miss an opportunity to have the last word, bustled after her for several paces along the passage. 'Don't you give me any lip, madam. Tek care you don't cut yersel in the knife drawer! You'll collect your cards for that bit of insolence. And don't bother comin' in tomorrer – theer'll be no job for thi to come to.'

'Well, that suits me fine,' Lucy staunchly replied, flinging her apron aside and slamming the vestibule door so hard the glass panel rattled. Once outside, all the fury drained out of her, leaving her weak and shaking with emotion. She had to go and sit on the kerbside for a minute and put her head in her hands while she wished, not for the first time, that her temper wasn't quite so hot; got from her Irish mother, Polly Pride, no doubt. Oh, lord, she'd done it now. What would her mam say?

'By heck, a chap has to watch where he puts his feet on his own front doorstep these days. It's that clean I could eat me dinner off it.'

Lucy turned to greet the newcomer with a ready smile. She liked Michael Hopkins. He was a big, well set up sort of chap with a friendly open face and a thatch of reddish-brown hair that hinted at a streak of Irish blood some-where in his veins, descended no doubt, as her own family was, from one of the immigrant Irish who had come to work in Manchester during the last century. Not that he sounded Irish. He was as Lancashire as hot pot, and never short of a jokey remark.

'Your aunt's got a bit of brawn for your dinner,' Lucy told him. 'And you'd best take care you eat it all up.'

Michael pulled a wry face. 'Happen she thinks I need it.' And with the last traces of her ill temper gone, Lucy laughed, tidying her hair and wondering if she had any lipstick left on, for she hated to be caught looking anything less than her best.

'If that's the way of it, she must be blind as well as . . .'

'Deaf? Daft? Or just plain cussed?' He stood with his hands in his pockets, smiling down at her. 'You and she been having another barney?'

'I've been given me marchin' orders.' Lucy screwed up her face and rolled her eyes in a wicked parody of her employer.

'Again?'

'I reckon she means it this time. Says I've to collect me cards.'

'I don't think we've any to give you, have we?'

Lucy gave a rueful sigh. 'It's me own fault, I was a bit rude to her. I've not to come tomorrer, she says.'

'By heck, that's serious. What'll I do wi'out you, Lucy? Who else could I get to come every day and face me aunt's constant carping, yet still do her every bidding with the

15

kind of tongue-biting patience you display?'

'I didn't bite me tongue hard enough today.'

He grinned. 'Let rip, did you?'

'She started it,' Lucy protested, and then flushed guiltily at this childish remark.

Michael came to sit beside her on the kerb, resting his elbows on his knees. Lucy cast a sideways glance at the strong biceps beneath the rolled shirt sleeves, the flush of freckles and sheen of golden hair on his forearms. 'She doesn't mean half what she says,' he explained. 'It's only her way of letting off steam. I reckon she just enjoys the drama of a good row. Livens a dull day.'

Lucy gave a disbelieving snort. 'She's a nasty-minded old . . . sorry, but she's got me all a-flunter. Accused me of having a fancy man. As if I would! What does she take me for? Tom could be home any day now. It's ages since I've heard owt, but they say everyone'll be home in a month or two.'

'Ah.' Michael attempted to look sympathetic but his heart was squeezed by an odd sort of pain as he watched the way joy and sadness chased across her lovely face. Flecks of gold sparkled in the hazel eyes one minute and were clouded with uncertainty the next. Brown curls danced as if with a life of their own against the flushed curve of her cheek and he longed to reach out and run his fingers through them, to kiss the rosy mouth, savour the softness of her against him. He knew for a fact that Tom Shackleton had rarely penned a line to his wife for the entire duration. A man did not, in Michael's opinion, deserve to possess a lovely creature like Lucy if he couldn't be bothered to treat her with more consideration. Pulling himself back under iron control, he stared solemnly at the setts in the road. 'It won't be easy for him, Lucy, picking up the threads of civilian life again after so long away. He'll feel a bit at odds for a while. I know I did.'

Michael had been invalided out of the RAF in 1942, following a crash landing in a Lancaster bomber in which all the crew, bar him, were killed. He'd broken both legs, which had left him with a slight limp, and suffered burns to his arms and chest, injuries which had taken a long time to heal. The guilt of finding himself alive while his mates were dead never would. It was a subject he preferred to avoid and consequently had, at times, caused him problems. Some folk could be less than kind when they saw a man walking around in civvies during wartime.

'We'll be fine and dandy,' Lucy said, 'given time, which we'll have in plenty now this dratted war is over. Once Tom gets home I won't need to go down on me hands and knees scrubbing other folk's mucky doorsteps.'

Michael managed a weak smile, trying to imagine an existence that didn't contain the presence of this laughing, precious girl.

'You'll come to the do this afternoon?'

'Happen.' His eyes were fixed thoughtfully on her.

'But you must. Everyone will be there, the whole street. There's pies and sandwiches, jellies and all sorts of goodies. Even Mabel Radcliffe has contributed a whole ounce of butter and a plate of home-made sad-cake. What d'you think of that?'

'Miracles will never cease. She's not known for her generosity, isn't our Mabel.' Michael's blue eyes were twinkling now, no longer solemn.

'Starts sharp at three.' And so filled was she with the coming joys of a new life with her husband that Lucy impulsively kissed him full on the lips, then wagged a finger teasingly in his face. 'No argufying. Mam will have your guts for garters if you don't show up.'

'That settles it then,' he agreed, though having to clear his throat before he could get the words out properly. 'Your mam isn't one to cross. I'll be there.'

Lucy drew in a deep breath and, giggling like the young girl she still was at heart, skipped off down the street, joining in a game of hopscotch on the way as if she truly were a child revelling in the joys of life, before reaching her own front door quite out of breath.

Watching her go, Michael thought Tom Shackleton a very lucky man.

Chapter Two

Polly Pride was waiting for her daughter at the front door and, snatching her arm, marched her straight into the kitchen, exasperation in her voice. 'So it's home you are at last, you little heathen! Will ye never learn to guard that divil tongue of yours? Whatever possessed you to risk losing such a fine job? Sure and ye'll be the death of me, so you will.' The Irish in her always came out when Polly was agitated.

'How did you know?' Lucy gazed in mortification at her mother who stood, lips pursed, arms folded, disapproval oozing from every pore. She was a fine figure of a woman still, despite being very nearly fifty which seemed tremendously old to twenty-eight-year-old Lucy. There wasn't much Polly missed in Pansy Street but this was fast, even by her mother's standards.

'Didn't Maisie Wright tell me while we were standing in the Co-op queue, waiting to collect our divvy? She witnessed the whole pandemonium.' Polly considered admitting that she was in the same boat as Lucy but pride prevented her.

'Minnie Hopkins said some awful things about me cheating on Tom.' And Lucy's eyes filled with a sudden gush of tears, whereupon Polly's soft heart instantly melted and she wrapped her arms about her daughter.

'Aw, m'cushla, I'm sure she didn't mean them. I know cleaning is not what ye should be doing, a fine intelligent young woman such as yerself. And aren't I in the same boat, so who am I to throw the first stone?' It all came out then about Polly's employers laying off the women to make room for the returning service men. 'I dare say it's fair enough and we mustn't fret. Now the war is over, won't we get the business up and running again, so we will. Once our Benny is home.'

Lucy felt a quick surge of irritation. Why was it always Benny who did the right thing and not her? 'Our Benny might have his own ideas about that, Mam. Mebbe he won't want to go back to cleaning and cutting carpets. Anyroad, mebbe there won't be enough work for him. The business has been closed for years. It'd be like starting all over again.'

'Don't talk soft. Aren't folk just itching to buy carpets to smarten their drab homes? And won't everything be grand for us then? I shall go looking for premises first thing in the morning, something small and cheap till we get up and running. The last thing we need is for you to be jobless.' Polly's face clouded as she half glanced back over her shoulder down the lobby to the living room where she knew Charlie sat, reading the paper, as he'd no doubt been doing all day through no fault of his own. She dropped her voice to a whisper. 'We need some money coming in, me darlin'.'

Lucy's cheeks burned hot and red with guilt. 'I didn't lose the job on purpose but that Minnie Hopkins has the muckiest mind in all of Manchester. She just got me paddy up, that's all.'

Polly snatched up a sharp knife and started hacking a fruit cake to pieces. Strictly speaking it wasn't a fruit cake at all, since it consisted chiefly of dried egg and chopped prunes, but she liked to think of it as such. She wagged the knife recklessly in her daughter's face. 'Seems to me you fly too easy into a paddy, so you do. You need to clip a peg on that sharp tongue of yours, madam.'

'And where might I have got that from, d'you reckon?'

For a while neither woman spoke as each lapsed into self-righteous silence. They busied themselves preparing sandwiches for the party. Eventually Polly set two slices of bread and cheese together with a couple of pickles on to a small plate and handed it to Lucy. 'Tek that out to yer gran.'

'Why me?'

'Why not you?'

Lucy carried the plate, together with a large mug of tea, out to Big Flo who spent most days in the Anderson shelter that still occupied much of the back yard, waiting for the bomb she daily expected would carry her off. The girl was back in the kitchen in seconds.

'You should have stayed and made sure she ate it,' Polly said.

'Oh, Mam. You molly-coddle her. What am I supposed to do? Ram it down her throat?' And snatching up a plate of potted meat sandwiches, Lucy stormed out of the house, slamming the door behind her.

Polly found her legs were trembling so much she had to sit down. Why did she always find herself criticising Lucy, making it seem as if she didn't love her at all when in fact she loved the bones of her? But then, why did Lucy fly off the handle at the least thing? Daughters were surely difficult creatures, far more emotional and pigheaded than sons. Independent to a fault, Lucy was. But Polly did so wish they got on better. As well as she did with Benny, for instance.

The next minute she put her hands to her face and found they were wet with tears. They squeezed out between her fingers and dripped on to her clean pinny, though she really didn't have the time for weeping. For all her brave words about starting up her business again, inside she felt cold with terror. If only they knew what was wrong with Charlie. If only he was well and his usual cheery self then it wouldn't matter that she'd been sacked, and Lucy wouldn't have to go cap in hand to get her job back.

'*Polly?*' That was Charlie now, calling from the parlour.

He always told her not to interfere, to let her children live their own lives without advice or counsel from her. Wise words, if she could but bring herself to follow them. But then he was only their stepfather so how could he possibly know how a mother felt? Polly guiltily conceded that wasn't quite fair on Charlie, for hadn't he always supported her and been a fine father to her children, treating them as if they were indeed his own? It was simply that he'd not been quite himself lately, growing soft, or mard as he called it, in his old age, constantly complaining of aching bones made worse by his long days working on the freezing docks, so perhaps that was why he was less sympathetic. The pains had got so bad recently he could hardly walk and now had been laid off till he got over whatever it was. Aw, she was that worried about him.

And now, to add to her concerns, she and Lucy had both got the push.

'I'll not be a minute, love. I'll just see to these sandwiches then I'll fetch you a cuppa.' Polly stood up, dabbing her eyes on her pinny, knowing that the minute she'd done the washing up and got this food ready for the party, she still had to clean through. Saturdays were her only chance and she was never one for giving a lick and a promise as many women in this street were. Polly Pride liked her house to shine, from top to toe. She allowed not a speck of dust, nor a moment of self-pity either.

Soon as they got the business going again, they'd all feel more secure, she told herself sternly as she set out spam sandwiches on a plate. Life would get back to normal at last and Charlie could have a nice warm job indoors instead of working on the wharfs, which he hated. Polly was quite sure that was what had made him ill in the first place. Or he'd caught some nasty bug from that filthy river.

When she was quite composed again, she picked up the plate of sandwiches and followed her daughter outside, biting back a further admonishment as she saw Lucy shunting and banging plates about on the long trestle tables. Borrowed from the local Sunday schools and covered with well-darned sheets in varying degrees of whiteness, these straddled the cobbles down the centre of the street. Pop-eyed children hovered close, tongues licking rosy lips as they waited for the magic hour when the celebrations and, best of all, the eating, could commence, Polly's own grandchildren among them.

Her hands stilled in their arranging of plates and folding of napkins, greeny-grey eyes growing soft as she watched the children, eager to help for once. Young Sean, three years old, the image of his dad with his straight fair hair, and Sarah Jane, all dark and sulky, a budding Veronica Lake, tugging at her skirt.

'When can I put me party frock on?'

'As late as possible then you don't spoil it.'

'I'm hungry.'

'Have a banana sandwich then.'

Sarah Jane pulled a face. 'It's not banana. It's boiled parsnip with banana essence in it. I saw you make it.'

'Aw, who's a little clever-clogs then? Is it hungry you are or not?'

'No.'

'Please yourself.' Polly set the plate close by her grand-daughter's elbow, knowing she would take one the minute her back was turned.

Larders had been ruthlessly raided for this day. Not since before the war had there been such a spread and none of the children could remember anything but war. When it was over, hearts would still ache for loved ones not yet come home, and some, like Doris Mitchell from next door, would never see a son safe home again.

Oh, but what was Polly complaining for? Sure and wasn't she the lucky one? She had her two children and grandchildren safe and well. Charlie might be overworked and a bit below par but he'd mend, so he would, and at least he'd been too old to fight. Benny would be home soon, along with Lucy's Tom, and they'd all be happy as Larry.

And then it came to her why her daughter was so scratchy today. 'Is it afeared ye are that he'll no longer feel the same about ye, after all this time away?'

A moment's silence and then Lucy nodded, eyes brimming with tears.

'Aw, me little one, won't he love every hair on yer head, just as we all do?' But as she made to hold her daughter close again, Lucy turned stiffly away, as if rejecting her comfort.

Polly clenched her hands, trying not to mind for she knew there were many such concerns this afternoon, despite the sunshine and joy of the day. When would their men return? Would they be different, or damaged in some way? Would there be work for them to do? And how would each family settle down to the changes? Some women were reluctant to give up their own jobs, while others dreaded the return of an almost forgotten husband. And there were those simply concerned over whether their menfolk would bring their own ration book. But for an hour or two at least they could all enjoy the celebrations and forget about the aftermath of war and the new worries that peace might bring. Bellies would be filled, and some pleasure could be found in an otherwise grey life.

Conceding at last to the warm weather, Polly unbuttoned her cardigan, the wool of which had long since lost its stretch, this being the third garment it had supplied in six years. She'd go and take it off in a minute, have a good wash and put on her Sunday best. 'Is nobody going to mash some tea? I feel like I'm chewing sawdust.'

Lucy laughed, her ill temper melting beneath her mother's good humour and the sunshine of this special day. 'I'll make it.' She hurried indoors and grabbed the kettle, filling it from the single cold tap over the sink.

She really ought to go upstairs and start getting washed and changed herself but her mind was still on how next week's bills would be paid. It would mean eating into her savings but then how was she to know that her mam would be laid off too, on the very same day? Life was cruel. It would be difficult enough for Tom when he came home, and she'd made it no easier by losing one of her best paying customers. Two children to feed and her wages more than halved. Mam was right. She should guard her tongue better.

For a long time Lucy hovered by the stove, waiting for the kettle to boil, her mind turning over the problems, worrying about her children, about Tom and how it would be for them after a married life spent mainly apart. She even found herself anxiously going over Polly's business plans. All wishful thinking, in Lucy's opinion. Once Polly Pride Carpets had been busy and prosperous, had made them enough money to escape the mean streets of Ancoats and move them up in the world to a smart new house in Cheetham, but since the outbreak of war nobody had wanted carpets, even if such an item could be found, and the family had been forced to move again, to a more modest house in Castlefield, for all it was better than many in Pansy Street, where Charlie could get work on the wharfs and the womenfolk close by.

They'd got by well enough but starting up the business again would need capital as well as will power, and more hard work than perhaps her mother realised. Polly no longer had the youth or the energy she'd once enjoyed in abundance. Not that Lucy would mind having a go herself, given the chance.

As for Benny, his mother's pride and joy, perhaps he was no longer the biddable boy Polly fondly remembered. He'd always been streetwise, good at living by his wits as they all had once, yet also ambitious and filled with unrealistic dreams. Lucy wondered what these would be now, after six years of war.

Her troubled thoughts were interrupted by the sound of running feet then Sean was beside her, face scarlet with excitement. 'There's someone outside. I'm only allowed to say it's a soldier, Mam, and he's asking for you.'

Lucy froze then made a dash for the door, knocking a plate of fairy cakes to the floor as she ran, hardly noticing as she trampled over the fatless sponge treats. The soldier striding down the street towards her had light brown hair cut close to his bullet-shaped head and eyes of a familiar greeny-grey. Broad, almost stockily built, with powerful shoulders and a ramrod back, he did not carry a kit bag for the children gathered about him were doing that for him. But he did swing Sarah Jane high on his shoulders and caught a giggling Sean as the little boy leapt into his arms.

Joy warred with disappointment as Lucy's pounding heart slowed to normal. It was only her brother Benny, miraculously materialising out of her thoughts. Pleased as she was to see him, he was not her lovely husband. Then Lucy became aware of an eerie silence.

Somewhere a blackbird trilled its piercingly sweet note, not even the sound of a tram or shunting train marring the sudden silence. Nothing but the squeak of the telegraph boy's bike.

Not a soul spoke as he rode slowly towards the group of women hovering about the tables. Hearts stopped, mouths went ash-dry, skipping ropes dropped to the ground as even the children understood the implications of such a visit.

He paused by one old man but only to ask a question, then the bike squeaked on as the boy struggled to pedal over the setts, carefully avoiding getting his wheels caught in the tramlines. Why didn't he get off the damn thing and walk?

Seconds later the waiting was over, the orange envelope was in her hands and Lucy knew, even before she opened it, that Tom wouldn't be coming home next week or even next month. He wouldn't be coming home at all.

Locked in a state of disbelief, Lucy felt too numb to grieve, though a part of her was only too keenly aware that her world had just fallen apart and nothing would ever be the same again. She hadn't set eyes on Tom since before Sean was born, when he was sent out to Italy and God knows where since, yet she should surely feel something other than this terrible sensation of resentment? To lose a husband at the end of the war seemed especially unfair somehow, if war ever could be fair. She ached now to tell him all the things she'd never had the chance to say, to ask forgiveness for the quarrels they'd had, few as they were. She wished they'd made more of their marriage, that she'd been a perfect wife for him, since it was all the time they were to have.

Missing, presumed killed in action. Cold, unfeeling words that would live with her for the rest of her life. How could anyone *presume* such a thing? Yet she knew that to continue to hope year after year was a kind of death in itself. She'd seen it happen to neighbours: to Doris-next-door for one; Mrs Shaw at the end house for another. Even after they'd sent back what was left of her eldest boy, she still left his razor out on the shelf, just in case.

Lucy could never do that. It wouldn't be fair on Sarah Jane or Sean. She'd taken the children upstairs to her room and explained it all, as carefully as she could. They'd looked at her, dry-eyed and uncomprehending. Then, as if seeing their bewilderment brought it finally home to her, it had been Lucy who'd wept, which in turn started Sean off, and Sarah Jane had comforted them all.

After that Polly brewed tea, pot after pot, as if the hot

steaming brew could put everything right. Sarah Jane put on her pink party frock, Lucy her best blue costume in an attempt to celebrate Benny's return home on leave, though her heart was no longer in it. And as if things weren't bad enough, a row broke out as soon as Charlie emerged from the front parlour to find this young stranger lounging in his favourite chair by the kitchen fire.

'I suppose you think you're the only one who's suffered during this dratted war?' Charlie demanded, prodding a surprised Benny in the chest with one finger. 'Well, let me tell you, there's many a family round here can say different. Mary Lee for one. She went out to the Co-op for a bag of rations and came back to find her house and half of Hardman Street had been blasted off the face of the earth. There were many such tales.'

'It's good to see you too, Charlie,' Benny dryly commented. 'How are you?'

'He's not been too well and that's the truth.' Polly flapped around the pair of them, trying to keep the peace. 'Hush, hush, Charlie. Don't lay into him the minute he gets home. Glad we are to have our boy safe with us at last, are we not? Now sit ye down and drink yer tea and I'll get ye a bite of summat to eat.' She tried not to meet her son's puzzled gaze for Charlie had once been the gentlest of stepfathers. Whatever was ailing him was doing his temper no good at all.

People came and went all afternoon. Gran refused to

emerge from the Anderson shelter as usual, and the whole day took on a deep sense of unreality. They at least remembered to thank Aunt Ida for her contribution of a tin of spam and Uncle Nobby for enough lettuce and tomatoes from his allotment to turn them all into rabbits. But nobody felt like eating, for all the sacrifices that had been made to provide such a spread.

Every now and then Polly would squeeze Lucy's hand or whisper that Tom would come home one day, see if he didn't, that *presumed* only meant the authorities hadn't the first idea where he was at present. Some sort of bureaucratic mix-up and he was even now on his way home, no doubt. Lucy tried to find comfort in these words and consistently failed.

The only time any of them truly managed to lift their spirits was for the sake of the children. Later that evening, Sean, bewildered by the strangeness of what should have been an extra special day, marched into the kitchen and made a grab for his uncle's leg. 'Have you not fetched me a present, Uncle Benny?'

Benny, enjoying a glass of stout and a quiet read of the paper while his mother and Lucy washed up and tidied the table around him, gazed mystified about the room. 'Did you hear summat, our Lucy? I reckon we've got a squeaking mouse in the house.'

'I hope not,' Polly said, with equal seriousness.

'Well, if we have, don't expect me to oil it,' Benny

warned, making them all laugh and lightening the tension a little. Sean squealed with delight as his uncle swung him upside down before setting him back on his feet and suggesting he dig deep in his rucksack. 'Fancy me forgetting. Fetch Sarah Jane. Go on, you. Have a shufty in there. You might both find summat of interest.'

Sarah Jane came running, half glancing at her mother as if wanting reassurance that it was all right to take pleasure in a gift on this sad occasion. Lucy smiled and nodded at her to dig deep.

'Happen yer too old for toys now?' Benny idly commented, helping the children to search. Then he held out a yellow duck for Sarah Jane, and a small brown and grey dog for Sean.

Two pairs of shining eyes met his. 'Oh, no, Uncle Benny. I haven't had much in the way of toys, there being a war on, you see,' Sarah Jane gravely explained.

'Me neever,' Sean agreed, reaching for the dog. 'Can he sit on my pillow?'

'I reckon he'd like that,' Benny agreed.

There was a box of mints for his gran, cigarettes for Charlie, a scarf for his mother and silk stockings for his sister. 'No questions asked,' warned Benny, tapping the side of his nose with one nicotine-stained finger, which for some reason took some of the pleasure out of the gift for Lucy, though not for the world would she say as much.

*

The excitement and trauma of the day meant it took a while to get the children to sleep, and their new playmates naturally must be suitably tucked up too. But then, as she lay listening to the even rhythm of their breathing in the bed beside her own, Lucy finally succumbed and sobbed out her grief, stuffing the pillow into her mouth so that she wouldn't wake them. The hours of darkness seemed to protect her from prying eyes and gave her at last some release from the pent-up emotion, if not from her heartache. She slept for a few short hours after that, out of sheer exhaustion, but the first shafts of a grey dawn found practical matters once more occupying her mind.

Her dreams of being able to spend more time with Sarah Jane and Sean were like bitter dust in her mouth. She was particularly sorry about Sean. The boy was growing a bit wild and although Lucy did what she could, he was sorely in need of a father. Her life had always been hard and she didn't need telling that it would become even harder without a husband to provide for their future. She might still get her allowance from the army, little as that was, but the long hours and backbreaking drudgery would continue indefinitely. Even when she'd finished work there was still all the washing, ironing and endless make-do-and-mend to do at home, not to mention the daily worry of finding something to eat.

And what about fun? she asked herself with a bitter twist of self-pity. She was still a young woman, with all her life before her. When did she start to enjoy life? Never, by the looks of it, for all the longed for peace had finally arrived, which brought on a fresh spurt of tears.

Losing one of her best clients had made things worse. She'd worked five mornings a week for Minnie Hopkins. In the afternoons she cleaned for Mrs Shaw, the Beckworths and the Taylors, while on Fridays she went right through the house behind the corner shop for the Benson sisters. Now, with one gesture of stupid defiance, she'd lost nearly half her week's wages.

There was no help for it but to do as her mam suggested, swallow her pride and go and apologise to Minnie Hopkins. Temper or no temper, Lucy needed that job or they'd all starve.

Chapter Three

'So, tha's had second thoughts, 'asta? Tha's remembered them as doan't work, doan't eat.' Minnie Hopkins stood on her spotless doorstep, arms folded, queen of her own domain, and treated Lucy to her most blistering glare.

Lucy drew in a calming breath, gritted her teeth and forced a smile. It made her face feel all stiff and uncomfortable. 'I thought you'd happen be having second thoughts yourself. After all, somebody has to clean this place for yer. It's a big house.'

'Aye. And theer's plenty'd be glad of the chance to work here.'

Silence fell while the two women sized each other up, Minnie weighing up whether she could get Lucy back on reduced wages. The lass worked hard for all she was a bit lippy. For two pins she'd let her go but Michael had a soft spot for her, which was why he paid her too much, daft git.

Yet Minnie knew she'd be hard put to find someone else willing to take on the job of cleaning this great house. Stuck at the end of Pansy Street, a cut above the rest, it had been the bane of her life ever since the pair of them had been left rattling around in it. A real white elephant it was with its seven bedrooms and three reception rooms, for all it had a fine Edwardian front to it, complete with stone pillars, and one doorstep more than everyone else.

Lucy was wondering how much more humiliation she could bear, whether she should appeal to the woman's sympathy, or tell her she could keep her blasted job. She did neither.

With her chin up, back straight, Lucy kept her mind on her two children, the gas bill that had landed on the mat that very morning, and the sight of her mother's face when she'd opened it. As if Polly didn't have enough on her plate, what with losing her own job, grieving with Lucy over Tom, worrying over Charlie who was frequently in a sour mood these days, not to mention Benny lording it over them all the minute he came downstairs, prattling on about how he was going to make his fortune on Civvy Street the minute his demob number came up and he was home for good.

'Aw, indeed you are so, and isn't that all settled?' Polly had agreed, placing a substantial breakfast the like of which Lucy hadn't seen in a long while before him. 'We'll be getting the business going again and you, m'cushla, can be me right hand man.'

Benny had laughed as he dipped a thick chunk of bread into his egg while Lucy's mouth watered to watch the precious yellow yolk run. 'Nay, Mam. I haven't med me mind up yet. Happen I'll be lookin' for summat a bit more substantial like than second-hand carpets. Something that'll make proper money.' Just as if he could take his pick of jobs.

'Don't talk soft. And what else would ye be doing?' Polly had laughed at his dismissal of this precious dream but Lucy could see the hurt in the way her face stiffened. 'Carpets made us plenty of money before the war, did they not? Brought us out of Ancoats and saved the lot of us from near starvation at one time.'

'That's all in the past,' Benny told her.

'So, they can make us money again in the future. I mean to buy machines to offer a service for cleaning and steaming. Now won't that be grand?'

'Sounds like too much hard graft to me, Mam. I've had enough of hard labour and square bashing. I'm looking for a job which brings in good money for less sweat and toil, if you know what I mean.' And, grinning, he'd sliced the egg in two and put half of it into his mouth. Lucy had walked out at that point, unable to bear witness to the waste of such good food.

She was fond enough of her brother, but he didn't seem to appreciate how hard it had been for them all during the long war, what sacrifices they'd had to make. Money had been so tight at one time, she remembered scrabbling in the muck and wet of the gutter when she'd dropped a precious loaf of bread, washing it under the tap and baking it crisp again in the oven. And Lucy couldn't remember the last time she'd tasted a fried egg since she gave her meagre ration to her children, which brought her troubled thoughts right back to where they'd started. Sean was already through the soles of that pair of shoes she'd got from Lily Gantry's rag shop less than two months back, and Sarah Jane showed an indecent amount of knickers in all her little frocks. Oh, yes, for all she'd a bit put by and, for now at least, she'd continue to get something from the army, she needed this job.

Lucy smiled steadfastly at her hated employer. 'I could mek your dinners an' all, if you want?' she recklessly offered. 'Michael's allus asking me.'

Minnie Hopkins popped a pear drop into her mouth and sucked on it while she thought about this proposition. 'For t'same rate? We can't afford to pay any more.' The beady jet eyes seemed to pierce right into Lucy's soul and she could do nothing but comply.

'Yes, all right, for the same rate.'

'Reet. Tha mun get back to work reet now. I'm noan feeling too champion this mornin'. Get me a cuppa, good and strong, then you can start by scrubbing t'back yard.'

'My favourite job,' said Lucy dryly, reaching for her sacking apron.

'What didsta say?'

'I said, just the job.'

'A thank you would be more appropriate.' The old woman's hearing was a sight too sharp at times, Lucy thought, offering her thanks as humbly as she was able. She brewed Minnie a strong pot of tea, even offered a slice of the 'fruit' cake left over from the street party as a peace offering. As she headed for the backyard, bucket in hand, Minnie called after her.

'Only cook for two, mind. Thi con mek thee own dinner when thi gets home.'

Lucy gritted her teeth. She'd be half starved by then after all this extra work, and Benny would no doubt have eaten them out of house and home.

Lucy baked a pie, consisting chiefly of vegetables but with a bit of pork added to make it tasty. The new regime meant she had to work harder and faster than ever in order to be home in time to pick up her children, but Michael was delighted. He had long since tired of his aunt's paltry attempts at cooking. He made no mention of the fact that Lucy was back after only recently being sacked. Nor did he ask why she'd suddenly agreed to do the very thing she had always resisted.

Once she'd served up, Lucy quickly untied her apron and, reaching for her coat and basket, headed for the door.

'I'll be in tomorrow then, as usual.'

'Right you are,' Michael said, pushing back his chair and insisting on showing her out, despite some caustic comment from his aunt about the girl being able to find her own way. 'I didn't like to say owt in there, in front of Aunt Minnie, not after all that kerfuffle the other day, but I'm sorry about Tom.'

'Thank you.' Lucy didn't know what else to say, and kept her face turned away as she fussed with coat buttons, bag and scarf, not wanting him to see the quick rush of tears.

'If there's anything I can do . . .'

'What can anyone do? He's dead, for God's sake.' Lucy realised she'd spoken more sharply than she'd intended, and instantly apologised. 'Sorry. I'm fine, really I am.'

'Are you?'

'I will be. I have to be. Anyroad, how can you grieve for somebody you haven't seen in three years, hardly even heard from?'

'You can if you still love them.'

She'd been all right until he said that, and until he gently touched her arm. Then, before she could stop herself, Lucy turned her face into his broad shoulder and began to weep, overwhelmed by emotion and his ready sympathy.

Michael's arms slid about her, strong and firm, holding her tight as he murmured soothing words of comfort against her hair, his mouth so close to her ear she could feel the soft vibration of him whispering her name into it.

It made her shiver with a new, strange emotion. The clean, soapy scent of him, and the firmness of a strong male body pressed so hard against her own, created a tension between them, one that even Lucy, despite her distress, recognised as dangerous.

They broke apart, the storm of weeping over almost as quickly as it had begun, and Lucy dabbed at her eyes with the flat of her hand, flushed with embarrassment.

Michael felt hot with shame at the fierceness of his need. His arms were still imprinted with the feel of her as he stood awkwardly on the mat, studying the downcast tilt of her head. The roughness of his jacket had rubbed a red patch on her cheek and he watched, dry-mouthed, as a tear trailed over it, managing only by a superhuman effort not to put out a finger to catch it. He did offer her a handkerchief, one of his old airforce blue ones but spanking clean. 'It does you good to open the floodgates once in a while, for all you've soaked me through.'

Managing to smile through her tears, Lucy took the handkerchief from him and blew her nose then shyly met his gaze. 'I'm all right now, thanks.'

'Well, you know where I am if you're not.'

'Yes.' She hesitated another fraction of a second, then turned on her heel and fled, her heart pounding in time with her feet on the stone paving slabs as she ran home. What in heaven's name had she done now?

*

Belinda Clarke had been pleased and excited to get her call-up papers back in 1940. She'd volunteered for the ATS, for special radio training, and later for service overseas — anything that sounded remotely exciting, to bring some colour into her plain, drab life.

She'd certainly succeeded. She'd enjoyed her time in London, but best of all were the years in Malta and Cairo where, in spite of the war, there'd at least been sun and a social life, even if warding off the good-time johnnies was a bit of a trial at times.

It hadn't all been fun, of course. There were times when she'd been thoroughly browned off, and at others scared witless, which was more than could be said for many, so by rights she should be grateful to be coming home. She'd spent the last eighteen months of the war in South Wales of all places, and had left the demobilisation centre at Aldershot in the second week of September with per-ilously little cash, thanks to the prevailing live-for-today attitude, a few clothing coupons and a travel warrant. But what she lacked in material possessions, she more than made up for with plenty of optimism and energy at the prospect of a new beginning.

She'd forgotten how plain and drab life in Cherry Crescent could be.

Belinda dropped her bag and pressed the polished brass bell. Somewhere from within the depths of the house came the familiar jangling sound. She smoothed a hand over the grain of the polished wood. Blistered and cracked, it looked in dire need of a fresh coat of varnish, if such a luxury could be found. Someone had tried to clean off the strips of protective brown sticky paper from the red and green panes of glass in the leaded bay windows, and not made a very good job of it. If this were the depot, she'd have the perpetrator brought back and made to finish the job properly. Belinda smiled and again rang the bell. Where was everyone? Finally she tried the door, found it unlocked, and walked into the cool hall.

A solid, semi-detached house, sufficiently unlike its neighbours to lend it some pretensions to superiority, it nevertheless looked smaller than she remembered. Shabbier. But then, she hadn't been home for – how long? Oh goodness, she couldn't remember. Too long, perhaps. There was the old grandfather clock that seemed to fill the narrow hall, ticking dully, and still ten minutes slow. The same brown panelling and green paint, her father's ancient barometer which he tapped every day on his way to the office, and the cumbersome Victorian hatstand with the wonky hooks. She'd forgotten how very ugly that was. She flung her hat neatly on to it, watching it spin and settle on a hook, and grinned.

'Is that you, darling?'

Belinda went to the foot of the stairs to smile up at her mother. The sight of her, looking as serene and beautiful as ever in a lavender cotton housecoat that flowed over the curves of her girlishly slender figure, made Belinda feel instantly jaded and unwashed.

Her own demob suit was a dull brown, creased and dusty after hours spent squashed on an overcrowded train. Her laced brogues were more sensible than fashionable, for all they were highly polished. In her bag, apart from one decent silk dress from her days out east, there were a couple of outdated summer frocks among the serviceable underwear, two tin plates and an old army blanket she'd felt duty bound to bring home as a memento.

Belinda Clarke herself, however, was very far from being either dull or plain. At twenty-six, she was fit and slender, athletic and yet feminine. Her cheek bones were high, mouth wide and prone to easy laughter, and if her hair was cut mercilessly short yet it glowed honey-gold, and her blue eyes sparkled with ready mischief. Her whole bearing exuded confidence, as befitted someone who had attained the rank of Corporal.

Her mother was scolding her for not having rung from the station.

'I took a bus.'

'Darling, with that bag? You surely haven't carried it yourself?'

Belinda let out a peal of laughter. 'Mother, I've been carrying my own bags for five years. Are we to continue this staircase conversation indefinitely, or will you come down and give your only daughter a hug?'

'Darling, of course.' Joanna Clarke half glanced back

over one shoulder, as if reluctant to leave whatever she'd been doing, then floated down the stairs on light slippered feet, offering a scented cheek to be kissed. 'We'll have a glass of sherry in the conservatory. Just you and me.'

'I'd rather have a bath. I'm filthy.'

'No, no, not now. In any case, you look marvellous, and you've hours and hours to make yourself beautiful before this evening. I want to have you all to myself for a while.'

Belinda was instantly on the alert. 'This evening? Why, what's happening this evening?'

Joanna giggled, the girlish tones sounding oddly false. 'Everything's going to be splendid now you're home again. We've invited the Fentons round for a little welcome-home party. You remember Frank Fenton? You and he had quite a "thing" going once.'

Belinda groaned.

'No pouting, darling. Your father is quite set on it. You must at least make the effort to be nice to dear Frank, even if you have no wish to pick up where you left off.'

'Which I certainly haven't!'

'You know that Ron has gone into the business, don't you?' Joanna said, filling the sherry glasses to the brim as she very sweetly changed the subject.

Belinda let out a peal of laughter. 'Little brother working? Whatever next?'

'Oh, he's grown quite ambitious. It will be just like old times, all together again. Exactly the way it used to be.'

Heart sinking, Belinda followed her mother into the overheated conservatory, lush with vegetation and sickly sweet flowers, wondering how she was going to get it across to her overprotective parents that it could never be as it used to be. The naive, obedient daughter who had fled their fireside seeking adventure five years ago had not returned, and never would.

The dinner party was not a success. They all sat stiffly around the oversized mahogany table in the gloomy dining-room. Hubert drank too much wine and dominated the conversation with talk of Council matters and his hopes of being elevated to a position of even higher office next year, laying one finger against his broad nose as if to indicate it was all rather hush-hush. Brother Ron, seated opposite, wore his usual sour expression and seemed intent on not speaking to anyone while he devoured everything in sight.

Belinda upset her mother by refusing to wear the frothy pink number bought by her 'specially for the purpose, choosing instead a sensible green suit that had seen better days. The skirt draped softly over her slender figure but nobody could call it elegant. She brushed her hair until it shone, added the faintest touch of lipstick, but could see that neither of her parents was impressed with the result. She was soon to learn the reason.

The Fentons were well known to Belinda, the owners of

a large chemical dye works on Liverpool Road. They were quiet, unprepossessing people, despite an air of self-satisfaction which seemed to proclaim they need make no further effort since they had already made their place in the world. Their greatest asset was their son Frank. He had followed them into the business, working hard to do his bit despite being excused military service, as they were at constant pains to point out.

Belinda had dreaded seeing Frank again, remembering all too well his spotty face and eager bonhomie, so was greatly relieved when he didn't put in an appearance, hoping she could now relax and enjoy the meal. Her mother was evidently deeply offended, clearly believing that an invitation to her table far outweighed any other possible commitment which might have claimed his attention.

'He mustn't feel shy with us,' she said, and suggested Ron go round and persuade him to change his mind.

'He isn't in,' George Fenton insisted, as irritated as the Clarkes by his son's defection. 'Haven't the foggiest where he is.'

'Trying to avoid us, eh?' joked Hubert, though with little sign of good humour.

Always apt to talk too much when she was nervous or distressed, Joanna launched into a lengthy discourse on how pleased she was that hostilities had ended, whether the authorities would be able to rectify the terrible destruction in the city, and how dreary it had been for her to be evacuated for the duration to Aunt Cora's in Scotland: 'But Hubert was most insistent that I be safe.'

The very idea of anyone, even a German, daring to bomb Cherry Crescent, seemed sacrilege beyond belief. Belinda managed, against all the odds, not to say so, deciding that at least the enforced evacuation would have given her father some respite. Perhaps that was the reasoning behind his idea. The thought brought a smile, and very nearly a fit of laughter, so that she had to dash off into the kitchen under the pretext of checking on the apricot pudding to get herself back under control. Belinda stood at the back door, sneaking a quick drag of a cigarette. This proved to be a mistake for when she returned, still coughing slightly, it brought attention firmly back to her.

'Don't you agree, Scotland was a good idea, darling?'

Belinda resolved to hold her ground. 'If it suited you, Mother. Unfortunately we couldn't all escape to Aunt Cora's. Some of us had to fight the war.' She regretted the remark instantly as being unnecessarily unkind for Joanna looked wounded and batted her long eyelashes in obvious distress.

'I did my bit, darling. I spent a great deal of time knitting dull scarves and countless balaclavas. For the poor sailors, don't you know?'

'I'm sure they were most grateful,' Belinda said, sucking in her cheeks and wondering if she dare dash out again.

Her mother's soft mouth trembled. 'Cora got involved with the VAD but I truly couldn't. The sights she saw . . . quite dreadful. I would have been ill, I swear I would.' Joanna pressed a lace handkerchief to her pretty nose, which had never smelled anything more unpleasant than cheap cologne when she couldn't find any of her favourite Evening in Paris perfume. She looked about the table with brimming eyes, seeking understanding and ready sympathy, which she instantly received.

'Don't upset your mother,' came Hubert's voice from the head of the table.

'I didn't. I never meant . . .' Belinda bit her lip, hating to find herself in the wrong on her very first night home.

Then George Fenton, obviously wishing to assist by changing the subject, enquired as to her future plans, now that the war was well and truly over. Before Belinda could think of a suitable reply, her father's voice boomed out yet again.

'There's no need for a daughter of mine to work,' pronounced Hubert Clarke, as if he were at a Council meeting. 'Ron works with me in the business, of course. Belinda will help her mother at home and get involved in summat useful, to give her an interest like.' There were red blotches on his plump face and the implication behind his words was plain to everyone. She would stay at home until the right young man came along. Hubert drank the last of his soup with a loud slurping noise, then smiled beneficently at

Belinda. 'You won't find me niggardly when it comes to giving you a good send-off.'

'Sent off where?' she asked, in her coolest tones. 'Haven't I only this very day arrived back? Besides, perhaps I won't want to stay at home. I haven't yet decided what I wish to do.'

'What is there to do but find yourself a good husband, and a bit smartish like? You aren't getting any younger.' Hubert, as he constantly reminded his family and friends, came from Bolton and prided himself on never mincing his words. 'Father knows best, eh?'

Belinda, who was used to holding her own against whole squadrons of joking men, who had been responsible for the welfare of other girls in her care and was no longer the shy, convent-educated girl who had gone away to war, merely smiled. 'Really, Father, that all sounds rather Victorian, don't you think? I'm not a child any longer, you know, and I do believe I'm capable of choosing my own job. I doubt radio operators are much in demand in Manchester these days, but I hope to find something a bit more interesting than helping Mummy with dinner parties or serving at coffee mornings.'

Councillor Hubert Clarke turned a dull shade of purple. He was not accustomed to having his word flouted by anyone, least of all a daughter at his own dining table. He would have said as much there and then, had it not been for the Fenton woman taking an obvious satisfaction in his discomfiture. Even so, he wouldn't have his guests think him weak or be bested in his own house. Hubert considered himself a man of some importance thanks to his credit trading business, ably assisted by his son who ensured the customers kept up their regular weekly payments of a shilling in the pound for goods purchased. Hubert had never stood any nonsense in that department, war or no war. If they didn't pay, he sued or pursued them until they regretted their lack of thrift. He hadn't become a self-made man of means without learning a trick or two. He was also becoming a force to be reckoned with in the city, with many useful contacts which served him well. He reminded himself of this fact now.

Joanna had placed a small chicken before him which he began, with great ceremony, to carve. 'We all appreciate how you volunteered to do your bit, Belinda, as we have too in our different ways, even your poor mother.' He wagged the carving knife at her. 'But it was your own choice to join the military and run wild. A feverish whim, no doubt, that got a bit out of hand. We're only thankful the war is over at last and our little girl is home again, safe and sound.' He beamed round at everyone before sinking the knife into the plump chicken.

'Feverish whim?'

'This is the reality now, lass. You can forget all that daft ATS nonsense and smarten your ideas up. You'll never catch a chap in that mannish suit, with your hair chopped off. Your mother will take you shopping tomorrow and sort you out, won't you, love? I've got some spare coupons I'll willingly donate for the purpose.'

If it hadn't been for the sheen of embarrassment on George Fenton's upper lip, not to mention Muriel Fenton's stifled snigger, Belinda might have imagined she'd misheard him.

'I know you were never one for the glamour stakes,' Hubert relentlessly continued, 'but we can't have folks thinking my lass a dowd, now can we?' He passed her a plate of chicken. 'Eat up, and put some flesh on those bones. Chaps round here like summat to get hold of on a woman.'

Belinda felt the surge of anger run up her spine and freeze it rigid. 'How dare you? How *dare* you? I'm perfectly capable of buying my own clothes, and I wouldn't *dream* of putting on weight simply to please a man. Besides, I'm extremely fit and intend to stay that way. And there are other things in life besides marriage.'

'Nay, lass. Hold your horses. Don't tek on so,' he mildly chided her.

Ron stopped masticating his chicken long enough to comment, 'Dad's only concerned for your future – that you shouldn't let the side down like.'

'Side? What *side*?'

'That's right. We can't have you rusting on the shelf.' Hubert Clarke had never been one to know when to shut up and draw a line under a point. He always had to score it deep. 'All I'm saying is, you've had your bit of fun. Now it's time to settle down and be the good daughter we deserve. Marry well and provide us with grandchildren. Don't you reckon we deserve that, George? Muriel?' He appealed to the Fentons, busily stuffing their scarlet faces with chicken.

For Belinda it was all too much. She was on her feet, pushing back her chair and actually gaping at him. 'Fun? *Fun, you say*? Oh, yes, I've had loads of *fun* these last five years. It's been one long laugh from start to finish! What can be more amusing than picking up pieces of bodies and trying to match which bit belongs to whom? Or watching a friend's leg turn to green slime and then seeing her hobble about on crutches when they relieve her of it? Now that really *was* hilarious.'

It was unforgivable, of course, to relate such horror stories in front of her timid mother, and at a dinner party too.

Vaguely aware of Muriel Fenton rushing to the bathroom, Belinda watched in fascinated horror as her mother very elegantly slid off her chair into a dead faint on the carpet, her napkin still clutched tight in her hand, as if even in an unconscious state, she must not be found neglectful of her table manners. If it hadn't been so desperately sad, it might have been exceedingly funny.

As it was, Belinda simply folded her own napkin,

dropped it on the table, and walked from the room. She'd start looking for a job first thing in the morning, come what may, and a place of her own to go with it.

Chapter Four

Polly stood in line for broken biscuits with a patience born of long practice. Far from disappearing with the end of the war, queues seemed to stretch even longer and black marketeering was as rife as ever, causing a lot of bother in certain quarters though it was no skin off her nose, she supposed, if the government lost out a bit. There were times when Polly wondered if they really had won the war or whether it was all a big con.

'Are you queuing for owt good?' a passer-by enquired.

'We don't know till we gets theer, missus,' said one wit.

Not that Polly minded queuing. Here at Campfield market it gave her time to look around and chat with friends. She had always loved markets, had stood on one herself in her younger days. Just watching Billy the Potman juggle with his dinner plates and beat down his own prices never failed to make her laugh. What a showman! He should be on twice nightly at the Queen's. When she'd queued at the butcher's and got a nice long red-skinned polony for tea, she'd take a little saunter down Tonman Street. She might find a cheap frock there for Sarah Jane.

'Here y'are. Don't eat 'em all at once,' Madge Sullivan cheekily remarked as she deftly spun the bag to produce an ear at each corner and handed it over to Polly. Her wide girth seemed to fill the space behind the stacked stall, leaving her skinny husband hardly room to breathe let alone reach the biscuit tins.

'Fat chance with my lot.'

'Got home safe, Poll, 'ave they?'

Polly explained about Tom being missing, and Madge tried to assure her that there was still hope. Other women in the long queue chipped in with tales of various friends and neighbours whose loved ones had come home, against all odds, and she nodded in agreement, without actually believing it possible. For all she'd been an incomer from Cheetham Hill, the folk of Deansgate Village had accepted her as one of their own, Madge Sullivan included. Polly loved the intricate network of canals and railway arches, the locks and bridges, and the wide sweep of the Bridgewater viaduct straddling it all.

'Millie Bradshaw's husband had been missing for four year when he turned up, nice as ninepence and just as brash.' Madge leaned closer over the biscuit tins, causing them to wobble perilously and a few stray biscuits to fall on the stone setts where they were gobbled up by an opportunist dog. 'And how's your lad, Polly? I hear he's home safe and sound at least.'

'Hey, missus, we'll be here next Preston Guild if you don't shape thissen,' said one chap, clearly growing impatient with this feminine chit-chat. 'I wants to get home today, tha knows, not tomorrer, if it's all t'same to thee.'

'Why don't you save yer breath to cool yer porridge, you? Yer lucky if yer've got an 'ouse to go to. There's plenty 'oo 'aven't.'

Polly, anxious now to get away before the rest of the queue lost its good will and turned nasty, said, 'Benny'll be bright as a new pin and raring to go once he's had a good rest, so he will.'

'Yer a lucky woman.'

'And isn't that the truth?' And she hurried away, making no mention of her worries over Charlie. Nor did she refer to the rebellious stand her son had taken the minute he'd arrived home for good, threatening not to come into the business with her at all. Not that Polly gave much credence to such daft declarations of independence for all they'd shaken her a bit at first, admittedly. Like a slap in the face it was, but then mebbe she'd rushed him, hadn't put it quite right nor properly outlined her plans. Why, she hadn't even mentioned her dream to go into new carpets. Full of grandiose schemes he may be but in his mother's opinion Benny could do no better than stick with the family business. Wouldn't he come round fast enough once he'd had time to settle? For this reason alone she preferred to keep family concerns private.

She sauntered down Tonman Street, enjoying a rare bit of time to herself. At a second-hand stall she found a frock for Sarah Jane – blue gingham. She'd look a picture in it. To avoid any squabbles between her precious grandchildren, Polly bought a gaudy glass bobber for Sean's marble collection, then treated herself to a mug of hot Vimto, which went down a treat. After that, she turned off by St Matthew's Church and made her way along Liverpool Road where she'd heard of a warehouse to let. If she could get at least a part of it at a rent she could afford they'd be up and running in no time. Charlie could work indoors again and be his own boss, which he preferred, and Benny would soon see the sense of coming in with her. Pity Big Flo was no longer the woman she'd once been, or she'd have given him what for, wouldn't she just, at rejecting such a fine offer. But the loss of her own three sons, one after the other over the years, had finally turned the old woman's mind. Didn't even know what day of the week it was half the time, poor old soul. Pride Carpets was still remembered, though, a name to be reckoned with.

The warehouse had already been taken, the landlord informed her, but softened her disappointment by mentioning another he'd heard going vacant, over towards Knotts Mill. Polly decided to take a shufty now, while she had the time. After all, Big Flo was being well taken care of. She'd left Benny in charge, giving Lily Gantry, who usually sat with the old woman while Polly was working, a morning off.

The future, Polly steadfastly decided, was looking bright.

Benny didn't quite share his mother's belief that family responsibilities were good for him. Fond as he was of his grandmother, Big Flo was an old woman, she'd had her life, while he was young and eager to be out and about to savour his freedom. What sort of a homecoming was this, to sit in the back yard with a seventy nine year old who was only tuppence to the shilling?

He'd been shocked when he first saw her. Once a big woman, with arms on her like an all-in wrestler, Flo now seemed shrunken and wizened. When Benny took her the meal his mother had left keeping warm between two plates over a pan of boiling water he found Flo, as usual, staring into space in the shadowy depths of the Anderson shelter, a strangely blank expression upon her face. The place had that sweet-sour smell of decay, of mustiness and the old tippler closet against which it leaned. It made him want to puke. On a table beside the old woman's chair lay a large book covered in newspaper clippings.

'He was my son, tha knows,' Big Flo reminded him, with a hint of her old sternness.

'Aye, 'course he was.' Benny stared at the face of his own

father, Matthew Pride, who'd been killed in the riots back in the thirties, protesting over the means test. Ancient history so far as Benny was concerned. He remembered grieving for him though as a young boy, and hating having to live with his Uncle Josh who'd taken over their lives completely. In the end, so far as he could remember, Josh too had turned a bit queer in the head, but Benny had no wish to live his life gazing over his shoulder. Look to the future, that was the way.

'Did you know my lad then?' Flo's wrinkled face broke into a childish grin, false teeth clicking loudly, as if this were a new discovery. Benny stifled a desire to ask how would he not know his own father? Instead he set the tray quietly before her.

'See, Mam's med you some nice lentil broth. Eat up,' he urged in jollying tones. 'Put some flesh on them old bones, eh? You should come inside, Gran, it in't warm here.' The damp was getting to him already. Why didn't his mother pull the shelter down?

' 'Oo art thee to tell me what to do?' Big Flo's voice boomed out, as forceful as ever. 'Thee's nobbut a lad. Fourteen next week, Joshua Pride, so don't get high-handed wi' me. Yer not too big fer me to clock you one.'

Oh, lord, Benny thought. Now she thinks I'm me own uncle. 'All right, don't get yer dander up. Eat yer dinner afore it goes cold.'

Big Flo showed no sign of touching the food and after

a long silence in which Benny struggled to think what to say that wouldn't upset her, he came suddenly to a decision. 'How about a walk? That'll put some colour in yer cheeks. Fresh air, that's what you need.' He couldn't bear to stay another minute stuck in this Anderson Shelter. He'd go as daft as her.

He went upstairs and brought the old woman's coat and hat, changed her felt slippers for a pair of sturdy shoes, tucked a scarf about her neck. 'Exercise is good for you, Gran. Do us both good, eh? How about a tram ride? You like going on the tram, eh?' He'd go down to the Council offices, ask about jobs or shop premises to rent, then he could do a bit of buying and selling on his own account. He had his demob money burning a hole in his pocket. There must be something good he could do with his future besides steaming and cleaning old carpets. Some way he could be independent.

Big Flo was remarkably easy to steer, if a bit wobbly, rather like an old car that kept stalling. Only once did she enquire where they were going and Benny told her the truth: that he was seeking employment. Unfortunately this set her off on tales of the hungry thirties again and all the way in the tram she scolded him about his false pride over Polly working when he wasn't.

'I'm Benny, not me dad,' he tried to say, but she wasn't listening so he gave up, humouring her as best he could.

He parked her on a bench, just outside the rating office,

instructing her sternly to sit tight while he went inside. 'I'll be back in a jiffy,' he told her as he disappeared through the door.

Benny only needed a small shop, just to get him started. In truth that would be all he could afford, though once he'd a bit more saved up, he'd go for something bigger. What he was going to sell in the shop he wasn't too clear. Clothing maybe. Or, better still, furniture. Whatever he could get his hands on. There'd be a good future in retailing once the utility rules were lifted. One shop, two shops . . . who knew where it might lead?

He marched smartly along the dimly lit corridor, boots ringing on the tiled floor. There were several men already waiting at the office to which he was directed, and a young woman sheltering behind a newspaper. Benny ignored them all, stood at the small square window and pressed the bell. He could see a man bent over a ledger in which he was writing in crabbed lettering. The clerk did not even glance up at the sound of the bell.

Benny pressed it again.

A woman in a tweed skirt and grey cardigan glanced briefly in his direction before returning to clacking the keys of an ancient typewriter. Benny wasn't used to being kept waiting, particularly by civvies. He drummed his fingers on the window ledge but neither paid him the slightest attention. Anger curled deep in his belly. He'd risked his life for idiots like this, penpushers who'd hardly taken their backsides off their easy chairs.

With one knuckle he rapped sharply on the window again. ' 'Scuse me,' he said in stentorian tones. No response save from the woman who, without pause in her typing, half glanced at the clerk, then quickly away again. Benny decided that the man was either stone deaf or pig ignorant. 'I haven't all day to stand here, tha knows.'

From behind him came a stifled snort of laughter. He rounded upon the perpetrator, and stopped dead.

Bright blue eyes danced with merriment above the open newspaper in the kind of classical face that might be considered plain or beautiful, depending perhaps on her mood or on those who looked upon it. She was certainly arresting. A fresh, almost schoolgirl grin, straight nose and a neat chin. The kind of beauty you could get to enjoy looking at. A beauty that showed breeding and class. The kind Benny Pride didn't usually get anywhere near.

'I've been here two hours,' she said, twisting her mouth into a moue of disbelief. Relaxed again, it became wide and laughing once more, a mouth he experienced a strong desire to taste. 'And it's not the first time. I've been here more times than I care to recall. It's always the same. He deals with you eventually. In his own good time. You just have to be patient.'

Benny was slowly gathering his wits. 'Two hours, my foot! Nobody meks a monkey out o' me.'

The girl giggled and ran her fingers through ridiculously short honey-gold hair. Benny preferred long curls that fell enticingly over a girl's face and red heads rather than blondes, more the Rita Hayworth type, but it suited her all the same, no doubt about that. 'I shouldn't think anyone would try,' she said, and Benny puffed out his chest, aware he'd developed a good physique while in the army, and that this girl seemed to appreciate the fact.

He rapped on the window again, harder this time, meaning to impress. 'Hey up. I'd like a word, if you don't mind.' He'd no intention of being ignored while those bewitching cornflower blue eyes were fixed upon him.

The clerk lifted his head and adjusted his spectacles to consider Benny briefly. 'Wait in line. You'll be attended to in due course.'

In one fluid movement Benny pushed up the small window, stuck his hand through the gap and, grasping the man by the only bit of collar he could reach, hauled him to his feet. 'Stand up when you speak to me,' he bawled, in a voice the men in his platoon would have recognised. 'Straighten that tie, jump to it, and *get your bleedin' hair cut!*'

The clerk's jaw hung loose with shock as his dazed eyes took in the size of Benny. He was quite unable to free himself from the clenched fist that held him in its iron grip. 'I b-b-beg your pardon?'

'No bloody pen-pusher tells me to wait in line. Is that understood? I've done all the waiting I'm doing. Six years of it. Now the soddin' war is over, and I haven't helped win it to wait about for fools like you to walk all over me.'

'Bravo!' cheered the girl softly from behind him, followed by a smattering of applause from the rest of his audience.

Benny's hand tightened on the clerk's collar, pulling the alarmed face closer to the window. His voice was low and uncompromising. 'You'll deal with this young lady first. *She* has been waiting fer *two hours*. You'll call her "ma'am", and you'll be polite. Then you'll deal with me.' Benny ignored the fact that there was a queue of men waiting before him. That was their problem. 'And you'll call me "*sir*". Have you got that? Is that simple enough for your clerk's brain to understand?'

The man wagged his head, not without difficulty.

'Good. Get on wi' it then.'

'Right away.'

'*Sir*.'

'Right away, sir.'

And to do the man justice, he did. In a surprisingly short time he had dealt with the girl and produced a list of empty shops, albeit a short one, for Benny to try.

Out on the pavement, Belinda thanked Benny for his help, though she had been less successful in her search for accommodation. The list the clerk had given her was for rooms only and the rent would soon eat away at her savings. 'Not that I've found a job yet,' she complained.

'Five years' hard labour for my beloved country and what do I get at the end of it?'

'Two hours in a rating office and the satisfaction of seeing authority crawl,' Benny replied, making her laugh again, a ripe gurgling sound that he instantly warmed to.

'I did enjoy that, I must say.'

She was perfectly delightful. As well as being stunningly attractive, she had a soft, well-modulated voice, indicating that she came from a better part of the city than himself. Happen up near Heaton Park or them new houses off Cheetham Hill, he decided. He wanted to know everything about her. Most of all if he could see her again. 'What were you then? A WRN?'

She shook her head. 'ATS. Corporal.'

Benny saluted, giving her a cheeky grin and a wink. 'Sergeant. Border Regiment. We must have quite a lot in common.' He was struggling to soften his Lancashire accent. It wouldn't do to put her off.

Clear blue eyes regarded him with undisguised interest. 'Maybe we do.'

A stillness fell upon them then and both seemed momentarily lost for words. As she half turned to go Benny felt a desperate urge for her not to walk out of his life as easily as she had walked into it. 'How about a cuppa? Or a bite of dinner? I'm fair starving.' He could have kicked himself. A girl like this would call it lunch, not dinner. He felt suddenly unsure of himself, the cockiness he'd displayed in the rating office now quite evaporated. He even wished he wasn't still in uniform but instead wearing a smart suit, maybe a double-breasted pinstripe, to show her he meant business.

Belinda was remembering that breakfast at Cherry Crescent had been even more fraught than usual that morning, so much so that she'd left without eating a thing. But then, tension had mounted daily since the ill-fated dinner party while she insisted on searching for work and alternative accommodation. Her father objected to everything she did, even to the clothes she chose to wear. Trousers, in his opinion, were unfeminine and gave the wrong impression, whatever that might be. He was furious that she'd declined to go shopping with her mother or to have her hair curled. Even the fact that she refused to go to bed when her parents did only served to spark off a row every supper time. If, as a result, Belinda barely stayed in the house long enough to sleep, let alone eat, was it any wonder?

She grinned up at Benny. 'Me too. Haven't eaten a thing all day. I wouldn't mind a bit of dinner myself.'

In no time at all the two of them were laughing together over home-made pie and chips in a small cafe off Deansgate, swopping jokes and war stories, funny ones only permitted. Belinda recalled diving into the toilets on Victoria Station, attracted by the faint blue light over the door when a doodlebug had been about to drop.

'Trouble was, it was the gents. Fortunately it wasn't in use at the time.' And they both laughed like drains. People turned and smiled, entranced by the lovely girl who sounded so happy with her young man.

Then they moved on to their dreams and ambitions, what they would do now that hostilities were over. She told him of the difficulties she was encountering at home, how her father was attempting to organise her life, her mother wanting to turn her into something she wasn't. 'And my brother Ron is no help at all. If Pops says jump, he jumps.'

'Nobody makes me jump if I don't want to,' Benny bragged. Eager to impress, he told her how he meant to have his own business. 'I'd start out modest like to begin with, just to test the market,' he explained, as if finance were not a serious consideration. He got so carried away by the intentness of her cornflower blue gaze that when she enquired what he might sell in his shop, and from where he would find his supplies, he found himself claiming skills he didn't possess. 'I've allus been good at making things with me own hands. This utility stuff won't last. Folk want summat better, so if I can't find it, I'll mek it.' Pure fantasy, born of hopes and dreams and the need to impress a beautiful woman. Belinda took it all in with flattering attention.

'I'm me own man,' he declared, rather grandly and somewhat inaccurately.

In view of how well they got on, it seemed natural for Benny to ask to see her again. He'd always been a bit shy around girls – the way they giggled behind their hands, and were only keen on spending his hard-earned brass. But this one seemed different, this one wasn't daft and silly like the rest. She wasn't some tart on the make. She showed style, had class, and probably a bunch of smart young officers queuing up to take her out. If he'd embroidered his ambitions a bit, let his dreams run wild, what of it? Wasn't that the only way to be noticed by a smart lass like Belinda Clarke? He certainly wasn't going to admit he'd only been offered a job cleaning mucky old carpets. When she agreed to see him again, he couldn't believe his luck.

'When? Tomorrow?'

Her eyes were dancing up at him and Benny felt the blood race through his veins. Yet again he was filled with worry. Was she laughing at him or did those wonderful peepers naturally behave in that lively fashion, out of sheer happiness? Benny did hope so. He felt dazed, dazzled by the perfect loveliness of her face in exciting and startling contrast to the mischievous rebel he glimpsed beneath.

He walked her to Piccadilly bus station, watched her climb aboard the red and white corporation bus, still bemused by his good fortune. Only as it pulled away did he smack the palm of his hand to his forehead and start to run after it, shouting to her as she clung to the rail on the platform that he didn't know her address, or even her last name. And they'd arranged no time for their next meeting. 'Meet me in Heaton Park by the band stand,' he shouted above the roar of the engine. It was the only decent place he could think of, on the spur of the moment.

She was still laughing as the bus swung round the corner, and when he finally stopped to draw breath, Benny became acutely aware he was standing like a great cart horse in the middle of Portland Street, running a grave risk of being ploughed down by a passing tram whose driver clanged its bell furiously at him.

And he hadn't the first idea whether she'd heard him or not.

He turned smartly on his heel and started to walk home. So captivated was he by her, so bemused by his own good fortune at meeting this lovely girl, and so concerned over whether she'd turn up for their date, that he quite forgot parking an old woman on a bench more than an hour before. It wasn't until he marched through his own front door and saw his sister set the frying pan on the stove and start tossing in slices of black pudding that he remembered. He stopped dead and swore softly under his breath.

'What's wrong? You've gone white as a sheet.'

'I'm in dead lumber, Lucy.' Thank heaven his mam wasn't home yet. He turned and raced straight out of the house again, Lucy's voice echoing after him, yelling to ask if he'd taken leave of his senses. He'd just have to hope Big

Flo was still sitting tight on that bench.

His hopes, sadly, were in vain. The bench was empty. The half-demented old woman had vanished.

Chapter Five

Polly was furious. Having found the untouched midday meal in the Anderson shelter with not a sign of Big Flo, she was frantic with worry by the time Benny returned alone from the city centre. Couldn't he manage a simple task like minding one old woman? she wanted to know. Didn't she have enough to worry over without having to supervise her own son? And much more along similar lines, punctuating her words with frequent slaps about his shoulders and upper body which bounced off Benny as if they were made by a fly. Polly was all for calling the police without delay, or for dragging the canal basin at the very least. Minnie Hopkins, who came galloping down the street at the first whiff of trouble, advised caution.

'Give her till tea time. Her stomach'll fetch her home by then.' Even so, the entire street turned out to search for Flo.

All afternoon they hunted high and low, trailing the length of Deansgate, through St Anne's Square, along

Cross Street, Market Street, even checking all the surface air-raid shelters around Piccadilly Gardens in case she'd taken a fancy to one. Then back to Deansgate Village and Castlefield where they searched beneath every railway arch, trawled around every likely wharf and tramped over practically every dingy stalk of grass down by the canal basin without seeing hide nor hair of her.

It was Lucy who found her, quite close to home, sitting in an air-raid shelter, of course, on a stretch of wasteland. It was growing dark by this time and nobody could begin to guess how she'd got there or when. Big Flo had her gas mask on, which she always carried in her portmanteau-sized handbag, and her only response when Lucy gently scolded her for wandering off and not waiting for Benny was to tell her that Jerry was sending buzz bombs now.

'Like a bleedin' homing pigeon,' said Lily Gantry, in her usual colourful language.

'At least she's nearing the end of the war,' Lucy said with a wry smile, once they had the old woman safely asleep in her own bed, a warm meal inside her and a hot water bottle at her feet. 'She might reach VJ Day soon, you never know.' Mother and daughter laughed, though not unkindly for it wasn't really a laughing matter.

'I wouldn't bank on it,' Polly mourned. 'She's hardly with us these days, is she?' and felt a pang of guilt that she'd left Flo to Benny's tender care. 'Jesus, Mary and Joseph, she doesn't ask for much, does she? All she wants is an

Anderson shelter fitted out with a bed, and a gas mask, and she's happy as a bug in a rug. It's my fault, it is so. I shouldn't've left her.'

'You're not to blame,' Charlie insisted. 'Benny should've had more sense than to take her into town. Mind like a feather pillow, that boy has.'

Polly quickly changed the subject, eager to tell Charlie all about the warehouse she'd found, close to Knott Mill Iron Works and with easy access to Castle Quay. 'I've agreed to take the ground floor which has plenty of space for the big machines I have in mind. We can just about afford the rent, so long as we all pull together and get the business going pretty smartish.' Polly thought of the savings she'd kept hoarded away in the bank for just such a day as this when war was at an end. They weren't made of brass, as Big Flo would say, but they could manage if they all worked hard.

'And what if I can't pull me weight? What if these dratted aches and pains of mine won't go, even when I'm working inside?'

Polly couldn't bear to think about such a prospect. She'd have him back up St John Street to see that doctor like a shot. Useless though he'd been the last time, claiming it was nothing more than age creeping up on him — as if Charlie were in his eighties instead of not yet sixty. 'Then you can sit in a comfy chair in a swanky office and do the paperwork, and won't that be a relief? You know how I hate doing it.'

Charlie was only too aware that paperwork was something Polly never shunned. She'd sat up night after night making her plans: endlessly going over the estimates for machinery she'd sent for, drawing up lists and costings, yet she always made it sound as if she couldn't manage without him, as if she were weak and helpless, when all the time she was the strongest woman he knew. But then, he wouldn't have her any other way. Charlie looked at her and loved the way her eyes shone with confidence and optimism for this new venture. He loved the way her head tilted and the impish grin that puckered her lips, the way she brushed back her hair with a languorous gesture. As always it made him want to kiss her and he wasted no time in doing so.

'I'm the luckiest man alive and not a day over twenty-five in me head at least,' he whispered, leading her upstairs to their private domain.

'And isn't it about time you realised that?'

When Benny got home the following afternoon he felt greatly in need of sympathy after failing yet again to find a job or shop premises, not to mention his keen disappointment over the fact that he'd waited two long cold hours in the park for Belinda, who hadn't turned up. She mustn't have heard him after all, over the roar of the bus engine, and since he didn't know where she lived, or even what her last name was, this had put him in a self-pitying frame of mind. Yet no one seemed in the least interested in his troubles. He could almost feel the family shunning him.

Sean had apparently howled all the way home from nursery because it was closing the following week. Lucy was almost as distraught, worrying over how she could possibly earn a living if she had no one to care for her son. It was all apparently due to the fact that since husbands had come home from the war, wives could now go back to being mothers instead of factory workers and child care facilities were no longer needed. But where did that leave her and others like her? she kept asking.

The small boy was now in the throes of a tantrum, drumming his heels on the floor with a sound fit to wake the dead, while Sarah Jane wept in sympathy. Polly was struggling to instruct a confused Big Flo on how to pull back an old blue and white cardigan, on the grounds that if she could keep the old woman occupied, she might not wander off again. She'd seemed even more vague since the incident.

Benny looked at the scene in despair. 'Bloody hell, its pandemonium in here. Can't a chap find a bit of peace in his own home? Isn't somebody going to shut that child up?'

'Will ye mind yer language?' Polly tutted, casting a nervous glance at Big Flo who, in her better days, would have clipped him about the ears for defying her Methodist morals so blatantly. 'And leave the child be. He'll shut up when he runs out of steam,' she finished, in a tone even Benny didn't dare to argue with. He tried a different tack, by complaining that he was hungry, but nobody heard, or troubled to answer if they did.

'I said, I've had no tea.' He addressed this directly to his sister. 'Or any dinner either for that matter.'

'You'll have to get it yourself for once.'

Benny looked appalled, as if she'd asked him to build Blackpool tower in their front parlour. 'Mek it meself?'

Polly set down the ball of wool she was winding with a sigh and got wearily to her feet. 'We thought you'd've got something while ye were out. I'll make you some dried scrambled egg.'

Lucy protested. 'Mam, you've done enough. You look fair wore out. He can surely get it himself for once. There's some cold sausage in the larder.'

Benny felt as if he was still being punished for his mistake over Big Flo. 'Cold sausage? Dried scrambled egg? Don't I deserve a proper meal? I've fought in this war, not you. I'm the one t'Germans have been tekkin pot shots at.'

Lucy pulled a warmed nightdress over Sarah Jane's head, thankfully noticing that at least the arrival of Benny, Sean's idol, had stopped his screaming and he was listening with interest to the escalating argument. 'Don't exaggerate. You never went overseas like my Tom. You had it soft. You worked in the stores for ages, and the most trouble you had was finding the right size of uniform.'

Benny was incensed by his sister's casual assessment of his war effort. 'Stores is a responsible job, I'll have you know, and that were only me first job anyroad. I went on to others – training men to fire machine guns for one. I may not have been sent overseas but there were planes going over all the time, firing at the base.'

'We've had a few bombs dropped on Manchester an' all,' Lucy hotly protested, determined not to let her brother have it all his own way. Hadn't they all enough to worry over, without him adding to it? Oh, she could see how it was going to be now he'd come home for good: arguing the whole time, selfishly thinking he could be waited on hand, foot and finger. Well, he had another think coming.

Benny, embittered by the keenness of his disappointment over Belinda, couldn't allow his sister to belittle his war career. 'I were wounded once in me leg, when the roof of our billet caved in. And you can't even be bothered to get me a bite to eat, you bl—'

Big Flo suddenly lifted her great head and fixed him with a glare. 'Tha's been told once. Watch thy language, lad, if tha knows what's good for thee. Tha's not too old to have thy mouth washed out wi' carbolic soap.'

They were so stunned at the old woman's return to the fighting talk they'd once taken for granted that they all burst out laughing.

'Will ye listen to yer gran. Doesn't she talk sense?'

Sheepish now, Benny went to the larder and made

himself a sandwich with the cold sausage. Polly placed a brimming mug of scalding tea on the kitchen table before him, and another beside Big Flo. 'Get that down yer neck, Mother. Ye deserve it after sorting that lad o' mine out.'

But Big Flo shook her head. 'Nay, I'm feeling a bit peculiar like. I couldn't face one. I reckon I'll go and 'ave a lie down.' They all tensed, ready to block the back door when she attempted, as was her wont, to go down the yard back to the shelter. Instead she opened the stair door and climbed wearily up to bed. They were all so startled that both Lucy and Polly ran to fill the stone hot water bottle, realising she must indeed feel poorly.

'Don't fuss, I'll be wick as a snig tomorn,' she tartly informed Polly as the bottle, carefully wrapped in a flannel cloth, was slid in beside her feet.

Polly expressed doubts on her mother-in-law wriggling like any eel the following morning, no matter how much she might protest to the contrary. 'You're all clammy and cold. Couldn't I leather our Benny for losing you, so I could. I'll fetch you some Fenning's Fever Cure, in case yer getting a temperature. And you're having a day with your feet up tomorrow and no argument.'

Big Flo gave a weak smile as Polly tucked the covers tight. 'Thee allus manages to have yer own way, lass. Allus did, I seem to recall, even against our Josh. Only one I know who ever dared to stand up to him.'

Polly was startled. This was the first time in years that

the old woman had spoken of her dreadful son in the past tense. She'd grown used to hearing Joshua Pride referred to as if he were still with them, as if Big Flo expected him to walk in at any moment. And with such conviction that there were times when Polly would glance over her shoulder and shiver. She hated to be reminded of her brother-in-law's malice, thankful only that she'd beaten him in the end, if at a price. He'd intended to emigrate but had ended his days in an institution for the mentally insane and his mother had never quite recovered from the shame of it.

Polly made up a fire in the bedroom, then piled extra blankets on the big high bed.

'Don't forget the blackout,' came the forceful voice, and realising there was little point in arguing, Polly dutifully pulled down the black paper blind and drew the curtains over it, but she didn't return to the kitchen. Instead, she sat with her mother-in-law, sipping quietly at her tea, her eyes on Big Flo's face, remembering a time when the pair of them had been constantly at odds, forever at each other's throats, just as Benny and Lucy were now. She could hear them continuing their quarrel down below. 'Will ye listen to the pair of them? Ye'd think they'd be sick of war and want a bit of peace, wouldn't ye now?' Polly said, but the only answer was a heavy snore and she smiled, letting her own eyes close. Wasn't it grand to have a minute's peace herself?

After a while she heard Benny go out and Lucy climb

the stairs to put the children to bed. The house was filled to bursting so it was. Oh, but she didn't mind a bit. Didn't she enjoy having her family about her?

It was a good house, for all she'd have preferred to stay on at Cheetham Hill had they been able to afford. But they'd three bedrooms which was one more than most in Pansy Street, save for Minnie Hopkins at the top house with seven. Even so Benny was forced to sleep in the alcove bed downstairs since Lucy and the children were crowded into one, and Big Flo had this little box room. Downstairs, the front door might open directly on to the street but the long lobby led the way to a living room as well as a front parlour. At the back was the kitchen with a few steps leading down into a backyard which they shared with no one, and wasn't that a treat? They even possessed a good-sized cellar, which was where they'd spent much of the war, though Big Flo had always favoured the Anderson shelter of course. One day soon, when Polly was feeling brave, she'd have the dratted thing pulled to pieces, so she would.

She smiled down at her mother-in-law, sleeping peacefully like an old war-horse herself. She thought how different things would have been if Matthew had lived. Not that she didn't love Charlie. She'd been fortunate to have two good husbands in her life. She and Matthew had enjoyed many happy years together, not like poor Lucy who'd lost her own husband far too young. Yet somehow, Polly knew she'd manage. Didn't you always, when you'd no choice in the matter? This reminded her that her first task tomorrow was to help Lucy find someone to mind Sean for when he could no longer go to the nursery, otherwise wouldn't she be landed with the job herself? And much as she loved the little tyke, she needed to get her business going and not spend her days baby minding. But it needed to be someone trustworthy and reliable to take care of her grandson. She worried a long time over this.

Charlie came in, urging her to go to bed and get a bit of rest, but still she refused to leave Big Flo. Much later Polly heard the front door bang when Benny came back from the pub, and the sound of his stumbling feet going along the lobby. He was singing some raucous song and bumping into the furniture. Wouldn't she clip him one if he woke the poor old soul up, not to mention those children in the next room? Polly had changed into her old dressing gown by this time and pulled it close about her before tiptoeing downstairs, ready to give him a piece of her mind.

In the dim light of the kitchen fire she saw him slumped in a chair, head flung back, loud snores emanating from his wide-open mouth. A stink of vomit filled the tiny kitchen. Polly punched her son in the chest.

'Will ye wake up, yer good-fer-nothing lout? Is it come to this, that ye defile yer own mam's hearth?'

Benny woke with a start, mumbling apologies that he'd only been celebrating his own homecoming, though he was clearly having difficulty focusing on exactly who it was he was apologising to. With a snap Polly pulled down the alcove bed that nestled in the wall by the kitchen fire. Cramped it may be for a lad as big as Benny, yet it was warm and snug and more than he deserved, drunken sot that he was.

'See you wash yer face and tek off those filthy boots afore you get into it, ye useless tyke.' She wagged a finger at him, stabbing him in the chest with it to emphasise every word. She could feel her whole body begin to shake with fury. 'First you leave your poor old grandmother wandering the city like a lost soul, so is it any wonder she's sick with a temperature and possible pneumonia? Now ye come home the worse for drink. 'Tis me da all over again, to be sure, and see how he ended up – dead as a nail. I'll not have it. Not in me own house. Couldn't I just batter yer daft head in?'

Benny flinched as he saw her snatch up the dish cloth, but it was only to wipe the sick and spittle from his face, just as if he were a lad still. He jerked his head away, anxious to avoid her ministrations, but knew better than to argue, not when she was in this frame of mind. In truth he was secretly ashamed of his drunkenness. By trying to drown his sorrows over Belinda, he'd succeeded only in worsening the poor opinion his mother already had of him. He could see her winding herself up into a fair paddy. In addition he'd made himself ill and would no doubt suffer a thick head in the morning.

Polly poured a jug of cold water over her son's head, soaking him through. 'Tomorrow ye'll come to the warehouse with me and no more nonsense about being yer own boss or finding yer own job. There's enough work there to keep us all busy and don't we need all the help we can get?'

'Aw, Mam. I've told you already, I'll not work for you in the warehouse, I'll not. I mean to mek me own way.'

She could hardly believe what she was hearing: her own son still stubbornly refusing to work with her, and after the way she'd given him his first job when he was no more than a whelp. The Irish temper rose in her so fierce that a flush of red seemed to suffuse her vision. 'Jesus, Mary and Joseph, ye'd make a saint swear, so ye would. I'm thinking yer too stubborn for yer own good. Ye'll pull yer weight as I tell you to, or it's out on the streets for you, ye daft galoot.'

Benny drew himself up in the chair to his not inconsiderable height, concentrating hard so that he didn't fall off it while he put this very important point, enunciating each word as slowly and carefully as he could. 'I'll pleashe meshelf. I'm warning you, Mam, I've had enough of folk tellin' me what to do. I'm going to pleashe meshelf in future.'

'Oh, is that so, to be sure? Then it's a bill you'll be getting every week for yer bed and board.' And, swinging on her heel, Polly strode from the room, ignoring his plea of: 'Aw, Mam, you can't do that. I've no money yet.'

At the door she stopped and wagged her finger one last time. 'Then ye'd best earn some or it's the warehouse for you, like it or no. I don't want to spend every day doing battle with me own son, but if it's a war ye want, then it's a war ye'll get. Only *I'll* win.'

After an achingly long and uncomfortable night, necessitating frequent trips to the privy down the yard, Benny felt worse rather than better as daylight approached. He couldn't believe what he was doing. How had he imagined he could take on his mother? Wasn't she notorious for getting her own way? Why couldn't he just agree and accept the miserable job? What was so marvellous about independence anyroad? He never did find the answer to this one before merciful oblivion took over.

At some time during her long vigil, Polly must have closed her eyes and slept, too, for when she next woke with a start it was to find the night-light had guttered, the fire gone out and the room felt strangely cold for early summer.

Polly drew back the curtains and lifted the paper blackout blind a fraction so she could see to find a match to relight a candle. The moon still hung in a pale grey sky, sending a shaft of light into the bedroom, eerily outlining the figure which lay so still in the high brass bed. That was the moment in which Polly realised her mother-in-law was dead.

For once in her life, without making any fuss, Big Flo had slipped quietly away when no one was looking.

Polly sat on the polished seat of the pew, her family gathered silently about her, and tried to take in the words of the minister as he droned on about Florence Pride, our dear departed sister. The small chapel was almost filled with family and friends, some in severe black, others wearing well-used arm bands over their ordinary coats. Aunt Ida was there, almost as stoic as Big Flo herself had been in a lifetime of troubles. Uncle Nobby, looking pale and solemn and smelling faintly of the manure he'd put on his rhubarb patch that morning. Lily Gantry, putting her hand on Polly's arm. 'Eeh, lass, I'm reet sorry. She were a grand woman, in her day.' Minnie Hopkins dressed in a funereal black coat that had a greenish cast to it from long disuse, but her shoes were well polished and she'd put her teeth in for the occasion. The two women sat together like a pair of old crows.

Behind them came other neighbours. The Taylors and Beckworths, Maggie Stubbs, Maisie Wright, Harry Entwistle the joiner, and Mrs Shaw from the end house. Then of course there was Doris-from-next-door and Gladys and Vera Benson, the two sisters who ran the corner shop, for all they too, like Polly, were Catholics and would have some explaining to do for even being present in a Methodist chapel. The sisters had managed to find a bit of ham and pickles from 'under t'counter', for those who wished to go back to the house for a bite of refreshment afterwards.

Every now and then Polly would sniff into her hanky and Charlie pat her shoulder, or Sarah Jane would feed her little brother a toffee to still his chattering tongue. He'd surely be sick if he had many more, Polly thought, watching them. Benny was looking unusually sombre in his drab demob suit, as if the bomb Big Flo had been expecting for so long had finally fallen and he'd been the one to bring it. And so he should, for in a way he had.

Polly could hardly believe she was sitting here, calmly taking part in Big Flo's funeral. The old woman had seemed indestructible at one time, larger than life itself. Now, all because of Benny's neglect, she was gone. She swallowed the tears that blocked her throat. Sure and she'd be hard pushed to forgive him for his carelessness, so she would.

Michael Hopkins, occupying the pew immediately behind the diminutive figure of his aunt, leaned over to whisper a few sympathetic words and while Polly nodded vaguely, Lucy turned her head to smile a radiant response.

'Look at that little madam,' came the hissing voice of Lily Gantry to her companion Minnie Hopkins, overriding the muted tuning-up from the organ. 'Making eyes at that nephew o' thine at her own grandmother's funeral. You'd happen think her a merry widow instead of a good

Catholic wife to a soldier declared missing.'

Polly felt as if someone had struck her. How dare they? *How dare they*! If she weren't in chapel, she'd give them a piece of her mind for uttering such blasphemy. She cast a sideways glance at Lucy, who was using her hymn book to hide her scarlet cheeks.

'Blethering idiots,' Polly whispered.

The minister was asking them to rise, hymn books were being opened, throats cleared and the organ straining to find the right notes. Then good Methodist voices soared up to the gallery, *The Day Thou Gavest Lord is Ended*, and Polly felt the tears roll unchecked down her cheeks, to make little splashes on the blurred words in the book. Aw, but she'd miss the old dragon, so she would.

Chapter Six

Outside the chapel Michael Hopkins hovered at Lucy's elbow. 'Will you be coming to work tomorrow, as usual?' he asked.

'Of course.' Lucy sounded surprised for didn't she have her living to earn?

'Only I'd like a word.' He meant about the whispers they'd all clearly heard in chapel but even as he disappeared amongst the crowd she didn't dare watch him go, too keenly aware of his aunt's all-seeing eye fixed upon her and evil tongue still wagging. Lucy contented herself with tugging Sean's collar into place and hustling Sarah Jane into the waiting car to cover her embarrassment.

The cortege of two funeral cars, hired by Polly to show they could still hold their heads high, unemployed or not, carried the entire Stockton and Pride family and various close friends along Lower Byrom Street on the way back to Pansy Street.

Benny took no part in the polite attempts at conversation around him, too concerned with his own troubles. He'd loved Big Flo. Hadn't she spoiled him rotten as a boy for all her sharp tongue? And he'd never meant her any harm. Yet he could sense that everyone blamed him, just as if he'd deliberately left her sitting on that bench in the hope she'd catch pneumonia. Coming home seemed to have been something of an anticlimax. There'd been no Welcome Home banner for him. Arriving at the same moment as the telegram bringing news of Tom's fate had scuppered any chance of that. The longed for Civvy Street was, in reality, a bleak and lonely place. He still hadn't sorted out his future and he'd even messed up his chances with a wonderful girl called Belinda.

It was as the cars turned into Liverpool Road that he saw her. For a moment he thought his eyes were deceiving him, that he'd conjured her out of a fevered and overworked imagination. He couldn't think what she might be doing here, at Castlefield, but he would have recognised her anywhere, even in a floppy red beret that hid half her lovely face from his view. She was standing at the corner of Fenton Chemicals, talking to a young man, wearing a light grey costume that seemed to mould itself to her slender figure. Benny thought she looked even more beautiful than he remembered.

'Stop the car.' He was shouting at the driver and Lucy was slapping his arm, telling him to be quiet and show more respect. But the car did indeed stop and within seconds he was beside Belinda, grinning from ear to ear.

She looked startled, as well she might, to have him appear out of nowhere. There was a slight puckering between her straight brows as she gazed at him with those mesmerising blue eyes. Perhaps, he worried, she didn't even remember him. Benny was about to remind her who he was when her brow cleared and she laughed.

'Of course, you're the chap who got me served in the rating office.'

Benny beamed. 'You remember me.'

'How could I forget?'

She introduced him to her companion, Frank Fenton no less, the son of the owner. He was thin, not very tall, with light brown hair and eyes, pale pockmarked skin and a faintly sulky expression on his boyish face. A nondescript in Benny's opinion and he took pleasure in paying the fellow scant attention. 'I'm glad I caught you. I must've missed you the other day.'

Benny couldn't take his eyes off her, saying the first thing that came into his head, foolishly asking how she came to be here in Liverpool Road, as if it mattered so long as he'd found her again. She told him that her father had business interests in the area and they were soon chatting twenty to the dozen until Lucy shouted to him to hurry up. Benny turned and yelled back, to tell her he'd be along later, and she slammed the funeral car's door in a most inappropriate fashion. Benny hastily explained he couldn't hang around for long as he was at this very moment on his way back from his grandmother's funeral, earning himself a softening of those dazzling blue eyes as a result.

'I'm so sorry. Don't let us hold you up,' Belinda murmured, in that wonderful voice of hers.

'You could come and have a bite with us, if you wanted? There's plenty.' He'd no idea whether there was or not but he was anxious to hang on to her, wishing Fenton would take the hint and vamoose. Instead, the man simply stood there, foursquare, as if he owned the flippin' road as well as the factory.

'Oh, we wouldn't dream of intruding, would we, Frank?'

The young man shook his head. 'Indeed not. Our commiserations to your family.' He took hold of Belinda's arm as if he had every right to do so. Benny longed to shove him off and take hold of her himself, but she wasn't the sort of girl to appreciate a tug-of-war between two warring suitors.

Panic struck. Benny knew he must do something to delay her, to make sure they met again. Then he was pulling out his pocket book, asking her to write her name and address in it, and she was laughing up at him in just the way he remembered.

'And my telephone number too, I suppose?'

She had a telephone? Hadn't he known she had class.

'Of course,' he casually agreed, and watched with satisfaction as a frown marred Frank Fenton's brow as Belinda carefully noted the details down, closed the book and handed it back to Benny.

'Good to see you again,' she said quite lightly but, he was sure, with absolute sincerity.

'Happen you'll be seeing me sooner than you think.' He saluted, and then remembering he wasn't in uniform, held out his hands by way of apology, making her giggle. How he loved her laughter!

Benny strode away at such a cracking pace it took him a moment or two to realise he was going in quite the wrong direction so was forced to double back and march past them both again, making her hoot with laughter all the more, Frank Fenton smirk, and his own neck and cheeks fire up. Still, he was beyond caring, he was so pleased at his good fortune. He'd never have thought such a bit of luck could come out of such a sad day. If it wasn't disrespectful to think so, happen his grandmother had fixed it for him, from the other side, to show that she at least had forgiven him. Benny rather hoped so.

At seven o'clock that evening he was kicking his heels outside a certain house in Cherry Crescent, plucking up the courage to make his presence known. Feeling surprisingly nervous, yet determined not to show it, he finally pressed his thumb to the bell. A portly, red-faced man came to the door, looking down his bulbous nose at Benny as if he were a beetle that had crawled out from under a stone.

'I've called to see Miss Belinda Clarke. Would she be in?' Benny politely enquired, somewhat overdoing the carefully practised phrases.

'Indeed she wouldn't,' came the brusque reply. Not to the likes of you anyway, Hubert might have added had he not been interrupted at that moment by Belinda herself.

'Yes, I am, Father. Don't be silly. Oh, hello, Benny. Wait there, I'll get my coat.'

And as he stood grinning with pleasure, Councillor Hubert Clarke fidgeted on his own front doorstep itching to give the young soldier a piece of his mind for his impudence in calling without an appointment. 'I thought you were stopping in tonight,' he tried, as his daughter brushed past him. 'Frank will be round, don't forget.'

'No, he won't,' she said, tucking her arm under Benny's. 'I told him not to bother. Don't wait up, I might be late.' And the pair of them strolled off, Belinda smiling, Benny looking as if he'd swallowed a whole dish of cream. Hubert Clarke looked as if he'd been given a lemon to suck.

Benny took Belinda to the Gaumont, which was the most expensive cinema he could afford, to see *Meet Me in St Louis*. He curbed his natural impatience by contenting himself with merely holding her hand and she didn't seem to object. They came out dancing and singing the *Trolley Song* all along the tramlines, just as if Belinda were Judy Garland. To Benny's mind she was every bit as fabulous as any film star. She must have enjoyed herself for she agreed to see him the next afternoon too. Benny took her for tea at Lewis's because he thought that was what classy young women liked to do. Two weeks and several dates later he was beginning to worry that at this rate he'd spend all his demob money in no time, so risked making a suggestion.

'I'd tek you home to meet me mam and Charlie and our Lucy, only you'd happen think us a bit – well – a bit humble like. Clean and honest but ordinary folk, us.' He'd chosen his words with care, so that she'd feel obliged to agree. And she did.

'Don't be silly, I'm ordinary too. And I'd love to meet them,' she said, with genuine warmth in her voice, exactly as he'd hoped.

Beaming, Benny tucked her arm in his. 'That's settled then. Lucy'll be back from her cleaning job by now, and she'll mek us a cuppa.'

'I wouldn't want to get in her way, though, if she's busy.'

'You won't be. She likes a bit of company, does our Lucy.' He was anxious for the two girls to meet for, if they got on, Belinda might take to calling. He hadn't much cared for the red-faced old geezer who'd opened the door to him that first evening, though the house had been a real eye-opener, much bigger and grander than he'd expected, and with a garden front and back. But if Belinda didn't think much of her father, then she'd happen take to coming round to his house regular like, and he'd be more sure of her. He was almost certain she and Lucy would hit it off.

In the event he was proved right. His sister and Belinda liked each other on sight, the two girls soon laughing and talking as if they'd known each other for years. The children climbed all over Belinda's knees, vying for her attention, and when it was time for her to go, Lucy went with them to the door.

'You must call any time, I'd be glad of your company.'

'Me too.' They smiled at each other. 'You could come to the pictures with us some time,' Belinda added.

Lucy glanced at her brother's face, noted the quick frown and chuckled. 'I wouldn't want to play gooseberry.' Belinda laughed, making it clear she was perfectly capable of choosing for herself: sometimes she would go with Benny, sometimes with Lucy, or all together. And so it was agreed.

The two girls became firm friends. Belinda would call regularly and, if Polly was working, Doris-next-door would baby-sit for Lucy and off they would go, window gazing along Deansgate or, if they were a bit flush, on a trip to the pictures. On these occasions they were two young lasses again, not a wife worrying about a missing husband or somebody's daughter trying to hang on to her battered independence. They cheered when Dane Clark won the war, stamped their feet when the cavalry chased the Indians, and wept unashamedly when Ingrid Bergman lost her man.

On other occasions, like today, Benny was with them, and the three of them would walk arm in arm, laughing and joking, their young voices ringing out, singing songs from the movies, making up fantasies of how it felt to live in a vast Hollywood mansion. Afterwards they'd treat themselves to a fish supper or walk along Liverpool Road eating a meat and potato pie, hot and succulent, giggling as the gravy dribbled down their chins. There was nothing better on a cool autumn evening.

'Wait till I get me own business,' Benny announced, swaggering a little in front of Belinda. 'Then I'll happen get me own car and drive you somewhere smarter even than the Gaumont. Mebbe all the way to the seaside for a day.'

'What about Mam?' Lucy queried, bringing him back to reality. 'I thought you were helping her with the carpets?'

Benny flushed for he had done a bit of work for his mam since so far he'd been unable to find premises or a job to suit him. 'I can do better than that, Luce, see if I can't. I mean to set up on me own, you know I do.'

Smiling fondly at him, Belinda said, 'I remember you telling me how good you are with your hands, that you'd like to try joinering and make your own furniture to sell.'

'Aye, happen so,' Benny agreed, with not too much conviction in his tone. He could feel himself becoming more and more embroiled in this lie, surely only a white one since he had done quite well in woodwork at school, yet he seemed unable to do anything to extricate himself from it. 'There's going to be a great call for good furniture. That's certainly true.'

Lucy snorted her disbelief but, smiling to herself, left him to his harmless fantasies.

Belinda chipped in, 'I think you're ever so brave, but wise too, to start up on your own right away, now peace is here. The best way to make money is to work for yourself or so Pops tells me, and judging from his success I have to believe him. Of course, you'd need premises.' And so flattered was he by her interest, in contrast to his sister's negative attitude, that Benny couldn't resist expanding on his theme.

'Oh, aye. I'm keeping an eye open for summat suitable, though they're hard to come by these days, shop premises. Once I find a place I'll set it all up wi' a bench and tools and everything. Then customers'll flock to me door for whatever I produce.'

'I could help you look.'

'Aye, why not?' He felt almost breathless with hope. She liked him. She really did. Happen he was in with a chance after all.

Lucy had heard enough of his foolish bragging and

sought for a way to change the conversation. They were walking past the Co-op which was still open and doing a brisk trade, for all it was late, the shop's bright lights spilling out on to the wet pavements. They could see Lily Gantry barging her way to the front of the queue. Lucy shook her head in despair. 'What a woman! D'you remember what she said at Big Flo's funeral?' And she related the words that had caused her such hurt at the time.

'The old witch,' Belinda said, and put her arm around her friend's waist, giving her a comforting squeeze. 'Take no notice. She's only jealous of your lovely youth.'

'Aye,' Benny agreed. 'Who'd fancy her, an old goat wi' whiskers on her chin?'

Belinda gave a merry chuckling laugh. 'Who is this Michael Hopkins? What's he like?'

'A rather private, reliable sort of man. He's my employer, and a good friend,' Lucy explained. 'He's rather nice actually, a sort of Trevor Howard type.'

'And our Luce is panting for him,' Benny said with a snort.

'Ooh, I never am.'

'You mek his dinner every day fer nowt. That sounds pretty keen to me.'

'I'd no choice. That flippin' dragon Minnie Hopkins made me.'

'Why don't you invite him to come to the flicks with us?' Belinda suggested.

'Then you can canoodle on the back row,' Benny teased, thinking this a good idea as it would leave him free to do the same with Belinda. Having his sister tag along too often hadn't been the plan at all. Lucy's response, however, was to knock him over the head with her rolled up umbrella.

Belinda laughed as the pair of them tussled together in a play fight. 'Mind you don't drop your pie, Lucy.'

'Quite right. Let's keep our priorities in order. Eat first and I'll batter his brains in later.'

Over the next weeks, as the days shortened, Belinda continued to see almost as much of Lucy as she did of Benny and seemed content to have it that way. Not that they weren't pretty inseparable as a couple, and Lucy envied them that contentment. Yet within the family disagreement rumbled on. Benny seemed determined to be independent, refusing any sort of commitment beyond a bit of temporary employment now and then with his mother. Polly was clearly upset by his continued stubbornness in this matter and went about tight-lipped. Knowing her mother as she did, Lucy could see the situation exploding in Benny's face if he didn't make a move to find himself a proper job soon. Polly's patience with her one and only son, much as she adored him, would surely only stretch so far.

But Lucy was happy for him, she was really. Belinda was a lovely girl, though what she saw in head-in-the-clouds

Benny she really couldn't imagine. Maybe she was jealous in a way for wouldn't she just love a man of her own; a life other than one with herself and two children crammed into the spare room of her mother's house.

That Christmas the Ministry of Food handed out free Christmas puddings and one was given to Lucy, since she was bringing a family up alone. A part of her resented this act of charity but she accepted it all the same. Every day she was forced to remind herself that Tom was only *missing*, as if she needed to drum this fact into her head. Yet however much she might do so, deep down she held no hope that he would ever return, which left her feeling like a widow with all the problems that brought. But what if she wasn't? Others, besides Lily Gantry and Minnie Hopkins, didn't see her as such, so how could she ever rebuild her life, ever start again with another man, if she did not know for certain one way or the other.

She missed having someone to confide in, to chat with, to open her heart to as she used to be able to do with Tom. She didn't always see eye to eye with her mother, though it was admittedly true that Polly had never been one to interfere and when she offered advice, it was usually wise. Like the time she'd urged Lucy to apologise to her employer for those sharp words. Nevertheless even a loving mother or a friend like Belinda, however valuable, couldn't make up for the loss of a soul mate, husband and lover.

As always Lucy took refuge from her troubles in hard

work. It was the only way she could cope with her grief. Every morning she went to the end of the street and cleaned number 179, keeping a well buttoned lip despite much provocation from Minnie Hopkins. Lucy still couldn't stand her but at least she'd kept her job, one she needed and enjoyed, and they became reconciled to a state of what might be called armed truce. Generally speaking they managed to keep out of each other's way, circling whenever they met like a pair of sparring dogs.

Lucy enjoyed looking after Michael. He was a kind and gentle man, had even stood up for her when she'd asked if she could have Sean with her while she worked, since the day nursery had closed. Minnie had been vehemently opposed to the idea, but Michael very reasonably pointed out that if Sean didn't come, neither would his mother. And by that time even Minnie had come to appreciate the excellent dinners the young woman cooked for them, so had grudgingly accepted the situation.

To Lucy this was a huge relief as it eased the pressure on her over-full day. Sean, though curious about the big house, was no trouble and seemed to benefit from spending more time with his mother. He played either in the long back yard or safely in the small front garden, little bigger than a pocket handkerchief with a few stalwart marigolds surrounded by a privet hedge. The boy seemed content with his chalks and slate, toy soldiers or bowl of soapy water for blowing bubbles, and Lucy could keep an eye on him from out of the many windows as she rubbed them clean.

Yet she was aware as Michael returned each dinnertime from the haulage depot where he worked as foreman that he watched her with concern, often remarking that she worked too hard, that she'd lost weight and looked worn out.

One day when Lucy had made a delicious mutton hot pot he insisted she sit and share it with them. Minnie looked outraged but for once, wisely perhaps, kept her opinions to herself. Lucy was equally opposed to the idea but the more she protested, the more Michael insisted. Cushions were placed on a chair for Sean and, finally succumbing to the mouth-watering aroma of good meat, the like of which Polly could rarely afford since all her spare cash was being poured into restarting the business, Lucy urged the small boy to be on his best behaviour and seated herself beside him. She was aware throughout the meal of Minnie Hopkins's grim silence, apart from the clicking of her false teeth as she sucked on the mutton bones.

Afterwards Michael walked the length of the street with Lucy while Sean skipped and hopped along in front, riding his imaginary cowboy horse. As they approached number 32, among the more tightly packed terraces where Lucy lived, Michael said, 'You still look tired. What you need is a rest, a day off.'

She laughed out loud at that. 'What chance do I get for

a rest? Today I have to pick up our Sarah Jane on her way home from school, then mek a bite of dinner for everyone. That's my job, d'you see? Mam usually makes supper. Then I'm off to Taylor's this afternoon to do their weekly clean through. That's after I've washed the dishes and dropped our Sean off next door and Sarah Jane back at school. Pick the kids up again at four. Then there's only all the washing, ironing and mending to do, which never stops with two childer, plus my share of the housework. After that me time's me own!'

'You do too much,' he said, and she pushed the brown curls behind her ears as she laughed up at him.

'Well, when you come up wi' a way of earning brass without having to work for it, let me know.'

Michael was thoughtful for a while as they walked on before returning to his argument. 'I still think you need a day off, a day all to yourself. And, by heck, I'll see you get one.' He was gripping her arms now, swinging her round to face him, and the heat of his touch was doing peculiar things to her insides. 'You could have a day trip to Belle Vue, or Blackpool. I'll tek you mesel, Lucy Shackleton.'

'Belle Vue? Blackpool?' She stared at him in wonder, as if he had suggested a trip to the moon. 'And who'd tek care of the childer, if I did?'

'The childer would come wi' us, you daft ha'porth.'

A day in Blackpool. A ride in a tramcar, a dance in the Tower Ballroom, sucking on a stick of rock and paddling her feet in the sea. Eeh, it sounded grand! Lucy couldn't remember the last time she'd been. Yes, she could, with Aunt Ida and Uncle Nobby just before the war. They were no more than courtesy titles, them being old friends of Charlie's, but they'd always been good to Lucy even so. They'd stayed at a boarding house in York Street for a full week, in one of those tall terraced houses with stairs that seemed to reach all the way up to heaven. But she wouldn't say no to an afternoon at Belle Vue either. Near as it was to her home, she'd rarely visited this magical place, scarcely had the money since the children were born. A few hours with nothing to do but gawp at exotic animals, lick candy floss like a big kid and whiz on a whirligig. Oh, wouldn't that be grand?

For a moment, as Michael's big broad hands gripped hers, she felt dizzy at the prospect of such heady joys. The temptation was so great, happiness so nearly within her grasp, that Lucy almost flung her arms about his neck and said yes, she'd love to, before reality drenched the madness.

She couldn't let Michael pay for them. That wouldn't be right. Both the children needed new shoes, and hadn't she enough trouble finding money to pay the bills, let alone to waste on whirligigs and candy floss? She was supposed to be saving hard for a place of their own; her children deserved a bit of space and privacy, even if they no longer had a dad. So she firmly refused his kind offer. 'Me, take a day off? When 'ave I got time?' she scoffed. 'You must be soft in the 'ead. Anyroad, it'll be too cold. Happen next year, eh?'

'Is that a promise?'

Lucy could hardly meet the intentness of his gaze. It seemed to be burning her up. 'Barring accidents, as they say,' she commented brightly. Yet it stayed in her mind, this foolish dream, and she couldn't help but wonder what Michael Hopkins would look like dressed up smart, instead of in his blue work overalls.

Chapter Seven

Lucy was keenly aware that Sean missed the nursery and also missed his dad. For all he had never known him, she'd made sure that he kissed Tom's photo every night and he'd got it into his head that his father would one day come home, play football with him and teach him how to fish. It was all her fault if the little boy now felt let down, as if a promise had been broken.

'When is me dad coming home? He hasn't forgotten me, has he?' And Lucy would explain that he might never come back, that she didn't know the first thing about fishing or football and he should ask Uncle Benny. But Uncle Benny was always too busy with his own affairs these days, looking for the shop of his dreams and taking Belinda out. When Sarah Jane had gone back to school at the beginning of the autumn term it was hard for the little boy to accept that he couldn't go too. It made him feel even more left out of things.

'You can go next year – perhaps by next summer, if the teacher will let you. You'll be four and a half by then, love,' Lucy told him.

'Dad'll be home soon, won't he?'

'No, love. I don't think so.' And at that he'd picked the photo up from where it stood on the dresser and flung it to the stone floor where the glass had shattered into a dozen pieces. Sean was a child with a determined nature. Lucy tried to explain this to Michael one morning after he'd found her weeping as she swept the endless stairs in his aunt's house.

'I can't bear to see you cry, Lucy.' He laid a hand on her shoulder and something inside her seemed to unfold at his touch, as if her body were reaching out to his.

'It's our Sean, I'm that worried about him.'

'Don't be.' And to her surprise he reached over and pressed his lips very gently upon hers. It was nothing more than the sweetest breath of a kiss but it left her with a strange sensation of anticipation, not to mention a trembling breathlessness in the pit of her stomach. Then next minute his arms were tight about her, holding her against him and offering her such wonderfully solid comfort that her heart was thumping like an express train.

Afterwards she swore to Polly that she hadn't been distracted at all, that of course she'd been keeping a proper eye on Sean. He'd asked to go down into the front garden to play and she'd thought it perfectly safe, with the small green gate fast shut and the sneck tied up, since she was aware how resourceful he was. But while she stood in the dark intimacy of the stairs with Michael's arms about her, out in the garden Sean dealt quite easily with the bit of string that held it fast and was soon marching smartly up Pansy Street, straight as a soldier, just like his Uncle Benny.

He knew where the school was. Hadn't he walked with Mam and Sarah Jane often enough? He turned the corner quickly and kept on marching, trying not to look at the round things at the crest of the hill that looked like bogey-men's heads, but which Mam had once told him were chimney pots. He wasn't sure he could believe her. Grown-ups didn't always tell the truth. Mam had said his dad was coming home. Now he wasn't.

The school yard was empty when Sean arrived, which threw him for a minute. Then he realised that the children would be in their classrooms having lessons, and all he had to do was walk down the long corridor to find Sarah Jane's room, and she'd tell him which was the right class for him. But first he had to cross this busy road.

Lucy and Michael leapt apart when Minnie came to find her. Lucy began to sweep for all she was worth, brandishing the stiff hand brush with vigour while Michael attempted to adopt an air of casual interest. She wondered if her lipstick was smeared and that was why Minnie glared at her so fiercely.

'Do you realise you left the front gate open? Anybody could have walked in; perfect strangers who might have murdered me in my bed. If I'd still been in it, that is.'

Lucy stopped sweeping, a small cloud of dust settling about her head as she froze and stared up at Minnie Hopkins. 'What did you say?'

'I said, I could've been . . .'

'No, about the gate.'

'I've told you, it were wide open and . . .'

Lucy dropped the brush and, scrambling to her feet, almost fell down the stairs in her haste, heart racing. She saw the gate swinging open and stood transfixed before turning and flying back through the house, calling his name. 'Sean! Are you there, Sean? *Sean!* Oh, my God, where is he?'

Minnie, puffing down the stairs after her, caught some of Lucy's alarm and her beady black eyes widened. 'I never thought of t'lad. He's probably hiding somewhere. Playing some sort of daft game.' Michael dashed out to the back yard, flinging open the doors on to various outhouses. None of them contained a small boy.

Panicking and quite out of control, Lucy couldn't begin to think. 'Oh, please God, not the canal. He's kept on pestering me to take him fishing. I kept saying no. What do I know about fishing?'

'He can't have got far,' Michael said, trying to calm her, but she was running and Minnie wasn't far behind, her short legs having a hard time to keep pace. Michael caught up easily. 'I'll search down by the wharfs and the canal.'

While Minnie scoured Pansy Street from top to bottom, Lucy tackled the wasteland where the abandoned air-raid shelters were. It was just like Big Flo all over again, only this was a small boy who could wriggle his way into all sorts of tiny, dangerous places. Heart in mouth, Lucy searched every place she could think of yet could find no sign of him. She was considering calling the police when she suddenly saw Sarah Jane and her teacher walking down Duke Street beneath the railway bridge. Clutching tightly to Sarah Jane's hand was Sean, tears making tracks down his grubby face.

'I didn't know whether to hug him or smack him,' Lucy told Michael that evening as she sat sipping a welcome sherry in the Dog and Duck on the corner of Pansy Street. He'd decided that she deserved one, for the shock, and although Polly had disapproved strongly of her going out, giving her a hard time and accusing Lucy of the kind of carelessness she'd expected only to find in Benny, Lucy wouldn't for the world have refused Michael's invitation, even if it only stemmed from kindness. She had to see him, to be with him, however innocently. It made her feel good just to see him smiling at her.

'I've no doubt you did both. Mothers usually do.'

Still pale to the lips, Lucy sighed. 'The teacher was very

kind. She told him that if he was a good boy and didn't run away again, she'd let him start half time in the nursery class next Easter, when he's four. I could've kissed her.'

'Some good came out of it then?'

Her face clouded as she recalled putting the tearful small boy to bed. 'It still sounds a long time off to Sean. Trouble is, he won't believe that Tom is dead. He can't picture it, you see. Death, I mean. He was so looking forward to having a dad.'

Michael said nothing and a silence fell between them. At length he continued, 'He won't be the only child without a dad, not these days. Or the only dad without a child for that matter.'

'I know that but does he? He finds it all so hard to understand. He's still so little.'

'Perhaps Tom isn't dead. The telegram said missing *presumed* killed.'

Lucy shook her head so vigorously her brown curls bounced. 'I'm not going down that road. He's dead. I'd know inside of me if he was still alive. Aunt Ida agrees. She thinks I should be wearing black, grieve for him properly and be miserable all the time.'

'And what do you say?'

'Nothing. She's not one to cross, isn't Aunt Ida, for all she's not really me aunt at all. Besides . . .'. Lucy flushed and hid her embarrassment with a sip of sherry. 'There are times when I find it hard to remember what Tom looked like. It's so long since I saw him. Does that sound awful?'

'No. We all suffer from that problem, it's fairly normal. We don't want to remember, that's why. Memories bring fresh pain.'

Lucy looked into his gaunt face. She didn't think this was so in her case. Yet she realised, for the first time, how little she knew about him. Unlike her, Michael Hopkins had not lived in this street all his life. He was a newcomer, having moved in shortly after he was invalided out of the RAF. 'You sound as if you speak from experience. What sort of pain did this dreadful war bring you?' She asked the question gently, but hastily added, 'It's all right if you don't wish to talk about it.'

He answered directly, without any prevarication. 'It killed my wife. Blasted her and our small son out of existence.'

'Oh, Michael,' she breathed, and he told her in one further crisp sentence about the bomb that had flattened his house. She asked no questions about the woman he had loved and lost, or his beloved child. It seemed far too intrusive with such a private man. Instead, she found herself saying, 'Enough of this gloom, the war's over. This is supposed to be a new beginning. What about that day out you promised us? Is it still on?'

'It certainly is. We could take young Sean on that fishing trip he's so desperate for. Or maybe that day at Belle Vue if the good weather holds. Please say yes? I want to see you smile again.' For a long moment he looked into her eyes and Lucy did not turn away. Then as if by some compulsion over which neither had any control they drew closer till they were a mere breath apart. This time when Michael placed his mouth against hers, capturing it completely, she instinctively opened her lips to his.

Lucy only vaguely heard what he said after that, details of tram times and picnic baskets, fishing rods and umbrellas. She was staring at him entranced, feeling bubbles of unexpected excitement starting up somewhere deep inside her. Feelings she'd thought never to experience again; the kind a woman with a missing husband had no right to be feeling. No right at all.

Lucy, Michael and the children disembarked from the tram at Belle Vue bursting with excitement. Sean had been sick before they'd even reached the end of Quay Street, filling Lucy with embarrassment though why she really couldn't imagine because Michael was charm itself, holding the little boy on his knee for the rest of the journey so he could see out of the window. He'd already taken him down to the canal and given him a short lesson on how to catch fish with a rod and a net, while giving stern lectures on how he mustn't go anywhere near either the canal or the River Medlock by himself. Michael had also promised to teach the boy how to swim and the two were now fast friends.

And now here they were at Belle Vue.

This was a place loved by all Mancunians for its zoological gardens and amusement park, dirt track racing, various exhibitions, dancing, and even a circus at certain times of the year. Folk were attracted to its pleasures like bees to a honey pot.

'Can I go on the Caterpillar?' Sean wanted to know, jumping up and down with excitement.

'And be sick again? No fear,' Lucy told him.

'I want to go on an elephant,' Sarah Jane put in.

So many dangers. The thought of her children let loose amongst all these rides filled Lucy with terror but Michael swiftly put an end to her concern. 'They'll be safe enough with me,' he assured her, and she cast him a shy glance of gratitude as they went through the turnstiles, for of course they would, in more ways than one.

But then she had to remind herself strictly not to read too much into his kindness. It was one thing to spend time with this man as her employer, even go out with him on a Saturday afternoon all dressed in their best, quite another to look upon him as anything more than that. Even so, she felt a bit sick with excitement herself, and wondered how they would get on.

She needn't have worried. The day was a great success.

They giggled at the monkeys climbing all over their rocky mountain. Sean and Sarah Jane rode on the Bug and the Bobs and of course the miniature railway. They all went on the Caterpillar and squealed when the green hood came over and made it all dark. Then it was time for the elephant ride. The elephants of Belle Vue were famous. There were three of them there today. Mary, Annie, and of course Lil, the most famous of all. These were led by a dark-faced man in oriental robes who went by the even more exotic name of Fernandez. Perched high in a precarious swaying chair, the children squealed with delight. Lucy could hardly believe that outside the turnstiles lay Gorton with its factories, rows of dark red brick houses, shops and pubs. Here, inside Belle Vue, was a magical kingdom, a wonderland of fun and entertainment.

The elephant ride was so popular that Michael paid for the children to go again, which gave the two adults a few more precious moments to themselves. And somehow this seemed to be particularly important, possibly because summer was almost over and this soft September day was an unexpected treat.

'Are you happy now?' he asked, breathing the words softly against her ear, and Lucy could hardly bear to look at him as she whispered her agreement, flushing like a schoolgirl.

After the elephant rides came far more candy floss and vanilla ice cream than was good for them. Sean demanded to see the fireworks which he'd seen illustrated on a poster and Michael had to explain they'd been cancelled because of the war. Both children groaned, Sarah

Jane looking as if she was about to cry.

'Why does the war spoil everything?'

'Good question, but they'll start again soon, when things get back to normal,' Michael promised.

'We'll have to come again then,' Sarah Jane firmly announced and he agreed, glancing quickly across at Lucy.

'We'll make that a date, eh?'

'*Yes!*' both children squealed so loud that Lucy decided it was time to take control.

'How about some dinner? Fish and chips all round?'

'Sausages, sausages!' yelled Sean, jumping up and down so violently that Michael picked him up and swung him round in the air like an aeroplane, leaving the little boy gasping for breath and giggling so much Lucy had to calm him down all over again. She scolded Michael for encouraging him even while her eyes sparkled with laughter.

'If you're very good,' Michael solemnly promised, wagging a calming finger in the children's eager faces, 'we'll go and watch the dirt track racing after we've eaten.'

Lucy gave a mock groan. 'Now I'll never have a moment's peace whenever Sean goes out on his bike. He'll think he's a speedway star rider.'

Both children did indeed love the race track on the corner of Hyde Road and Hunter's Lane, the roar of the engines filling their ears as they watched in breathless excitement the bikes tearing around the track, frequently overtaking and sometimes slipping and sliding in a perilous manner. Michael told them about how he used to come here often before the war to watch the riders, Frank Varey, known as the Red Devil, being a particular favourite on his Scott motorbike. He tried to imitate the noise it made, making them all laugh.

Later, while the children were more restfully building castles in the sand pit, the two adults took a breather by renting a couple of deck chairs to enjoy the last of the sun-shine.

'You look all flushed and sun-kissed,' he said, and Lucy laughed.

'I'll be red as a turkey-cock tomorrow with my fair skin, but I don't care. I'm having a lovely time.'

'I'm glad.' She opened her eyes to look at him and some-thing shifted and lurched inside her, as if her world had turned upside down. 'I am right about what passed between us the other day when I kissed you, aren't I?' asked Michael, very softly, and she could only manage a nod.

'Then I wouldn't mind repeating it.' When he leaned across the narrow gap between the deck chairs to pull her close by one arm, she did not resist, did not even glance in the children's direction, hoping against hope they were busily playing in the sand. His lips closed over hers and she gave herself up to the pleasure of it; soft and warm, smelling sweetly of sunshine and something indescribably masculine. It had been so long since she'd felt like this with a man, she could hardly believe it was happening. Then his warm breath was against her ear and he was kissing that too, murmuring her name against the pulse-beat in her throat, telling her how much he had longed to touch her in this way, and in other ways too. Pleasure soared through her, making her heart beat like a mad thing against her breast.

'It must be a sin to feel this happy,' she said, unable to tear herself from his hold.

'Happiness is never a sin, but even if it was, I'd very much like to sin some more with you, Lucy.'

'Me too.' She gave him her lips again, shamelessly opening them, aching to be rid of the dratted chairs and to savour the hardness of his body against hers. And why not? Her mind was telling her that Tom was dead, that they'd barely had any sort of marriage in any case because of the war, and now she was a widow and free to do as she pleased.

'Mam, Mam, look at our sand castle! It's got two towers. Look, look!'

The spell was broken. Riddled with guilt and confusion, Lucy rummaged in her bag for a comb and powder compact, trying to avoid Michael's smiling eyes before admiring the children's creative efforts.

They had to be back at Lake Entrance Corner by six and then it was a tired and happy little group that climbed back on to the homeward bound tram. Sarah Jane couldn't stop chattering about the delights of the day, her one regret being that there hadn't been time to try out the boating lake. Michael carried a sleepy Sean, still making vroom-vroom noises following the thrills of the speedway, aloft on his shoulder.

The tram swung into view as it curved around the loop by Gorton Town Hall. Then, while the driver walked through it, the trolley-boy used a long pole to reconnect the wire with the opposite end of the tram. Only then was everyone allowed on board and Lucy, Michael and the children collapsed on to a seat with a sigh of relief.

'I'm fair wore out,' Lucy complained, cheeks rosy with happiness.

It had been a good day, and as Sarah Jane and Sean slept all the way home, it gave the two adults ample opportunity for some serious conversation and even to try out one or two more of those delightful kisses.

Polly stared at her daughter as if she'd gone mad. 'Marry Michael Hopkins? May the saints preserve us, are you not already married?' She was sitting at the kitchen table, little piles of money set out before her on its scratched wooden surface, a task she did every week; one heap of coins for the gas man, another for the coal, one for the rent, a few bob for the electricity meter, and whatever was left would feed them. For all money wasn't as tight as it had once been, she couldn't get out of the habit of careful budgeting.

'Tom is dead,' Lucy stubbornly pointed out.

'*Presumed* dead. Michael's a lovely man, I'll grant you, but you can't marry again until you know for sure, one way or the other, m'cushla. Don't you know that's true, in yer heart?' A pile of coins fell with a clatter, as if echoing the destruction of Lucy's dreams.

She sat gazing into her mother's sympathetic eyes and as Polly talked, explaining the reality of her situation very clearly and concisely, all the excitement of the day drained out of her. Even the sun's heat on her cheeks seemed merely to stiffen the rosy skin.

'I know it's too soon,' he'd said. 'That it's wicked even to think this way. But one day, when you're good and ready, I want you to know that I'll be here. Waiting.'

But by the time Polly was done, Lucy knew her mother was right. It had been no more than a dream, a foolish fantasy, and for the first time she felt some sympathy for her brother and his own fanciful ambitions.

The next day Lucy could hardly bear to look at Michael when she broke the news. Even the weather had changed from brilliant September sunshine to solid sheets of rain, entirely in keeping with her mood. She watched it swirl down the gutter, washing away the last of her hopes while she stood on his doorstep hands thrust deep into her rain-coat pockets.

'Why?' he asked. 'Why won't you marry me?'

'I didn't say won't, I said *can't*. Because I'm still married to Tom.'

'Come in, for goodness' sake. You're soaked through.'

So they stood in the narrow hall, because Lucy refused to go any further in case his aunt should overhear, and she repeated what she had already told him. She explained how the magic of a sun-filled day at Belle Vue must have gone to her head to make her forget such an important fact. 'I'm ashamed for even considering such a thing so soon, with Tom posted missing only a few short months ago for all it seems longer. But that's only because it's years since I last heard from him. Mam says I'll have to wait seven years before I can get a death certificate.'

'Seven years?' Michael looked aghast for a moment but then had to admit that he should have known, if only he'd stopped to think. 'I must have been carried away too, by your sweetness and your beauty.' He kissed the tip of her nose, and she flapped a hand at him in agitation.

'Don't. What if your aunt should come?'

'She's in the parlour listening to *Band Wagon* on the wireless. I can't help but want to kiss you.' Lucy was suffering from much the same problem. Her hands were clenched into tight fists in her pockets so they couldn't sneak out and betray her. Almost to her disappointment, Michael made no attempt to touch her again. They both stood for a long moment, looking deeply into each other's eyes, not daring to reach out for each knew they might never let go.

'Seven years is a long time,' Lucy said at last, her voice barely above a whisper. 'I can't expect you to wait for me that long. I'll be thirty-five.'

'Mercy, quite old. And I'll be thirty-eight. Even older.'

'Don't tease me. This is awful. I shouldn't even be thinking this way, not with Tom only just . . . I have to go.'

'I'll wait, Lucy.' Michael was earnest suddenly, his eyes unnervingly solemn. 'I don't care how long.'

She turned away quickly, not trusting herself, making a great business of pulling up her head scarf and tying it in a businesslike fashion. 'I've left the children with Doris-next-door, I must go.'

Michael attempted to rally them both. 'Don't worry, Lucy. We'll sort something out. All isn't lost yet. We can at least still be friends. I'll wait, I tell you. I love you.'

Then he did kiss her, pulling her into his arms with a ferocity that robbed her of the last breath in her body, as if by holding her so tightly he could make her a part of him.

Chapter Eight

By the end of May 1946 everyone declared the country to be on the verge of bankruptcy which meant they all had to pinch and scrape more than ever. The ration book Polly guarded with her life wouldn't buy nearly as much as it used to. Butter, margarine and other cooking fats had been cut from eight to seven ounces a week. Even bread was rationed now, and pretty awful it was too: greyer and tougher than the Victory Loaf due to a lack of wheat apparently. And now people were queuing to get divorced as well as buy sausages. What a sad mess of people's lives war made, Polly thought.

Even so, she was pleased with the way things were going. The warehouse she'd found was large and spacious, even if the windows were still mostly boarded up and you needed to keep your coat, scarf and gloves on against the cold of a late spring.

She'd had a gas fire installed in the two offices where she

and Charlie worked, which meant the pains in his joints had eased somewhat, but she hoped to put proper heating in the rest of the building eventually. In the meantime she'd purchased a few paraffin heaters and urged her employees, mainly women, to wear plenty of clothes and keep moving, allowing them to take regular tea breaks in the warmth of the main office.

She'd installed new machinery for steaming and cleaning carpets but still had plans to expand into new carpets one day. Folk seemed to be itching to spend money on brightening up their homes now the war was over, and a new fashion for fitted carpets was taking hold, one Polly hoped to take advantage of one day. She dreamed of buying one or two looms to make new carpets at the standard twenty-seven-inch width which could be stitched together. The problem, as always, was capital.

She'd used every penny to get the business set up again, and was reluctant to borrow from the bank until she knew how successful it would be. Nevertheless she intended to think positive. Polly believed the future to be bright. The warehouse had a good location with easy access to Castle Quay, which meant transport was not a problem. All that was required was a van to deliver the carpets to customers. She bought a large green one and had 'Polly Pride Carpets' painted on the side. One evening over supper she suggested it should be Benny's task to drive it. He refused.

'Jesus, Mary and Joseph, what'll I have to do to persuade you to see sense?' She slammed his supper down on the table in front of him, hoping he'd take the hint that someone had to pay for it.

'There's nowt you can do, Mam. Leave me be. I'll sort me own life out.'

'And would that include getting a permanent job, d'you reckon?'

'Only if I must,' he said. 'I'd rather have a shop.'

'I'll swing for him, so I will.'

Lucy, washing her hair in the sink, kept her head down, not wishing to get involved in the argument. She wished her mother would say that living on the dole and lounging about the streets all day looking for shop premises in King Street and other places he couldn't afford, as he'd been doing for months, wouldn't get him anywhere; that it was time he pulled his weight as the rest of them had to. In Lucy's opinion Mam was far too soft with him.

Polly did indeed feel a strong urge to remind her son of how tough life had been when they were in Ancoats, how she'd sold all their worldly goods and chattels in order to start her own little business in the first place. That if she was cautious it was because she remembered those days of poverty so clearly, and had no wish to return to them. She'd imagined that life would get easier since the war was over and she could get back to what she most loved doing.

But she'd love to have Benny with her in these exciting new plans of hers.

She glanced across at Charlie, one eyebrow raised as if asking for his support, but he picked up his knife and fork and winked at her, grinning broadly. 'Why should you imagine that Benny would always agree with you? Isn't he a chip off the old block? Give the lad time to find his feet.'

Polly had to laugh, because of course he was and she wouldn't have him any other way. A determined young man with a mind of his own. 'Or enough rope to hang himself?' she wryly suggested, but she was grinning too. Charlie was right, shouldn't she be encouraging Benny in his desire to be independent, not putting him down all the time? Hadn't she had a similar reckless belief in herself once? She certainly had no intention of fracturing family relations purely over business matters.

Lucy, frantically scrubbing at her hair with the towel, could have wept.

Councillor Hubert Clarke was not without influence, largely due to his prominence in business and local Council affairs. It was gratifying to see how eager people were to keep friendly with him, ever willing to perform small tasks or favours for him. Look at the way George Fenton was as anxious as he to encourage his son to court Belinda, despite her obstinate lack of interest. All too often, she wasn't even in the house when the poor boy called.

This morning they'd had their usual heated exchange of words; Belinda refusing to eat her breakfast and going off in a huff, with much slamming of doors. She'd got herself a job in an insurance office, which he thought quite unnecessary and still stubbornly insisted on wearing those hideous trousers on her days off. Today, however, they'd returned to their favourite sparring topic: why she was spending so much time with that unemployed squaddie. He'd let her go in the end since her stubbornness was making him late for the office, which really was insupportable.

When she was gone, Hubert sliced the top off his egg as if he wished it were Benny's head and decided it was time to start exercising some of his influence. He'd shilly-shallied long enough, which was most unlike him.

He glanced across the table to where Ron, his only son and heir, sat noisily crunching toast, the sports pages of the morning paper collecting smears of jam and butter from the dishes it was propped against. A surge of irritation ran through Hubert but he had the common sense to curb the impulse to insist he remove it. If he fell out with Ron, who could he depend on then? The boy's tall, rangy body was flung out with abandon, as if he had no pressures on him at all, unlike Hubert who felt every burden like a lead weight on his chest. At least Ron did as he was told without argument. Hubert got little if any support from anyone else, not even from his own wife, who usually hid in the kitchen during these spats. Anyone would think he was the villain, simply for striving to save their daughter from rushing disastrously into the arms of her working-class lover.

'What do you know about this chap?'

Without taking his eyes from the paper, Ron took another bite of toast and shook his head. 'Nowt.'

Again that hot flood of fury in his veins. Hubert drew in a steadying breath, knowing it was bad for his heart to get too excited. But he could not allow his only daughter to ruin her life, ruin all their lives, by making a fool of herself. What on earth did she see in this common jack-me-laddo from the worst part of town, when she could have Frank Fenton, a chemical dye works that served a good third of the textile trade in Manchester if not all of Lancashire, a large house close to Heaton Park and access to huge family wealth?

And there was no denying that such an alliance would do his own credit trading company no harm at all.

As if on cue, the young man himself appeared at the door of the breakfast room and Hubert stifled a groan. He really didn't have the strength for any more thwarted love, not this morning.

It was Ron who spoke, again without lifting his dark head from the paper. 'You've missed her. She's just left.'

'Oh!' Frank looked thoroughly nonplussed. 'I-it's usually the other way around. You've both gone by now and Belinda's just starting her breakfast. That's why I popped in. It's often a good time to catch her,' he explained, rather lengthily.

Hubert spooned egg into his mouth, catching dribbles of yolk on his moustache. 'I'm surprised you can spare the time. I'm in a bit of a rush myself.'

'Er – I've got the day off.'

Joanna came out of the kitchen, neat in twin-set and pearls, a pink floral apron tied about her waist. She started stacking cups and plates on to a tray. 'Hello, Frank. Belinda's gone, I'm afraid. You can come and talk to me while I wash up the breakfast dishes. I expect she'll be back later.' And like a lamb, he followed her into the kitchen.

Hubert dabbed at his mouth with a folded napkin and grunted. The boy was too weak for his own good. Faint heart never won fair lady. He really couldn't sit back and do nothing while his own daughter scuppered his chances of advancement on the City Council by going about with a chap from Castlefield, mebbe even marrying him or getting herself into bother. At this thought, his heart began to pound and the heat in the room became utterly intolerable. Reaching across the table, Hubert snatched the newspaper from his son and tossed it aside. 'Shift yourself. We've work to do.'

'What?' Pale blue eyes narrowed enquiringly. He knew Ron was always interested in his plans. They usually involved putting the skids under some poor fool who owed him money. Before they'd finished paying for one item, a coat maybe, they'd usually been persuaded by Ron to buy shoes to go with it, or some item of furniture for their home. Inevitably their greed led to debt, which Hubert never tolerated. It was up to Ron to sort it out, which gave the boy a surprising amount of satisfaction. But then they hadn't got where they were today by being overgenerous to layabouts. Quite the opposite. 'Someone being difficult?'

'You might say so. Fetch the car to the front.'

Hubert watched him leap up to bring the Wolseley to the door. It spent most of its time in the garage, lovingly polished and taken out only when there was no sign of rain. He placed his folded napkin precisely by his plate, walked from the breakfast room to collect his greatcoat, bowler hat and briefcase, and, standing by the kitchen door (he never set foot in this female domain), called out to his wife.

'Tell Frank I'll have the matter in hand by next week at the latest. She'll see him in quite a different light by then, mark my words.'

Then he left the house without demanding the usual farewell on the front doorstep, largely performed for the benefit of the neighbours. Joanna stood transfixed, her hands in the sudsy water and her eyes on Frank. She looked oddly bleak, not wearing at all the happy expression you would expect from a mother who's just been told her daughter will soon see sense.

The family argument rumbled on at odd intervals throughout that day and the one after it and in the days following, with Benny constantly propounding his theories on how the second-hand carpet business was a dead duck. 'Finished. Caput. Don't waste your time on it,' he would say whenever he could get Polly to listen.

Not that she had much time to listen, what with working long hours at the warehouse as well as looking after Charlie. Osteo-arthritis had finally been diagnosed, exacerbated by a desperately cold winter, so working in the freezing warehouse had done him no good at all. Sometimes the pain was so bad he couldn't even get up but lay in his bed, moaning in agony. Polly could hardly bear to see him suffer so, and when she came home spent hours rubbing his shoulders, back and knees with embrocation, which brought little more than momentary relief from the crippling pain.

All of this put more pressure on her as the breadwinner. She spent night after night with her little piles of coins, juggling finances, robbing Peter to pay Paul. She'd heard of a loom going cheap, out Hebden Bridge way, and meant to have it. She was determined to break into manufacturing as the best way forward. Perhaps then Benny would come in with her. She knew that a business either expanded or died, and she couldn't let that happen.

She had never been short on courage yet this seemed an enormous risk. And buying the loom was only the beginning. She'd need more than one, lots more, and there were bobbins, spools, work benches and fitted shelving called cribs needed to hold the raw wool; a machine to wash it, maybe another to dye it. Money would need to be found for all of this. Polly often wondered if perhaps she was getting too old to face the risks involved but then chided herself for such self-pity. She could do anything she wanted to do, she told herself. Always had.

But tired as she was, how could she find the patience to deal with an obstinate son blocking her plans, on top of everything else?

Today the argument had blown up again because she'd insisted Benny stand in for Charlie whose knees had swollen up so much he could barely stand, let alone deliver carpets. It was true that Benny had done the work, as asked, but Polly wasn't in the mood to listen to him blathering on about his own dreams and aspirations. She felt only irritation that this young whippersnapper could stand in her office after a single day's graft and think himself an expert on a business she'd devoted her life to. Now he was saying he might come in with her after all, if she made him a full partner and let him have an equal say.

Polly pooh-poohed this ridiculous notion and told him in her no-nonsense way that he could start at the bottom like everyone else. But Benny had a chip on his shoulder after six years of being told what to do, and absolutely refused this option.

'You'd soon learn, move up the ladder,' she replied. 'I mean to get into manufacturing one day, once we have some money coming in and can afford to buy looms and equipment. Second-hand carpets are what got us started in the first place. It's what we do best. Cleaning and steaming is our bread and butter, was literally — for a number of years before the war.'

Benny pulled a face, still not satisfied. 'The war's over and done with, Mam. It's history. Now it's time to move on. You shouldn't wait too long. After all, you could always borrow on the house.'

'I don't like to borrow.' Polly was loath to abandon the skills she'd acquired throughout those hard early years, insisting it was surely not impossible to move forward with new ideas while hanging on to the old. 'I don't want to take any risks till I can find the capital.'

Benny scoffed at this. 'Everyone borrows in business. Anyroad, there are other things that'll make more money without buying looms and taking on too much labour. We could sell furniture and household goods, for instance. Belinda's father makes a fortune out of stuff like that.'

Polly threw back her head and laughed at him. 'So now

we're to become a grand furniture store, are we, or is it a huge joinery factory you've a mind for?' She clicked her tongue with annoyance. 'Tush! And where do ye imagine we'd find the capital to expand the business in such a way?'

Benny's voice took on a note of urgency as he leaned across her desk, eagerness lighting his young face. 'Nay, listen to me for a minute, Mam. If you're short of capital, you shouldn't be wasting it on second-hand stuff, or on all these workers you have to employ to deal with old carpets.' He waved a dismissive hand in the direction of the humming work room. 'All that expensive labour, is it worth it? You'd do better lending yer money to me. I'm young. I'm the future. With enough capital behind me I could buy a proper shop, in the city centre, and really make me way. All you have to do is back me.'

Polly gaped at him. 'So now my carpet business is as dead as the dodo, is it, and I should give all my money to you? I don't think so.'

Benny scowled. 'You'll do nowt for me, will you?'

'I've done everything for you, ye daft galoot, if only ye'd the sense to see it. One minute a partnership, the next a fancy shop. I'm thinking ye should get your feet planted back on this earth with all speed.' She didn't mention that the last time he'd had his head in the clouds, he'd mislaid his own grandmother who later died, but the accusation was there somehow, in her face, as she confronted him.

Benny's greeny-grey eyes, so like Polly's own, flashed with anger at his mother's intransigence. 'And I reckon its time you came out of the ark — time you listened to someone else's ideas besides your own.'

Polly was shocked to the core. She was on her feet, fists planted on the desk in front of her as she glared across at him. 'Will ye listen to his divil tongue? I'm old and past it, am I? Out of the ark, am I? Haven't I paid a high enough price for this business in the past?' She certainly didn't intend giving it all up because her own son had taken some daft notion into his head to sell furniture. She shook a fist in his startled face. 'Find the money some other way, I'll not finance your crack-brained schemes. Leave me out of it.'

He was shouting at her now in his desperation as Polly remained unmoved. 'Watch me then, and don't think for one minute that I won't succeed.' And with this parting shot he tossed the van keys on to his mother's desk and strode out of her office, slamming the door behind him.

Benny was tired and in a foul mood as he marched home. He hated quarrelling with his mam in that way. Why had he done it? He knew the reason. Because he was desperate to have his own business so that he could ask Belinda to marry him. Hadn't he bragged from the start that he was going to be his own man? What would she think of him if he failed? What chance would he have with her then?

He might have agreed to go in with Mam if she'd let him have some say, be a full partner. But no, everything had to be done her way, the way things had always been done. Why couldn't she understand that he needed to make his mark, not be an underling? He'd no time for starting at the bottom, for all being part of a growing concern like Pride Carpets might win him a bit more credibility with Belinda's family and he wasn't totally against the idea. But nobody would listen to *his* ideas. And he knew why. It was because of Big Flo. The whole family still blamed him for her death, and it mortified him.

His first call as he turned into Pansy Street was to Benson's corner shop for more cigarettes. He usually had plenty of fags but had finished his packet during that boring delivery run. He was wasted driving a van. If only he could make Mam listen. Benny swaggered out again and strode off, looking about him with the air of a man who knew he was on his way up in spite of his ill-fitting suit and the pathetically few quid in his pocket.

Since it was a Saturday he expected Lucy to be at home, perhaps even Belinda as well if the two girls had been to a matinee. They'd have his tea ready for him and a bottle of stout to go with it. Benny rather enjoyed this sort of attention after six years of war and NAAFI food, particularly if he could share it with Belinda.

He'd promised to take her out for a drink tonight, or to the flicks. He could hardly wait to see her again, but then he was always like this before one of their meetings, all tense and sick-feeling inside. He wondered if she felt the same when she was waiting to see him. He really must convince her that he was going all the way to the top. It was his only chance. If she thought he was a no-hoper, she'd drop him like a stone.

He found the door locked and the house in darkness. Women, he thought. Completely unreliable. The silent, empty house seemed to echo the bleakness of his day, convincing Benny that not a soul cared. In a fit of pique he took himself off to the Crown on Byrom Street. Here he downed a couple of pints, expounding at length on his plans for the future to anyone who cared to listen. This cheered him a little and at half-past seven he decided the girls must have arrived home by now and be wondering where he was. He liked the idea of Belinda worrying about him but couldn't bear to wait any longer. Besides, he was feeling a bit peckish, ready for his supper.

He was passing the end of Camp Street when a dark figure suddenly lurched out of the shadows. The next minute he was flat on the ground with his nose pressed hard into the pavement.

'Were you wanting yer thumbs cut off?'

Benny tried to say that he wasn't but couldn't seem to manage it. His teeth were grinding into the paving stones and an elbow was applying painful pressure on the back of his neck, which was having a disastrous effect on his windpipe. Then he felt his head lifted by a hand grasping a fistful of hair and shaken vigorously from side to side.

'Is that a no?'

'Yes,' he croaked. 'No. Yes.' He was growing confused, could feel the wet dribble of blood on his chin and wondered how many teeth he'd broken.

'I'm glad to see you're paying attention.' The voice was calm, controlled and entirely unfamiliar. Benny had terrible memories of being bullied as a boy and wasn't taking kindly to this treatment. He'd thought himself past all of that and could feel a terrible anger gathering in his veins.

'Get yer bleedin' hands off me afore . . .'

'Before what? I don't reckon you're in any position to make threats, do you?' The face came down close to his, the voice hissing in his ear, so soft and melodious it sounded like rushing water. 'I'm here to ask – nay, to *inform* you – to leave our Belinda alone, right? Lay one finger on her, or try to see her again, and I'll chop them fingers and thumbs o' yours right off, followed by yer chattering tongue. Do you understand that, soldier boy?'

Benny might have grunted a response, had he been able. Anger was coursing through his rigid limbs, his vision blurred by a haze of red fury, but his position, face down on the hard unyielding pavement with the weight of the other man on top, left him helpless in his rage. If he could just break free he'd paste the floor with the bastard.

'The message comes from her father. He don't like to be

crossed, don't our dad.' Benny's head was jerked upwards for one last neck-crunching twist before being smashed down on to the pavement. He did not hear the terrible ringing sound it made as blackness closed in.

Chapter Nine

Lucy had indeed gone to the Saturday afternoon matinee with Belinda. They didn't hurry home because they knew that the children were with Doris-next-door, and that Polly would still be at the warehouse, trying to cope with a pile of paperwork and worrying over how she should develop the business. For once Benny would be there too, helping with deliveries. Do him good to put in a full day's work, Lucy thought.

It had started to rain and they were sheltering in a doorway when they saw the shop.

'Look at this.' Belinda was staring through the filthy windows. 'What did this used to be?'

Lucy said, 'Lord, that was Netta Abram's tripe shop. She sold the best pig's trotters I've ever tasted. Quite a delicacy.'

'What happened to her?'

'She died.' Lucy filled her mouth with hot fish cake,

147

spitting bread crumbs as she talked. 'She was reluctant to go, mind, her only being ninety-eight at the time.'

Now they were both peering through the dirt-encrusted glass but someone had painted it on the inside so it was impossible to see in. 'Wouldn't this be just the thing for Benny?' Belinda said.

'Our Benny? I thought he was looking for summat grander.' Lucy rubbed at the filthy glass, aghast at the very idea.

Belinda pointed out that the prime thing the shop had to recommend it was its position, situated as it was so close to the Co-op, it would never be short of customers, assuming it had something of interest to sell. She sounded optimistic, almost excited. 'Why not? It's what he wants — to make furniture. He talks about it often.'

'Aye, that's the way he is. All talk. He'd never have the gumption actually to do it.' Lucy wiped her mouth and looked at Belinda curiously. 'I can't make you out, a girl from Cherry Crescent going with a chap like our Benny. He's a bit of a rough diamond, isn't he? Harmless enough but gormless like.'

Belinda smiled. 'Perhaps I find him a refreshing change after the hypocrisy and snobbery of my own family, not to mention the endless machinations of my father to find me a husband.'

Lucy gave a snort of laughter. 'Well, you're safe enough there with our Benny. He'd run a mile at any sign of a wedding ring.' She popped a chip in her mouth. 'What about your own brother? What does he do?' Lucy had noticed that Belinda rarely spoke of her family.

'Ron managed to spend the duration working part-time for the Post Office, delivering mail, and the rest feathering his own nest, as you might say.' Belinda frowned as she wondered, not for the first time, just how he'd managed to evade call up. 'He's in the business with Pops. Bit of a yes man, to be honest, which suits my father down to the ground.'

'And you're the opposite?'

'Seems so.'

'Well, don't expect our Benny to follow in your family's footsteps. He couldn't win an argument, let alone run his own business. Forget it.'

Belinda wasn't listening. 'Let's look inside, for goodness sake. I'm soaked through.' Giving it a push the door swung open.

'Hey, what you doing?' Lucy had exactly twenty minutes to spare, then she must collect the children from Doris-next-door, and she'd promised to peel some potatoes for Polly's and Charlie's supper. Both girls stepped inside and at once put their hands to their noses in disgust.

'Cats!'

'Better than dry rot,' Belinda said, shaking the rain from her mackintosh and hair.

'It might have that an' all.'

The room, lit by a single electric light bulb, was not large but adequate for Benny's purpose. Belinda pointed out how the work bench could sit under the window, for maximum light. 'Tools could be hooked along the wall and there would still be enough space to store furniture as it was made.'

'What does our Benny know about joinering? Nowt.' Lucy kicked aside bundles of newspapers and other unspeakable rubbish. 'Besides, it's filthy.'

Belinda had gone through into a back kitchen where she found a large stone sink and a rusted gas cooker. The windows were encrusted with so much grime hardly any daylight filtered through. She slapped the sink with a delighted grin. 'Somewhere to make the necessary brew of tea. Basic but definitely promising. It's perfect.'

That was not the word on Lucy's tongue.

Upstairs there were, as expected, two sizeable empty rooms. The paint was a nauseous brown and wallpaper hung from damp walls, behind which no doubt lived a multitude of wildlife.

'No bathroom?' Belinda enquired, showing her ignorance of this style of property.

'Oh, aye, down t'yard. There's probably a bath next to the lavvy with gold-plated taps.' Lucy began to giggle then stopped as she noted the intent expression on her friend's face. 'You weren't thinking of actually living here?'

Belinda hadn't but it didn't seem quite appropriate to

say so. After all, Lucy's family lived in a fairly humble back-to-back themselves. Nothing quite so reckless had entered her mind, however, despite the fact that mealtimes at Cherry Crescent continued to operate like a war zone. She tactfully explained that it was Benny she saw living up here, over his own shop. 'It could be cleaned, scrubbed out and whitewashed with lime to kill the bugs. Isn't that what you do?'

Lucy pursed her lips before replying. 'We don't have bugs, so I wouldn't know.'

Belinda looked stricken. 'Sorry, I didn't think. It's just that I'm so thrilled, so excited to have found it. This is the first decent empty shop we've seen in months. Like gold they are. It's too good an opportunity to miss.'

'It must be,' Lucy dryly commented, feeling bound to point out that her brother might be less enthusiastic.

Belinda was so keen to tell him about it there and then that she rushed Lucy straight back to number 32 Pansy Street, only to find the house empty. 'He would be late, today of all days,' she said, leaning against the slopstone quite out of breath.

'He'll be downing a jar with his mates,' Lucy agreed, shaking the rain off her coat and putting the kettle on. She'd just get it going then nip next door for those two tearaways. 'You'll not clap eyes on him again till closing time.'

'But the shop could be gone by tomorrow.'

'That's his loss, not yours.'

Belinda's eyes suddenly lit up and she grasped Lucy's hands. 'We'll keep it a secret. You're right anyway. He'll be much more enthusiastic once we've given the place a thorough clean through, and a lick of paint.'

Lucy gaped. 'We?' But there was no gainsaying Belinda. Within half an hour she had found the landlord, beaten him down from a pound to seventeen shillings and sixpence a week rent, and paid the first month's in advance. The deal was done.

'Won't Benny be pleased?' she said.

'Over the moon,' Lucy agreed, but with less conviction in her voice.

Polly stood, arms akimbo, and looked pityingly at her son. 'Ye great daft galoot, you'll sober up before you sit at my table.'

'I'm not drunk, I swear I'm not.'

Any defence he might have uttered dissolved under her critical glare and while Charlie hid behind his paper and Sarah Jane stood by giggling, Polly made him stick his head in the sink while she poured cold water over it. Benny yelled like a banshee but she paid him no need. 'Hush yer wailing. If ye didn't pour ale down your throat then you wouldn't get into these scraps, now would you? Ye've only yerself to blame.'

He tried to protest his innocence, that he'd only had two

pints, but his mother scrubbed his raw wounds with a loofah daubed with carbolic soap, a repetition of the kind of sympathetic nursing he used to receive from his grandmother.

'Hush, ye big babby. Isn't Belinda upstairs with our Lucy putting young Sean to bed? Did you want for her to find you the worse for wear?'

This sobered him somewhat and Benny began worrying over whether or not he should tell Belinda that it'd been her own brother Ron who'd done him over. He wondered whether Ron was, at this very moment, watching number 32, knowing Belinda was here, and would set on him again the minute he stepped out the door.

Yet why the hell should he give her up? He liked her. Loved her, in fact. Belinda was special. He couldn't risk losing her. Surely it was not beyond the bounds of possibility for him to keep her in the manner to which she was accustomed? Though it worried him a bit how he might manage such an enormous task since his mam was proving so uncooperative and he still hadn't found the right sort of premises, he was determined to hold on to his dreams. Maybe Polly would reconsider her offer if she knew he was seriously contemplating matrimony. Or was he rushing it a bit? he wondered. Would Belinda be more likely to accept if he got a business going first? It was so much more difficult in real life to think and plan than it was in the army, where all decisions were made for you.

When Belinda came downstairs with Lucy he was washed, shaved and changed into a clean shirt even if there were still signs of bruising around his nose and mouth. Painful bruising as it turned out, that would put paid to any kissing and canoodling this evening. Benny expected her to lay into him for getting himself into a punch-up but to his great surprise Belinda ran to him and threw her arms about his neck. 'Benny! How lovely to see you.'

He winced slightly as she planted a hearty kiss on his cheek, but was thankful that she made no mention of the bruises. 'By heck, its good to see someone cares,' he said, preening himself at her fervour. She didn't scold him for looking like a prize fighter, or even complain about the stink of beer on his breath which she usually hated. He was so relieved to be let off the hook that he barely noticed she didn't tell him where she'd been either. Both girls were acting a bit daft and giggly but he put that down to normal behaviour following an afternoon out together at the flicks. He'd got her eating out of his hand for sure, so her brother could go hang. No bully boy was going to make him give up his lovely girl.

Hubert was late for the auction so had to stand at the back, which he hated. Today it was largely second-hand goods which were going under the hammer. He preferred bankrupt stock, new and modern, but wasn't too fussy, so long as he got what he wanted at the price he was prepared to pay. He and his cronies had come to their usual agreement before the auctioneer had even lifted his gavel. None of the dealers present believed in pushing up prices unnecessarily, certainly not Hubert.

He'd laid his mark on some rolls of barbed wire, evidently no longer required by the authorities but which he was certain he could sell on at an interesting profit in the right quarters. There was also a sizeable dinner service, amounting to over five hundred items in all, from cups and saucers to tea, breakfast and dinner plates. They bore a crest marking them as the property of His Majesty's Royal Navy but Hubert wasn't fussy. He'd make a killing out of them, split up into smaller sets.

The auctioneer was calling for order, wanting to make a start. He'd deal with the smaller items first, Hubert guessed, to keep everyone hanging on for the best items later, and this was confirmed when the auction began with a collection of cast-iron cobbler's lasts. After that he moved on to other ironmongery goods, ladders and various tools.

It was then that he saw Belinda. Hubert jerked to attention, itching to push through the crowds and go over to demand what the hangment she was doing here. He strained to see over shoulders then thrust people aside, earning some fierce glares which he ignored, wishing he could tell what it exactly was she was bidding for. He saw her hand go up once or twice and knew something had been knocked down to her. If it had anything to do with that no-good piece of dross, he'd give her what for, he would really.

He saw her make her way up the crowded room to a table, where she handed over some notes, then turn and quietly leave the building.

Hubert forgot all about the barbed wire and the dinner plates as he followed his daughter out into the street, keeping a safe distance away so she didn't spot him. Where was she going? To arrange transport for whatever it was she'd bought? Damnation but he wished Ron was here. He'd be much less conspicuous. Despite the risk, he continued to follow her, maintaining what he hoped was a safe distance. Hubert saw her turn into Pansy Street and thought she was going to that young blighter's house, but then she peeled off down Nelson's ginnel, which threw him completely.

By the time he'd reached it and rushed down to the far end, he was thoroughly blown for breath and his daughter nowhere in sight. By heck, but he knew where to watch for her now, though. He'd set Ron on the task first thing tomorrow.

It was the second Saturday in June when Belinda told Benny she had some marvellous news. 'Come with me. I can't wait to see your face.'

'Me neither,' said Lucy, with a wry smile.

Benny stood looking at the shop, utterly dumbfounded, wondering why on earth she'd brought him here. Chuckling, Belinda took a key from her pocket, unlocked the door and led the way inside. To Lucy it looked even worse without the last fading rays of the afternoon sunshine to lift the gloom, for all it had been cleaned and scrubbed and painted inside and out. It was also fully equipped with a work bench and a battery of tools which any good journeyman joiner would need. A glance at her brother's face told Lucy that all her fears had been justified.

'Good God, whoever owns this dump? What a load of junk. I wouldn't give 'em tuppence for the lot,' he said with brutal frankness.

Belinda went white. Lucy, seeing she was too upset to speak, was the first to find her voice. 'Benny Pride, sometimes I could swing for you, I could really.'

'Why? What've I said?'

Belinda quickly interceded. 'It's all right, Lucy, if I've made a mistake, the fault is entirely mine. I thought Benny wanted a shop like this. Obviously I was wrong.' There was a tremor in her voice despite her brave words. She was thinking of all the effort she'd put in, the money she'd spent, not simply on things like wallpaper and furniture for the two rooms upstairs, which she still had to show to him, but on the equipment to get him started. 'I thought you'd be pleased. Its position is excellent, right next to the

Co-op and close to the main road. What more could you ask for?'

'My say-so for a start.'

'But you said you wanted your own joinery business, that you were looking for premises. You *agreed* I should keep an eye out too. We've been looking for months. I thought you'd be pleased.'

This was undeniably true. But then he hadn't expected her to take him quite so literally, let alone actually take on a place and do it up so that he was committed without so much as the chance to say yea or nay. 'You should've told me,' he grunted, unable to think of anything else to say.

'It was meant as a surprise.'

'Shock, more like.' Benny pouted, feeling cornered. Had he been wrong to fall so badly for Belinda? The Clarke family must all be a bit queer in the head. On the one hand there was brother Ron bringing messages from *Pops* to keep out of his precious daughter's life, and on the other Belinda herself taking over Benny's life, lock, stock and barrel. Desperate as he was to have her, the cheek of it left him momentarily breathless. 'What the hell do you know about joinery tools anyroad?'

'Don't use foul language on me, *Sergeant*.'

'And don't you dare organise my blasted life, *Corporal*,' he shouted back.

Belinda had never felt more angry and exasperated and, yes, disappointed, in her life. Tears smarted at the backs of her lids though not for a moment would she allow them to fall. '*Drat you*,' she yelled, as if joining in the slanging match made everything better. 'You were right, Lucy. I should've listened to you.'

Lucy didn't answer, merely backed away, not wishing to get involved.

Belinda was struggling against a ridiculous urge to cry. She'd been so certain he would be as thrilled as she was by the way the shop had turned out. A rough diamond he may be, but she liked Benny Pride. He was cheerful, considerate and quite good-looking in a roguish sort of way, and there was something about him that excited her. Perhaps his hunger to make something of himself, his youthful arrogance, so sure he could do anything he wanted in life now he was out of the army. Let's face it, she fancied him like crazy though she certainly had no intention of giving him the satisfaction of telling him so.

She gathered up an armful of tools and flung them at his feet with a resounding clatter. 'There! Be a bloody joiner. That's what you said you wanted.' She was panting with the effort of controlling her emotions, which made her breasts heave in the most delightful way, a phenomenon Benny didn't fail to notice. 'Don't think I care one way or the other what you do. You're not at all the sort of man my father would choose for me, nowhere near as eligible as Frank Fenton, for instance, but . . .'

'A damn' sight more exciting,' Benny finished for her.

'I didn't say that.' Belinda was furious with him and didn't quite know why. What did she want from Benny Pride anyway? For him to sweep her into his arms and promise to spend his life building a business and a home for them? Or did she just want a bit of fun before moving on to someone more suitable? She had the strangest feeling that, unsuitable or not, she was already more than half committed to this man so he might at least show some gratitude for her efforts on his behalf. What was wrong with the fool? Just because he didn't find the shop himself, she supposed. Wounded male ego.

She bit her lip, looking up at him from under her lids. 'I got this lot at auction. At a good price too. But don't worry, if it's no good I can get rid of the stuff again.' She flung the words at him with such force he could feel the warmth of her breath before she flounced away to stand at the window with her arms folded. When he didn't come after her but remained sunk in silence she added, in a voice tight with anger, 'At least it's my own money I've wasted.'

'Oh, aye, and you've money to burn of course?' His tone mocked her.

All the heat and fury drained out of Belinda, to be replaced by a rush of sympathy as suddenly she understood. She'd insulted Lucy over bugs she didn't have, now she'd insulted Benny over money. She turned and ran to him, grasping him by the arms. 'That's it, isn't it? I've hurt you by using *my* money. Is that all? Why didn't you say?'

She put back her head and gave her full rich laugh and, unable to help himself, Benny found his eyes drawn to the slender whiteness of her throat, moving down to where it dipped into the open vee of her shirt and swelled into full firm breasts.

'I've money of me own, tha knows,' he said, thinking that perhaps he should go on letting her think this was the reason, so he could perhaps salvage the ruins of their promising friendship before it was too late. He was beginning to appreciate that he might have shot his mouth off a bit too far, and all because she'd called his bluff. What he knew about joinery could be written on the back of a chisel.

Maybe he should try it anyway, he thought, reckless with need, for if he didn't have her soon he'd go mad. Maybe she was worth the sacrifice of his other dreams.

Mind you, if she ever told her father that she'd loaned her 'soldier-boy' money to get started up in business, he'd really be in hot water then. Benny didn't care to think just how hot it might be. 'I'd pay back every penny, and it would have to be our secret,' he said, just to be on the safe side. Good God, he thought, what am I saying? Why am I agreeing? This was all a terrible mistake. Her lips were moist, full and sweet, and the pain in his loins was mounting so that he was certain he'd shame himself soon. He wondered desperately if there was something else he could do with the place other than joinery and despite the work

bench and array of tools. It certainly wasn't big enough for
a furniture store.

'What does money matter?' She was smiling at him
again, and it was as if the sun had come out, warming him,
searing him with new heat. 'You can pay me back when you
get going. Oh, Benny, you silly man.' Then she had her
arms about him, pressing that ripe luscious body against
his, and he thought he might burst with pain. She was
kissing his cheek, his mouth, saying something about not
letting pride stand in the way of what could be a good
future for them, though her voice came from such a distance away he wasn't too sure.

From the corner of his eye he saw Lucy quietly closing
the shop door as she slipped outside. Belinda was telling
him she had yet another surprise waiting upstairs and
Benny made no further protest for he knew now that he
must go along with the plan whatever the cost. He was lost
completely.

Chapter Ten

Hubert made up his mind that it was long past time he cracked the whip and brought his recalcitrant daughter to heel. He set out his shaving brush, soap mug and cutthroat razor on the bathroom shelf with painstaking care while his mind buzzed with plans. Ron was supposed to have seen off soldier-boy but she was evidently still mooning over the young whippersnapper.

It wasn't like Ron to fail. The one good thing about his son was that he had very little brain and even less imagination, and therefore was always willing to carry out whatever task his father set him. What he lacked in the brain department he more than made up for in native cunning. If a child told him her mam wasn't in, he'd wait round the back of the house till the woman emerged and then squeeze a bob or two out of her even if she did claim her family to be starving. And if it were a chap who refused to pay, Ron usually found another way to make him regret that daft notion.

So why hadn't it worked with young Benny Pride?

Hubert began to lather his chin with his best badger bristle brush. This was the cause of half his problems at the moment, of course. Folk weren't listening any more, and they weren't paying up. The world had gone haywire and everyone thought they could avoid irksome responsibilities just because the war was over. Added to which some of the returning service men objected to coming home and finding their wives in debt. As if it were *his* fault that they couldn't find a job.

Hubert had an appointment today with Colin Wilnshaw, his accountant, and didn't expect the news to be particularly good. He'd made a lot of money over the past few years but sadly had spent a good deal of it almost as fast. But then he did have a lot of commitments, some of them quite delightful ones. The thought brought a smile to his face as he applied the soap with greater care. He needed to look his best today. After the accountant he had another meeting, a much more interesting one.

Myra was the kind of woman any man would hock his soul for. Unlike his wife, for whom he had every respect, naturally, as the mother of his children, Myra knew how to excite a man. She knew how to peel off her stockings in the most tantalising way imaginable, how to carry out a chap's every fantasy while adding a few of her own. Her fertile imagination had provided them with countless sensual diversions and she knew better than any of the many women he had enjoyed over the years how to bring him to a fierce climax yet still leave him panting for more. Myra was a bad girl, in the best possible sense of the word.

So if he'd been a touch too generous with her out of gratitude of late, didn't she deserve it? This slight cash flow crisis could quite easily be rectified, given time and energy, of which he still had plenty, thank God. Credit trading was suffering just at present. The firms who supplied his clients with goods were getting greedier, cutting their discounts, demanding payment up front. And the bank was squeezing him to reduce his loans, fearing the change of government might damage trade, that the coming of peace had bequeathed them all as many problems as it had solved. But he was impatient to further his ambitions and move ever upward in the city of Manchester, without sacrificing these pleasant diversions which surely any hardworking businessman deserved.

Hubert slid his cut-throat razor over his throat, the scraping sound it made on his rough skin echoing in the stark Victorian bathroom. An alliance with Fenton Chemicals would have fitted the bill nicely, providing him with the extra kudos he craved; would perhaps have led to himself and George Fenton fixing up some sort of partnership deal. Hubert was not averse to having his fingers in many pies.

He nicked himself and cursed, sticking a piece of tissue paper on it to stop the bleeding. Myra preferred a close shave which wasn't always easy to achieve, but then nothing worth having came easy. Despite the difficulties there was no question that he would survive. The answer, surely, was to increase his holdings and thence his profits.

His accountant, at their lunchtime meeting held at the Rising Sun, confirmed this diagnosis, adding that Hubert's latest set of tax returns were even now in the process of being prepared. They in no way revealed the true state of his affairs, naturally, for what the Inland Revenue didn't know couldn't hurt either them or Hubert. Much of his trading was done on a cash only basis (Hubert never referred to it as the black market), with no invoices or paperwork of any kind to show that it had taken place. All those details were in his head with the money carefully deposited in obscure places, saved for a rainy day and his old age.

'The difficulty is, Hubert, that this kind of trading will gradually disappear,' Colin informed him. 'So you need to look in other directions to expand.'

'There'll always be those who prefer to deal in cash.'

'True, but opportunities will be reduced once the rationing of materials is relaxed. Nothing lasts forever, Hubert, old chap. You need to be thinking more creatively.'

He puffed on his excellent cigar and smiled through a swirl of smoke. Creative thinking, when it came to business, had never been a problem. 'Right then, let's order another malt and put our brains to it.'

It was pointed out to him that, in the past, he'd often taken over a failing enterprise in lieu of debt. That this was, in fact, a useful way of building an empire and there was really no reason why he shouldn't do more of that in the future. The secret was to latch on to a business that was new and overstretched, suffering from insufficient capital or some other problem such as an unsettled workforce or division between the partners. There were a surprising number, once you started to look. Hubert judged this idea a fruitful one to pursue.

Tactics and planning were, of course, of the essence. He couldn't simply go barging in but must carefully manoeuvre and manipulate his target into just the right weakened state for a takeover, like a cat baiting a mouse. Fortunately he was strong on patience and could devise all manner of interesting tactics to bring this happy situation about. All he had to do now was keep his eye open for a likely victim.

Yet another awkward breakfast was over. Belinda had taken a week's holiday from her job as she hadn't been feeling too well lately, though it wasn't turning into quite the rest she'd imagined as there was still a great deal of work to be done on the upstairs rooms at the shop. She packed sandwiches and a flask of tea into the bag she took with her each day.

She'd never intended to let things go so far the day she'd taken Benny upstairs to the rooms above the shop. She'd meant only to try to explain to him how much better the rooms would look once she'd finished the painting and decorating, and that with one or two bits of furniture he could enjoy the independence he'd so craved. But somehow the explanations had got lost in their need to touch, to kiss, to express the burning passion they felt for each other. Within moments he'd had her backed up against a wall, her legs up around his solid waist while he thrust into her, her cries sounding embarrassingly loud in the empty room.

Now, it seemed, she must rue the consequences and still hadn't got round to telling him – or her father. Belinda hadn't even allowed herself to dwell on the problem, preferring to push it to the back of her mind, but time she was only too aware was fast running out. The problem could no longer be ignored.

'Frank's called here regularly, most days in fact, and you're never in,' Hubert was saying, sounding peeved.

Belinda reached for a couple of apples and stuffed those into the bag too, studiously refusing to allow him to rile her. 'I've already told him that it isn't on, that whatever there was between us before the war, if anything, is well and truly over. We were little more than children, which we definitely are not now. He understands. Why don't you?'

Her calmness inflamed her father. 'Don't take that tone of voice to me, young lady! Show some respect when you're living in my house. Who do you think you are, running wild, not helping your mother properly, wearing trousers – not to mention refusing to have owt to do with a fine young man from a good family? You're so determined to make yourself cheap, you can't even be civil. Are you listening to me madam?'

'No, Father. There's really nothing more to be said and I don't have to stand here and listen to anything.' Belinda picked up her bag and swung it on to her shoulder.

'You will if I say you must. You'll marry who I tell you to marry and be thankful someone is prepared to have you, plain lump of codfish that you are.'

Belinda froze and whatever remnant of feeling she had left for her father finally faded. 'As a matter of fact, I doubt Frank would have me now that I'm expecting Benny's child.' She strode towards the door.

Hubert could feel the blood pounding in his ears, a haze of red expanding before his eyes. 'What did you say?'

'Oh, I think you heard. I'm just on my way to break the happy news to Benny.'

'You *whore!*'

She'd taken no more than two steps when, in one swift movement, Councillor Hubert Clarke wrenched the bag from her shoulder and flung it across the room. It hit the sideboard, smashing the thermos flask on impact and sending a vase of roses crashing to the floor, spraying water and flowers everywhere.

'Oh, Hubert, what have you done?' Joanna, rushing in from the kitchen, gasped in distress and instantly went

169

down on her hands and knees to gather up shards of glass and broken stems.

'Stop it, Mother.' Belinda, aghast by what had happened, ran to help. 'Stop it, you'll cut yourself. Let me get the dustpan and brush.' Hubert, colour coming and going in his flaccid face, thrust past them both and without a backward glance carefully removed his coat, bowler hat and briefcase from the hall stand and walked from the house as if it were a perfectly normal day.

'It's all my fault,' Joanna sobbed when they were alone. 'All my fault.'

Belinda, feeling she really couldn't cope with her mother's hysterics on top of her father's display of temper, briskly began to sweep up debris. 'Don't be ridiculous, Mother. How can it be your fault? Pops simply won't come to terms with the fact I can make my own decisions now. As a matter of fact . . .'

She might very well have broken the news to her mother at this point, except that Joanna, still kneeling on the carpet, interrupted, 'No, I mean about Frank. He doesn't come here to see you. That's just a ploy, an excuse. He comes here to see *me*. We're having an affair.'

Within three weeks Belinda and Benny were married. They had a small reception at the Co-op, then moved into the two rooms over the shop. It wasn't what either of them had planned but there didn't seem to be any alternative.

✤

Having his daughter elope with a ne'er-do-well was, to Hubert, an unmitigated disaster. Not what he'd planned at all. Where was the benefit in it to him? he asked Myra, watching greedily as she lazily unhooked her skirt. But as she slid beneath him and he pounded out his frustration into her warm yielding body, he knew that he mustn't throw in the towel too easily. There had to be some way he could turn the situation to his advantage, some way to bring his daughter to heel.

The next day he put this very point to Ron. 'Who do we know that can put a spoke in his wheel?'

'What would be the point?' Ron commented, picking his teeth with the blade of his penknife. 'They're wed now, aren't they? What's done is done. Anyroad, I give him a thorough dust up like you said, but it didn't work.'

'Everything can be mended, you daft lout. It has to be. I'll not be made a laughing stock. You've heard of divorce, I suppose, or annulment? We must find some way to prove the marriage wasn't legal, or to make certain that lass o' mine has learned her lesson and is ready to come home with her tail between her legs.'

He'd already cut off her allowance. Now he would drive her almost to the brink of starvation if necessary to make her see the folly of her ways. Once hunger and desperation set in, she'd come home fast enough, chastened but wiser. Didn't she appreciate her father wasn't a man to cross? He'd certainly proved this point to Joanna years ago, that he wouldn't stand for his name to be sullied, not at any price. His wife had learned to toe the line if she was to continue to enjoy the comforts in life she so craved, and so must Belinda.

He let his mind range through the people he knew, the contacts he'd made. Then he smiled. Of course, John Riley, Secretary of the local branch of the Board of Trade. Riley owed him a favour or two and Hubert had always been good at calling in those. Soldier-boy might find it less easy than he imagined to get himself the necessary licences, once Hubert had had a quiet word in Riley's ear.

Belinda was beginning to discover that nothing had turned out quite as she'd expected either. Without question, life with Benny during that first wonderful week was fun, exciting and wildly unpredictable, and there was undoubtedly passion between them. She loved his looks, his physique, the way he clearly adored her and paid her so much attention. But most of all, she loved his ambition; the way he wouldn't let anything stand in the way of it.

Every morning he'd bring her tea and toast in bed, which was just as well since she felt horrendously sick. Even then she could spend a good twenty minutes throwing up. Having babies clearly wasn't as much fun as she'd been led to believe.

If she were honest, marrying Benny had been not only expedient but a means of escape, as well as a crazy form of retribution. The relief of being released from the machinations of her father had felt glorious. To build a new future with a man of whom Councillor Hubert Clarke did not approve seemed like a marvellous way of expressing her independence.

Yet she was genuinely fond of Benny, and anxious that their marriage should be a success. She meant to be a good wife and to help him rise in the world. But as she huddled shivering beneath the covers in their sparsely furnished bedroom Belinda began, for the first time, to experience doubts. The shop seemed smaller than she remembered and the two rooms over it, where they must live, positively poky. They were also perishing cold despite it being early summer. God knows what would happen when winter came.

On the Monday of their second week together Belinda got up first for once and cooked porridge on the old gas stove which they'd had brought upstairs into the other room which they used as a living-kitchen. Benny watched, giving instructions, for he was surprisingly good at cooking himself, his hands and lips teasing her so much she could hardly work for laughing. They ate the porridge, which was dreadful, at the table, the only piece of furniture they possessed save for the cooker, a small sink and one armchair. Afterwards she expected him to start sawing wood or whatever must be done to make furniture but he didn't even get dressed, being still in his pyjamas. Instead he began pushing her back into bed.

'Here, what are you doing?'

'I need to recover after eating your lumpy porridge. Anyroad, there's plenty of time.' They were on honeymoon after all, weren't they? he reminded her, and she protested no further. Besides, bed was the warmest place.

As they rolled about in the tumbled sheets, laughing and giggling, the silk of her blouse ripping slightly in his eagerness to drag it off her, it dawned on Belinda that it would be her task to cook and clear away breakfast every morning, and tidy through, when he'd started work.

'I've never done much cooking before,' she gasped, for he was kissing her now and she could barely think while he busied himself with the buttons on her skirt.

'You'll have to learn lots of new skills then, won't you?' Sliding off her silk knickers with a practised hand. 'Though we could always employ a French chef if you like.'

Her giggles changed into gasps of excitement as his fingers explored her, even as that tiny voice at the back of her mind reminded her that, fun as it may seem now, they couldn't spend their entire lives eating fish and chips in bed. She didn't even know if she could cook anything more complicated than porridge. She'd never had to do it. There'd always been her mother or the NAAFI to take care of such matters.

The next day she was again up first while Benny lay

sprawled on his stomach and the silence of early morning folded around her. Outside the narrow, grimy window she could hear the rattle of milk churns, the sound of cart wheels on cobbles, and somewhere in the distance a church clock started to chime. Seven o'clock. She'd wake Benny in a minute, persuade him to find something to do in his workshop, or better still go down to the Council offices and sort out the delay over the issuing of an allocation licence. Without that, apparently, he couldn't buy any wood.

On slippered feet she padded downstairs to collect the post and, seeing a brown envelope lying on the mat, thought it might have come. Excitement flared in her and she'd barely paused long enough to scoop it up and slip it in her dressing-gown pocket preparatory to taking it up to him before the shop door bell jangled, making her jump. She turned the big rusty key and opened it a crack.

Frank stood on the doorstep, a sheepish grin on his face. Without waiting for an invitation, he pushed open the door and walked in. 'Sorry to barge in but I wondered if you could spare me a minute?'

'I'd rather you didn't come round here at all. I don't think we have anything to say to each other.' She felt no sense of annoyance towards Frank. Had she been in love with him, she supposed his and her mother's behaviour would have been the ultimate betrayal. But even though this was not the case, she still felt used and certainly saw no reason to be civil to him. 'I'd really prefer you to go.'

'I won't take a moment of your precious time,' he said, closing the door behind him as if he owned the place. 'There's trouble.'

She didn't want to hear. Whether her father suspected his wife of having an affair or if her parents' marriage would survive Belinda had no idea, nor any intention of investigating. It was really up to them. 'I've told you, Frank, I really don't want to . . .'

'Are you deaf or summat?' She hadn't heard Benny come up behind her but, clearly irritated to find his one-time rival stepping uninvited over his own front doorstep, he told Frank to leave this instant if he didn't want his head battered in.

Frank looked slightly taken aback by this, as well he might though he steadfastly stood his ground. 'It's about your mother, Belinda.'

She looked from one to the other of these two young men, and for all Benny's undoubted sexual attraction, wondered if she would have been quite so ready to marry him, baby or no baby, had her mother not confessed to her affair with Frank Fenton and her father tried to bully her into submission. Impossible to say. Nor was it a question Belinda cared to examine too closely. Despite her qualms, she invited Frank upstairs for coffee, more to compensate for her husband's ungraciousness than from any concern for Joanna. It was her own dash into matrimony which was now beginning to seem like madness, a dangerous impulse made in a fit of pique.

Belinda served tea since she didn't have any coffee and listened with what patience she could muster to Frank's account of how her mother was sorry for the upset caused, how she needed her daughter home, how it wasn't too late to save the situation.

'On the contrary, I think it is. Much, much too late.'

'Aye, and time you slung yer hook,' Benny interrupted, feeling he'd been ignored long enough and noting with pleasure the outrage on Frank Fenton's face. 'This is *my* shop, if you haven't noticed, and it isn't even open yet. So hop it! You're upsetting my wife and we've work to do, right?'

Belinda spun about, excitement lighting her face. 'You mean that letter I gave you is your licence for the allocation of materials?'

Cornered by this small lie, Benny shuffled his feet. 'When I say work, I mean paperwork. Sorting out this bureaucratic muddle for one thing.'

'Oh!' Belinda looked disappointed, as if it were his fault in some way that he couldn't get the dratted licence.

'It'll be here any day, I'm sure of it.' Benny fingered the envelope in his pocket, wondering how she would react when she learned that it had brought further trouble. 'Besides, I've me tools to sharpen, a vice to set up, workshop to clean and . . .' He ran out of ideas '. . . other jobs that don't do themselves. So, if you wouldn't mind?' He opened the stair door and shouldered Fenton towards it. The gesture had a hint of aggression in it, which Frank didn't miss. Nevertheless, for all Benny's bullish attitude, he made a valiant attempt to hold his ground.

'I haven't finished speaking to Belinda yet.'

'Oh, aye, I think you have, mate. She don't look too pleased to see you, from what I can gather. So off you go, afore you feel the warmth of my boot on thy backside. This is my property and you're trespassing.'

Belinda, watching this small skirmish, was at first amused and then, belatedly, incensed. She'd spent the last half-hour forcibly putting forward her argument that what Frank and Joanna did in their private moments was no concern of hers. She'd called him a liar and a cheat, accused him of using her, but had assured him finally that he hadn't broken her heart. Throughout her discourse, Frank had stood there calmly and smiled, exactly as her father might have done when she was a child in the midst of a tantrum. Infuriating. Now, perversely, she swung to his defence.

'Hold on a minute. I live here too and pay my whack, so I've as much right as you to decide who comes calling.' In point of fact, Belinda paid more than her whack. She'd paid all of the rent so far, but didn't think reminding Benny of that fact right now would be entirely tactful.

As if aware of these unspoken words, he glowered at her. 'I'm yer husband. You should ask my permission before you invite another chap into my property.'

Arms folded, she tossed back her head in disgust and the sunlight glinted on the golden sheen of her hair. It was growing now, forming sleek wings of colour against each cheek. 'Damn you, Benny Pride. I've just told you – it isn't *your* shop, it's ours. And don't you try telling me what to do. I've had enough of that at home to last me a lifetime, thanks very much.'

The dressing gown was of embroidered silk, dark brown in colour and clinging to her pale skin like chocolate. Benny would have liked to lick it off her there and then. He cleared his throat. 'The lease is in *my* name, don't forget.'

'Look, I didn't mean . . .' Frank began but Belinda didn't hear, she was too occupied in prodding a finger into Benny's broad chest as the argument spiralled into one of their more passionate and all too familiar rows.

'I've agreed to stand at your counter, brew your tea, look after our home, even deliver whatever you sell or repair, if you want me to. But, *goddam it*, I'm in charge of my own life, and nobody else. Not you, not my parents. I'll not be bossed about by anyone. Is that clear enough? To both of you?' Blue eyes sparked like polished steel, magnificent in her anger, making both men fall silent as they stared at her mesmerised, enthralled by her beauty. Belinda was shaking with fury but her voice rang out clearly, echoing in the half-empty rooms. 'I've been in the army too, in case you'd forgotten. I've fought in this bloody war, suffered agonies, lost good friends, grieved. So I feel I've earned the right to have some say in how I spend my peacetime. Being someone's daughter, or even your wife, Benny Pride, doesn't take away that right. OK?'

Benny's face was set tight and had turned an angry dark red, for all he itched to rip that dressing gown off her. He always fancied her more when she was all fired up like this. 'The women's army has certainly taught you how to swear, Corporal. But I outrank you. I'm the bloody Sergeant here.'

For one long furious moment each outfaced the other and then, to Frank Fenton's complete bafflement, they burst out laughing as one and almost fell into each other's arms.

Chapter Eleven

It wasn't till long after Fenton had gone and they'd re-established good relations to their joint satisfaction that Benny remembered the envelope in his trouser pocket. Lying back comfortably on the pillows with Belinda's head warm against his shoulder was as good a time as any, he thought. He handed it to her and watched as she read with dawning disbelief.

Belinda sat up. 'It's from a Harry Entwistle — says he has a shop on Collier Street and that he and all the other carpenters in the district have signed a petition to stop us opening.'

Benny took the letter from her hand and tore it up, letting the pieces fall to the floor. 'Aye, trade's bad, he says, and they can't afford the competition. Says we might as well pack up and go somewhere else.'

Belinda stared at him, devastated. 'Move? After all the work we've put in here. We can't do that. Where would we move to? I've searched the area with a fine-toothed comb and there are no other shops to let anywhere. Not that we can afford.'

'We're staying put,' Benny said, perversely determined to hang on to the shop he'd so despised, now that it was under threat. 'Nobody pushes me about, not if I've owt to do wi' the matter.'

Had Benny been aware that he owed this particular piece of misfortune to his father-in-law, he might have known better how to fight it. Yet weeks later the shop remained closed for the allocation licence had still not been issued. Benny sweated with worry, earning little more than a pittance from whatever part-time labouring jobs he could pick up on the docks or wharfs, yet was no nearer to achieving his dream of becoming his own boss. He'd have taken a permanent job now, if he could've found one, but work of any kind wasn't easy to come by and he refused to go cap in hand to his mother, for that would have been admitting failure.

At least he and Belinda were happy, despite everything. She believed utterly in every one of his many boasts, including his competence as a craftsman. She promised to treasure him, to support him utterly in everything he did, and, once he got going, to save every penny she could so that within no time at all they'd move out of the two squalid rooms and rent, maybe even buy, a proper house of their own. This was Benny's dream too and they would spend most evenings talking over how it might be achieved.

'This is but the beginning,' she would say. 'You can do it, I know you can. Big clever boy like you.'

Trouble was, they couldn't even make a start without the materials, and they couldn't get those without an allocation licence. Time and time again Benny called at the various council offices asking about the forms, stoking up his failing belief in himself, that if he could only get his hands on that essential bit of paper, no petition on earth would prevent him from opening. He really couldn't understand what the hold-up was. Despite countless promises by countless different officials, no licence materialised. He was tired, he was hungry, and just when he least needed reminding, Belinda pointed out she would have to give up her own job soon, that babies were expensive, and that the pair of them couldn't continue to live on lumpy porridge indefinitely.

'Talk to your family then,' Benny bitterly responded as they sat huddled in bed eating yet another dreaded bowlful of the stuff on yet another drizzly wet morning. The day ahead, rather like his life, stretched out before him, grey and dull and completely without hope. 'They're the ones with brass. Why don't they help us? They could lend me a bob or two. I'm their son-in-law after all.'

'I'd rather starve than ask them,' Belinda coldly responded, stiff-lipped with pride.

'Aye, well, we can happen arrange that for you.' And frustration suddenly flared in him so strong that he broke into a cold sweat and out of sheer frustration, picked up the bowl and flung it right across the room. It hit the bedroom wall and slid down it, leaving a trail of sticky porridge over Belinda's pretty pale blue paint. Stunned by his own violence Benny was shocked into silence for a whole half minute before murmuring, 'Sorry, love. Don't worry. I'll scrub it clean.'

'You certainly will. It's a shocking waste of good food. I should make you lick it off.' And she gave a throaty chuckle. 'Though perhaps we're not quite that starving hungry yet.'

'Well, I'm certainly not licking that mucky wall,' Benny scoffed, grinning sideways at her, and then they were both laughing, the outburst seeming to have done them both good. Happy, silly nonsense, two young lovers squabbling and enjoying each other, trying not to take life too seriously despite its being very serious indeed.

They made love, tenderly, and with all due care for their coming child, but with undoubted passion. Afterwards they lay warmly entwined and reverted to their favourite pastime of planning a solid future, a prosperous business, a loving home life for their child. This was the dream, but how to bring it about?

'What will you do if you never get the licence?' Belinda murmured from the warm hollow where she'd settled herself beneath his chin. 'Would you change your mind about taking Polly's offer?'

His reply was a long time in coming but she didn't hurry him. Belinda knew it had to be Benny's decision.

'I might think about it,' he conceded at last. 'But I'd want my ideas to be listened to. I'd want a proper say in the running of the business. It all depends what she's offering.'

Another long thoughtful pause, this time on Belinda's part. She stirred softly in his arms. 'Why don't we ask her and Charlie round on Sunday and find out?' She'd been seeking the right moment to broach this suggestion for some time and even now held her breath in case it brought a stormy response.

Instead he gently disentangled himself and, shrugging into his jacket, declared his intention of trying one more time at the Council offices, and taking no nonsense this time. He wrapped his muffler round his neck, tied the laces of his boots, and just when she thought he wasn't going to mention it, said, 'You'd have to include our Luce and those two tearaways.' Benny spoke with affection for he adored his nephew and niece.

'You'd trust my cooking then?'

'Reckon our constitutions are tough enough to take the risk. But tidy this place up, Corporal, or it's jankers for you.' She was kneeling on the bed, her hands caressing the swell of her stomach, lips twitching upwards into her bewitching smile. Benny only had to look at her to agree to whatever she asked. Giving her belly a quick kiss while pinching her bottom at the same time, he swung out quickly through the door before she could land him a fourpenny one in return.

She scrambled from the bed to blow kisses to him through the window, now cleaned of its grime and shining bright. With one hand still on her stomach, as if by this simple gesture she could protect the baby growing inside her, she waved to him lovingly with the other, knowing that the next few months would be even more testing, particularly after the little one was born. Perhaps Sunday would give her an opportunity to speak to Polly on the quiet, talk to her about whether Benny was right to stick out for a business of his own or whether he should go in with his mother after all.

Belinda understood his need for independence but she also knew how vital it was for them to get a regular income coming in soon. If they were successfully to adapt to civilian life again, build a home and a marriage together, then there had to be give and take on both sides.

And if sometimes she thought with nostalgia of the more intellectually challenging and less domestic life in the forces, then that was something she must put aside as over and done with. She pressed her forehead against the cold glass so she could catch a last glimpse of his retreating figure. She did love the stupid tyke, dreamer or no.

*

Benny issued the invitation on his way back from yet another fruitless argument with officialdom and found Polly up to her elbows in machine oil, struggling to get one of her fancy new machines working properly. Laughing at her hopeless efforts he took off his jacket, rolled up his sleeves and got to work.

'How's Charlie. Better?' he asked, as he soon had the steam rollers moving again.

Polly's voice thickened with the emotion that suddenly blocked her throat. 'He's up and down. There must be something else wrong with him, Benny. I'm that worried. I'm trying to persuade him to see the doctor again, but will he? Accuses me of fussing. Stubborn as a mule, so he is.'

Benny refused her request for him to hang around long enough to help with the next delivery run, insisting he had his own fish to fry. She even tried telling him that Charlie was working too hard and could do with a break but he marched off, head high, to nowhere in particular. Polly stood at the door of the warehouse and shouted after him.

'And now who's stubborn? Sure and aren't I surrounded by fools and idiots?'

'Come to yer dinner on Sunday,' he yelled back. 'We'll be expecting you.'

Polly shook a furious fist after his rapidly retreating figure. 'Sure and wouldn't I grab at any opportunity to put a flea in yer stupid ear?'

When he'd gone she strode back into her office, buzzing

with irritation. Where in heaven's name he got such obstinacy from she really couldn't imagine. And then she gave a shout of laughter for of course she knew only too well. Well, at least he'd fixed the machine for her, bless his kind heart.

Benny also called at number 179, to issue a similar invitation to Lucy. He thought she took an unconscionable length of time to come to the door and then wouldn't let him over the threshold, saying both her employers were out and it wouldn't be right to let him in when the house was empty. Then after they'd spoken, which took less than half a minute, she quickly closed the door in his face and he could've sworn, as he turned to go, that he heard a man's voice. Yet how could he have when she'd said the house was empty? He instantly dismissed the puzzle from his mind as he hurried home, anxious to return to his lovely Belinda.

When Sunday came, Belinda's determination to be considered an equal partner in the whole of Benny's life and not just on the domestic front led her slap-bang into the most serious marital discord to date. Benny informed her that he was off down to the Dog and Duck for a quick pint while she cooked the dinner.

Her first reaction as he reached for his jacket was to ask how he could afford a pint since he hadn't had much in the way of regular work lately because of bad weather but she guessed he'd probably have a few bob left of his demob money and wouldn't be above accepting drinks from his mates. She tried pointing out that, what with his family coming over, he could perhaps stay and help her in the kitchen. Benny looked askance at this, insisting he'd only get under her feet and there was loads of time.

Belinda gave in, smiled and said, 'OK, why not? A drink sounds a good idea. I've got the roast already in the oven. Give me a minute to put in the potatoes, then I can come with you.'

Benny's jaw dropped and his mouth fell open. 'Come with me? You can't do that.'

But she made it abundantly clear that she meant to do exactly that. Paying no attention to his spluttering excuses, she slipped the piece of brisket, circled by potatoes, back into the warm oven. The piece of meat was one of the cheaper cuts. Even so, Belinda hadn't realised it could cost quite so much. For the first time in her life she'd begun to worry about money, wondering how long her savings would last since there was precious little left in her account and no more allowance coming from her father. Still, Benny would surely have the business up and running long before she ran out of funds. She put on her coat and beret and took his arm with a proud smile. 'So long as we're back by one, it'll be fine.'

It was only as she walked through the double doors of the Dog and Duck that she realised what a very big mistake she had made. A hush fell as she entered, there not being another woman in the place, and every eye turned upon her.

She'd been used to dealing with male hostility on many occasions in the past, but this was something else. You could have cut the atmosphere with a knife. It was so oppressive that she very nearly turned tail and ran. It might have been the done thing for Corporal Belinda Clarke to share a pint with fellow soldiers, male and female, but this wasn't the army, this was Pansy Street, and these were not fellow soldiers. These people had a set pattern to their lives, certain customs and traditions, and she had just broken the holiest of them all.

On Sundays women must cook while men must drink.

Well, she was here now, so she'd have to stick it out. The next hour was the most difficult Belinda could ever remember. Every word and gesture told her that she'd no right to be here, that she'd overstepped an invisible line. Her place was in the kitchen, seeing to her man's dinner, as their own wives were at this very moment. She certainly shouldn't be standing at her husband's side in the vault room of a public house.

'She's got the shackles on yer now, lad,' said one old codger, winking at Benny and making him go red with embarrassment and anger.

'Aye, watch out, she'll have you clocking in and out next.'

Belinda went home alone well before one o'clock simply

because Benny refused to come with her. She was relieved
to find that the joint was only slightly overcooked, and the
potatoes nicely crisp. Not bad for a first effort. She'd
already made an apple pie which stood cooling on the
window sill.

Lucy arrived with the children moments later, along
with Polly and Charlie, and they all ate the meal in a
silence which might have been called companionable. Polly
offered high praise on her Yorkshire puddings despite their
being a touch leathery while Belinda gave an entertaining
account of her visit to the pub. No comments were made
upon this, and no one enquired where Benny was. She
quite lost her nerve about asking whether there was still a
place for him in Polly's business. When Charlie politely
enquired how they were managing, she assured them that
Benny had been getting plenty of work on the wharfs in
recent weeks and had the matter of the licence all in hand.
Then she offered them a slice of apple pie and the subject
was dropped.

By the time Benny deigned to come home his family were
long gone. He'd made sure that they would be, having no
wish to have his mam picking over the ragbag of his life
once again. It also left him free to play the heavy husband
as his mates had insisted he should, getting him tanked up
so that he could do it right. He swaggered in, tossed his
cap and coat on the back of a chair and demanded Belinda

fetch him his dinner, good and hot. 'And that's the last time you'll shame me in such a way, woman,' he announced, quite spoiling the ferocity of his voice by hiccuping loudly at the end.

Belinda cast him a withering glance as she placed the dried remains of his dinner on the table before him with commendable control. She'd never seen him in such a filthy temper but had no intention of being cowed by it. 'I accept that perhaps my coming with you to the pub was a mistake, though by rights it shouldn't be. I'm your wife, and entitled to the same relaxation as you. Besides, I'm used to such places, having been in the army myself, remember.'

'You shouldn't be drinking anyway, being pregnant,' he muttered, rather self-righteously.

'I only had a half shandy. However, I offer my sincere apologies if I embarrassed you.'

Benny subsided into an aggrieved silence, not quite knowing how to proceed now that she had so quickly capitulated. His advisers had been quite certain that she wouldn't, that he'd need to throw his weight about a bit. They'd said she'd be in a mood because this was the first Sunday lunch she'd ever cooked for his family, but she wasn't behaving as he'd expected at all, even her apology sounded genuine. Which made it look as if he was in the wrong.

As he chewed on the dry tough meat, half wishing he'd had the pleasure of eating it when it was still hot and tender, he stubbornly offered no forgiveness, no soft words of reconciliation. A man, his advisors had assured him, must make a stand. Start as you mean to go on. Show who has the upper hand. He regretted having to treat Belinda in this way, but they were clearly right. He couldn't have a woman dictating his life, as if she owned him. It wasn't the way things were done round here.

Belinda seated herself at the opposite end of the table and started to tell him about the lunch, about how Charlie was looking much better, and how relaxed and happy Lucy seemed to be, almost glowing with health these days.

He gazed at her, growing increasingly annoyed that he'd missed this happy family occasion yet justifying his anger by insisting that she still hadn't got the point. 'Have you heard a word I've said? I'll not be med a fool of in front of me mates.' His carefully nurtured reputation would vanish like fog in sunshine if she did anything half so daft again, he told her. 'Then where would we be? Up Queer Street.'

Belinda gave him that crooked smile of hers, which made the blood pound where it did most damage. 'Oh, I heard all right, but I'm a lady of determination as well as great talent, Benny. Make no mistake about that. I've already apologised for embarrassing you but we're equal partners, remember. Isn't that what we agreed? And I'd really like to be treated as such.'

While Benny swallowed his anger along with his rapidly cooling dinner, Belinda went back to discussing bits of gossip and the funny things the children had done, as if the problem were settled. 'Sarah Jane is a sweetheart, but young Sean is a little devil. He must've been downstairs for an age playing with those sharp tools of yours before anyone missed him.'

As she chattered on, Benny ceased to take any of it in properly. The beer and whisky were fuddling his head and doing a war dance with the food in his stomach, making him feel decidedly queasy. He ruefully contemplated a whole list of worries that tormented him; his lack of success in his business venture for one. He'd spent the afternoon in a rebellious, and illegal, game of black jack that he could ill afford, in an attempt to recover some of his lost pride and credibility. All he needed was that licence, though how he would explain to Belinda when he finally did get hold of some new wood that he wasn't quite the skilled carpenter she imagined, nor had the first idea how to make a chair even, he wasn't quite sure.

He felt himself starting to panic, overwhelmed by his own fantasies which had somehow turned into barefaced lies without his meaning them to. He now bitterly regretted treating his mother's offer with such contempt but then how had he known that he'd be making this headlong dash into matrimony? That's what had done for him. In his present mood of maudlin self-pity, Benny felt tempted to put the entire blame on Belinda's shoulders. She'd been the one to take on this white elephant of a shop, after all, without even a by-your-leave.

If only he had more capital then it wouldn't matter. He could change direction, do something other than joinery. But how could he even buy stock for the shop in his current state of penury? He'd asked Polly for help in this direction and she'd refused. There was only one more avenue worth exploring.

'We'll 'ave to go and talk to your dad,' he found himself saying, the words popping unbidden out of his mouth. 'If we put it to him right, I'm sure he'll help.'

'With the licence?' Belinda laughed. 'Like hell he would. It could well be him who's putting the block on it.'

Benny stared at her, stunned by this new insight into Hubert Clarke, never having considered such a possibility. He tried insisting that she must be mistaken, that he'd surely be prepared to help since she was his only daughter after all, perhaps with a loan so they could buy stock for instance, but Belinda calmly refused even to consider the possibility.

'I've already told you, I won't ask for help. I'm done with them. We'll make it on our own in the end, I know we will. However,' she continued, in that low, sexy voice of hers, running her fingers through his hair, 'returning to our earlier conversation, I'd prefer it if you did not address me

as "woman", and don't ever shout at me again, Benny
Pride. I won't stand for it.' She rubbed noses with him,
gazing intently right into his greeny-grey eyes. 'I deserve
some respect as the mother of your child, for all I may be
making a few mistakes. You should've been here for lunch
with your family. It was your duty to me, as well as to
them.'

Weak with fresh love for her, Benny could do nothing
but agree. And his mam would give him gyp next time she
saw him.

While Belinda went to put the kettle on to make him a
fresh pot of tea, Benny pushed aside the half-eaten meal, a
bleak expression tightening his jaw, bitterly aware that for
all their undoubted love for each other, the marriage was
equal only in the sense that they occupied the same flat
and the same bed. Apart from that, Belinda supplied the
money and he spent it.

Hubert sat back in his chair and steepled the tips of his
fingers together. His smile, if you could call it that, under
the thin moustache brought very little humour to his eyes
beneath their beetle brows. He'd unnerved the lad, or so
his sources reliably informed him. But stubborn as Belinda
herself, Benny Pride still hadn't given up so which card
should he play next? Hubert never liked to lose.

It took very little effort to discover the name of Benny's
landlord. The handing over of a few paltry pounds elicited

an agreement to evict the pair from the premises at the first opportunity, on the grounds that they'd never opened the shop.

Chapter Twelve

Summer changed into a damp autumn when the rain never seemed to stop, and as the days shortened and winter approached Belinda was forced to give up her part-time job at the insurance office because of her advanced pregnancy. Several local cotton mills had closed and there was talk of a coming coal shortage, not that they could afford much in any case. Benny was more worried about the threat to nationalise ports and road haulage as these were the only areas where he was finding work. Permanent employment now seemed an impossible dream, and he'd lost all hope of ever getting an allocation licence so bought a few bits of second-hand wood from a mate and set about fashioning a stool. He'd thought this would be easier than a chair but somehow memories of woodwork at school had grown surprisingly hazy and, after hitting his thumb with the hammer several times and almost slicing a finger off, he announced he'd changed his mind about being a joiner. The dream was dead.

He stuck an advert up in the fish shop window and sold off the work bench together with all the tools for the first half decent offer he got for them.

'Something will turn up,' he told Belinda with a confidence he didn't quite feel. 'Just you wait and see.'

What did turn up was the eviction notice. Benny stared at it horror-struck. It seemed like the last straw. How were they going to manage without even a roof over their heads? The prospect of going back home to number 32 and the pair of them squeezing into Big Flo's single bed seemed too much like defeat for Benny to swallow. There'd been severe flooding in September when the River Irwell burst its banks in neighbouring Salford and he knew they were lucky to have a roof over their heads at all. Housing was in short supply and the floods hadn't made it any easier. The last thing he wanted was to have to take Belinda to a municipal lodging house. He'd die sooner.

Desperate not to upset her, since she'd spent most of the morning feeling ill and all afternoon sleeping, he tucked the eviction notice into his pocket, hoping for some inspiration before it was taken into effect. He'd have a word with Percy Sympkin, the landlord, and make it clear they were up to date with their rent, though how much longer that state of affairs would last, he couldn't say. Surely no one would be so cruel as to turn a pregnant woman out on the streets?

✻

Polly was keeping a close eye on the goings on of her son and daughter-in-law. She'd enjoyed the Sunday dinner Belinda had made for them, the meat a touch overdone perhaps and the potatoes a mite greasy but then it was the girl's first effort. That Benny hadn't turned up to eat it had troubled her a bit at the time, but the fact there'd been no invitation since concerned her even more, seeming to indicate that there were problems the young couple weren't owning up to. Polly was so concerned she could barely stop talking about them.

'It's nowt to do with us,' Charlie constantly warned her. 'Don't interfere.'

'I'm not,' Polly protested, even as she worried over what she could do to put matters right. She could guess what it was. Benny hadn't found work and was too proud to crawl back and accept her offer. She'd grown tired of persuading, deciding to let him stew in his own juices in the hope that would bring him round quicker. It didn't seem to be working. Perhaps a quiet word with Belinda wouldn't go amiss, woman to woman, as it were.

She saw Belinda rarely but once or twice caught sight of her out shopping and felt again that twinge of worry as the girl quickly hurried out of sight, as if not wanting to be seen. But then she wasn't exactly blooming. Pregnancy didn't seem to be sitting well on her and so far as Polly was aware, Benny was still stubbornly waiting for that dratted licence.

Christmas came and went, dull and damp, the shortages seeming to bite ever deeper. Lucy was having a hard time finding the money for presents for young Sean and Sarah Jane. Michael Hopkins managed it, though, buying Sean a fire engine and Sarah Jane a high chair for her dolly, of which Polly didn't entirely approve. After all, as she constantly reminded Lucy, Tom was only *missing*.

One Monday morning in early January Polly decided to pop round to Belinda's for a quick cuppa. Uncle Nobby and Aunt Ida were keen for them all to attend a New Year Coffee and Bun Social at the Methodist Church. Not being a strong Catholic, Polly had no problem with this, particularly since Big Flo had been strong chapel throughout her long life. Maybe she could persuade Benny to bring Belinda along. It would certainly make a good enough reason for Polly to call on the grounds it might do the lass good to have a night out.

She was appalled to find the flat freezing cold despite the haze of steam coming from the wash tub in the back scullery. The swollen figure of her daughter-in-law sat propped on a kitchen chair, evidently trying to catch her breath before starting the mangling. Mindful of Charlie's warning, Polly tried not to show the shock and concern she felt at sight of her. There were dark patches under the girl's eyes and she looked far too thin for so late a stage in her pregnancy. 'And how are you this fine day, me lovely girl?' Polly said.

'Fine, apart from feeling a bit sick, as usual,' Belinda confessed. 'It never seems to get any better.'

'Then it's a cuppa you're needing, and one of these lovely custard tarts I've brought you.' Polly helped her up the narrow stairs to the small living room, insisting she take ten minutes' rest at least. While she waited for the kettle to boil she went in search of a few scraps of wood and coal to light a fire, but found none. The coal man, Belinda told her when she tentatively enquired, had forgotten to come this week.

Polly managed to bite her tongue though she felt sure it was more likely her dozy son had forgotten to pay the last coal bill. She couldn't think what had got into the daft eejit. She put a penny in the meter and switched on the small electric fire instead, more expensive but there seemed no alternative. Something would have to be done, of that she was certain. 'Sickness is common enough,' she said brightly. 'And you've nought to be afeared of, a fine healthy girl like yourself.'

'I'm not frightened, just over-tired, that's all. This little monster keeps me awake half the night, kicking and churning inside me. I'm lucky if I sleep a wink.' Belinda rubbed at the burning stitch that ran down the inside of her right leg but Polly didn't notice as she was brewing the tea.

While she poured out Polly told her about the Coffee and Bun Social and watched with increasing concern as

Belinda quickly took a scalding sip and then bit deep into the custard tart as if she hadn't eaten a square meal in days. 'Wait till the baby comes,' Polly consoled her with a cheery grin. 'You won't sleep at all then.'

'Thanks.' But Belinda did see the funny side and gave a little smile. 'I'm sorry you've found me in a bit of a state. I got up late this morning so now the dolly tub will be under our feet all day.' It took ages because she found it hard bending over the galvanised washtub, not to mention operating the heavy, copper-bottomed posser. Even so, when they'd finished their tea and enjoyed a bit of a crack, as Polly called it, Belinda insisted on returning to the washing. Polly took hold of the posser, a long wooden stick with its disk of copper on the bottom, and started swirling and thumping the sheets.

'Where is the lazy tyke? If he's no work on, he should at least be giving you a hand.'

Benny had brought the tub in from the yard for her and helped to fill it but then had dashed off on important business, or so he'd claimed. Belinda chuckled, easing herself into a more comfortable position, feeling better already for having eaten the delicious tart. She couldn't remember the last time she'd tasted anything as good. 'Benny's very good and tidy about the house, army training you know, but that'll be the day when a man helps to wash grubby sheets, eh?'

'Aye, the sky will fall on our heads, and that's the truth.'

'According to him, of course, having a baby is a perfectly normal state, which doesn't prevent washing being on the line by nine, ten at the latest.' He'd grown surprisingly critical of her lately, an attitude which was not going down too well. Belinda knew why, of course, all because she wouldn't ask Hubert for help, but since he refused to work for his mother you'd think he'd understand.

Polly frowned, wisely refraining from enquiring as to what it was that had got her son into such a lather. He'd never shown any interest in when the washing got done before. There had to be something more important on his mind than that. 'Well, 'tis certainly true that having a baby is a perfectly natural state of affairs, but that doesn't mean you shouldn't treat yourself to a bit more rest. I'm sorry yer having this difficulty, lass, I'd no trouble at all with either of mine.'

'Are you saying it's all in the mind?'

'Indeed I'm not. I'm thinking it's in yer belly,' Polly said with a grin, and, startled by her mother-in-law's flippancy, Belinda burst out laughing. She realised at once that it was the first time she'd laughed properly in days and it felt good. 'Aw now that's brought a bit of colour into yer cheeks. Yer looking better already.' Polly returned to her mission with increased vigour. 'It would do you both good to have a night out. And wouldn't I welcome the chance to have a word with the daft galoot and give him a piece of my mind for neglecting you so? If ever you should feel poorly again, send our Benny over. Won't me or Lucy be glad to come and sit with you for a while.'

A rush of tears came into Belinda's eyes, in gratitude for the warmth in Polly's voice. 'There's really no need. It's just getting me down, I suppose, being stuck in this place every day.' Pregnancy, so far as Belinda was concerned, was proving to be a far from joyful experience. Her legs throbbed, the sickness lingered on, her blood pressure was up and her spirits were sinking lower by the day. And though Benny continued to get some casual work, which just about kept the wolf from the door, she'd begun to despair of him ever getting a business off the ground. But how could she admit this to his own mother?

As if reading her thoughts Polly asked, 'And what about the shop? Has any progress been made?'

Belinda shook her head. 'You've seen that the work bench and everything has gone?'

'I have.' Polly sounded grim.

'No demand, apparently. He's looking for something better, he says. And I'm sure he'll find it – eventually.' Belinda rubbed a hand down the inside of her thigh, then quickly stopped when she saw Polly glance at her with an anxious frown. 'We're just running out of time, that's all.' Giving a rueful smile. 'This baby seems to be growing bigger by the day.'

Polly dragged a soaking wet sheet from out of the dolly tub and, insisting Belinda remain seated, began to wring it between her hands for all the world as if it were her son's neck. Sweat was pouring off her by the time she was done. 'Sure and I'll have a word with him about that too.' Tight-lipped, Polly handed Belinda one end of the wet sheet. As they folded it and set it ready to go through the mangle, her mind was racing. She'd have to do something about this. Independence was one thing, sheer pigheadedness another thing entirely.

Never short on courage, Polly wasted no time in calling on Hubert Clarke to confront him with the seriousness of his daughter's situation. She watched as his lips thinned into a tight line of disapproval even as he offered her a seat in his plush mahogany-panelled study, after sending his wife scurrying for coffee.

'I don't believe in interfering in young folk's business,' he sanctimoniously and falsely announced, knocked a bit off balance by Polly's bluntness. 'It's up to them what they make of their lives. Nowt to do wi' me.'

'Oh, I do agree,' Polly said. 'But there are times, like this current situation with Belinda pregnant and in need of good food and care, when no one but a heartless beast would ignore the poor girl's plight. Which I know you aren't, Councillor Clarke.' Giving him the benefit of her fine Irish smile so that even Hubert was slightly mollified.

'Aye, well,' he blustered. 'She's her husband's responsibility now, by my reckoning.'

'And hasn't Benny done his best? Couldn't he have had a fine job with me in the carpet warehouse, had he not wanted to prove himself and be independent, the daft galoot?' She slanted her greeny-grey eyes at him, hoping her charms hadn't quite faded, and again offered the benefit of that soft smile. 'Couldn't you find it in that great heart of yours to give your son-in-law a first foot on the ladder? He'd mebbe take it from you, rather than his mam.'

Hubert's mind had been working overtime through all of this. Not until Polly had mentioned the carpets did he make the connection. Of course! What a blind fool he'd been not to realise before. Pride Carpets, an up-and-coming firm which his accountant had mentioned to him more than once. Now that little gem of information, Hubert thought, put an entirely different complexion on the matter and would demand careful thought, maybe even some revision of his plans. Funny thing about life. It could often throw up a wild card that turned out to be the very one you were seeking.

He was saved from answering by the door opening. Joanna appeared, looking flustered and precariously balancing a silver tray laden with coffee jug, cups and saucers, and tiny petit fours. Hubert got briskly to his feet and took the tray from her in a gesture of good will which left her standing with empty arms and mouth open in an '*Oh*' of surprise.

'Now then,' Hubert said, as he magnanimously started

to pour coffee, 'what are we going to do then, for these youngsters of ours?'

'Whatever it is,' Polly said, agreeably pleased by his unexpectedly positive response, 'it must look as if it has come about through their own efforts. Not a hint of interference on our part, d'you not agree?'

Hubert took a slurp of coffee before beaming upon his guest. 'Indeed I do, my good lady. Indeed I do.'

They talked for some time over the delicious coffee and cakes. When he had showed his visitor out Hubert returned to his study, closed the door and lit one of his best Havana cigars while he considered the implications. In his fixed opinion, poverty was the fault of the individual. The fact that Benny wasn't alone in failing to find full-time employment or to get a business going in post-war Britain cut no ice with him at all. Hubert didn't hold with this newly created Ministry of National Insurance or the Family Allowance Bill, which only encouraged laziness. If a couple were bringing a child into the world, they should be entirely responsible for it. The lad must be daft if he'd had a good job offered him by his mother, and refused it.

And wasn't Pride Carpets exactly the sort of enterprise that Hubert enjoyed swallowing up in his own greedy maw? This acquisition would be a particular pleasure.

Lucy sat in a corner of the school hall where she could watch Sarah Jane and Sean sliding up and down the polished floor with their friends. Everyone seemed to be dancing and laughing and having a good time except her, which only made her sense of anticipation bite even deeper. At least from here she could keep an eye on the door. She longed for Michael to come, yet worried over how she could possibly face him in front of her family and friends without showing plainly how she felt about him.

The slightest inkling of the way things stood between them and the matriarchs of Pansy Street would soon have the pair of them torn apart by their malicious tongues. Lucy had seen the groups of women gather, heard the scrape of chairs as they pulled closer together at their front doors to exchange salacious details.

At least Belinda and Benny seemed happy. Lucy could see them now, dancing a quickstep, the skirts of Belinda's dress, clearly silk and a beautiful peacock blue, swirling about her legs with a grace that seemed to bely the fact that she was only a matter of two months from giving birth. She might well complain it looked untidy, with its let-out seams and her bump making the hem lift at the front, but to Lucy she looked marvellous, about as out of place in this room as a butterfly would be in the Anderson shelter.

Sitting on the hard Sunday School chair watching everyone dance and laugh, Lucy felt quite old and dowdy in her navy two-piece, its plainness relieved only by a double row of buttons down the front and a touch of white at the collar and cuffs. But then she supposed it was perfectly appropriate for a widow, and if nobody asked her out on to the floor, what did it matter? There was only one person she wished to dance with.

'Please may I have the pleasure of this dance?' She started but it was only Johnny Parkinson grinning down at her. Determined not to show her disappointment, she grinned back. 'Hey up, chuck. Etten t'dictionary for thy tay, 'asta?' she teased, using pure dialect to make him laugh. Grasping the blushing young man's hand she let him lead her out on to the dance floor, then wrapped his arm tight about her slim waist and pressed herself close against him, making him go bright red to the tips of his ears. 'Pity it in't a tango. Very passionate dance, a tango.'

Belinda, seeing this pantomime, laughed at her sister-in-law making herself out to be a vamp. Nobody could make fun of themselves quite so effectively as a Lancastrian and Lucy was incorrigible. She looked pretty and relaxed with her light brown hair curled into soft rolls on the top of her neat head, as if a glow lit her from within. Nor did Belinda miss the many glances she cast throughout the dance in the direction of the door. A woman with a secret perhaps?

It was past nine o'clock and still Michael hadn't come.

Perhaps he wouldn't come at all and, despite her rebellious thoughts, Lucy's heart sank at the bleak prospect of sitting like a wallflower all night. She could see Johnny

Parkinson had gone over to ask Belinda to dance now, the pair tripping about the floor in some fancy two-step. Poor boy, he looked bewildered by his good fortune before being grabbed by his own mother and waltzed away, clutched tightly to her bosom. She thought Belinda looked slightly relieved as she quickly returned to her seat.

'Would it be too much to ask a lovely young lady to dance wi' an old man?'

Lucy beamed. 'Uncle Nobby.'

'I've two left feet, tha knows, but they're starting a slow waltz so I might manage it. I can count to three.'

Laughing, Lucy readily got up to join her favourite courtesy uncle on the dance floor. Nobby did a little reverse turn, swinging her round in a manner so accomplished it quite belied his modest statement about his two left feet.

'Methodist or no, you've been dancing before,' she teased.

'Oh, aye, its true,' he said in his low, rasping Lancashire tones. 'I larned, like many another, in t'Tower Ballroom when I were nobbut a lad. We're not all po-faced, tha knows. Even your Aunt Ida can tread the light fantastic, if she's a mind. But don't let on I told you. That's where I met her, in Blackpoo'. As you well know, we went every year after that, staying at Mrs Nelson's guest house on York Street. Eeh, them were the days.'

Lucy burst out laughing. 'Oh, I remember. I loved those holidays. Uncle Nobby, you're as good as a tonic.'

'Now that's another thing yer Aunt Ida likes, a bit of tonic wine. What a sinner she is, on t'quiet. Not that she wants it bruited about, you understand, her being so strong in the chapel department. She says she's too old fer dancing and only come to t'do toneet because she's on t'committee. Eeh, on t'committee for everything is our Ida. But she'd not've missed this daft fandango for owt. I'll persuade her up later, see if I don't.' He grinned, spinning Lucy round in such a whirl of intricate steps that she had to struggle against her giggles in order to keep up with him.

'Did you have a dance when you went wi' that Michael Hopkins to Belle Vue?'

The quick change of subject startled her so much Lucy very nearly missed her step. But before she could find any sort of answer, she saw that Michael had at last arrived. He was leaning against the doorjamb as if he'd been there an age, watching her, when she knew he must only have walked through the door a minute since for hadn't she been looking for him all night? He smiled at her and then she did lose her step and trod on Uncle Nobby's foot. 'Oh, I'm so sorry. I lost my concentration.'

Nobby too glanced across the hall. 'Aye, I'm not surprised. Nice chap.'

'Yes.'

'Widowed?'

'I believe so.'

'They say he's a conchie?'

'*What*? That's not true.' She was so upset, Lucy stopped dancing and Uncle Nobby led her back to her chair, one arm about her waist, his eyes kindly.

'I want only t'best for thee, love. Since Charlie's not well enough to think on these matters hissel these days, I thought it my place to put in a quiet word. If I've over-stepped the mark, you'll have to put it down to nosy old age. It's just that folk are talking.'

'Folk are always talking. I don't listen.'

'Sometimes you can't help but hear.'

'Then if that's what they're saying, they couldn't be more wrong. He was in the RAF, invalided out in 1942 after his plane went down.'

'You've only his word for that. He arrives here in civvies, in the middle of a war, so folk are bound to gossip. We know nowt about him, so he meks up some yarn to shut yon gossips up. Who can blame 'im? Nay, don't tek on, just think afore thi meks any snap decisions, that's all I ask. Yer husband might well have died fighting fer 'is country, remember. Or he might still be alive some place, trying to get back home to thee.' And having said his piece, the old man walked away, leaving Lucy desolate.

'Hello!'

She felt her heart constrict. 'Hello,' she said, outwardly demure, inwardly on fire. Sickness was invading her flut-tering stomach. Could she possibly be going down with 'flu, or something far more serious? Michael didn't ask if she wished to dance. He simply took her hand as if he knew she'd been waiting for him to do that very thing, and led her into it. It was a 'Paul Jones' and soon they were galloping round with the rest to *Here We Go Gathering Nuts in May*.

'You look lovely,' he whispered into her ear. For a whole five seconds she was in his arms, feeling the exciting closeness of him. Then the music changed and they were back in the circle again. Yet it was astonishing how many times, when the two circles of dancers stopped, Lucy found herself opposite him.

'What a coincidence. You again,' she'd say, amused and highly flattered by his swift detours across the floor to be by her side.

'Fancy that.'

Neither of them noticed the interest they were causing, not least among Lucy's own family. Benny's face, as he watched Michael's antics, grew dark as thunder. When the dance finished, it seemed quite natural for them to collect their supper and sit together.

'Just as well,' Lucy said. 'I'm fair clemmed.' And giggled as she tucked in to the food. She wasn't really very hungry but had noticed Michael had started limping again on his bad leg and didn't like to mention it. A rest would probably do it good. And she was looking forward to a quiet chat. Then Minnie arrived, bearing down upon them with a laden plate in her hand. 'So there y'are, lad. Thought I'd lost thee. Hutch up a bit, lass, and make room for a little 'un.' And she plonked herself down between them.

They exchanged glances of pure anguish but could say nothing, confining themselves to eating their supper in silence while Minnie demolished hers with several refills, never stopping talking once.

Chapter Thirteen

Later in the evening they managed to escape. Lucy complained of being hot and Michael led her outside when he thought no one was paying them any attention. It felt cold in the school yard for the air was sparkling and fresh, with a clear view of a myriad of stars glittering high in the heavens. Lucy slid her hand into his, revelling in this moment alone. Even so she kept looking back, imagining shadowed figures watching them. 'We must be careful.'

'It's all right,' he urged. 'There's no one here.'

Standing under the shelter in the school playground, he rubbed her bare arms, slid her inside the warmth of his jacket, urging her not to get cold. She didn't feel cold, despite the crispness of the night air. Every nerve ending was on fire, her limbs glowing with the heat of the passion she felt for him, her lips burning for his kiss. Unable to resist, Lucy could feel her body growing languorous with desire.

When the kiss came she melted into him, became a part of him, grafted on to the hard planes of his body. He slid the buttons of her little navy jacket apart and when he struggled with the last one, she helped him. His hand on her breast was icy but that only added to her excitement. She could never remember feeling this way before. Certainly not with Tom.

'We could go home.' His voice rasped with passion. 'No one would notice, they're all busy dancing. Our house is empty. We could be alone for once.' How could she resist? 'The children,' she murmured against his hot kisses, still desperately trying to.

'We could be back in half an hour. Thirty whole precious minutes.' Enough to make her his for all time. Dare he risk it? His mouth teased hers open, his exploring tongue only making her want him all the more. 'They'll never miss us. I love you so much, Lucy.'

She kissed him again. Oh, but she loved him too. The thought of his naked body hard against her own, of his exploring hands gently urging her to a climax, was tempting beyond endurance. She even found herself shamefully glorying in the fact she was wearing her best underwear, handmade from parachute silk. What she wouldn't do with him, given half a chance. 'Maybe . . .' she began.

'*Lucy*! Are you taking a breath of fresh air, m'cushla?'

They broke hastily apart, Lucy doing up her buttons with clumsy fingers, in a fever not to be found anywhere

218

near Michael Hopkins. 'Lord, it's Mam. She'll flay me alive. Quick, hide.'

By the time Polly crossed the dark playground and reached her, Michael had ducked into the boys' lavatory and Lucy was alone, leaning against the stone wall in her little navy two-piece as if it wasn't actually starting to snow and she now freezing cold.

'Saints preserve us, is it pneumonia yer wanting to catch?'

'No, just a bit of peace, Mam.'

'Aw, is it that yer missing Tom, m'cushla?' And Polly put sympathetic arms about her daughter, holding her tight, urging her to have faith and patience and her husband would be home in no time, so he would. Lucy despaired of ever making her understand.

Michael slowly emerged from his hiding place. He loved Lucy, wanted her, and didn't care if the world knew it. Lucy, however, did care and had a reputation to protect.

He made his way around the perimeter of the yard, his bad leg aching from the cold and dragging a little. He really shouldn't have done so much dancing, he thought, and then stumbled across a group of men huddled together, obviously a card school; not unusual in these parts. Michael heard the clink of coins, a few choice words uttered in anger. He tried to avoid them but a scuffle broke out. One man was on the ground, another on top, and in seconds fists were flying. He hesitated, wondering if he should get involved. They were grown men after all and it wasn't his quarrel. Everyone else seemed to be standing back in a wide circle, egging the combatants on.

'Come on, Benny lad. Hit him hard.'

There was no doubt about it then. Benny Pride, the young fool, fists and feet flying, blood streaming from his nose, no doubt thinking a bit of fisticuffs could solve everything. Michael ploughed into the mêlée, knowing he could hardly stand by while Lucy's brother was being pulverised.

A hand grabbed his lapel and shoved him away. 'What's it got to do wi' you, mate? They're just sorting out a bit of family business, right?'

Michael could see now who the other combatant was: Ron Clarke, Benny's brother-in-law. Perhaps it wasn't any of his business. Or should he call for help? It could all become very nasty if they turned on him. Then Benny was struck square in the jaw and flung sprawling over Michael's feet. Reaching down and neatly avoiding a flying fist, he hauled Benny up. Ron was back on him in a second, clinging like a leech, but Michael wasn't for letting go, not this time. 'Stop it, the pair of you, or somebody'll get seriously hurt.'

Others, fortunately, had reached a similar conclusion and the two were finally dragged apart, though not without difficulty or colourful protests. Ron vanished in a trice but Benny, raring to go after him, had to be held back, under protest and far from grateful.

'Leave it. Let him go,' Michael urged, anxious to put an end to this dispute so he could get back to Lucy and enjoy the evening.

'What the hell has it got to do wi' you?'

'Nothing.' Michael started dusting him down but Benny shook him off. 'Except that I thought Belinda might object if you were killed, but perhaps I'm wrong. Not very sensible though, is it, to fall out with your in-laws when you're trying to get started in a new business?'

If there was one thing Benny didn't need it was to be reminded that after six years away fighting for his country he was unemployed and on the dung heap. This wasn't the way it was meant to be. Ron Clarke had just taken great pleasure in explaining why he couldn't get a licence or permission to open his shop, and never would if Hubert had anything to do with it. Benny could hardly believe his father-in-law could be so vindictive and certainly had no wish to explain any of it to Michael Hopkins, or admit to his lack of success in keeping his lovely wife in the manner to which she was accustomed. It was far too shaming. He'd no idea what he could do about the situation. Benny knew he was in dead trouble. He'd even lost his latest job on Castle Quay, Ron Clarke claiming credit for that as well by telling his employer that Benny was a rabble-rousing unionite.

And there was still the eviction notice hanging over his head. The landlord had given him a month's grace but where next month's rent would come from he hadn't the first idea. Worse, Belinda had no money either. Benny knew it was up to him to save them, though how he was to manage it, he hadn't a clue. Frustration and anger waged war in his head. What was he supposed to do? Why was everyone against him?

'It's none o' your goddammed business,' he shouted, and threw off restraining arms to snatch up his jacket and shrug it back on. He straightened his tie and slicked down his hair, dabbing at the blood on his chin. Apart from a slight bruise on the left cheek bone, no one would know he'd been in a fight. At least he hoped Belinda wouldn't. If Michael Hopkins hadn't interfered he might have succeeded in settling his score with Ron-interfering-Clarke. They were married, for God's sake. Why couldn't Hubert accept the fact?

He pushed his face up close to Michael's. 'I'll settle up wi' Ron Clarke another time, make no mistake, when there's nobody to save his cowardly skin. But then you'd understand about cowards, wouldn't you, being one yourself?'

Michael said nothing to this though his jaw tightened and a nerve flickered at the corner of his mouth.

'In the meantime, you keep your nose out of my affairs, *conchie*, and your wandering hands off our Lucy. Don't think I didn't see you slobbering all over her when you were dancing. It may not seem like it but she's still a married woman, and *my* sister. If you come anywhere near her again, you'll be sorry, that's all. You'll be bleedin' sorry.'

'Will I indeed?'

'Aye, tha will.' Confidence restored by this show of aggression in front of his pals, Benny dusted off his hands as if he had soiled them by touching Michael Hopkins and thrust back his shoulders with cocky arrogance. He strolled away and his mates smacked him on the back, as if he'd won a great victory.

For the rest of the evening Lucy dare not go anywhere near Michael, yet it seemed she couldn't avoid him. Too frequently, as if by instinct, their glances met and held for a fraction of a second before hastily turning away in case anyone should notice.

When everyone got together to do a progressive barn dance, the Okey-Cokey or the Teddy Bears' Picnic, she made a point of dancing with anyone but him. Even so it was difficult to avoid him. She would quake with anticipation whenever he came near. It was pure torture as his fingers linked possessively with hers for the merest second; more agonising still if he put his hand on her waist while he whirled her round. Her anguish as he moved on with another partner was almost more than she could bear. She very nearly called him back.

At one point Benny waylaid her as she made her way back on to the dance floor. 'Yer mekking an exhibition of yerself. Remember, yer a married woman.'

Lucy snatched her arm away. 'And you remember it's none of your damn business.'

At the end of the evening she collected her coat and made her way outside with Benny and Belinda, Polly and Charlie. They were all tired but happy, little Sean and Sarah Jane half asleep already, for it was well past their bedtime. But what did it matter once in a while? Lucy thought, hugging them to her. And she'd enjoyed the dancing, for all she'd longed to spend more time with Michael.

Then Sean realised he'd left his cap in the Sunday school cloakroom and she called out to the others not to wait for them while she ran back to fetch it. After a hasty search Sarah Jane found the cap in a corner.

'Here it is, Mam.'

'Dozy Joe,' Lucy teased, pulling it tight on to the little boy's head where it nodded against her shoulder. After sitting down a moment to tie his shoe laces which had worked loose they set off again, Sean in her arms and Sarah Jane holding her hand, singing *Here We Go Round the Mulberry Bush*.

It happened so suddenly. One minute Michael had appeared out of the darkness to wish her and the children goodnight, the next he was falling, blood spurting everywhere. Lucy screamed, watching in horror as he hit the ground as if in slow motion.

'*Conchie. Conchie. Bloody, bloody conchie!*'

There was a hissing voice that she heard without quite registering as she fell to her knees beside Michael, desperately trying to staunch the blood with her scarf, her handkerchief, whatever she could find. She could hear Sean starting to cry, Sarah Jane shouting Michael's name. Where was all this blood coming from? And she must have been shouting for help too, for it came in the form of running feet, noisy shouts, yet no one came to kneel beside her. When she finally glanced up it was to find herself surrounded by a small group of curious onlookers.

' 'Ooever it were 'it him wi' that brick, love,' said one.

'It'll need stitching will that,' agreed another.

'Aye, proper mess, eh?'

Lucy looked into their faces and knew that for all they were happy to gawp, not one of them was willing to offer help. She'd always believed this to be a neighbourly district with the kind of people who, despite their predilection for gossip, would rally round if someone was in trouble. Salt-of-the-earth types. They'd bring food to the sick, wash bed-linen, mind a woman's family while she was occupied producing yet another mouth to feed. They'd make sure the old folk had coal in their buckets in winter and always found time to stop for a bit of a natter on a front doorstep. But these same people had lost sons, husbands, lovers in the war, and not one was prepared to lift a finger for an alleged conchie. Lucy struggled to lift him, feeling as if her fury might choke her. At least he was conscious now, thank God, and then Minnie Hopkins came galloping out of the darkness, her skinny legs and arms pumping like pistons, and Michael was finally helped to his feet. There was no sign of Polly or Benny or Belinda.

'Thanks for nowt,' Lucy shouted to the gathered crowd as she pulled her children close and offered her own shoulder for Michael to lean on. 'Thanks for bloody nowt.'

Later, when she'd got the children safely tucked up in bed, she marched straight round to the shop and accused Benny of throwing the brick. He'd vehemently denied it, of course, saying he might be a bit of a loud mouth but crude violence wasn't his style.

'And what's that then?' Lucy mocked, pointing to the bruise on his chin. Benny rubbed it, looking shamefaced and privately thanking his lucky stars that Belinda was in bed.

'I'd have a straight and fair fight with someone but I don't go in for them sort of tactics. I don't hit folk behind their backs, or on their head wi' a brick. What d'you take me for? Anyroad, I've enough troubles of me own without tekkin' on yours an' all.' He looked so hurt by her lack of belief in him and so sincere in his protestations of innocence that she felt half inclined to believe him. But then, if Benny hadn't thrown the brick, who had?

The next day, calmly shredding lettuce in Minnie Hopkins's kitchen, Lucy rehearsed how she would explain to Michael that they must not see each other alone again, not till she'd got things sorted out in her head. She was thankful that no real hurt had come to him beyond a cut on his head that Minnie's nursing skills would soon mend, but those stolen moments together in the shelter had made her think.

Lucy made up her mind to write to the army, to ask them if it was true that she had to wait seven years for Tom to be declared officially dead. It sounded like forever. She knew in her heart that no one could hold on that long, not loving each other as much as she and Michael did.

A rat-tat on the door knocker. She wiped her hands and went down the hall to find Lily Gantry standing on the clean doorstep with an expression like sour milk on her face.

'Thee's to come home at once.'

'Has something happened? Is it Sarah Jane? Sean?' There was panic in Lucy's voice. Aunt Ida had promised to collect them both from school. Now fear flooded through her even as the old woman shook her grizzled head.

'Nay, nowt like that. But yer to come quick.'

Minnie appeared, scowling with disapproval at this interruption of the morning's work, wanting to know what was
going on, but Lucy was already reaching for her coat. She
was quite certain something terrible must have happened
and the old besom was trying to break it to her gently.

Minnie interrupted her. 'Tha can't run off wi'out a by-
your-leave. Tha's not done yet. What about us dinner? Our
Michael'll be home and wanting his dinner in half an
hour.'

'I'll be back by then,' Lucy said, wrapping a scarf
about her head and, since she could hear rain pattering
on the windows, starting a search for an umbrella. If
Sean had run off again he'd be wet through by the time
she found him. Oh, lord, where would he have gone this
time? The air-raid shelters where Gran was found? She
really must hurry. She half ran along the passage to the
front door where Lily Gantry stood watching events
with interest. Minnie gave chase and brought her up
short.

'Aye, but what if you're not? What'll I give 'im?'

'What?' Lucy paused long enough to think and draw
breath. 'Uncle Nobby brought us some fresh vegetables
yesterday so I was in the middle of doing a nice salad, and
I've already made the Californian meat cakes from the
recipe Aunt Ida left me.'

'Californian meat cakes?'

'Yes, I know. Aunt Ida has been as close to California as

I've been to the Sahara Desert but all they are is corned beef, chopped onion and mashed potato, mixed together with beaten egg and formed into patties. I've done all of that, even rolled them in bread crumbs, all you have to do is fry them and prepare the salad. You can manage that, surely?'

Minnie was about to remark that with her standard of cooking, they could turn into Lancashire coal mine meat cakes but the front door knocker rattled again.

'What is it this time? If something's happened to our Sean, I'll kill him,' Lucy gasped, rather contrarily. The last thing she needed right now was trouble with her son. Wasn't it difficult enough hanging on to this job? Pushing past both Lily Gantry and Minnie, she flew to the door and flung it open.

But it wasn't young Sean standing in the small front garden, nor Sarah Jane, but a stranger, his coat collar turned up almost to the brim of his trilby hat against a brisk wind that had blown up.

'If you're wanting Michael,' Lucy began, irritated by this interruption, 'I'm afraid he isn't home from work yet.'

'Lucy, don't you recognise me? Benny told me I'd find you here. Don't scowl at me, lass. All I ask is a friendly welcome.' And the stranger took off his hat so that she could see him properly. At which point, for the first time in her life, Lucy fainted.

*

Minnie had galloped off for Michael the moment she realised who their unexpected visitor was and he arrived, out of breath and clearly in torment at this realisation of his worst nightmare. He focused on Tom's lopsided smile and decided instantly that he couldn't compete.

'They told me you were dead.' Lucy sat in the kitchen facing her husband, hands clenched tight in her lap. Michael could see she was shaking, her face ashen as if she were sickening for something. 'At least,' she remembered the exact wording of the telegram, 'missing, presumed killed in action.'

'They presumed too much then. Here I am, fit and well. Never better.'

She looked at him oddly for a moment, then said a strange thing. 'I'd forgotten how full of confidence you always were.'

Michael called it arrogance.

Tom was also tall and thin with fair hair cut close to his head. His shoulders were broad, skin tanned as if from years in the sun, not at all the yellowish tinge usually seen on POWs. He had the kind of good looks and easy smile that any woman would fall for. Michael had no difficulty in seeing why Lucy had loved and married him. It was a wonder she saw anything in himself to love at all, after living with such a demigod.

Now she'd fallen silent, seemed struck dumb by events,

overwhelmed perhaps by her good fortune at Tom's return
from the dead or too dazed to deal with the reality of it,
let alone work out all the implications. It was up to him
then, Michael decided, to ask the relevant questions about
where Tom had been stationed and where he'd been since
the war ended, which he proceeded to do, at length. He
heard in return a convoluted story of how Tom had
escaped from prisoner-of-war camp some time before the
end of the war, crossed the Italian Alps, fallen ill and been
nursed back to health by a generous and kind French
family.

'So where exactly were you imprisoned and how did you
manage to escape?' Michael persisted, still puzzled. 'Were
you alone? I mean, why didn't you let Lucy know you were
safe?'

Tom seemed to be searching his head for facts, dragging
them out reluctantly, one by one. 'I had malaria. All sorts
of wounds and sores, barely alive for months.'

'Malaria? How could you catch that in Italy or France?'

Tom answered sharply, as if suppressing an angry reaction, 'I was also stationed in Africa and Egypt for a while.
Anyway, I was too ill to write.'

'You could have got someone else to write for you.'

Lucy interrupted, putting out a hand as if she couldn't
bear any more questioning, the appeal in her eyes almost
breaking Michael's heart in two. 'It's all right. I'm sure Tom
would have let me know, if he could.'

' 'Course I would. Later it seemed a better idea to come and surprise you.'

'You've done that all right,' Michael said, hearing the sour note in his own voice and hating himself for it.

Lucy was actually shaking. 'It's been such a sh-shock. I'd best get off home, speak to Mam and Charlie. And find you somewhere to sleep tonight.'

'I rather thought I'd be sleeping with my wife.'

A small silence fell in which Lucy put a hand to her head, as if it had suddenly started to ache. Michael felt his jaw tense and sweat break out on his brow but managed to address his rival with perfect calm for all there was deep bitterness in his tone. 'I think patience is called for here. Can't you see how stunned she is? Give her time, for God's sake.'

'When I want advice on my marriage, I'll ask for it,' Tom coolly replied, and taking hold of Lucy's arm, propelled her towards the door. Michael instantly stepped in front of them, blocking the way. Speaking softly to Lucy he said, 'Go home, love. Get a good night's rest. You look worn out. We'll talk tomorrow.' And then to Tom, 'You can stop here tonight, if you want. We've plenty of spare bedrooms – till you've time to sort something out.' He issued the invitation like a challenge which, for one awful moment, he thought Tom Shackleton was about to refuse. But then he turned to Lucy with that winning smile.

'Why not? It has been a shock, I dare say. And there'll be plenty of time, the rest of our lives after all.' And he met Michael's glare with what could only be described as a smile of triumph.

Chapter Fourteen

After what seemed an endless afternoon of talk and family excitement, Tom did indeed go up the street to number 179 when darkness fell, though he made it clear it was only to give Lucy time to make more satisfactory arrangements and insisted he would be back for his breakfast, sharp at eight.

Lucy didn't sleep a wink. She couldn't stop shaking as she lay flat on her back in bed, with her children for once cuddled beside her, even though liquid fire seemed to be coursing through her veins. Her brain couldn't seem to digest all the facts, or work out what she should do about them.

Sean and Sarah Jane had been by turns delirious with delight and oddly shy and bemused. It had taken hours to settle them so that in the end she'd relented and let them into bed with her. Lucy lay with her arms about them, breathing in their sweet scents, feeling calmed by the rhythm of their breathing and thinking what it meant to them to have their dad back home. Sean in particular was beside himself with excitement. All he could talk about was going fishing.

'Aye, 'course I'll take you,' Tom had promised, tickling the little boy under his chin and making him giggle. Sarah Jane had hung back, shyly clinging to her mother, while Tom had laughed and patted his knee, asking her to come and sit on it.

'Do I have to?' she'd softly asked, and Lucy had leaned down to kiss her cheek and whisper in her ear that she didn't have to do anything she didn't want to.

But the implications of Tom's return were far wider ranging than Sean and his fishing. Where would he sleep tomorrow? The idea of having him in bed with her so haunted Lucy that she couldn't settle either. It seemed a longer, even more agonising night in many ways than the one following the news of his supposed death. Perhaps on that day it hadn't been quite such a shock as it might have been because it was so long since she'd seen or heard from him. Since then, she'd never, not for one moment, expected him to return. She'd been absolutely certain he was dead.

Not that she was sorry he was alive, how could she be? Once she would have given her life for this man. She'd loved him from being a young girl but her feelings had changed, there was no denying that fact. She loved Michael now, wholly and completely for all they'd never actually become lovers in the true sense of the word. Oh, but that wasn't from lack of desire. How she loved him, as if he were a part of her very soul. How could she go back to a marriage she'd thought was over for good?

On the other hand, how could she begin to explain all of this to Tom, poor man, or turn him out on the street? A soldier returned from the front, an escaped POW, her own husband and the father of her children. It was clear that he'd nowhere to go. No job, no home even – since she'd been forced to give that up years ago and move back in with Polly. And more important perhaps, he no longer had a wife. Only when the first cold rays of dawn poked fingers of pale light into the room did exhaustion finally overwhelm her and she slept.

What seemed only moments later she opened her eyes to find Polly, clearly delighted by the return of her son-in-law, bringing her a cup of tea in bed as a treat and volunteering to take the children to school for once. Lucy expressed her gratitude. It would give her time to talk to Tom, to explain things before the Lily Gantrys of this world did the job for her, and to make some decisions.

Lucy meant to be firm and she was, though it took more courage than she'd expected. In one way it seemed perfectly normal that they should be sitting together at the kitchen table with a pot of tea between them as they had done years ago. Yet in another they were like polite strangers, unsure of each other and afraid of saying the wrong thing. She kept to her resolution. 'As you see, Tom, things have changed. I genuinely believed you to be dead.'

'So I gather. Didn't take you long to find a substitute, did it?' His voice was hard, caustic and critical, jaw rigid.

'That's not fair. If you'd written, I would have known you were all right, wouldn't I?'

'So it's my fault, is it?'

'Don't be ridiculous.' She got up from the table, disguising her distress by fetching a pan, a pot of dripping and fresh kippers from the pantry, busying herself preparing breakfast for him as she tried to explain. 'It's just that I've no wish to deceive you. I feel you have the right to hear the truth.'

He pointed out that she was still his wife, that he also had a right to expect her to wait for him, and all Lucy could do was keep repeating how she'd thought him dead, how she hadn't planned on falling in love with Michael; that it had taken them both by surprise.

Her cheeks flushed with embarrassment. Her slender body wrapped in a long white apron and her hair tied up in a turban, she looked like a young girl still. Tom watched her small neat hands flip the kippers over in the huge frying pan as he listened to her halting tale and asked himself why he had stayed away so long. She was far more attractive, this young wife of his, than he'd remembered.

He should have come home months ago. Years. He could have written. Why hadn't he?

He knew why. She'd become almost a stranger to him during the long years of war, a distant figure whose face he could barely recall. Even his children hadn't seemed quite real. And then there were other reasons, some best not spoken of. He'd found his new life exciting and been reluctant to give it up, might never have done so if things hadn't got sticky. But what she didn't know wouldn't hurt either of them, particularly himself.

She was asking him a question. 'What about you? Didn't you meet anyone else in all these years you've been away? What stopped you from writing? A letter would have eased the shock, Tom. It would have given me hope, something to live for. Why didn't you?'

He felt the familiar surge of anger. Questions, questions, he was sick of bloody questions. People never left him alone. Everyone he met always had the same questions. Where had he been? Why? When? What? Who was he with? He was mightily sick of it. He certainly wasn't going to take being interrogated by an unfaithful wife so dismissed her curiosity with a snort of laughter. 'What are you accusing me of? Are you implying I deliberately didn't write? I was ill. Haven't I told you that already? I'm the injured party here.' And Lucy cringed with shame as she slid a pair of kippers on to his plate.

'Whatever Michael and I might feel for each other, and

I don't — can't — deny that I'm very fond of him, we've done nothing about it.'

'So you say.'

'It's true.' But watching her husband tuck in to his breakfast, for the first time Lucy almost wished that it weren't.

The newspapers the following day were saying that 50,000 couples were waiting for a divorce. They spoke of too-lengthy separations and too-hasty marriages, of infidelity and of wives waking up and finding themselves married to a stranger. Lucy knew just how they felt. The Archbishop of Canterbury, however, spoke of the serious lifelong obligations of marriage. Lucy didn't want obligations. She wanted love.

The next few days were difficult for everyone. She made up the alcove bed that Benny used to sleep in and desperately tried to come to terms with being a wife again. Tom, it seemed, just wanted to sit in the kitchen or in the front parlour, watching the world go by through the window. He had no wish, he said, to step outside the door or start looking up old friends. Not yet. He certainly wasn't ready even to think about finding a job. Lucy accepted all of this with calm equilibrium. What she found harder to accept was the fact that he expected her to stay in too.

'I can't stop at home, I've me living to earn,' she told him, but he insisted she owed him a few days of her time at least, so they could get to know each other again.

'I'm not sure I want you working up at 179 anyroad, not with that Michael Hopkins around.'

'Don't be silly. He isn't around, or only after he's finished work. Besides, we need the money.'

'Now I'm back everything must change,' Tom pointedly reminded her.

It was a bleak thought for she liked things the way they were. Lucy realised that she had no wish for her life to change, not in this way. But perhaps he had a point. A little time together wouldn't be a bad thing, so long as he remained in that alcove bed. Give them time to sort things out in a civilised fashion, without harming the children. Reluctantly she sent word to her clients, including Minnie Hopkins, that she was taking a week off to spend with her husband.

That week seemed endless. Both Polly and Charlie tried to talk to Tom but few further facts emerged. Any hopes Lucy might have had for a heart to heart with her mother about her worries, or to admit that she didn't feel the same about Tom, died in her throat as the warnings came thick and fast that she must be patient, give him time to adjust. Besides, Polly was busy with her own concerns over Charlie and the warehouse and once she recognised her daughter was depressed, assumed it to be because Tom wasn't yet sharing her bed. Somehow Lucy never seemed to find quite the right moment to explain that she'd much rather sleep with her lover.

The children soon lost interest in him, maintaining a shy distance. This man who was supposedly their father was yet a stranger to them and they found it difficult to accept him as anything more at this stage. Even Sean began to avoid him, saying only, 'You never took me fishing.'

'I could take you now.'

'It don't matter. Michael took me down the canal.'

Lucy made a decision not to interfere. If he wished to get to know his children, Tom must set about the task himself. Despite her feelings of guilt at her own apparent betrayal, she still harboured resentment that he had sent her no word that he was safe, nor warned her that he was coming home. Even the authorities seemed to have let her down. There'd been no letter from his commanding officer either, not a word to indicate that he was alive and well. Tom insisted that it was not uncommon for it to take six or even twelve months before relatives were informed a man had been found, a fact she found hard to believe but without hard evidence couldn't dispute.

Only Benny seemed enthusiastic over his brother-in-law's return. 'Great to see you again, old chap. We'll go for a pint or two one night, eh?' And he flashed Lucy a challenging glare, as if saying that he'd warned her all along that Tom would be back, and wasn't that why he'd disapproved of her friendship with Michael Hopkins?

'Did you ever discover who threw that brick at Michael?'

Lucy asked, without thinking that it might seem as if she were defending him.

Benny's eyes flashed dangerously, the natural rivalry between brother and sister instantly sparking. 'You're not still blaming me? I wasn't even there. Belinda and me were well on our way home by that time. Anyroad, he deserved it.'

'Was that because he's a conscientious objector?' Tom asked.

Lucy instinctively opened her mouth to deny this but then the thought flashed into her mind that Tom couldn't possibly know the rumours circulating about Michael. Not unless he'd arrived home a good deal sooner than he claimed and had overheard someone talking. She gazed thoughtfully at her husband's expression of interested enquiry and wondered if it were genuine. Wisely she decided not to pursue the matter, resolving to think about it later when she'd recovered from the shock of his unexpected return. Instead she changed the subject, reminding Benny that Tom wasn't well enough to start drinking yet. 'Hasn't he only just arrived home?'

Perversely, Tom said, 'How about tonight? We could go to the Dog and Duck, if you like.'

'But I thought you were ill and didn't want to go out?' Lucy protested, surprised by this contrariness.

'It's only to the pub. I can manage to go there, for God's sake.'

He was often contrary, she discovered in the days following. Once, she offered to put his things away and he went mad, snatching the shirt she'd picked up right out of her hands. He always insisted on folding his shirts and ties himself, personally stowing away each item with painstaking care. He'd put his cuff links in a box and lock it away in a drawer with other items he never showed her, almost as if he expected her to steal things when he wasn't looking. On one occasion she caught a glimpse of shining metal and asked if he'd brought home a German gun. She knew many soldiers did, as a memento. He was furious, shouting and raving at her, asking if she thought he was a madman. She never went near his things after that.

Benny explained that it was because he'd spent so much time as a POW. 'Affects 'em that way. Makes 'em very possessive because of the terrible living conditions they had to endure. Give him time.'

If anyone else told her to give him time, Lucy thought she might scream. What about her? Who was going to give her time? How was she supposed to adjust? She had no desire to coax him into her bed, as everyone seemed to think. She was hoping and praying he would never ask, that he'd be content to stay in the alcove bed in the kitchen for a long, long time. Or at least until she had found a way out of this nightmare.

*

On Sunday night, thankful that her days of being confined in the house with Tom were nearing an end, Lucy put on her coat and announced that she was just popping up to see Minnie Hopkins and her other customers, to let them know she'd be back at work the next day as usual. 'We need some money coming in, and I don't want you starting work till you feel ready.' She felt stifled, desperate to get out as well as to see Michael again. She prayed he'd be in.

'Don't be long,' Tom warned. 'I want you back within the hour.'

'You what?' She laughed in disbelief that he should think to give her orders. 'I'm used to coming and going as I please. I'll not be dictated to.'

Tom picked up the newspaper, shook it open and began to read. 'I've told you, things have changed now.'

Lucy felt a quick surge of anger well up within her but he merely glanced at her over the top of his paper with that odd, disconnected expression in his eyes and she remembered Polly's warnings to give him more time, and Benny cautioning her about ex-POWs being difficult. Tom wasn't himself. She must remember that. This man had almost died for his country, might well have endured torture and inhumanity that he couldn't even bear to talk about, and all for his wife and children. She bit back the protest. Perhaps if she didn't argue he'd get over his jealousy quicker and in time they'd sort everything out in sensible fashion without hurting anyone.

'I'll do my best to be quick then.'

As she went out through the door, his voice followed her. 'You'll do more than your best, Lucy. You'll learn to do as I say. And you won't talk to that Michael Hopkins ever again. Is that clear?' Lucy mumbled something unintelligible as she hurried out into the night.

Minnie was alone when she arrived, surprisingly sympathetic and avid for news. The old woman explained that Michael had gone to bed early for once, since he hadn't been sleeping well lately which Lucy didn't wonder at. But she did offer her a cuppa in the kitchen, admitted to being captivated by the whole situation and clearly itching to know more. 'What a pretty pickle, eh?'

'Upsetting and confusing, yes.'

'It would be. You fancy our Michael then?'

Startled by the older woman's bluntness, Lucy realised she'd led herself up this dangerous path by spending too much time with him at the Coffee and Bun Social. Well, she'd already made the situation clear to Tom, so there was no turning back now. What did she have to hide? She stood up, walked to the sink to fetch a dish cloth to wipe up a spill of tea, anything to avoid direct eye contact. 'I do, yes, as a matter of fact. And he fancies me. And if you've anything to say against that, you'd best get on and say it.'

'Aye, I thought as much. He allus has had a soft spot for thee, lass.' Minnie's calmness surprised Lucy, as if she didn't mind the fact that her nephew was 'bothering with a married woman', which was how the self-righteous gossipmongers would see it. 'Thee has more than thy fair share now, eh?'

'Of trouble? You're right, I have. The whole street will be talking about it by tomorrow, I've no doubt.'

'I meant of fellas. Two a penny, eh?'

Lucy tried to smile, used to Minnie's black humour, then leaned across the table, her face serious again. 'At least I stick up for him. I meant it about the gossip. It won't be pleasant. They've already had a go at Michael.'

' "Sticks and stones may break my bones but calling never hurt me." In't that what kids say?'

'*They* say he's a conchie. That's why someone threw that brick. Didn't he tell you?'

Minnie looked startled, her mouth curling in upon itself till her lips almost disappeared. '*Conchie?* Where the hecky thump did they get that from?'

'You know what folk are like. All because they've never seen him in uniform.'

Minnie was silent for a whole half minute, quite a long time for her. 'Come on, and don't mek a sound. I want to show thee summat. Summat tha'd best see if that's the way the wind blows.'

Back at number 32 Tom Shackleton took the opportunity of an empty house to visit his wife's bedroom. Polly and Charlie were down at the warehouse and Sarah Jane and

Sean were fast asleep, curled up like a pair of spoons in the single bed they shared in the corner. The brass double bed which had once stood in a bedroom in his own home occupied most of the rest of the floor.

Tom resented the fact that they had to share a house with Lucy's family though he could see it had made sense for her, while he was away at war. But a man should have his own place. He also bitterly resented only being offered the alcove bed downstairs when there was this big one here, which he should be sharing with his own wife. He'd certainly no intention of sharing her with that conchie. It amused him that Lucy had no idea he'd seen them together, kissing and canoodling in the school yard. Bit of luck that was. He chuckled now to think how Benny had got it in the neck for something he didn't do. If Lucy knew that it'd been he who'd thrown that brick, she might not even offer him the alcove bed.

But he meant to start asserting his rights soon. It wasn't that he meant to hang around longer than was necessary. Once she'd had time to get used to the idea and accepted him back in proper fashion, as a good obedient wife should, they'd be off, out of this dratted street and this drab city. He'd never shared Lucy's love for Manchester and he'd taken a big risk in coming back, like a rat to its hole, he thought to himself with a smile. One he had to make worth his while.

For now he turned his attention to quietly opening and

closing drawers in the chest which stood beside the bed. After some moments of searching he found what he was looking for. A small tin. Inside was exactly what he'd expected, a collection of coins and one or two notes. Like her mother, his lovely Lucy believed in careful budgeting. Old habits never change. He smiled again as he pocketed the money, leaving no more than a coin or two in the bottom of the tin. What was hers was now his. She was his wife after all. Then he let himself quietly out of the house and headed for the Dog and Duck. The children would be all right on their own for once. No bombs were likely to drop after all, since hostilities were over, and they were hard and fast asleep.

He'd just slip out and do what needed to be done, then have a quick half and be back long before Lucy returned.

Woken by the click of the front door, Sean sat up in bed and started to cry.

Filled with curiosity, Lucy followed the old woman upstairs. On the first landing Minnie opened a door and led her quietly inside. In the centre of the large double bed, Michael lay breathing softly, deep in sleep.

Lucy stepped back, alarmed, but Minnie merely put one finger to her lips, urging her to be quiet, and pointed to something on the floor. Peering into the shadows by the big high bed, Lucy saw Michael's boots, the ones he wore every day, always brightly polished. But they looked somehow different as they stood on the bedroom rug. One was quite ordinary, the other taller, as if they weren't a proper pair. And then it came to her what she was looking at and her hand flew to her mouth to stop herself from crying out loud.

Back in the kitchen the two women faced each other once more. 'So, now you know,' Minnie said matter-of-factly as she poured Lucy a fresh cup of tea and popped in two saccharin tablets. 'This so-called conchie left half his leg behind when he crashed, his foot anyroad. Happen you should tell the gossips that.'

'Oh, God, that's awful. So that's where the limp comes from?'

'Aye.' Minnie's expression was solemn. 'He never mentions it because he doesn't want folk's sympathy.'

'I want you to know that, missing a foot or not, it doesn't make any difference to the way I feel about him. It's Michael I love. I can't think of Tom as a husband, not now. I suppose I should, because we were happy once, but I can't.'

'Thee's still a married woman.'

The tea was cooling in the cup before her but now that she'd started, Lucy couldn't stop talking. 'I know, and maybe those feelings would come back if I let them, but somehow I doubt it. I'm desperate not to lose Michael yet I feel so guilty. I was the one who betrayed my own husband – not that we've – I mean – I've betrayed him in my mind – by loving another man.'

Minnie had the grace to smile. 'Nay, lass, don't be too hard on thisen. They told you he was dead. It's fair enough if tha believed 'em.'

'The letter said the army *presumed* he was dead, not quite the same thing, though it felt it at the time. I feel so confused. What am I to do? Tom expects everything to go back to the way it was. He's told me not to see Michael, nor ever to speak to him again. But how can I bear to do that? Should I ask Tom to leave, insist on a divorce? Everyone seems to be getting one these days, so why not me?' She gave Minnie no opportunity to offer any opinion as she continued with bitter pain in her voice, 'Yet it seems so unfair when he nearly died fighting in a war for us, doesn't it? I'm just being selfish and ungrateful.' Lucy could feel herself growing all hot and bothered, her throat constricting with tears and her chest tight with fear.

'Nay, nay, don't tek on so. Bide yer time, lass. Bide yer time. Give the lad chance to settle and yersel time to get used to the idea. Problems have a way of sorting theirselves out in the end, though the cat doesn't always jump the way you expect.'

This old woman, whom Lucy had always thought of as her enemy, looked so sad, so full of sympathy, that she felt an odd sort of kinship with her, as if she understood. Perhaps some time in her own youth Minnie Hopkins had loved and lost. 'Yes, you're right. It wouldn't be fair to bombard him with demands when he's only just arrived.

Oh, Minnie.' And the old woman gathered her up in her skinny arms while Lucy rested her head on that flat chest, breathing in the scent of violets and pear drops, and thought this cantankerous old dragon suddenly seemed to be her only friend.

Later, as Minnie showed her to the door, they found an envelope on the mat that someone had pushed through the letterbox. Inside were three white feathers.

Chapter Fifteen

Coming home to find her son in a lather of distress and Sarah Jane in floods of tears, not knowing where to find either of her parents, filled Lucy with the kind of anger she'd never experienced in her life before. Perhaps it was just as well that her negligent husband didn't come home till the early hours, far too late to discuss the matter then. She'd also discovered the near empty tin which she used to save coins for her share of the household expenses. It wasn't difficult to guess what had happened to the money either.

But it wasn't until after supper the next day that the subject was raised. Lucy had been quietly fuming all day and as she ladled out meat and potato pie everyone ate in a subdued silence, aware of a storm brewing. Even the children were quieter than usual. As soon as the meal was over, Polly offered to put them to bed while Charlie did the clearing away, shooing the pair off into the front parlour.

The minute the door was closed Lucy calmly enquired where exactly Tom had spent the previous evening. 'And don't say you went for a swift half because you didn't come home until after two in the morning. No doubt spending the money you stole from my tin.'

'I won't tell you anything, since you seem to know so much.'

Lucy had vowed that she would remain calm. Now she almost screamed at him: 'How could you leave the children alone like that?'

His response was cold to the point of icy. Picking up the paper as he always did when he needed to put a barrier between them, he said, 'They were perfectly safe. Many kids have been left in worse places during this war. Anyroad, you're their mother. You shouldn't have left them either.'

'But I left them with *you*, while I tried to hang on to my job.'

'I've decided I don't want you working for the Hopkinses any more. You won't be going there again, or on any other cleaning jobs for that matter. You'll stop at home in future and look after me and the children.' He didn't even glance up from the paper, the tone of his voice hard and unyielding, as if the matter were settled and there was really no need for further discussion.

Lucy's eyes widened in disbelief. She was half laughing at his obstinacy. 'You can't be serious? Of course I'll be going again. It's a good job that pays well. How would we manage without it?'

'I shall find a job. No problem. Till then, we can go on t'dole or benefits.'

'Don't be ridiculous.'

He flung the paper aside so violently she took a quick step back, startled by his anger. 'Do you need it spelling out? I thought I made it clear last night, Lucy. I'll not have you seeing Michael Hopkins every day, lusting after him.'

She wrapped her arms about herself in a defensive gesture and drew in a trembling breath, trying to keep steady and composed. 'I've already explained, Tom, nothing ever happened between us and it won't while you and me are still man and wife, so there's no reason for you to be jealous. But you can't expect things not to have changed. I'm prepared for you to stop on here for a bit, till you've time to sort yourself but . . .'

His hand snaked out to grasp her by the hair and push her back against the wall, making her squeal with surprise, quickly stifled as she didn't wish to alarm the children upstairs. Tom's face was less than an inch from her own, his angry words spraying her with spittle. 'Listen! You're *my* wife, not his. And always will be. I've no intention of giving you up. Not to anyone, and certainly not to a bloody conchie.'

Lucy felt the first nudge of fear, a worm of unease that wriggled like a maggot at the back of her mind. 'It was *you*, wasn't it? You put those feathers through his letter box.'

'What if I did? I threw the bloody brick an' all. I saw him kissing and fondling you in that disgusting way in the school yard, so thought I had the right. He deserved everything he got – interfering with my wife.'

A wave of sickness hit her. Hadn't she felt as if someone were watching them from the shadows? Now she knew it must have been Tom, she felt fury more than shame, disgust and loathing at his cunning. 'Dear God, why didn't you speak? Why didn't you let me know you were there?'

'Because it was far more interesting to find out what you were up to while I was away.'

'*I've told you, nothing happened!*' She thrust him away, breathing heavily as she resolutely outfaced him. 'I'll have you know that Michael Hopkins is no more a conchie than you are, just not so lucky, and I have proof.' She told him then about Michael's false foot, watching with satisfaction as astonishment dawned on Tom's face, making him look like a foolish child.

'Poor man.' It was Polly's voice from the door which had quietly opened without either of them hearing it. 'A proud one too by the sound of it.' She walked in bearing a tray of tea cups and a plate of biscuits. 'Something to wet your whistle, eh? Sure and I thought I heard a funny noise? But then you could hear bread being buttered in this house, the walls are that thin.' She shrewdly considered her daughter as she set the tray down.

Lucy was shaking too much to answer the question, her eyes riveted on her husband.

Tom stroked a lock of brown hair back from Lucy's face, the tone of his voice surprisingly soft now. 'I was just persuading her round to my way of thinking. Necessary, I think, don't you? The man is obviously taking advantage and since I'm home now it wouldn't be proper Lucy, for you to work there any more. I'd prefer you to give in your notice. Don't you agree, Polly?'

' 'Tis true there could be talk,' she agreed, looking uncomfortable and backing quickly out of the room as if regretting having ventured into this private argument between husband and wife.

Lucy felt incensed that Tom should use her own mother against her and very nearly flung the tea at him but, determined to stay in control of herself at least, she quietly sat down and sipped it, for all it was scalding hot and the cup clattered against her teeth. 'That decision is up to me, wouldn't you say?'

'I'll not have my wife gossiped about.'

Lucy pressed her lips together, praying for patience. 'If the vindictive old hags in this street choose to be malicious, that's up to them. I don't need to ask anyone's permission about what I do.'

'No, but you need to ask *me*.'

Lucy slammed the cup back in the saucer and was on her feet, shaking with temper, her fury overwhelming her efforts to remain cool, calm and collected, careless of her mother hovering at the other side of the door and probably listening to every word. '*Over my dead body!*' she yelled at him. 'You don't rule me, Tom Shackleton, husband or no. I'll make up me own mind what's proper and what isn't.' Whereupon she flew from the room, tears of rage and frustration streaming down her face.

Hearing her run upstairs, Polly turned to Charlie in distress. 'It's not working, them living here with us. They need a place of their own.'

Fifteen minutes later Polly found her daughter half packed, two sleepy children brought from their beds and already dressed.

'You're not going to him, this fancy man of yours, not because of a silly argument?'

Lucy turned to her children. 'Go on, get yourselves downstairs and wait by the front door. Sarah Jane, don't you dare open it till I come.'

After the children had gone, each clutching the soft toy Benny had given them, Lucy confronted her mother, face set in stubborn resolve. 'I've done my best but I don't love Tom any more, for all he's still me husband. And I'll not have him lording it over me, ordering me about as if he alone can decide what I can and cannot do. He left our Sean and Sarah Jane on their own for hours yesterday evening when I went up to Minnie's about me job. That wasn't right. *And* he admits to attacking Michael and sending him three white feathers, which is unforgivable.'

'That was jealousy.'

'Whatever the reason, it was a wicked thing to do. Michael's a brave man who fought for his country like the rest, and lost his foot in doing so.'

Polly sat down on the bed while Lucy continued to stuff clothes into a bag, not bothering to fold them. 'You love him, don't you?'

She didn't attempt to deny it. 'And he loves me.'

'So you'll risk the vindictive old hags talking, being ostracised by everyone?' Polly quietly watched her daughter.

'If he'll have me, which I believe he will, yes. I'd be his wife in the eyes of God at least, if not the law of the land. Like it or lump it.'

Polly was shaking her head. 'Aw, Lucy, m'cushla. If only life were that simple. Sure and wouldn't the shame of it drive you apart in the end? Look what the gossips are already doing to him.' She reached out a hand, but Lucy snatched up the bag and backed away.

'No, don't say anything. I've made up me mind.'

And then Polly did what she'd promised herself she would never do – set about interfering in her daughter's life. 'Listen to yer old mam for once. Haven't I warned you how Tom needs time to heal? As a prisoner-of-war, he knew what he had to do. Wasn't it all set out for him, plain as the nose on his face? He had to escape and so he did. If he forgot to write, or was too ill to do so, can you not find it in yer heart to forgive him? He came home as soon as he could and if it's hard for him to adjust then you must be patient. Hasn't the war damaged us all? No one said that getting back to normal would be easy because it never is. But the poor boy is devastated. He thinks he's lost you by his clumsiness. It's a place of yer own that the pair of you need, not to be crowded in our front parlour or in separate beds. You need to give this marriage a chance, to try and make it work for the children's sake at least. Don't they love their da now? And doesn't Tom love you, bless his heart?'

Lucy was staring into her mother's face and tears were again running unchecked down her cheeks.

'I don't know.'

'I want you to be happy so I do, but running off with another man isn't the way, m'cushla, and it's sorry I am that you love him so. But if Tom has made mistakes, isn't it only out of jealousy and love for you? Who knows what he's suffered in the past? Ye have to give the poor man a chance.' And then Lucy was weeping on Polly's shoulder as if her heart was broken, as surely it was.

Losing her job was like losing her identity, not simply her independence. Lucy no longer had any money of her own but was entirely dependent upon what Tom handed to her each week out of his dole money. She even missed her daily sparring with the old dragon. And she rarely saw Michael these days. She found every excuse she could to nip out to the shops on any pretext, just on the off-chance she might see him. But she never did.

Tom wasn't an early riser and one morning, before he was even awake, Lucy slipped up the street to number 179 and waited for Michael to come out of his front door prompt at six-thirty. She had to see him one more time, if only to explain. He was startled to see her but his face lit up with delight. Grabbing her hand, he pulled her into Nelson's ginnel and in seconds was covering her face with kisses. It was several moments before either of them had the breath to speak, and then only endlessly to repeat the inevitable, Michael insisting she should leave Tom, and Lucy trying to explain why she couldn't. Not just yet anyway.

'How can I? The children. Mam. He's still not well but he's determined to make a go of things and he's trying to find us a house. It's all so difficult.'

He was kissing her again, hot fierce kisses that she couldn't get enough of. She felt herself weakening with every blistering kiss, every pulsing touch and caress. Lucy pressed herself shamelessly against him, her fingers threading through his hair, as if by moulding herself to him, she could make them one.

'I want you, Lucy.'

'And I want you.' It was the most desperately difficult

thing she had ever done but she finally summoned the strength to put a stop to the kisses, even if it was only to lay her hot cheek against his pounding heart.

Michael gently stroked her hair and her mind turned back to VJ Day, to the day she'd received the telegram and her world had fallen apart with the news that her husband was dead, leaving her in a state of shock and disbelief. Somehow she'd learned to accept it, to go on with her life. Yet only a few months later she'd taken a day trip to Belle Vue with her children and fallen in love with this wonderful man.

As she lifted her head and captured his mouth with her own, the joy was tainted and she felt sick with fear for the future. Nevertheless she was sure that her mother must be right; running off with Michael would only destroy their love and gain them nothing. She didn't protest when he slid open her blouse and caressed her breast, only moaned and threw back her head in an agony of pain and delight. She needed to savour every last moment with him. Did this wanton behaviour make her wicked? Did it mark her as a 'loose woman' as the self-righteous Lily Gantry would no doubt claim. How could it be wicked when it felt so wonderful, gloriously right? It surprised her that Minnie didn't class her as such. Minnie Hopkins was a constant mystery to her, the kind of woman whose opinions you could never predict.

How full of optimism they'd all been just a few short

months ago; glad that the war was over at last, that they were still young with all of life before them even if the first flush of youth had gone. How dark the future seemed now, knowing they could not be together once Tom had returned. They drew apart at last, Michael begging her not to abandon him completely, at least to meet him now and then whenever she could get away. Lucy was shaking her head, tears standing proud in her eyes as she backed away from him.

'How can I? Tom would find out. He deserves a chance, a home and a wife to come back to after what he's been through. I have to give him that chance. It's the least I owe him.'

'And what about me? Us? I love you, Lucy. I need you desperately.'

She gave a little sob and, turning, hurried away through the cobbled ginnel back to Pansy Street, for how could she resist such persuasive arguments when she herself needed him so badly?

Belinda stood holding open her larder door and gazed in upon empty shelves. Not even a heel of bread left in the bin. Her stomach ached with hunger since she'd had little more than a bowl of vegetable broth the day before which Polly had brought them. What they would have done without her mother-in-law during these last weeks, she didn't care to consider. But even Polly didn't know the whole truth for Belinda had learned to hide their penurious state, putting on quite an act in order to give the impression that all was well.

Pulling a shawl close about her head for warmth, she fished her purse out of a drawer and found that it too was empty. She dropped it back in with a heavy sigh. How much longer could she continue with this pretence? There was not a scrap of food in the house to feed herself, let alone the child growing steadily inside her. Whatever she'd hoped for in Civvy Street – a new career, a life of purpose and meaning, a way of using her intelligence and training – this was far from those dreams.

The papers said that London only had a week of coal supplies left. Well, she didn't have any. It was February and she was now keeping her gloves, scarf and coat on all day in order to combat the near arctic temperatures. Outside, the streets were thick with snow and slush. It was said to be the worst winter on record. Thousands of people had been sent home from work in Manchester as factories closed for lack of power. There was no coal to be had anywhere despite the fact that tons of the stuff was piled up at the pits; it couldn't be delivered as roads were apparently blocked by drifts as high as ten foot. Even the street lights had been blacked out again, to conserve power. She and Benny had been eating by candlelight for days now, and it wasn't in order to foster romance. In fact she rarely saw him these days, and when she did, he was exhausted.

He spent most of each day tramping the snow-packed streets looking for work, any sort of work. Gone were his hopes now, along with his dreams and the last vestige of pride. But even Polly wasn't able to offer him employment as she too was laying people off, struggling to stay afloat. Not that he would ever ask her.

For Belinda it was a living nightmare. Living in these two poky rooms had proved to be more dreadful than she could ever have anticipated. Sometimes she heard the landlord hammering on the door, shouting rude words at her as he demanded she come down and pay the rent she owed. She would pull the blanket over her head, for she spent most of the time there now as the only warm place, and shut her ears. How could she pay him? She had nothing.

Benny was doing his best, she knew that. And without question he loved her but nothing was quite the same. All the fun had gone out of life. They no longer had the energy to enjoy anything, not even their little spats which had nearly always led to love making. Quite out of the question now in any case, since she was due in about four weeks. God knows what would happen then. She daren't even think about it except to hope that they'd keep her in the nursing home for ten days or so. The doctor told her the baby was coming along fine. It must be all that healthy free orange juice he gave her to drink, plus cod liver oil and malt. She practically lived on the stuff and didn't dare tell him how meagre the rest of her diet had become.

Worst of all, Benny no longer believed in himself. Every night he railed at the state he'd reduced them to, and every night she would hold him close and assure him of her continuing faith in him. For all Lucy said he was a dreamer with unrealistic ambitions, Belinda didn't for one moment believe their dire state was all his fault. Perhaps she should have gone to see her father, tackled him face to face and found out just what he was up to. Perhaps she'd been a coward not to. She hadn't done so because she still fervently believed that Benny would make something of himself in the end. The fact that he'd kicked over the traces a bit after six years of grinding war service didn't make him bad, only foolish. And surely everyone was entitled to their independence, and their dreams. But hunger and frustration caused tears to roll down her cheeks, making her feel giddy and light-headed. Her ankles were swollen and there was a constant stitch in her side.

When Benny came bursting through the door later that evening, covered in snow and freezing cold, he glared at the bare table and then at her.

'Where's me dinner?'

Belinda shook her head. She knew he was at the end of his tether, that like her he missed the jovial company of his comrades, the routine of army life, even the excitement of war. The last thing he needed right now was to listen to a nagging wife at the end of another fruitless day. But she nursed a terrible fear for her child and their future and no longer had the strength to be mindful of his ego. The accusing words came out of her mouth seemingly of their own accord. 'Where's the money to pay for it?'

His round face grew so red that she thought he might explode. Then he thrust his hand in his pocket, took out a pitiful few coppers and flung them on to the wooden table. Three pennies rolled across its scratched surface, one tipped over the edge and rolled away into a corner. Belinda knew she'd hunt for it on her hands and knees later. For now she wanted only to erase the pain from his beloved face. 'Oh, Benny, what's gone wrong with us? Why do we quarrel?'

'If you'd stop blaming me for everything, we might not.'

'I don't blame you for anything. You know I don't.' She took her shawl and with it began to brush the snow from his hair, which lay flat to his head, dark and wet, no longer the glowing colour it had once been. She rubbed some life back into his icy cheeks, pulled off his soaking wet coat and hung it up to drip even if there was no heat to dry it. It all came out then, all his pent-up emotion, his sense of failure and hurt pride.

'I've spent days – weeks – looking for a job, a way out of this hole, anything,' he groaned, 'but there isn't one.' Just reading the disappointment in her lovely eyes filled him with guilt, for all it might be tempered by a glimmer of resentment. She'd let him down too, this woman he'd loved so much. She hadn't lifted him out of his world, only driven him deeper into it thanks to her dratted family. Not that he could say as much to her for he knew in his heart that nobody could tell Hubert Clarke what to do. Instead he said, 'I didn't ask you to take on this poky shop, did I? Look what trouble you've landed us in. I could've used me demob money for summat decent if I hadn't been saddled with this white elephant.'

Belinda wrung out the sleeves of his coat, trying not to let the words hurt her, for she knew he didn't truly mean them. He was just hitting out at the injustice of life, as she was. 'I thought it would help.'

'Well, it hasn't, has it? There's hundreds of soldiers, airmen and sailors all coming home from the war, looking for work, and now this bleedin' weather. What am I supposed to do?' It sickened him. Six years fighting to end up on the scrap heap.

Benny flung away his chair, face tight with anger. 'I'm going down to t'pub, happen I can win a bob or two on t'dominoes. I'll at least find a bit of peace.' And he stormed out, slamming the door on her sad face and his own guilt.

A voice prompted him at the back of his mind as he strode through the slush and ice: *If you don't watch out you'll lose her. Then where'll you be?* He got as far as the pub door then turned on his heel and marched all the way back again, gathered Belinda in his arms and wept.

'I'll get work soon. I swear it.' And that night they lay with arms wrapped about each other, as happy as they'd ever been.

The next day, when he'd gone to carry out this promise, Belinda pulled a cardboard box out from under the bed and considered its sparse contents. Clothes had never been particularly important to her. She'd never pretended to be a fashion plate. Even so . . . the peacock dress had been special. She remembered buying it in Cairo, and all the parties and dances she'd enjoyed in it, the friends she'd made. Laughter and sunshine to hold back the shadow of fear which was always present in war. Now she wrapped the dress carefully in newspaper and, pushing it under her arm, walked down the street, head held high even as tears rolled down her cheeks.

Her humiliation was complete when the pawnbroker gave her only five shillings on it, claiming he was being generous at that. She'd bought it at Harrods for twelve guineas in the days when she'd been young and foolish and money hadn't seemed to matter. Now she was using it to buy bread and cheese.

The invitation when it came the next day took Belinda by surprise. Recognising her father's handwriting on the envelope, she lacked the courage to open it and propped it against the teapot. It was Benny, coming in from the bedroom where he'd been shaving from a bowl of water in front of the cracked mirror, who ripped it open.

'He wants us to come to tea. On Sunday.'

Belinda was so startled she was forced to sit down before her legs gave way. Perhaps it was because she was having a baby that she couldn't seem to deal with emotional upset quite so easily these days. She told Benny that of course they wouldn't go and an argument ensued which lasted throughout supper, though since that was only soup and bread and dripping, Belinda really didn't have the energy to fight any more, and eventually Benny won.

Chapter Sixteen

Belinda hoped the buses wouldn't be running but when Sunday came they wrapped up well and caught one easily into the city centre, then changed to the number seventeen which took them up Park Road. There were heaps of dirty snow to either side of the road but at least they were able to get through. They got off at the end of Cherry Crescent and Belinda had never felt more nervous in her life.

'This is a bad idea.'

'They're your parents,' Benny insisted. 'It could be just the break we need. It's long past time you med it up with them.'

'But what if Pops tells me *never to darken his door again*?' She adopted a humorously dramatic tone though it came out sounding hollow and foolish. Hubert Clarke was an easy man to argue with but a hard one to cross.

'He sent for us,' Benny reminded her. 'He must have a reason. Happen he wants to forgive and forget.' And since she couldn't imagine this for one minute, Belinda lapsed into a brooding silence. She would be polite, calm, non-controversial, she promised herself, for he was still her father.

They stood at the familiar door with its cracked varnish and stained glass window while Benny pressed the bell. A jangling sound echoed along the hall and up the empty stairs behind it and Belinda couldn't help remembering the day she'd arrived back, fresh and still young, brimful of confidence. Now she felt old, and beaten by life.

It was her mother who answered. Joanna stood and gazed upon her daughter and son-in-law as if she had never seen them in her life before, nor had the first idea what to say to them now. Her eyes seemed to be riveted upon Belinda's voluptuous figure, as if the letter she'd received giving her this glad news months ago had not registered until this moment.

'Mother. How lovely to see you. Are you well?'

Joanna managed a half smile then stepped aside without a word, and let them precede her into the house.

The four of them sat in the chilly front parlour where they took tea, brought in on a trolley by Joanna as if they were strangers who had to be impressed with the best china and the sight of a neatly folded fan of white paper in the empty fire grate. Belinda thought it typical of her father's pettiness that he had denied them a fire for all he might blame the state of the country. It was so cold that frost rimed the inside of the windows, and she recalled with longing the warm fug of the kitchen with its huge old-fashioned Aga, where apparently they were no longer welcome.

Hubert sat ramrod straight in his wing-backed chair, glowering at them as he sipped at his tea or pinched the tips of his moustache between finger and thumb. He swallowed whole one or two of Joanna's tiny egg sandwiches, leaving the butterfly cakes and scones untouched.

The silence threatened to become oppressive. Benny set down his cup and saucer with a snap, glad to be rid of the bother of trying to balance it while he ate, drew in a deep breath and beamed proudly as he indicated his wife. 'She's looking well, eh? Less than a month to go now.'

All eyes turned to Belinda who felt herself growing bright pink beneath the scrutiny. She hadn't wanted this meeting, had only agreed to come because the larder remained frighteningly empty, like her savings account. She'd also realised that Benny was determined on this family reunion and nothing would change his mind until he saw for himself what a hopeless case her parents were. 'I'm simply going to have a baby, that's all,' she said. 'A perfectly normal state of affairs.'

'Bit of a shaker at first, mind,' Benny said, nudging Belinda and almost upsetting her cup. 'I were a bit stunned mesel' like, when I first heard. But think on it, Mr Clarke.

A new offshoot to the family tree, eh? That's summat to be proud of, eh?'

'I fail to see why, when it will bear your name and not mine.'

Benny looked nonplussed. This was the last reaction he'd expected. He had been absolutely certain that a man of Hubert Clarke's stature would be secretly delighted to welcome a new grandchild, that Belinda's condition had been the reason for the proffered olive branch.

Joanna saved the situation. She got up from her seat and went to her daughter, arms outstretched. 'Well, I for one am delighted for you, darling. Having a baby is a wonderful joy. May I – may I kiss you?' And after initial awkwardness on Belinda's part, mother and daughter were hugging each other, mopping up tears and laughter, both talking at the same time after which display of affection they disappeared upstairs, arm in arm.

Benny sank back in his chair with a sigh of relief, his grin stretching just about as wide as it could go. 'There we are then, all breaches healed. Don't it do yer heart good to see it?' In his experience, families might fall out but they always made it up in the end. Certainly his own did. No matter what cross purposes there might be at times between himself and his mam, or even with Lucy, they all pulled together in times of trouble.

'Indeed,' Hubert agreed. His tone was as cold as the ice feathering the bay windows.

'Perhaps now,' Benny earnestly remarked, 'you and I should talk, man to man as it were. Get matters on a proper footing.' He was so beset by sudden nervousness that he stuffed a whole triangle of egg sandwich into his mouth, quickly followed by a slurp of tea.

Hubert grimaced. 'That might be productive, certainly.'

Benny knew he'd been right all along. Wasn't a father supposed to help his daughter, offer a helping hand to a new member of the family? Everything was going to work out fine. 'Well, you go first. Ask me summat – anything you like, I've nowt to be ashamed of. Then I'll ask you. How would that be?'

Hubert smoothed the ends of his moustache. 'An excellent notion.'

Benny reached for another egg sandwich. They were so tiny he could eat a dozen but was managing to restrain his hunger. 'Fire away.'

'Where, and how, were you intending my grandson or granddaughter to be brought up?' Hubert coolly enquired, and taking this interest as a good sign, Benny carefully explained that although there were no jobs to be found at present because of all the returning service men, the bad weather and strikes and so on, he had plans. Anxious to impress he hurried on to outline them, saying how he needed only a modest amount of capital to set himself up in business.

'Buying and selling household goods and furniture,

that's the future,' he expounded, 'as I'm sure you'll agree.'

Hubert merely raised one eyebrow, saying nothing. Beginning to relax, Benny pulled a packet of Woodbines from his pocket, offered Hubert one, and when he declined with a shake of the head, lit up one for himself.

'Our biggest problem, apart from the lack of capital as I said, is where we're living. It's not good enough for Belinda.'

'I'm sure you're right.'

Pleased he was striking the right note, Benny ploughed on. 'It seems to me that a man of property such as yerself like, wouldn't want his grandson to be brought up in the vicinity of Pansy Street.'

'It's a pity you didn't consider the matter more carefully before things reached this parlous state.'

Benny wasn't sure what parlous meant but doubted it was complimentary. 'There's still time,' he reasoned. 'Yon child isn't born yet.' Eager to explain his plans further he shuffled forward in his seat so he could flick the ash from his cigarette into the fire grate. He missed and hit the faded Persian rug instead. Mindful of his manners, he got up and rubbed the ash in with his heel and swiftly apologised.

Manfully swallowing the choking sensation that was tightening his chest, Hubert asked, 'And how much — capital — did you have in mind?'

Benny leaned back in his seat, feeling increasingly confident that Hubert was genuine in wanting to help. He mentioned a sum and, seeing his father-in-law's expression of disbelief, hastened to adjust it. 'I reckon I could manage with less if you'd agree to us moving in here. Just till we get going like and can afford a place of us own. I mean, yer not short of space, are you? More bedrooms than you know what to do with, eh?' Benny was babbling now, and he knew it, but somehow felt himself too far down the road he'd chosen to back out of it. All he could do was hope for a good reception to his ideas, for Belinda's sake. 'And we only need one, for us and the babby. Belinda's mam could help look after it. She'd enjoy that, I'm sure, which would mean Belinda could get a bit of a job if she wanted one. I'm not a stuffy, old-fashioned husband like some. Belinda's a smart lass with a brain in her head. I've no objection to me wife working.'

'I'm sure you haven't. Your plans seem — substantial. You think big, I can tell.'

Benny swelled out his chest with pride. 'Oh, aye, I'm a born enter . . . entpren . . .'

'Entrepreneur?' offered Hubert dryly.

'Aye, that's it. Never short of ideas, isn't Benny Pride. It runs in the family, don't you know? It'd all be above board, of course. A proper loan. Only if I borrow from you instead of a bank manager, you wouldn't be likely to charge nearly so much by way of interest, now would you? It being all in the family as it were.'

Hubert leaned forward in his chair, hands lightly

clasped, elbows resting on his knees. His tone was mild, ponderous. 'Let me see if I've got this right. You wish to live in my house and have my wife help look after your infant while borrowing money from me at a low rate of interest so you can set up this plan to be an entrepreneur. Is that about the size of it?'

'Got it in one.'

Hubert's voice dropped to a whisper. 'And what's in it for me?'

'I beg yer pardon?'

'What do I get out of this scheme of yours?' The question took Benny by surprise but before he could formulate a reply, Hubert continued, 'I expect you think you can have an easy ride because you've married our Belinda. Well, in my view you've messed her life up.' His voice remained quiet, meditative even, but Benny didn't much care for what he was saying. If Hubert said owt wrong about Belinda, he'd clock him one, father-in-law or not.

'If I were to put up the money for this — enterprise, and I haven't said that I will yet,' holding up one cautionary hand as Benny's eyes kindled, 'I reckon I deserve a favour in return. Wouldn't you say that was fair? I'd have a few terms of my own.'

Benny frowned. 'What sort of terms?'

Hubert reached for the whisky decanter. 'Well, let me tell you what I have in mind.'

*

Charlie had seen the doctor again and his heart and lungs had been given the all clear, which was a great relief. Polly had been afraid he might have angina or leukaemia, something seriously life-threatening. When she'd expressed her relief about that, Charlie, twisted with pain, had said, no, he'd definitely live — unfortunately. The pain of the arthritis got him down at times, though he was making some improvement with the tablets the doctor had given him. Sometimes he allowed Polly to rub embrocation into his muscles at night. At other times he nearly screamed when she touched him. It made her feel so helpless. The doctor insisted that he should rest and not inflame the joints, which meant he was never going to be the fit man he'd once been. This meant it was even more important that she should make a success of her manufacturing plans.

Polly had invested heavily in washing and dyeing machines as well as the second-hand loom from the mill at Hebden Bridge. Despite the difficulties everyone was experiencing in these hard times, they were already producing several yards of carpet a week which the girls stitched together to fit any size of room.

When Benny burst in one Monday morning demanding to speak to her right away, she was helping her old mate Maisie Wright, whom she'd taken on as a spool setter, to arrange the different shades of bobbins in their correct pattern grid on a large square table.

'By heck,' Maisie said, 'lad looks like he's just landed in a parachute,' referring to Benny's dishevelled, excited appearance.

He was so full of himself that he was well on with his tale by the time Polly had ushered him into her office and closed the door. She regarded her son with greeny-grey eyes narrowed in shrewd speculation. 'Are ye saying that ye've changed your mind, that ye'll come into the business after all? Honest to God, I never thought to hear the day. So what brought about this change of heart?'

'I've been talking to Hubert.' Hands in pockets and rocking on his heels since he was quite unable to stand still, Benny tossed the name out as if he were on friendly terms with his father-in-law.

'Hubert?'

'Hubert Clarke, Belinda's . . .'

'I know who he is. But what does Hubert have to do with your coming into the business with me? Assuming I survive this terrible winter.' Though she thought she could guess, following their earlier discussion about their respective children, and almost smiled to herself to see Benny squirm with embarrassment. How he hated to lose face.

Relieved as he was to be offered help, Benny had, in fact, been rather shaken by the interview with his father-in-law. Hubert had made it crystal clear that whatever Benny had suffered thus far with problems over a licence, petitions and eviction notices, not to mention being set upon in dark alleys, was nothing in comparison to what could happen next if he didn't co-operate.

At first he'd almost been prepared to run the risk in order to hang on to his prized independence, rather than have his father-in-law take what seemed like complete control of his life, let alone interfere in his mam's business. But then he thought of Belinda, and the empty cupboard, not to mention imminent fatherhood, and somehow he'd managed to swallow his pride and hear Hubert out.

After a while Benny recognised many advantages in the plan, besides its providing the security that they desperately needed. He saw no reason not to go along with the idea. Wasn't it worth losing his pride and independence, he thought, if he got to keep his family safe? And who knew where it could all lead? The plan had the added benefit of providing a proper role for himself, as well as burying the hatchet as it were and pleasing both sets of parents in one go. All of which surely had to be beneficial for everyone concerned. He just had to persuade Polly to agree. 'I thought you wanted me to come in with you?'

'I do.' She decided to play along, resolving not to let him see she'd been the instigator of Hubert's sudden approach. 'I just don't understand what changed your mind.'

'Because I can recognise a good idea when I see one. Just for once, Mam, hear me out without interrupting. It'd work like this . . .' And he set about carefully explaining the deal. Polly's eyes narrowed thoughtfully as he talked and she sank back in her chair while Benny paced back and forth in the office.

Hubert, as a credit trader and wholesaler, would supply Polly with goods at competitive wholesale prices. She must buy exclusively from him to get the best terms but could then sell the goods either at normal retail price to her own customers or at a higher credit price to the club customers he sent her. They would bring with them a voucher to an agreed value which they paid off week by week at a shilling in the pound. Ron, Hubert's son, did the collecting, Benny explained, and if folk got behind in their payments or did a moonlight flit, it was Hubert who stood the loss.

This was the last thing Polly had been expecting, for Hubert to come up with a plan which included her. 'Why doesn't he sell his wholesale goods to his own customers direct?'

'Because that would turn his business into a retail operation. He'd have to take on shop premises, employ staff to display, sell and wrap the goods, which all costs money. He makes his profit by selling in bulk to his suppliers and through his credit club. He does well, Mam. There's no flies on Hubert.'

Polly dryly remarked that she didn't wonder at it since he seemed to be playing the fiddle from both ends but Benny wasn't to be distracted. He continued with his explanation. 'You can't lose. He already has the customers, just waiting for somewhere to spend their money. Of course you couldn't do all of this from the warehouse. You'd have to take on a shop, a big one, happen in the city centre.'

'No.'

'What?'

'I said no. The rates and rents of city centre premises are too high. They'd cripple us.'

This had admittedly been Hubert's response too when Benny had made the suggestion to him. Now he shrugged philosophically, conceding defeat. 'All right then, off centre, closer to Castlefield, Salford, or wherever you think suitable. Only it must be *retail* premises. No reason why you can't keep the warehouse on for storage and your carpet manufacturing, of course,' he airily added, as if money were no object. Polly, her mind racing ahead, homed in on this point.

'And where is all the capital coming from for such ambitious expansion plans, might I enquire?'

'Oh, you don't have to worry, most of the finance is all set up. You only need find enough to tek on and fit out a shop and Hubert will provide the stock on sale or return. He also says that if you need it, he can offer you ample credit on an interest-free loan. He can't say fairer than that, now can he?'

'Why?' Polly's eyes glinted with suspicion. 'Why would he be so generous?'

Benny's whole body became rigid with tension as he rested his knuckles on the polished desk, desperately holding on to his rapidly diminishing patience. Why were old people so over-cautious? Was it any wonder he'd refused his mother's invitation to work with her? This was an attitude which would have to change. 'Because we're family now. Because it's in his interest to get you up and running. I mean, the business can grow faster that way. The profit margins are high. High enough for us both to mek a good living out of it.'

Polly insisted he explain it all over again, from start to finish, till she had it clear in her head. But was sorely tempted by the offer of a secure customer base, and most of all by the prospect of having Benny come in to the business with her. What could be better than to be working with her own son, just as she'd always dreamed of, with peace declared between them at last?

'I'll give it some thought,' she promised him, while deep down she wondered how she could refuse when she herself had set the whole thing in motion?

Tom found them a house, just a few doors down at number 67. It would need some attention before they could move in, but a bit of painting and decorating would work wonders, he was sure. Weren't women supposed to be expert in such matters these days? It would keep Lucy nicely occupied instead of pining over that stupid job and Michael bloody Hopkins. She, however, was less than enchanted about the whole idea.

'Can we afford it?' Though out of guilt, or perhaps conceding much of what her mother said to be true, Lucy didn't feel able to dismiss the suggestion out of hand, despite her fear of resuming more intimate relations with him.

Tom assured her that they could, that he'd even got himself an interview for a job. 'At the dye works on Liverpool Road.'

'Fenton's place?'

'That's the one. It would be good money too.' He was so excited, so pleased with himself, that she couldn't help but feel glad for him. He'd fought in the war, been a POW for years, suffered untold horrors of which he refused to speak, had escaped and then returned only to find a wife who was having an affair with another man. No wonder he was scratchy. At times Lucy felt nothing but shame at her own behaviour. Tom surely deserved better than she'd been able to offer him. And it wasn't as if she even liked cleaning. If it weren't for this madness of loving Michael she would have been delighted to have Tom back, have welcomed him with open arms.

Tentatively he put out a hand to stroke her hair. He rarely touched her so she felt almost flattered that he felt able to do so now, while at the same time nervous it might encourage him to go further. 'I want to make you happy, Lucy. I want us to have a chance. We need time together and privacy like a proper married couple.'

She quietly moved out of his reach, aware that here, in her mother's house, they never had a moment alone and secretly welcoming that fact. Tom believed this to be the main problem between them, that once he had his wife to himself he could make her fall in love with him all over again. Lucy wondered if that were true.

She remembered how she'd once waited so eagerly for him to come home; how young and excited she had been when they'd first married, believing the war would be merely an interlude in their young lives, over in no time, not rob them of their youth completely. When she'd married him she'd been madly in love with Tom Shackleton for as long as she could remember, though perhaps she'd simply been in love with life, and youth, and the idea of marriage. He'd made it so enchantingly easy with his good looks and undoubted charm. Now she'd changed, grown up. They both had. Neither of them was the person they'd once been.

'I'll give it a try,' she sighed.

As they worked together, cleaning the little house, Tom's behaviour continued to trouble Lucy. Everything had to be just so. Sweeping brushes carefully washed after they'd been used and left to dry in the open, not put away dusty. The floors scrubbed over and over again. Every scrap of wooden skirting or window frame had to be scoured a dozen times before he would let her anywhere near with a paint brush. Not even cleaning cloths were allowed to become soiled and, if they were, he made her boil them till they were white again. It all seemed to be far more tiring than it need be but Lucy put it all down to the difficulties he'd experienced as a POW. He was ill and would get better, given time. Her one consolation was that he showed endless patience with the children.

Polly was right about that. Sean was enjoying having his dad around now, if being a bit silly and wild, always wanting to show off in front of Tom, which was understandable as the little boy craved his attention. Sarah Jane, on the other hand, remained shy but then she'd always been a quiet, timid short of child. She was old enough to remember the shock of losing her dad, and needed time to adjust to his reappearance. They all did. But he could easily tease her into blushes and giggles and very slowly she was coming round to accepting him. Polly said it was up to Lucy to encourage the relationship, for them to spend more time together as a family.

'Don't rush it, Mam,' Lucy would reply, still wary. Yet when they moved that was exactly what would happen. Lucy worried over how it would feel not to have Polly around, almost as if she needed her mother's protection — though from what, she couldn't imagine, apart from the increasing intimacy she dreaded.

She couldn't help noticing that the stories Tom told of his escape and illness varied slightly from day to day, depending on his mood. Sometimes he spoke of Italy, at other times France or even Africa, but never about conditions in the POW camp. All she knew was that he'd been taken to Germany after Italy surrendered.

But none of it quite added up and Lucy wondered just what he really had got up to during those missing years and felt certain there was something he was holding back. His letters had always been sporadic and, even allowing for the censor, oddly vague and unsatisfactory. Perhaps there was a woman in his past somewhere. A part of her rather hoped so, then she wouldn't be the only one with a guilty conscience.

He'd walked back into her life as cool as you please and seemed to think he could pick up exactly where they'd left off. When she'd needed him he hadn't been there for her, hadn't even written. Now that she was in love with someone else, he'd come home. How unfair life could be.

Later that day, scrubbing the stoneflagged kitchen floor in the house she didn't want to live in, with a man she could no longer look upon as a husband, Lucy could see Michael's face in the swirls of soapy water. She couldn't get her need for him out of her mind, out of her aching body, but knew that she must never seek him out again. Never. God knows what would happen if one of them didn't learn to exercise some control over their emotions. She must accept that whatever had been growing between them was over.

Tiring of the endless chores, she flung the scrubbing

brush back into the bucket, sending water spraying everywhere, and wasn't quite sure whether it was tears or dirty water that she wiped from her face.

Chapter Seventeen

The manufacturing of new carpets was progressing well for Polly. The wool arrived in soft, unwashed hanks from the West Coast of Scotland. The washing was done in a long trough with the wool being fed around huge drums on the same principle as a mangle. As she watched the process proudly, Polly was hoping and praying that her daughter's marriage would survive and that Lucy would be happy. Many weren't in these difficult times. She and Charlie had had it easy in a way, with no war to separate them and always having the family around. But the war had torn apart her family all the same. Soon, for the first time in their married lives, there would be just the two of them left at home. Not that she minded. Charlie might get more rest that way.

She walked from the washing room into the dyeing area, and quickly became embroiled in a long discussion on the various shades of green. Customers liked a strong pattern in their carpets but not necessarily strong colours.

'This bright green didn't sell so well, Polly,' Josh, her chief dyer, told her. 'Better to soften it to more of a leaf shade, don't you think?'

'And a pinky beige to go with it?'

Polly personally traced out the patterns on to squared paper, each square representing one tuft in the carpet, usually at a rate of seven to eleven tufts per inch depending on the quality. Drawing the designs was one of her favourite tasks. Sales were buoyant and she longed to expand and buy more looms, but was nervous of going too quickly and overextending herself. She'd always thought there was little point in building the business too big if her children weren't interested. Now that Benny had agreed to come in with her, the situation had changed dramatically. It would be a relief to have more help, for all she still held some reservations about Hubert Clarke and his scheme. By the time she'd finished the day's work it was past eight and she had energy to do no more than grab a meal and fall into bed.

'All this hard work,' she groaned, rubbing her aching back, 'and for what?'

'For us, sweetheart,' Charlie murmured sleepily into her ear. 'For our lovely family and to keep us in our old age.'

'And will we take the risk, as Benny wants us to?'

'Would it make you happy?'

'I think it would, Charlie.'

'Then do it. If you're happy, so am I.' And cuddling up like a pair of old spoons, they fell asleep in perfect contentment.

So Polly took the risk. She took out a small mortgage on her house, rented large shop premises at the Castlefield end of Deansgate and took delivery of a consignment of furniture from Hubert Clarke. Pride Carpets now moved in a new direction, into buying and selling, though she continued with, and even hoped to expand, the manufacturing of new carpet. Credit trading would not have been her first choice but if it made Benny happy, wasn't that something?

Benny felt like a real man again. From the very first day he stayed late without complaint and put all his energies into the job. On his first pay day, he gave Belinda a bit of money to spend on a new frock, if she could find one to fit, just to cheer her up, but she said it would be a waste and hoarded it away for when the baby was born. At least she was eating properly again. She queued at the butcher's for a bit of steak and kidney, which she made into a steamed pudding. They ate like kings and she bloomed as a result. It was worth all the effort to see her happy again.

All family differences seemed to be resolved with what might tentatively be called a reconciliation between Belinda and her parents. And Benny felt quite content to be working with his mother, for it was on equal terms.

This was only the beginning, he thought. As the business grew, moving ever onward and upward, nothing and no one would stand in their way. Since his father-in-law was a self-made man with innate shrewdness and business acumen, Benny had every confidence in his judgement.

Because he didn't like Belinda spending too much time alone, being so close to her time, she took to spending the afternoons with Lucy, though she was able to do little beyond brew tea and chat while her friend trimmed and pasted wallpaper, and climbed ladders to hang it. Nevertheless Belinda was happy and content, and there was much giggling when Lucy made mistakes or when Sean and Sarah Jane got covered in paste as they helped to mix it.

Sometimes the two girls would wrap the children up well and take them sledging on the waste ground, or for a walk along by the Manchester Ship Canal to watch the barges go by. Lucy would talk of her hopes for Tom to get well, never quite finding the courage to mention her secret love, and Belinda would talk about how content she was now that everything had come right for Benny at last, how happy they were, for all she sometimes missed her ATS friends.

'Though I'm sick of this great bump, and cry with frustration sometimes over the most simple task.' She giggled. 'Like starching Benny's shirt collars. I made too much starch the other day, and without thinking tipped the remains all down the yard, hoping it would mix with the snow and slush, but it made such a terrible slimy mess you took your life in your hands just crossing the yard to the lavatory.' And the two girls dissolved into helpless laughter, young and happy, despite all their recent problems.

Tom did not get the job at Fenton's Chemicals because he'd never gone for the interview. There was a problem standing in his way and, determined to find employment so Lucy wouldn't get any fancy ideas in her head about going back to work herself, he meant to solve it.

He called upon his brother-in-law and found Benny, surprisingly enough, in the new shop sticking price labels on a set of chairs. It was already open for business and several customers were browsing among the carefully arranged furniture displays. Tom leaned against the door-jamb and chuckled. 'I thought your job was to run the show from a fancy office and let some chit of a girl write out price labels?'

Benny grinned. 'I don't mind doing my bit. It's all profit in the till at the end of the day. Anyroad, we're a bit short staffed.'

'Sounds like I could be the answer to your prayers then, if you can sort out a little problem for me?'

'I wouldn't've thought you had any, now yer back in dear old Blighty.'

'I've made Lucy give up her job. She was seeing too

much of that Michael Hopkins.' Tom was relieved to see
Benny nodding wisely, as if he understood. 'But we have to
live, which means work, but before I can get a job, I need
papers. An identity card. Right?'

Benny frowned. 'Not if you have your AB64. Yer army
book will do just as well.'

'But I don't have one of those either. I lost it some
place.'

'So go to . . .'

'Look, it's not as easy as all that. Can we talk, private
like?'

Benny led Tom into his office, which was cramped and
not very tidy but he could at least close the door, take a
bottle of Scotch from a cupboard and pour them both a
nip without anyone seeing. He offered Tom a cigarette and
propped himself against the desk to listen. Within seconds
of Tom's launching into his tale, Benny's mouth was
hanging open and he'd forgotten all about the cigarette
which had burned to ash between his fingers. He disposed
of it and lit another.

'Arta saying tha weren't a POW at all?' Benny always
reverted to broad Lancashire when in shock.

Tom shrugged. 'I was wounded at Salerno, many were in
that quagmire of mud and misery, very nearly captured but
managed to get away. You see . . .'

'You deserted!' Despite himself, Benny was shocked.
Admittedly he'd had a safe war, more uncomfortable than

dangerous. Even so, he'd done his bit and didn't care for deserters, not one bit. Nobody did. Couldn't stomach them at any price, as a matter of fact. Yet this was his brother-in-law, married to their Lucy. Even so . . . 'Don't tell me any more. I don't want to know.'

'*I* didn't say I was a deserter. You did. I said I lost my papers.'

'You'll never get away wi' it. Someone will shop you.'

'Why should they? So far as the neighbours are concerned I was a POW, escaped, lost, and now home. End of story. There's plenty of other chaps coming home daily with similar tales to tell. Seems to me, Benny, since you were once in the same boat – seeking official documentation, that is – you'd understand my situation and be prepared to help.'

'Not me.' Benny felt relieved he could honestly wriggle out of this obligation. 'I never managed to sort out my licence. I'm having nowt more to do wi' either joinering nor bureaucracy. So how could I help?'

'By giving me a job – here. We're family, after all, and you want your Lucy to be happy, don't you? You wouldn't want her to run out on our marriage.' Benny scowled, for this was all too true. The last thing he wanted was for her to run off with Michael Hopkins, a known conchie. 'And wouldn't you just love to get one over on them bureaucrats for once, eh, by ignoring all the niceties of paperwork?'

Benny's cigarette had again burned away to ash and he stubbed it out in his glass, sighing deeply and not bothering to light another. This all sounded very complicated and not a little worrying. 'Nay, I don't know, Tom. I would help, if I could, you know that. But I'm not on me own here, tha knows. There's me mam to consider, and she allus likes things above board.'

'And what about Hubert Clarke? Is he so particular?'

Benny shrugged. 'Couldn't say. You'd have to ask him.'

'Mebbe I will. But not a word to your Lucy about this conversation, right? It's just between you and me. Man to man. One squaddie to another.' And since Benny thought it in his family's best interests for Lucy to stay with her husband, rather than go off with Michael Hopkins, he reluctantly agreed. What Lucy didn't know, surely couldn't hurt her. And who was he to judge? Salerno had been a mess, everybody said so.

Tom wasted no time in going to see Hubert Clarke who, after considering the young man with interest and some curiosity, agreed to look into the problem for him. It took little more than a week for him to produce the paperwork Tom needed.

'I'm grateful,' he told his benefactor.

'Happen I'll need you to show how much one day,' Hubert said. In his experience it never hurt to have folk owe him the odd favour.

*

Polly took no persuading to put her son-in-law on the pay roll, in the firm belief that she was doing her own daughter a good turn. Lucy, on the other hand, was less than delighted. She felt as if her nose had been pushed very firmly out of joint, since everyone in the family was now in the business except herself.

The job Tom was given, however, wasn't nearly so congenial as he'd hoped for, comprised chiefly of filling and emptying dye vats, and the money was poor. He grumbled about it constantly: the pay, the hours, the people he worked with.

'It's a start,' Lucy would say. 'Plenty of time to better yourself later, as you get fitter.' And sometimes, watching him work on their little house, she would be pleased and surprised at just how fit he seemed to be, for an ex-POW. He was making good progress and perhaps a part of her hoped that as soon as he was entirely fit and well and himself again, everything would either come right between them, or she could leave him to get on with his life without any sense of guilt. For, despite her best efforts, she still ached for Michael with every fibre of her being.

Lucy tried suggesting that they'd make more progress if she too went back to work but Tom wouldn't hear of it. He didn't approve of her going anywhere for that matter, not even to the pictures. She felt like the prisoner now. Lucy constantly chafed against the restrictions he imposed but even if she slipped out to the shops, or for a walk with

Belinda and the children, she had to leave a note, to say where she was and what time she would be back. She understood why he didn't trust her but it didn't make for an easy life. She could only hope the tension between them would ease as his mental health improved.

And, like it or not, she was forced to spend hours searching Campfield market for bargain cuts or cheap titbits of offal or pork scratchings. Anything to add a bit of flavour to a dull meal. Lucy would queue for hours if she heard there'd been a delivery of sausages, or smile sweetly at Mr Shaw the grocer in his long white apron in the hope that he had a bit of bacon or better still a pat of butter tucked under the counter somewhere. Sometimes she'd believe fortune was about to smile on her and then a man would come in and he'd always be served first, whether he marched boldly to the front or attempted to hang back; whether he'd fought at the front or done nothing more taxing than dish up stew for the pilots he was considered to be a war hero and would be treated as such. Sometimes, when she'd queued for hours and there was nothing left, it seemed grossly unfair, though not for a moment did she complain of any of this to Tom.

On one such occasion as she came hurrying away in triumph with half a dozen sausages, her head down because it was raining, she ran straight into Michael. She tried to back away but her heart was racing, her insides ached with need for him and her body simply wouldn't move in any direction but into his arms. He led her quickly under the railway arches where he wasted no time in kissing her, despite the rain having soaked both of them by this time.

'God, I love you. I need you so much. Why do you stay with him?'

'Because he's my husband, the father of my children,' she protested, craving more of his kisses, more caresses; a crazy mixture of emotion and divided loyalties churning madly within her.

'But you don't love him.' Michael was sliding a hand beneath her coat.

'He's ill. He needs me. How could I simply turn him out on the streets? It wouldn't be right.' Lucy took his hand and pushed it inside her blouse. The sensation of his cold wet skin against hers made her gasp and she missed what he said next, something about their being happy together for ever and ever. 'I know,' she murmured, teasing his mouth open with her tongue. Then he was grasping her by the arms, thrusting her from him and glaring fiercely into her flushed face.

'We could go away together, you, me and the children. No one would ever find us. Ever.'

'*I can't. I can't.*'

Then his mouth came down on hers without mercy as, crushing her to him, he half lifted her from the ground, and with her arms wrapped about his neck Lucy hung on, as if every atom of her happiness depended upon this man.

She was crying as she hurried home but nobody could tell because of the rain. She saw Tom the minute she turned the corner into Pansy Street, standing there in the pouring rain without cap or raincoat.

'You'll catch your death,' she said, but he didn't reply, only grabbed her arm and marched her smartly down the street in full view of every twitching curtain straight into her mother's house, just as if she were a naughty child. She could only feel thankful that Polly and Charlie weren't home yet. Despite the fearful thumping of her heart, Lucy calmly apologised for being late and, with fingers crossed against the lie, quietly explained that she'd been chatting with Belinda.

'You said you'd be home by six and you weren't. See you don't let it happen again.'

'Or what?' she laughed, determined not to be intimidated.

His face as he turned towards her gave the answer. Never had she seen such hatred, such anger. Was this what jealousy did? Lord, what had she done to him? Shame bit deep and Lucy watched in silence as Tom pulled his soiled work shirt over his head, tossed it to the floor and reached for a clean one off the airing rack.

'Are you going out?'

'Aye. So look sharp, I'm hungry.'

Wisely saying no more, Lucy quickly made the tea, fed and washed the children and put them to bed, then sat quietly mending his socks on the darning mushroom while he shaved, tied a muffler about his neck and shrugged into his jacket.

'Don't wait up,' he told her, and she agreed, with some gratitude, that she wouldn't.

It was on the first night together in their new home that Tom decided the moment had come to exercise his 'rights'. The children had been put to bed after the entire family had enjoyed the treat of a bag of chips each, to celebrate this new beginning, and because, with all the packing and unpacking, moving and sorting, Lucy hadn't had time to cook.

After supper she deliberately took her time fussing over her few clothes, laying the children's things away in their drawers, interleaved with lavender mothballs to keep them fresh. It seemed strange to them, having a bedroom of their own, and she read them two stories before they settled. Even then Sean came downstairs for a glass of water the minute she left him. 'Can't I go and sleep at Michael's house?' he asked, confused by the constant changes in his life.

Alarmed that Tom might have heard, Lucy quickly picked up the little boy and carried him back up to bed. 'Why would you want to do that when your dad's here?' she soothed. 'He might even take you fishing, if you ask him nicely.'

The boy brightened. 'When? Tomorrer?'

Lucy tucked her son back beneath the sheets, kissing Sarah Jane again so she didn't feel left out. 'Not another word. Go to sleep this minute.' And the pair of them screwed their eyes tight shut, still giggling as she slipped out of the room. At the bedroom door Lucy paused and whispered, 'Don't forget now, I'm only in the next room if you need me.' As she rather hoped that they might. Then, leaving the door ajar, she drew in a deep shuddering breath and went to wait for her husband.

She felt sick with nerves. This was worse than she'd imagined, worse than a new bride on her wedding night. At least then she'd been panting with love for him. Now here she was, lying rigid in her half of the sagging old bed which Tom and Benny had moved from number 32, and all she felt was dread. She could hear her husband downstairs, raking the coals, sliding the bolt on the back door. He'd already had his shave while she was fussing over the children – his description, not hers – so any minute now he would climb the stairs and get in beside her, and she didn't want him to, oh, she really didn't.

Then suddenly he was there, pulling back the bed-clothes, the weight of the mattress sagging still further and his body lying alongside hers, not touching, not speaking. He lifted one hand and switched off the light with the pull that hung over the bed-head. Darkness engulfed her and she could see nothing but Michael's face, luminous in her imagination. Lucy wondered if she would be able to hold on to this image during what was to follow. Too late now to regret allowing things to get this far.

She heard Tom clear his throat and took comfort from it. Perhaps he was as nervous as she. 'It's been a long time,' he said.

She agreed, her voice faint, hardly above a whisper. Then she felt him turn towards her, his hand come to rest on her stomach, and tried not to flinch away. Could he feel her heart beating?

'I'll not hurt you,' he said as he pulled up her nightdress. She wanted to put out her hand and stop him, to jump out of the bed and run, but some instinct told her to hold still, that it would be less of an ordeal if she surrendered with as good a grace as possible. He was her husband. She'd promised to give their marriage a chance, for the sake of the children. He started to kiss her but Lucy found none of the excitement in his kisses that she'd once found and, as if sensing her lack of response, he soon gave up. Then she could feel the swollen warmth of him pulsing against her, his hands drawing her resisting legs apart, and the urge to push him away and escape was overwhelming. When he thrust himself inside her, Lucy knew she was both dry and unwilling and cried out, though not with ecstasy, eyes opening in appalled shock as, ignoring her unreadiness, he only pushed harder, pounding his frustration into her.

'Next time,' he told her when the agony was finally over

and he'd withdrawn to his side of the bed, 'you'll put a bit more effort into it.'

She turned her face to the wall and lay staring into the darkness, silent tears rolling over hot cheeks, dampening her pillow, hardly daring to breathe until she heard the even rhythm of his snores. Only then did she get up and creep downstairs to the kitchen where she bathed her sore body with warm water and a soft flannel. It was as if he were not her husband at all, as if he had violated her. Yet that was nonsense, of course. The fault must be entirely hers, as he had said, for not even making any effort.

If Lucy had been unhappy before, she was utterly wretched now. Every day dawned grey and empty, devoid of hope or happiness. Try as she might she could not banish Michael from her thoughts and Tom's continued criticism of her, that he deserved better than a frigid wife after all these years away, began to seem justified.

It was Belinda who rescued her by suggesting they re-establish their regular trips to the cinema. It would be good for them both, she said, an opportunity to escape the confines of increasing domesticity. 'These last two weeks have seemed endless for me too. This baby feels like a lump of clay in my stomach, using up all my energy and managing to govern my life completely.'

Rebelliously ignoring Tom's rules, Lucy left the children with good old Doris-from-next-door and the two girls went to their favourite cinema, the Gaumont. It was the first of several such outings. Sometimes she left them with Uncle Nobby and Aunt Ida, who were always happy to have the children they said, telling her young folk should enjoy themselves. 'Isn't that what life is all about?'

Lucy eagerly snatched the opportunity to put on her glad rags, as Uncle Nobby called them, and if the matriarchs of Pansy Street gave her fiercely censorious looks, then she paid them no heed. Anything was better than stopping in night after night, living in dread of her husband wanting sex. Let them paint her as a scarlet woman if they'd a mind. She was young still, and life was for living. If she couldn't live it with the man she loved, at least she could have some fun going out with her friend.

Off the two would go, arm in arm, giggling like young girls again, dreaming of their celluloid heroes and a fish supper afterwards. At least the picture house was warmer than Belinda's flat, and she got to rest her swollen ankles. Celia Johnson and Trevor Howard in *Brief Encounter* proved to be one of their favourite movies. They saw it three times in two weeks and still came out of the cinema surreptitiously drying away tears.

'What a soppy pair we are,' Belinda chuckled. 'So deliciously sad. Do you think Laura meant to kill herself when she ran out to meet the express at the end?'

Lucy sighed, a deeply unhappy sound. 'Rather than live without him, you mean? I don't know but I'm glad she didn't. I'm glad she went back to her husband.'

'Heavens, no, what a bore he was. Far better to go off with her lover and be happy.'

'But would she have been? Happy, I mean?' Lucy argued, her friend's answer more important than she dared admit. 'They were both married. How could they be so selfish? It would have destroyed their love.'

'Utter rubbish. They might have made one person happy instead of making two miserable.' And Lucy couldn't help but laugh because it all sounded so simple when Belinda said it.

Following one such happy evening, Belinda arrived home to find her front door not only locked but with slats of wood nailed across it. The icy February weather had changed to a thin drizzle, and stacked against the rough stone wall of the shop were the few sticks of furniture which she and Benny had managed to collect: the kitchen table and two chairs, a broken box which held a few knives and forks and a blackened pan, even the bed and mattress, once a haven for their loving, lay in shaming view for any passer-by to see. She could hardly believe what her own eyes were telling her, that all her worldly goods had been thrown out on the street as, it seemed, had they.

Somewhere in the next street she could hear a vendor calling 'Hot peas and puddings', and felt thankful that at least her stomach was full and warm from the fish supper she'd enjoyed with Lucy, the days of near starvation long gone. She thumped on the door again in disbelief, though she knew Benny was at the pub with Tom so there was no one to hear her. Who could have done such a thing and why? It made no sense.

She was shaking with cold and knew she couldn't stay here, on the damp pavement, railing at injustice.

Lucy would be in, of course, but Pansy Street suddenly seemed as far away as the moon. Nevertheless Belinda set off, her back starting to ache with a vengeance from the effort it took just to walk in the chill of the increasing downpour. It was as she took a short cut through Nelson's ginnel that she felt a rush of warm liquid between her legs. Staring down at herself in horrified fascination, she saw a puddle of water forming at her feet, one that quickly took on a frighteningly scarlet hue.

Belinda cried out in shocked surprise then sank to the wet cobbles, sliding into a heap of dirty snow on a gasp of sudden pain. She glanced desperately about only to discover the ginnel deserted in each direction, black dark with not a single lamp lit. Freezing rain hammered and bubbled up on the glistening setts, gushing from the broken guttering of the roofs above her head, and within seconds she was soaked. Belinda neither noticed nor cared as she was swamped by pain, fierce darts of fire slicing through from her lower back to her belly, emerging as wailing screams that seemed to be swallowed up and spat out by the rain as it heedlessly drummed on dustbin lids and washed the scarlet stains from Benny's newborn son down the rusty grate.

Chapter Eighteen

Benny took some comfort from the fact that he came home early from the pub that night, leaving Tom to his self-pity and his moaning. Finding the shop door boarded up, he realised at once that the eviction notice had still been carried out even though he'd found a way to pay his debts and would have moved his family out anyway within a few months, business permitting.

Cold fear clamped his stomach. Ignoring the heap of furniture that stood getting soaked on the pavement, his one concern was for Belinda. Where the hell was she?

'Belinda? *Belinda!*' He screamed her name into the teeming rain and began to run.

He knocked on door after door, asking where his wife was — had anyone seen her, was she taking shelter? When he finally found her, in Minnie Hopkins's house on Pansy Street of all places, it didn't take the presence of the offi-cious doctor or grim-faced midwife to tell him the news was bad. He could sense it the minute he set foot across the threshold.

'Nay, lad, don't go in theer,' Minnie told him, blocking his way as he marched up the lobby. Benny thrust the old woman out of his way, not unkindly but with a desperate determination. He didn't care if she'd lost the baby, he wanted only to find his beloved Belinda.

She lay quite still on the sofa, in a parlour which seemed crowded with people, their anxious voices dying away to a dreadful hush as he approached. Someone had tried to light a fire and it smoked fitfully in the tiny grate. Beside it stood a bowl covered in a blood-soaked cloth. He averted his eyes from this and went at once to Belinda. A soldier's greatcoat was slung across her slender body, now showing no sign of the pregnancy. Her face, he thought, as he kissed her, had lost its strained expression and was once again exquisitely beautiful, eyelids curving up and outward at each corner, shadowed a translucent blue. Her lips too were smiling as they had been that very first day when he'd seen her in the rating office, but it was only when he found no response to his kisses, heard the soft catching of tears around him, that he realised what he'd lost tonight. The very meaning of his existence.

Minnie placed what appeared to be a bundle of rags in Benny's arms. 'Tek good care of that little mite. He's thy son, and all thee's got now.'

Benny gazed in stunned disbelief at the pink, screwed

up face staring knowingly up at him from the folds of cloth. He'd assumed the baby to be dead but here he was, alive and well and in his father's arms. He wished with a terrible intensity that it were not so, that it had been the baby who'd died and Belinda spared. He felt his knees start to shake as the awesome weight of responsibility closed in and sank on to a chair someone had thoughtfully provided, the soft bundle held awkwardly in his big hands. Dear God, what did he know about babbies?

He felt disorientated, set apart from the real world as if he were trapped in a bubble and couldn't reach through it, back to reality. He could hear, as if from a great distance, Minnie Hopkins fussing and arranging the baby in his arms, Lily Gantry and her cronies discussing arrangements to have Belinda moved to a Chapel of Rest, hushed voices wondering whether next-of-kin had been informed, and suddenly Benny needed his own mother. 'Mam,' he said, and Minnie gave his shoulder an awkward little pat, assuring him that Polly and Lucy had both been sent for. Nausea rose in his gullet at the pain and shock they were about to face.

He looked again upon his child.

He knew he should cry for his lovely Belinda but somehow no tears would come. Somewhere in his head he could see a gaping black mouth, hear a silent scream, and in his chest feel a tight sensation which felt like fear but wasn't. Then it was as if he was falling through that mouth, through a long black tunnel, and a voice was shouting in his ears: '*It's not true. She isn't dead. She's not! She's not! Bloody vultures! Get out, the lot of you. Get out!*'

The baby was gone from his arms, the room emptied in seconds. All except for Minnie Hopkins, who sat with the child on her knee.

'And you can bloody go too.'

She didn't move, just sat rocking the baby without saying a word, not even when he grabbed the aspidistra pot from its tall stand and smashed it against the mahogany fire surround. Nor when he swept all the books from her shelves, including the family Bible, and followed this by smashing the Westminster Chime clock given to her by her former employer. Minnie merely commented that she'd never really liked it.

It was then that Benny crumpled. Head bowed, he sagged to his knees and great racking sobs came tearing out of some black pit deep inside, one he couldn't reach the bottom of but somehow must in order to rid himself of this terrible pain.

'That's it, lad. Let it come.' But he really had no choice. For now that he had started, nothing would stop him. Benny put his head in his hands and gave in to his grief.

The entire street came to pay their respects in Polly's front parlour, which seemed more fitting than a funeral home. She set several candles around the open coffin and put a garland of flowers in Belinda's golden hair. Minnie Hopkins and Lily Gantry insisted every mirror in the house be covered, so that her precious soul could not be stolen by the devil. Lucy, who'd spent hours sitting with her friend, thought she had never looked more beautiful.

'It's such a waste,' she sobbed, quite unable to control her distress.

Polly took care of the infant, which Benny ignored completely.

The funeral took place the following Tuesday when, for the first time, the two branches of Belinda's family came together in one place. Benny was white-faced and rigid in his grief, Lucy clinging to his arm and Polly quietly weeping. All Belinda's friends and neighbours were there, too, more than she would have expected, being a modest, unassuming sort of person.

She would not have been surprised, however, to see her father, Councillor Hubert Clarke, in best funereal attire, watch chain displayed over the curve of his belly, take complete charge of the service whether it be reading the lesson, singing the loudest during the hymns or leading the mourners to the graveside and then on to a cold repast at the Tudor Cafe. Joanna's role, of grieving mother, was relegated to second place, and Benny, the distraught husband, was ignored completely.

Hubert knew where to place the blame for his daughter's death. He had completely erased from his mind the blocks he'd put on Benny's enterprise, though there was of course the small matter of the eviction notice. But then, if Benny Pride hadn't got Belinda pregnant in the first place, she'd have been alive today, eviction or no eviction. Hubert certainly had no intention of shouldering responsibility for his daughter's death and, just to be on the safe side, had taken the precaution of ensuring that the landlord didn't shoot his mouth off about why he'd decided to put the squeeze on the young couple by evicting them. Hubert was certain that his own role in the matter would never be mentioned. The subject was closed.

The need for justice, however, so far as he was concerned, was not. Not by a long chalk. If Benny Pride thought he could seduce Hubert's lovely daughter, get her pregnant and force her into an entirely unsuitable marriage, then keep her in abject poverty resulting in her death, he was in for a rude shock. Hubert meant to take his revenge for her loss. He meant to make Benny pay.

It was he, however, who was in for the first surprise. When he reached his office on Potato Wharf the following morning, it was to find Tom leaning against the doorjamb, waiting for him. 'What are you after now, Shackleton? More problems with your paperwork?' Hubert's voice crackled with annoyance. He'd a busy day ahead, with no time to listen to this nincompoop begging yet more favours.

'I thought I'd do you a service,' Tom mildly replied. 'At

least give you the chance before I went elsewhere.'

Hubert thrust his key in the lock, pushed open the door sufficiently to let himself slip through without giving any indication that the young man should follow. 'Give me a chance at what?' he barked, curiosity awakened despite his better judgement.

'I was out walking that night your Belinda copped it. Glad to be out of t'house, away from a nagging wife. You know how it is. I were on me way for a drink wi' me mates and I thought, Now, what's all this pile of furniture doing on the pavement?'

'They were evicted. My daughter was turned out on the street because she'd married an idiot who couldn't look after her properly.'

Tom took a step closer, his voice dropping to barely a whisper. 'Or because somebody decided to apply a bit of extra pressure. Put the boot in as it were. Somebody quite close to her, in fact, with his own axe to grind. Or so Percy says. You remember Percy Sympkin? He were Belinda and Benny's landlord. Good mate o' mine is Percy. We go back a long way. Used to work alongside him when I were in Ancoats, would you believe? Didn't you have a word with him on the subject of eviction only recently?'

Tom's mildly enquiring gaze met the blazing fury in Hubert's bloodshot eyes and seemed to find it amusing. The corners of his mouth tilted into his famously charming smile. 'Small world, eh? Lift up a stone and you'll always find a worm or two underneath. Or so I've found.'

'You'd best come in,' Hubert growled, and glancing up and down the empty street, allowed Tom Shackleton into his private domain.

The worst time for Benny was after the funeral, after Joanna had meticulously repossessed every item of her daughter's clothes and belongings, after everyone had gone home and all practical details had been attended to. Then he was, quite literally, left holding the baby.

What in God's name was he going to do with it?

That night his son lay in a crib in Polly's room. During the day Benny wasn't sure what happened to him, and didn't greatly care.

He'd moved into his sister's old room at his mother's house, now it was free, lying alone in the big brass bed he'd once shared with Belinda. Besides this there was a small chest of drawers and a single chair. These sparse surroundings seemed to suit his mood.

Most of the time his mind seemed locked in a blessed numbness, as if unable to take in the terrible event that had occurred. He would get up, wash and shave, go to work, come home, eat, give every appearance of normal behaviour. But every so often the numbing mists would lift and disperse and he would realise with a terrible clarity that his beloved Belinda was dead. It was then that the pain started and all he could do was to sit with his head in his hands and think of her: of her laughter, her teasing sense of fun, her lovemaking. No, he couldn't bear to remember her lovemaking. Not yet. For when he did, the pain became almost unbearable.

At other times he couldn't bear to think of her at all and would storm out, walk the streets, down several pints at the Dog and Duck where he became a frequent visitor, or occupy himself with some useless task at the shop or even in the warehouse. He'd stay all night if necessary, anything to keep busy, so that when he fell into bed, he would sleep instead of going endlessly over his loss.

Polly found caring for a tiny baby on top of a new business taxing indeed. If she didn't grieve for Belinda quite as intensely as Benny did, she still missed the girl sorely and felt she owed it to her to do the best she could for her poor motherless child.

'Benny will have to come round to it soon,' she groaned wearily to Charlie as she climbed from her bed for the second time one night and went in search of a warmed bottle. 'I'm too old for this caper, so I am.'

'Give the lad time,' was all Charlie could say, and perhaps, Polly thought, he was right. But then again, maybe Benny needed a bit of a push, if she could just think of the right way to give him one. In the meantime, she'd ask Lucy for a bit more help. Perhaps helping to care for Belinda's child would ease her own grieving. To her great surprise and disappointment, Tom refused to allow it.

'She has enough on her plate,' he tartly informed Polly, 'with our own two.'

'One more wouldn't be any trouble,' Lucy said, her voice thick with tears. 'He's so tiny, and he's family after all.'

'I say you've enough to do, and I'll hear no argument on the matter.' He glared fiercely at his mother-in-law. 'You should know better than to ask, since we've only just set up home together after all this time apart.'

'It would only be during the day while you're at work, as I am meself.'

'That's your problem, and Benny's. I've said no.' Lucy shot him an anguished glance but Polly conceded defeat. She'd not beg. It seemed every request, however simple, created bad feeling in her family.

'Thee should 'ave axed me, Polly love,' Doris-next-door chided her. 'Tha knows how I loves childer, and I could do wi' the money. The little mite'll be safe enough wi' me till his da's up to tekking over. What's he called?'

'Benny hasn't named him yet,' Polly said, her face sad.

'Poor little sausage, no name. Nay, that's a bad show, that is.'

From the very first day after the funeral Polly drew some consolation from the fact that Benny came to work as usual, as if he realised it was even more important now for him to bring home the bacon, try to make up to his son for the loss of a mother. Polly certainly didn't intend the child to want for anything. Hadn't she seen enough poverty in her time? Not for this babby a jam butty on a cold doorstep. He would have the best. When Hubert called in sometime in the second week, claiming Joanna had asked him to enquire about the arrangements for and well-being of their grandson, she was pleased to inform him that he was being well taken care of.

'Yet he lacks a mother,' Hubert rather pedantically stated.

'Aye, but he'll never lack for love,' Polly stoutly replied. 'Getting back to business, what about this new shipment of bentwood chairs you promised me? We're nearly out of stock and you know how popular they are. You can swop them for those heavy Victorian monstrosities you brought last month. I can't shift those for love nor money.'

He rocked back on his heels, thumbs in his waistcoat pockets, and scowled at her. 'Tha wants to put a bit more ingenuity into yer selling techniques, my lass.'

Polly itched to tell him that she wasn't his lass, that she could sell anything so long as it was worth buying, which those chairs were not, but managed to bite her tongue. There was enough ill feeling already. Benny spent every evening searching for Percy Sympkin, the landlord who'd turned them out on the streets. God help the poor creature if her son ever did find him.

'Well, aren't I learning all the time?' she agreed, giving

Hubert the benefit of her most winning smile. 'But then, we did agree sale or return, I seem to recall, so long as I took what you sent.'

'I'll make a note,' Hubert said, though as he didn't produce any paper or notebook from his pocket, Polly could only assume he meant a mental one. Mind you, she told Charlie later, if he didn't remember to have the chairs collected, irksome as it was, she'd remind him again next week.

At the end of each day Polly collected her grandson from Doris, as arranged, and took him home. Tired as she was after her long day at the warehouse, she fed him, changed him, bathed and burped him, then laid the baby safely in his crib, rocking it till he fell asleep.

'Don't I love the bones of him?' she said whenever Charlie asked if she minded the extra work. Benny himself did nothing for his son. What could he do? he thought. Looking after babbies was women's work.

After three more weeks of this arduous regime, Polly was feeling the strain. 'I need a night off,' she told Benny, 'a chance to get a bit of uninterrupted sleep.' And with some reluctance, he agreed to the crib's being put into his room.

'How will I manage on me own?'

'Saints preserve us, Benny lad, you'll manage 'cos you have to, as we all do. Wouldn't Charlie and me give a gold clock for the chance of a good night's sleep? I'm too old for this caper, so I am.' She went on to remind him gently that he was the child's da and, as such, must take a share in his upbringing.

She showed Benny how to mix the National dried baby milk into the bottle, how to hold and feed him, how to sit him up and rub the little chap's back so that he got rid of his wind. She even demonstrated how to clean his little bottom and change his nappy. Benny prayed that the babby would sleep through the night and he'd be spared the whole terrifying procedure.

It was a wish not to be granted.

He heard the first few little hiccups long before they turned into a cry. He lay there for a long moment, halfway between sleep and waking, which proved to be unfortunate because by the time he did scramble blearily out of bed the cry was a full-blown howl of distress. Benny hoped the noise might bring Polly running from her bed but again was disappointed. She was clearly determined that this was his shift, which seemed a bit unfair. He had to work all day too, after all.

He picked the baby up and carried him aloft down the stairs, holding him with outstretched arms some distance from him, though supporting the precariously wobbling head with his fingers. He propped the child against a cushion in the corner of the old kitchen armchair while he struggled to read the directions on the tin of dried milk powder and remember Polly's instructions. He could hardly think for the racket the baby was making, and it was some moments before he realised he hadn't even put the kettle on and then had to rush around filling it from the tap and putting a match to the gas, by which time the infant's face was screwed up into a tight red ball of rage.

In that moment he hated the child. *It* had surely killed his beloved Belinda. Hadn't *it* been the bane of her life throughout the pregnancy, making her sick and tired, coming between them at the very start of their married life together? Yet *it* sat there, alive and well while *she* was dead, demanding to be fed as if by right.

He picked it up, though again remembering carefully to support its tiny head as Polly had shown him. He ordered it to hush but still the screaming went on, the tiny fists clenched with fury, and Benny's own frustration and rage mounted, his patience threatening to slip. He was exhausted; the day at the furniture shop had been long and wearing, filled with stress and problems of one sort or another. How could he be expected to care for a small child on top of getting a new business going?

The kettle began to sing and he shoved the baby back in its corner, stopping his ears to its gasping sobs. Even as he set it down Benny realised with horror that it stank. After the feed, he'd be forced to change its dirty nappy after all. He almost ran to snatch up the kettle, anxious to put some distance between himself and the cause of his anger. As he mixed the formula, he didn't hear stealthy footsteps on the stair, was unaware of the door opening a crack or of Polly's eye peering through it.

'Right, shut up, you,' he said, turning back to his son. And then he remembered his mother's warning about temperature and tested the milk on his wrist. Too hot! Thank Christ he hadn't given it to the boy. It occurred to him in that moment that the child had no name. Having a baby had always been to Benny something that would happen in the future, not now, and not without Belinda to look after it and make such decisions. They'd never talked about names. Whenever he'd brought the subject up she'd always put the decision off, saying it tempted fate to decide too soon. Now, drat it, he supposed he'd have to decide.

The baby had worked himself into a lather of fury and distress and was sliding down in the chair. Benny didn't know whether he should run back and shove him safely back into place or keep holding the bottle under the running tap to cool it. Desperation closed in.

'*Stay still!*' he shouted but the screaming child didn't seem to hear or understand, behaving like a termagent. But then, of course, how could it understand? It was only a baby. Benny dashed across the room and caught him long before he'd wriggled anywhere near the edge but his heart was racing with fear all the same. He held the child securely in his arms, sat himself down in the chair and offered the bottle. Blessed silence fell.

The eyes closed in blissful contentment and Benny

looked down upon his son in wonder. He marvelled at the translucent blue of the lids, the soft down of golden fair hair with just a hint of red in it, and the vulnerable pulsing hollow on the baby's crown. Small fingers spread like tiny stars and he felt the tension ease out of the baby's body. As he pulled on the teat, Benny marvelled at his strength. He was a fighter this one. What a paddy he had on him.

'Still some Irish blood running in those veins, eh, little chap?'

And he was a survivor. Benny thought that one day he would have to tell his son how he'd been born in a back street on a pile of mucky snow and in the pouring rain, without any assistance save that of his own brave mother. The rhythm of the baby's sucking was steady now, punctuated with contented little gasps. Benny found it immensely soothing, almost therapeutic, to be sitting here with his son in the quiet of the night, as if there were just the two of them in all the world. 'Course, it wasn't the little chap's fault that his mam was dead. How could he even think such a thing? Neither of them had been given a choice in the matter. And he'd do well enough, that much was plain, even if he did have to make do with an amateur for a da.

'She would've loved you,' Benny said, unaware of the tears sliding down his cheeks. He'd tell him about Belinda too when he was old enough to understand how lovely she was, how spirited and determined.

He chuckled softly at the memory. 'We hadn't two 'a' pennies to rub together and there were times when we fought like cat and dog, but by heck, lad, we were in love. I worshipped the ground she walked on, and she never lost her faith in me, despite my fanciful notions at times. That was yer mam for yer. A survivor, like you.'

The baby's eyes opened for a brief moment, round and blue, gazing intently up at Benny as if memorising his father's face, as if he'd been taking in every word and agreed with it, before allowing the lids to droop closed again. And not once did he pause in his sucking.

Benny tucked him closer to his chest, protectively, as if shielding the baby from a harsh world. He saw, in that moment of intense emotion, how he could best pay tribute to Belinda's memory: by being the man she'd believed him to be. All he had to do was work hard and be a success.

He thought of his own father, bravely fighting for his country then coming home and being the best dad any boy could've wished for. Benny had worshipped him.

The baby was drowsy now, sated with milk, a small bubble forming on his pursed lips as Benny withdrew the teat. He lifted his son and laid him gently against his shoulder, just as Polly had shown him. 'Come on now, Matthew love, give yer old dad a good burp.'

On the stairs, Polly slipped quietly back to bed, tears in her eyes and a soft smile on her face.

Chapter Nineteen

So far as Lucy was concerned everything changed when Belinda died. Losing her dear friend felt like the end of everything good in her life. And she was haunted by that conversation they'd had about love.

'Why make two people miserable when you can make one happy?' Belinda had said.

Life suddenly seemed very fragile, as if every day must be enjoyed to the full for you never knew when it might end. Wasting it with a man she no longer cared for, and who gave no indication of truly caring for her, didn't seem the best way to spend it at all. Lucy felt as if she were living a life of pretence. Pretending she loved Tom, pretending she was happy, when what she truly felt was a desperate urgency to spend every possible moment with Michael. She was young still, and in love. There surely wasn't a moment to be lost. Yet how to gain her freedom? That was the problem.

She lay beside Tom night after night, longing for Michael's touch, for the excitement only he could instill in her, regretting ever having given him up simply for the sake of duty. Each morning she went about her daily routine like some sort of clockwork toy, cooking and cleaning, doing what was necessary without thought or reason, without even the chance of escape to the Gaumont with her lovely friend. Inside, her heart lay heavy and sick, robbing her of the last of her appetite.

Following their last parting she'd caught no more than a glimpse of Michael in the distance. Lucy convinced herself that he'd forgotten all about her, filled his life with other things, whereas she couldn't get him out of her mind. One evening she was so wrapped up in these thoughts that she put salad cream on the table instead of custard.

'I don't think this goes with rhubarb tart, Mam,' Sarah Jane giggled, and Lucy dashed about, trying to remember what she'd done with the custard jug.

'How could you cope with Benny's baby when you can't even manage a simple meal?' Tom said, his voice thick with sarcasm, as it was so often these days. 'Get off to bed soon tonight, then you'll be more awake tomorrow.'

'I'm not tired. I'm fine.'

'Do as I say. The children can see to themselves for once, and you can do the washing and clearing up tomorrow. Go to bed.' And she did, for it seemed easier to obey.

*

It was Whit Sunday and Polly had invited the entire family to lunch. Lucy and Tom began it with their usual morning toast and mug of tea taken largely in silence, which even so somehow led to an argument. It all started innocently enough. Tom complained about there not being enough butter on his toast and Lucy laughed, saying it was actually margarine and she couldn't remember the last time she'd even seen any butter, let alone had the money to buy it. That inflamed him and he accused her of mocking him for not earning enough to keep them.

She felt cowed by his domineering ways, by his constant carping and criticisms. Yet something of the old Lucy still remained, buried deep beneath the damaged self-esteem. Now she experienced an unexpected surge of rebellion against being repeatedly bullied, even by a husband scarred by war. Benny had been bullied as a boy but he'd won through in the end. Maybe she would too, if she held her nerve. She waited until the children were upstairs getting dressed and she was tying Tom's best tie for him. 'I was thinking of getting a job,' she announced, without giving herself time to think. 'Maybe that would help.'

'Don't talk soft.'

'I mean it. I'm bored out of me mind stuck here at home. It's not as if there's enough to do, what with our Sean at school now. I've worked for years anyroad. I like working, having a bit of money in me pocket. And we could surely do with a bit extra. We could happen afford butter then, eh?'

'There you are, see. You're saying I keep you short.' Tom bridled at the implied criticism and Lucy hastened to assure him that wasn't what she'd meant at all. Yet, as so often before, he absolutely refused to listen to her point of view or even to discuss the matter. 'You'll stop at home, where you belong. You're not even managing the house-work very well, are you? How could you possibly cope with a job as well.'

'I've told you, it's because I'm bored. Why can't I work? I could easily get my old job back with Minnie Hopkins for a start.'

'So that's it. You're still pining after lover-boy.'

Lucy sighed but was determined not to rise to the bait. 'All right then, mebbe Mam could find me a job at the warehouse. Everyone else is working for the family busi-ness, why not me?'

'Because you have childer and a husband to look after.'

It was no good, she could feel the pointlessness of arguing in her bones and afterwards would wonder what had possessed her to battle on. She smoothed his tie into place, handed him his hat and raincoat. 'I overheard you telling Lily Gantry at the funeral that you spent years in that prisoner-of-war camp in Germany, yet you told Michael and me that you'd crossed over the Alps into Italy *after* you escaped and then made your way through France.

Where, exactly, were you held then?' The thought had come out of nowhere, but she couldn't doubt that her words had hit home from the way he flinched.

Tom rubbed a hand over his face and started prowling about the kitchen, back and forth, like a lion in a cage. '*Michael and me*,' he cruelly mimicked her voice, and before she could guess what was about to happen, he'd brought the flat of his hand down across her face. The blow knocked her off balance, sent her reeling across the kitchen so that she stumbled and fell, catching the side of her head on the edge of the steel fender.

Tom was instantly contrite. Full of apologies, he hurried to fetch iodine and warm water, assuring her that he hadn't meant to lash out. It was the war that caused his temper to be so short, he explained, and jealousy of her feelings for Michael. 'All you have to do is agree to give our marriage a chance. You really shouldn't have provoked me,' he told her as he bathed the swelling on her forehead. 'It's your own fault.' And she thought that it must be, for otherwise why would he have hit her?

Polly met them at the front door and, in honour of the occasion, wasn't wearing the much knitted cardigan which she'd rarely seemed to take off in the six long years of war but instead a smart frock in navy blue with a crisp white collar. It made her look young again.

She hugged and kissed her daughter, saying how pretty

she looked. Lucy was wearing a lemon seersucker dress, cut on the bias, and it was quite apparent to Polly that she'd lost weight since Belinda's death so she intended to make sure that at least her daughter would get something inside her today. As Charlie led the way into the house, limping slightly on the stick he now used, Polly noticed a small bruise on her daughter's face and mildly enquired how she'd come by it.

'Oh, I bumped me head on the cellar door,' Lucy said. 'Shall I set the table?'

'Now isn't that something? A pair of willing hands for once.' Aw, and wasn't she proud of the lot of them? It made Polly's heart sing for all there was the sadness of an empty place at the table. 'And where are my two treasures?'

The children, having not long since filled their stomachs with their usual breakfast of bread and jam, were soon sprawled on the floor, flat on their stomachs, playing with toy soldiers, oblivious to the appetising aroma of roast beef and Yorkshire pudding that was making all the adults salivate with hunger.

Polly watched her only son with pride as he carefully spooned cereal into baby Matt's mouth which fluttered open like a young bird's for more every time the spoon was taken away. At three months, wasn't he the finest baby in the street if not the whole of Manchester? She tickled him under the chin, and thinking it was the spoon, the small mouth fastened itself upon her finger with a startling fierceness. Polly burst out laughing. 'Look at the precious soul. Isn't he the one? Won't he grow as big as his da one day, and just as greedy?'

Benny grinned, taking this as a compliment.

Seated opposite him was Tom, looking fitter than ever. What a fine, good-looking young man he was to be sure. He'd surprised Polly by proving to be quite diligent at his work in the warehouse, for all it was little more than labouring, though she'd agreed to let him drive the van occasionally. He was proving to be a useful member of the team.

She glanced across at her daughter, as if searching for clues as to her state of mind, but Lucy was busily laying knives and forks. Polly watched as Tom slid an arm about her waist, popped a kiss upon his wife's neck as she bent over and then merrily tweaked the soft brown curls on her brow. So everything must be fine and dandy between them, she thought, for all Lucy didn't return the gesture or even smile a response. Mebbe she'd best have another talk to the girl, just to make sure.

Serving out the meat and vegetables on every plate took an age, but nobody minded as by then they'd all consumed a fluffy slice of Yorkshire pudding topped off with onion gravy. As Polly handed out the brimming platefuls, she recalled a time when her family would think that humble dish alone would constitute a dinner fit for a king. Certainly it had gone down well one Christmas back in

Ancoats, for all there'd been no meat to follow.

'That's too much for me,' Lucy demurred, unloading half of the food on to her brother's plate.

'Nay, is that all you're having, lass? It wouldn't keep a sparrer alive,' Charlie said.

'I'm not very hungry.'

Polly gave Lucy a keen look and wondered if she'd been crying. But then losing her sister-in-law had been a blow to poor Lucy. The pair had been as close as two slices of bread stuck together with jam. Which reminded Polly for some reason of her grandchildren. She finally managed to drag them away from their toys and placed a small plate of dinner before each of them, all the while advising Lucy as if she was a girl still, and Polly's responsibility as a mother as strong as ever, to take better care of herself.

'Ye definitely look a bit peaky. Starvin' yerself will do no good at all. Belinda would hate to see you mek yerself ill, wouldn't she so?'

Benny, returning from putting Matt down in his crib, asked what it was Belinda would hate and Lucy irritably told him that it was only Mam nagging.

Tom chipped in. 'I'm at her all the time to rest more but will she listen? Stubborn to a fault she is. All she has to do is settle back and enjoy her children, instead of which she's fussing about going back to work again.'

Perhaps these words rekindled her rebellion, or maybe it was being in the heart of her family with a mother who had always worked outside the home which gave Lucy the courage to make one more stand. 'And why not? I don't have to spend me entire time wiping children's mucky faces or cleaning other folk's doorsteps. There might very well be summat else, something more interesting and demanding I could do.'

'Well said,' Polly laughed, applauding vigorously. 'And couldn't we just use all the help we can get at the warehouse, if ye'd a mind.'

Tom scowled at this apparent show of feminine solidarity. 'Leave her be, mother-in-law. Don't encourage her day dreams. A wife's place is in the home.'

Polly might have protested against this damning indictment of womanhood but Lucy, her dander up now, returned to the subject which had been exercising her mind more and more these days, wagging her fork at him across the table. 'Tell me, when you were wounded at Salerno, there was presumably a roll call?'

Tom looked startled by this abrupt change of subject, as did the rest of the family, while Polly clicked her tongue in annoyance. 'Sunday dinner is not the place to discuss the war, m'cushla. Besides, haven't we put all of that behind us?'

'I'd like to know.'

'It's all right,' Tom said with a patient smile, as if he were used to humouring his wife. 'Aye, there always is a roll call after a battle. Very shrewd of you to guess.'

She hadn't guessed, of course. Michael had mentioned it once and somehow the fact had stuck in her mind. 'And later when they'd collected all the wounded, they'd check again, wouldn't they? Scour the site for bodies, for instance.'

A nerve by the corner of Tom's eye twitched, and though he appeared to be searching for an answer, or even a way out of the conversation, he could apparently find none. 'Yer mam's right, this isn't a fit subject for dinner. Can we get on with it in peace?' He bent his head to the task without bothering to answer the question at all.

Lucy set down her knife and fork and leaned across the table towards him. 'But how come they didn't find *you*? Why did they rescue all the other wounded and not you? Why were you left behind to be captured and nobody else?'

'How should I know? I was unconscious. That was a bad winter. The mud – by the time I was well enough to walk about or ask questions, my battalion had moved on.'

'So *where* did you spend that first winter? Who found you? When were you taken to that POW camp? And how?'

No one else at the table spoke a word or even moved; every eye was upon Tom, every ear listening to the exchange, waiting for the reply which came eventually in a soft monotone.

'It wasn't quite then I was captured. That was later. An Italian family found me. They were very kind to me. Can we forget the war now, please? This beef is delicious,' he added, turning deliberately to Polly who smiled sympathetically at him, not quite understanding what was going on but clearly troubled by it.

Lucy pushed her plate aside, despite protests from her mother. She'd always been able to tell when Tom was lying and she knew he was doing so now, without question.

When the family had gone Polly toed off her shoes and sank into an easy chair to rub her aching feet with a sigh of relief. 'What a mystery they all are to me,' she groaned. 'I thought they were hard enough work as children, but there's still never a moment but what I'm worrying about one or other of them. There's our Benny upstairs, widowed and alone, poor soul, for all he's playing the devoted father.'

'Well, you should be pleased about that at least,' Charlie said.

'Oh, I am, I am. Though I'm none too chuffed to be tied up so tight with that father-in-law of his. He's a cold fish is Councillor Hubert Clarke.'

'But substantial. A self-made man.'

'Aw, he's substantial all right. Too many beef dinners there, for sure.' Polly chuckled though it soon changed into a frown. 'It's odd but whenever we reorder anything for the shop, he's nearly always out of stock. And when I ring and ask him to send the van to collect unsold stock, as we agreed, it's always occupied somewhere else and I have to keep reminding him. I've been waiting for over a week now to be rid of a consignment of bookcases. Like cardboard they are. I'll never sell them.'

'Ring him again then,' Charlie said, only half listening, his eyes closed.

But Polly's thoughts had moved on. 'Our Lucy now, is she happy d'you think?'

Charlie met her gaze with the frankness she'd come to expect from him over the years. 'No, I don't think she's in the least bit happy. I'd say, if I didn't know better, that someone had put pressure on her to stay in that marriage against her will. I hope, Polly me lass, that it wasn't you.'

Polly's eyes rounded with false innocence for all she felt a twinge of guilt. 'Now would I do such a thing?'

'You just might, out of your own twisted sense of loyalty.'

'Twisted, is it, to want me family to thrive?'

'Yes, it is, if you interfere too much. A person must make their own way in the world, not follow a path set by someone else. The only way a marriage can thrive is with love, and no one can order that to be present, not even a loving mother. I reckon you should have a word with your Lucy, and tell her that whatever she decides, we'll back her. There's not much wrong with Michael Hopkins, and if he makes her happy, isn't that what you want too?'

Tears standing proud in her fine eyes, Polly dragged

herself out of the chair to kiss her husband full on his lips. 'Sure and what would I do without you? Aren't you the wisest man in all of Castlefield.'

'Not Manchester?'

'That too. Come on, I'm whacked. Take me to bed.'

'Only if you fetch me stick first.' And they both burst out laughing.

Lucy was attempting to explain to her husband why she had asked all those questions, desperately striving to calm his irascible temper. She'd certainly had ample opportunity to regret her impetuosity as she put the children to bed and read them a story, delaying the moment she too must go to bed till the last possible minute.

'You questioned my honesty in front of your family,' Tom kept repeating, over and over. 'You'd no bloody right!'

'I wanted to understand, that's all. I need to know what you went through,' she prevaricated. 'How you managed to survive through all the humiliation and torture you suffered. That way I can perhaps better help with your problems. I want you to tell me, Tom. I feel that if this marriage of ours is to survive, then I need to know everything.'

'Why?'

She decided to take the risk and make her feelings plain. 'Because of the way you make love to me, even talk to me at times. You're harsh, unfeeling, even unkind. Perhaps it's because of what happened to you – back then. But if we could talk about it maybe it would go away, this anger which seems to be eating you up.'

Tom strode over to the fire where he took down a pack of cigarettes from the mantelshelf and shook one out of the packet, like an American GI. Lighting it, he inhaled deeply. 'And you're an expert on war veterans, are you?'

'I care about you. Despite everything that's gone wrong between us, I'd like to be able to put it right. Yes, I've been guilty of fond feelings for another man, but only because I thought you were dead. Nothing physical happened between us.'

He snorted his disbelief. 'So you say.'

'It didn't, I swear it. In any case, forgiveness of my supposed infidelity isn't enough. We have to be happy together. If we can't be, then there's little point in carrying on, is there?'

Having gone this far, Lucy was determined to continue. She smiled reassuringly at him, for all her hands were clenching and unclenching with nervousness. 'So let's talk, shall we? Properly. You can start by explaining what life was like in that camp, then how you managed to escape. Did you dig a tunnel or sneak under a fence? It must have been an incredibly dangerous thing to do. Were you alone or with comrades?'

He was still pacing about the kitchen, unable to settle, his voice high-pitched and taut with anger. 'Aye, 'course I was with comrades. I've told you, we got separated.' He bent over the fire, stabbed at the coals with the poker to bring the flames back to life, and Lucy could see his neck growing red. She wondered if it was with the heat he was producing or with annoyance. Whatever the reason, she couldn't curb her curiosity.

'Why? Were you chased?'

He turned upon her, brandishing the poker, eyes matching it for glowing fury. 'For God's sake, how many times do I have to tell you? *I don't like talking about it!*' Heart racing, Lucy saw that she'd pushed him too far.

'I'm sorry,' she murmured. Going to him, she took the poker from his shaking hand and slid it back in the stand, then rested her own soft hand upon his shoulder. 'Perhaps we should leave it for now.' He'd clearly suffered far more than she realised. Tom turned to her with a tight little sob and sank into her arms, burying his face against her. The raw vulnerability of his despair shook her and she helplessly patted his back, trying to share his pain as he gulped on his sobs.

Later, as he sat sipping the tea she'd made him, he talked a little and Lucy listened in shamed gratitude. 'You've no idea what we suffered in those camps. Starvation, torture, locked in solitary if we stepped out of line,' he fabricated, remembering what he'd read about such places in the newspaper reports he devoured every day. 'After I'd got away, I could've been recaptured at any time, tortured and killed. Can you imagine how that sort of terror feels?'

Lucy felt hot with shame and pity for having interrogated him so hard. 'Oh, Tom, I should keep me nagging tongue still, I really should. It was just that I wanted to understand what you've been through, so that I know how to help you.'

He put down the cup, looked her straight in the eyes, and there was such sorrow in his face, such an aching sadness, that a knot of agony rose in her throat. 'You can help me best, Lucy, by giving the final heave-ho to that Michael Hopkins. Getting him out of our lives for good.' Then, firmly and possessively, he pulled her close into his arms and kissed her while Lucy, as so many times before, did her utmost to respond.

The scent of the cigarette he'd smoked, the warmth and closeness of him, rekindled memories of long-forgotten pleasures they'd once enjoyed together. He was still an attractive man and even if she couldn't love him quite as she did Michael, she was fond of Tom and felt guilty for having let him down, causing him to mistrust her. Didn't he deserve some happiness at least, after suffering such untold horrors he couldn't even bear to speak of them? And now she'd forced him to recall those painful memories, made him break down. Her guilt intensified.

'How about that day's fishing you keep promising our Sean? It's Whit Monday tomorrow, a holiday. I'll put up a picnic and we'll have a day out, as a family. See how we get on.' He really didn't deserve to be hurt any more, not after everything he'd been through, and she should remember that.

He seemed pleased by the suggestion and Lucy asked no more questions, nor gave him any further arguments. She allowed him to take her to bed, hoping against hope that this time when he made love to her he would be patient. She laid her head against his chest, let him stroke her hair, her buttocks, her breasts, steadfastly setting the image of Michael aside. But, as always, he was hasty and clumsy. He turned her on her back and took her as if he were barely aware of her as a person, simply using her to satisfy his needs. Valiantly she fought against the tears that brimmed in her eyes. The only relief being that, as usual, it was over mercifully quickly, then he lay with his back to her on the far side of the bed.

'Goodnight, Tom,' she said. He didn't reply, but nor did he trouble her again that night, for which she was unutterably grateful.

Chapter Twenty

It was a gold and emerald spring day, the sky a bright blue with fluffy white clouds as fat as pillows and a light breeze to take the edge off the heat. They caught a bus along Oldham Road and walked down Ashton Road to Woodhouses. From here they followed the path down by the cricket club which led to the River Medlock, where it seemed they were deep in the countryside and the air was sweet while they were yet just moments from the city centre. What a wonder it all was. Birds sang, dragonflies skated on the quiet waters, and the grass verge was starred with oxeye daisies, red campion and stitch-wort. The children ran ahead, constantly chastised by Lucy not to go too far, or too near the water.

'What a worry children are. It's a wonder you decided to return, knowing all this responsibility was waiting for you.' She slanted a glance at Tom, half hoping he would snatch the opportunity she offered to admit he hadn't returned out of love for her but only because of a sense of duty to his children. Would knowing that fact release her from a sense of duty to him? Lucy found herself holding her breath while Tom stopped, as if needing time to consider, letting his gaze travel slowly over her.

Lucy felt herself grow hot beneath his scrutiny. Because she'd felt so down lately, much of the time she looked as if she'd dressed herself from the rag bag, a far cry from the Lucy of old; her hair was too often fastened up, as wartime fashion had dictated, in a scarf which she wore like a turban with the tails tucked in. Today she'd let her hair fly loose in the breeze and could feel her cheeks flushed pink. She felt his gaze linger on her lips, rosy with the lipstick she'd applied, as if inviting kisses. She wished, in that moment, she hadn't indulged her vanity quite so recklessly, when the last thing she wanted was to attract his attentions.

He drew her close to his side. 'Remembering the children was what kept me going. They're a part of you, so how could I wish to be without them?'

She felt strangely moved by his words, tears springing readily to her eyes. 'Oh, Tom, what a lovely thing to say.'

'Besides, I flatter myself that Sean and I are getting along better these days.'

'Which is the reason you are loaded down with fishing rod, nets and jam-jars,' she said, laughing.

'Exactly.'

'I'm going to catch a real whopper,' Sean announced, running back to them at the sound of his own name.

'Are you? Well, that'll solve what we have for us tea.' Lucy's eyes were dancing as she walked along beside her husband, almost as if they were a normal family out for the day, and she wondered if her foolish suspicions had made her misjudge him for all she felt sure he'd lied. Perhaps he was jumpy because he was finding it hard to settle.

It was indeed a delightful afternoon. Lucy's worries that Tom might try to kiss her dissolved as they ate a huge picnic from the basket she'd brought and lay about on the grass, content to watch the children play and giggle at silly jokes. Sarah Jane took great delight in waving to all the passing barges, declaring her earnest intention to live on one because she loved all those pretty flowers they had painted on them. Lucy said her daughter would be better suited to a coal barge, considering the state of her frock, while Sean was in his element fishing. He cast his line like an expert now, after Michael's careful tuition, Lucy thought, without any fear of ending up in the water himself. He even caught two fish, admittedly small, due largely to the patient assistance of his father. He didn't stop talking about them all day. Today Lucy saw a different Tom Shackleton, one who was his old self again, cheerful, joking and relaxed, as if anxious to re-establish himself with his family, and most importantly his wife.

After lunch they picked bluebells in the Clough then walked on, following the path by the river to Daisy Nook.

'I've thought of nowt but getting back home to you for years, wanting to make things right.' Tom turned his face away, gaze fixed with a melancholy sadness upon the rickety bridge ahead of them, so that Lucy wasn't able to judge whether he truly meant what he said. When he did turn to her, she saw a strangeness in his eyes, as if he were in some distant place where she couldn't quite reach him. 'But you're right, it has been hard coming back. I lived in a village in the mountains for a long time. It was an unusual sort of life but I grew used to it.' Lucy held her breath. Would he reveal more? She waited and hoped but he seemed to snap back to the present, a dreadful bleakness in his gaze. 'Don't *you* ever leave me, Lucy. How would I manage without you?'

'I do appreciate how hard it's been for you, Tom,' she said, alarmed by his plea, and could have sworn there were tears in his eyes, not for a moment considering they might stem from self-pity. 'Really I do. Perhaps if you talked about it more, it would make it easier. Don't you reckon?'

He didn't seem to hear her. 'I want us to be happy, to be safe. I want to make up for the time we've lost. I've got meself a good job, found us a house, even put a bit by for a rainy day. What else should I do? Tell me, Lucy, and I'll do it.'

She felt close to panic, almost as if she were being suffocated. She'd meant to break free, now she felt more entangled than ever. How could she leave him without it seeming she was letting him down when he needed her the most? 'I don't know – I really don't know what to say, Tom.' She was thankfully saved from her dilemma by Sean who came running pell-mell back to them. 'Mam, Mam! There's a lake, and boats. Can we go on one? Can we? Can we?'

They'd reached Crime Lake about which there were a multitude of yarns. It was said to be bottomless and there were legends of ghosties and ghoulies, no doubt all intended to keep curious children from venturing too near the water. Tom hired a boat and took them all out in it. Lucy lay back, trailing her fingers in the cool water, and felt a new confidence flow through her veins. They were at least getting along better. Today had been good for them both and perhaps in future he would relax more and not feel the need to bully her. He'd opened up a little this weekend. Perhaps that too was a good sign, one she could encourage.

It was after she'd put the children to bed, both of them near dead on their feet from the excitement of the day, when she was preparing vegetables for a quick stew, that it all started to go wrong. Tom began by saying what a lovely day they'd enjoyed and Lucy agreed.

'We could move, if you like?' he suggested, quite out of the blue and in his most reasonable tone. 'We could leave this house, this city, and go somewhere fresh. Just you, me and the childer. It's what I'd like.'

Lucy felt a jolt of cold panic. 'I don't want to leave. Manchester is my home.'

'There's plenty places just as good,' he smilingly told her. 'Happen I'll buy us a little business of us own, eh? Why not? Then you can work with me. Somewhere a bit smarter, abroad perhaps where the weather's better, far away from the grubby wharves of Castlefield and nosy old Pansy Street. Like I said, I've a bit put by.'

Lucy picked up a carrot and began to scrape it clean. What was he saying? She wondered how he could have come by any money. He surely didn't earn enough labouring for Polly to have much in the way of savings. She longed to summon enough courage to tell him that it was all over between them, that she'd no wish to work in a little business with him, that it was Michael she loved with all her heart and soul, with every ounce of her being. But she daren't take the risk. He was so volatile, with such mercurial changes of mood. Dear God, she couldn't deal with him like this, she really couldn't. It was Michael she wanted, ached for.

As if reading her thoughts, he hissed, 'Michael Hopkins isn't right for you. He's a weak fool. A bloody conchie.'

'He isn't,' Lucy hotly retorted, instantly on the defensive and going all hot and flustered. 'I love him.'

'No, you don't.' Tom lurched towards her so swiftly that she jumped back, startled by this burst of ferocity. The knife she'd been holding fell with a clatter to the floor and he snatched it up. Holding it in his fist, he stabbed the table in front of her, over and over in a ferocious outburst of temper, punctuating every word. '*You only went with him because you were missing me.*'

She was stunned by this outburst. Shocked by his violence.

'Lots of women had affairs during this war, but when their husbands came home they gave their lover-boys up.'

Lucy could only gaze in horror at the row of holes in her table, fear crawling up her spine.

Seeing her expression, Tom let his shoulders droop and placed the knife back on the table. He straightened it meticulously then grinned up at her, shamefaced. 'I'm sorry, I didn't mean to alarm you. I get carried away sometimes.' Very gently he reached out one hand to stroke her cheek and she managed not to flinch as his voice dropped to a soft whisper. 'But it's all right. I've forgiven you, Lucy. You should be grateful I'm prepared to let the past go. I can't say fairer than that, now can I? I mean, you wouldn't want me to have to defend my honour, as it were? Or for owt nasty to happen to lover-boy, now would you?'

She gave a tiny shake of her head, anxious to appease him, to put an end to this appalling conversation before his temper flared again. What did he mean, about something nasty happening to Michael? It was all going terribly wrong, sliding out of her control.

But he was still smiling at her, saying what a lovely day they'd had and how they must repeat it some time soon. 'Now, is this dinner ever going to be ready? I'm sick of waiting.' And he reached for a potato and began to peel it, taking painstaking care to bring off the peel in long thin slivers. With shaking hands, Lucy picked up a carrot.

That night Tom cried in her arms, whimpering that he might have hurt her through his ungovernable temper and all because of what the war had done to him. He begged her again not to leave him and Lucy felt that the fragility of his mind was such that if she did, he might break down completely and God knows what would happen then. How could she possibly escape? And if she did, might he hurt himself? Might he hurt her, or even the children? She knew she should run far, far away but couldn't quite summon up the courage. There seemed nothing for it but that she must continue to live as a dutiful and loyal wife.

But Lucy also knew that neither could she give Michael up. The sacrifice would be too great. Since Belinda's death, she needed him more than ever. Life was too short to turn her back on the man she truly loved.

She invented a new friend, Sally, and claiming she lived in the next street, persuaded Tom to allow her to continue with one evening out a week at the flicks. In truth she would be seeing Michael but Tom agreed without demur, making no comment as he sat quietly watching her apply lipstick, sweep her hair into a roll and select a pretty frock to wear. It renewed her hope that he was becoming more reasonable, that he truly regretted his outburst.

Michael was more than willing to meet her and they took a bus as far away from the twitching lace curtains of Pansy Street and the bustling wharves of Castlefield as they could get. They would hold hands and talk, simply glad to be together again. Week after week they met this way. Sometimes they'd sit and cuddle on park benches, in dreary little cafes or on the back row of anonymous picture houses, never noticing what was on screen. And once Michael took her for lunch to a seedy hotel out in Ashton-in-Makerfield.

'You're mad,' she told him, excitement coursing through her.

'I'm in love.'

They sat in a drab dining room that smelled of stale cabbage and endless fry-ups, yet barely recognised the fact. They paid even less attention to the curiosity and amusement in the eyes of the landlady who served them fatty pork and jam rolypoly for pudding. All they wanted, all they needed, was each other.

'Will you be wanting to use the facilities?' the woman enquired when the meal was over, not quite with a wink but plainly enough for them both to understand that she was not discussing the bathroom arrangements.

Lucy gazed across at Michael and, embarrassed by what

she read there, dropped her eyes to the grubby tablecloth, blushing furiously. Then somehow, without any conscious thought, she was smiling up at the woman and saying thank you, that would be splendid.

Michael handed over the money to buy them an afternoon of privacy, an hour or two away from reality.

No time was wasted in preliminaries. They were tearing at each other's clothes the moment the bedroom door was closed, Lucy shivering with a new intensity of longing when Michael caressed her breast. The excitement of warm naked flesh meeting for the first time was too overwhelming for them to spare a glance at their surroundings. Neither noticed the fly-spotted wallpaper or the dingy curtains. They were too absorbed with tasting, sharing, loving, becoming one with the other, lost in a private world of their own where they could express the pent-up emotion and passion that they felt. Afterwards, lying with arms wrapped tight about each other, they could hardly bear to get up and dress and return to cold reality.

'You realise this is wicked? It should never have happened,' Lucy whispered, nuzzling close against the warmth of his body.

'Ask him for a divorce. Explain you believe there is no hope for the marriage.'

'I did try, but failed. It's too soon.' Lucy related parts of their conversation but made no mention of the knife. She believed Tom regretted that moment of lost control, that he would never do it again.

'Try one more time. Please, Lucy.'

'I will. As soon as he's more settled in his new job, more used to civilian life and has come to terms with whatever is eating him up about his past.'

'I can't bear to give you up.' And then Michael was rolling her over on to her back, placing feathery light kisses over her throat and breasts, making her gasp with new desire. How could she resist, when she needed him so?

Over the following weeks the dingy hotel in Ashton-in-Makerfield became a favourite haunt for the two lovers. The landlady came to welcome them as old friends, asked no questions, simply took their cash and left them alone. It felt to them both as if it were only here, in this grubby little room, that they truly came alive.

It amazed Lucy to find how adept she became at lying. She returned home that first evening, as on every other following, smiled at her husband, asked how the children had been, as if they were a normal, happy family and she had not just betrayed him with another man. But she knew in her heart that it couldn't go on like this indefinitely. Decisions would have to be made.

But Lucy feared that if she tried for a divorce she might risk losing the children for wouldn't she, in theory, be classed as the guilty party? Not for a moment did she consider giving Michael up. She'd felt suffocatingly trapped in a marriage without love. Now she gloried in the love she found with Michael, bloomed with the wonder of it, so that her hair shone, her face glowed and her eyes sparkled with happiness. Yet she continued to shy away from making any decision. Much better to leave things as they were. Tom didn't suspect. How could he? They were very careful. 'Who is getting hurt?' she would ask and then answer her own question. 'No one. Tom is reasonably content, and I can deal with Mam if she starts interfering again.'

'But I want more than this, Lucy, more than a hole-in-the-corner affair,' Michael would protest. 'I want you to belong to me utterly. For us to be man and wife.'

'I know, love, so do I. Oh, what are we going to do?' And her heart would melt with need for him, so that they would have to make love all over again.

Polly, still keeping a close eye on the goings on of her family, was surprised one evening in late-June to see young Sean walk into the warehouse, bold as you please. 'Jesus, Mary and Joseph, and where did you spring from? Where's yer mam?' She peered out through the door on to an empty street.

Sean grinned at her, jumping up and down on one foot with excitement. 'I come all by meself, Nan.'

'What, all the way, on yer own, across the canal basin? Even under the railway arches and over the canal bridges?'

Sean nodded vigorously, evidently proud of this feat.

'Glory, isn't that a brave thing to do?' Polly said, trying not to alarm the child while hugging him tightly to her breast. Later, when she'd taken him back home and found the house empty save for Sarah Jane, who was going frantic with worry, she fed them both, giving them stern lectures about strangers who ran off with small children and Jinny Greenteeth down by the water who ate them. Then, having thoroughly frightened her beloved grandchildren into staying closer to home in future, Polly read them two cheering stories and tucked them up safe in bed. After that she sat in the kitchen and waited impatiently for Lucy to come home. Within seconds of her daughter's crossing the threshold, Polly was laying into her, determined to frighten her witless for her neglect of the children, using words like 'irresponsible', 'dangerous', 'wanton', 'lazy' and 'hair-brained eejit'.

It made no impression on Polly that Lucy insisted this was her one evening out a week, that Tom had agreed to stay in and mind them. Polly had been too frightened by the little boy's adventure and told Lucy in no uncertain terms that the task of child minding was, first and foremost, the mother's responsibility. 'Did you even remember to ask Tom? For sure he would've been here if ye had.'

'Oh, so he's innocent and I'm to be found guilty without even the benefit of a fair trial, is that it?'

'Where was it ye had to go that was so urgent? And

don't try and lie for ye know I can allus tell.' And Polly watched the tell-tale signs of guilt wash up her daughter's throat to mantle her cheeks with pink. 'So that's the way of it. I might've guessed. Aw, Lucy, have ye no sense?'

Any hopes Polly might have had of talking sense into her daughter then were demolished as Lucy flounced out of the room, refusing to answer any more questions. Undeterred Polly went instead to see Minnie Hopkins and demanded she tell her what was going on between Michael and Lucy.

The old woman folded her arms across her skinny breast and sucked on her teeth, which for once she had in, and shook her head. 'I didn't know owt was going on. Anyroad, it's nowt to do wi' me.' Nor you neither, her expression seemed to say.

'Saints preserve us, of course it's summat to do with you. Isn't he yer nephew and Lucy a married woman? It's a sin for sure. Aren't they committing adultery, apart from the unholy mess they're getting them poor kids into?'

' 'Asta getten religion in thy old age, Polly lass? After all, tha's suffered from it in the way of bigotry in the past.' Polly had the grace to blush but persisted with her concern for Lucy, saying that no good would come of it, that they could both end up getting hurt.

'Don't be too hard on t'lass. She's sticking with Tom, po-faced and shifty though he is, just as thee axed her to.'

Polly was startled. 'Shifty? And who says so?'

'I do. Never looks you straight in the eye. Theer's allus a reason when folk won't do that. And don't thee try telling me how much he's suffered. We know about suffering in this house. He looks pretty fit to me.'

'She's neglecting her children, going out night after night . . .'

'It's only one night a week, so far as I'm aware, and any woman has a right to that much. But if yon lass is doin' summat she shouldn't then it's for her and that husband of hers to sort out, not thee.' And Minnie terminated the discussion by firmly changing the subject to the coming Bring and Buy in the church hall. Polly was forced to make a tactical withdrawal if not an absolute surrender.

The following Thursday, Lucy was late leaving as Sean had been fractious, trying to persuade her to take him with her to the pictures. She'd had to run to catch the bus and could hardly believe her eyes when, the moment she jumped on board, there was Polly, large as life in her tweed coat and head scarf, seated next to some toothless old dear in a rain hood. 'Hello, m'cushla, and where are you off to?' She might very well have added 'at this time of night' for it was written plain in her bright enquiring eyes that she'd caught the bus on purpose to check on Lucy.

She took a moment to answer while she found a seat opposite, fumbling in her pocket for some loose change for the conductor, thrusting a collection of carefully hoarded halfpennies into his hand. He jiggled them and wisecracked, 'Carol singing started early this year, has it?' and gave her a broad wink as he clipped her ticket. Lucy tried to smile, her brain whirling.

'I'm going out with a friend,' she said at last, unable to find a better excuse.

'And who might that be now?' Polly softly enquired. Her neighbour removed her rain hood so that she could better hear the reply, shaking drops over everyone seated nearby. 'I thought they all lived in Castlefield? This bus is going to the city centre. Now who d'you know who lives there? No one at all, I'm thinking.'

Lucy met her mother's shrewd, probing gaze and surrendered, mainly because a friend was the thing she needed most in all the world. There were times, like now, when she ached to have Belinda to talk to, but her dear sister-in-law was gone. 'All right, I'll tell you, but you mustn't blame me too much. We couldn't help it.' Lucy became embarrassingly aware of how silent the bus had become as ears positively twitched in their eagerness to listen in to this fascinating discussion. While Lucy hesitated, Polly pressed on with her interrogation.

'I suppose you're going to tell me that you love him?'

'I suppose I am.'

Polly's neighbour sucked on her gums and gave a brisk nod of her grizzled head. 'God meks 'em and the devil pairs 'em.'

Lucy shot the woman a fierce glare. The bell pinged and the bus lurched to a halt, the conductor calling out for them to mind the step. There was the usual jostling crowd waiting at the bus stop, anxious to get on before people had had time to alight. Lucy waited until the conductor rang for the bus to start again then was on her feet in a second and jumped off the moving vehicle.

She waved cheekily at Polly as it roared away for, not unnaturally, her mother's face was tight with annoyance.

Polly might very well have pursued the matter more vigorously in the coming weeks, were it not for the fact that she had a good many other matters on her mind.

Chapter Twenty-one

During the long hot summer of that year, Lucy struggled to cope with her difficult and loveless marriage. How she envied the young Princess Elizabeth as her romance progressed smoothly towards what would undoubtedly be happiness. The young couple were so clearly in love. But then Lucy's life too had once seemed equally full of hope and promise until the war had changed everything, destroying the Tom Shackleton she'd once known and loved and leaving in his place this hard, unfeeling person.

Despite his protestations to the contrary it was as if Tom was barely aware of her as a person. He would sit mute throughout family meals, barely register her presence as she went about her household chores. To her enormous relief his lovemaking, if you could call it that, became less frequent though it remained as hasty and clumsy as ever. Lucy could barely bring herself to tolerate the intimacy, let alone respond, though fearful of arousing his irascible temper, she never refused him. It was always over blessedly quickly and then he would turn his back to her and be snoring in seconds, leaving her to stare up into the darkness and silently nurse her despair.

With Michael it was entirely different. She only had to see his smile, look into his eyes, to feel herself bursting with love for him. He would stroke her with such a loving tenderness it made her cry. He would kiss her warm eager mouth and groan with desire as he pressed against the soft silkiness of her skin, their bodies melded together as if created for that sole purpose.

And if she ever suffered a pang of guilt for acting upon their love then Lucy would remind herself of how cold and unfeeling Tom was, of how he could have written and told her that he lived yet had chosen not to do so. She was utterly convinced that there was much he could tell her, had he a mind to, and that if she could but discover the truth about those missing years, then she would be free.

Lucy watched with some envy as Benny slowly rebuilt his life, caring for his son, working with his mother in an easy and friendly fashion. Her own relations with Polly remained distant following her shameful behaviour on the bus. Twice Lucy plucked up the courage to go round to Polly's house specifically to apologise and talk about the problem. She longed to unburden herself and ask advice on what she should do, or rather ask how she could leave her husband without suffering guilt, a seemingly impossible quest. On one occasion Polly wasn't in; on the second Lucy found her putting a cold compress on Charlie's knee which, as well as being swollen with painful arthritis, sported a massive purple bruise.

'I were only weeding the marigolds along the back yard wall,' he ruefully admitted.

'You're supposed to be resting, not gardening,' Polly scolded.

'I'm tired of resting and it isn't doing any good. Trouble is, the knee doesn't always behave as I tell it,' Charlie joked, but this incident, not the first by any means, had so clearly upset Polly, it somehow didn't seem the right moment to impose further worries on her mother. Lucy brewed tea for them all and sat for an hour, listening and sympathising over the agonies Charlie suffered and the various treatments and 'cures' they'd tried, not to mention the pressures of Polly's business, and then went home without ever mentioning her own troubles.

When the precious Thursday came round again, Lucy put on a new frock, one she'd made herself, finding the money for it by pinching a penny here and there out of the housekeeping. But for once, Michael failed to notice for his distress over their situation was growing. Lucy strived to placate him, to make him understand that however much they might want to be together, Tom needed her more, for now. But Michael's pleas grew so heated they came near to quarrelling.

'And what about *my* needs?'

'We must be patient.'

'For how much longer? I love you, Lucy, and want to spend the rest of my life with you, not simply snatched moments in this seedy hotel.' And looking out through the smeared glass of their bedroom retreat on to a dingy back street piled high with rubbish and rust-caked dustbins, Lucy couldn't help but agree.

She unbuttoned her dress, let it fall to the floor in a soft whisper, heard Michael's stifled gasp as she stood before him in her brassiere and French knickers, his eyes riveted to the outline of her nipples pressing against the flesh-coloured silk. His voice, when he found it, was hoarse with longing. 'It's marriage I want, Lucy. A proper life for us both.'

She put her hands to her cheeks and began to cry.

'Don't! Don't! Jesus, how I want you.' He went to her then, smoothed back her hair and cupped her face in his hands. 'You know I love you. Once I thought we could run off and live together but, much as I want to be with you, it's no good pretending that would be an easy decision because it wouldn't. In the eyes of the whole world we'd be living in sin.'

She slid a hand up about his neck and kissed his chin, his mouth, the roughness of his cheek. 'I don't call it a sin to love someone as we do.'

'Folk like Lily Gantry would have a field day.'

'I don't care. Let them do their worst, we'd be happy at least.' She felt desperate suddenly to get away from Tom, to feel safe and start life anew with the man she truly loved, yet knew she lacked the courage to ask Tom for a divorce. Perhaps living together was the only way out for them. What was so shocking about it? She pressed closer, pushing the softness of her breasts against the hardness of him, teasing him and bringing a smile to his lips at last with her display of wantonness. 'Tom would give up the fight to hold on to me, once he saw how happy we were together.'

Michael's face was in her hair, breathing in the sweet, exciting scent of her. 'What about the children? How would they feel about it? They'd be ostracised at school, all their mates teasing them that we were living o'er brush.' He asked this in such a quiet, sensitive way that Lucy dropped her chin so he couldn't read the fear in her eyes. If they didn't solve this problem would she lose him? Dear God, she couldn't bear that.

'It wouldn't matter. They both adore you, you know they do.'

'Try talking to him first, Lucy, sensibly and honestly. I'd come and speak to him myself, only that would be more likely to inflame him. Tell him you've done your best but that we need to be together, no matter what. Ask him for a divorce. I'll find the money to pay for it somehow.'

He stroked her cheek, and meeting the loving urgency of his gaze Lucy felt, for the first time in months, a surge of hope for the future, a new sense of freedom. 'All right. I'll try once more, I promise.'

'Be firm this time,' Michael insisted, pulling her down beside him on to the grubby sheets so he could remove the last silken impediments to their loving with his own eager hands. 'Be firm but kind. Show him you mean it this time.'

'I will.' Lucy was drowning in her need for him, helping him with the buttons and hooks. 'I shall be absolutely determined. Believe me.'

The next week passed in an agony of indecision. Time after time Lucy attempted to summon up the courage to broach the subject. But life was going along quite smoothly for once and she felt a reluctance, a fear almost, to spoil it. Tom even allowed her to have little Matt one afternoon, to give Doris-next-door a rest, which was lovely.

So the following week when they met she admitted to Michael she hadn't yet found the right moment to mention divorce. He looked so hurt and disappointed that she struggled to explain her reluctance. 'Tom is working hard, settling in nicely at his new job. I'm afraid to risk upsetting him. It isn't easy for me, Michael. He can be up one minute and down the next. Life is so much better when he's calm, as he seems to be at the moment.'

'Better for you maybe,' Michael grunted, disappointment causing an uncharacteristic bitterness to curl his lips. 'Not for me.'

'Are you suggesting that I didn't really try?'

'How should I know? What proof do I have? I'm just your *fancy man*.'

'Don't say such a thing. You know it's not like that. You *know* that I love you, and want to be with you.' Not for the world did she want Michael to suspect this foolish fear that was growing inside her that Tom was only too aware of where she went every Thursday evening, yet chose not to mention it. Why she thought that she couldn't say, but if she was right then it somehow made her extra wary of raising the subject of leaving him, as if one word from her might topple him from this knife edge of patience upon which he balanced.

As summer progressed and the country talked of little else but the hope of a Royal wedding it became ever harder to keep Michael happy. Even Lucy began to shudder at the stained sheets they must lie on, the cobwebs festooning the cracked lamp shade above their heads, and the fly-spotted mirror as she replaced her lipstick after their lovemaking. It all began to feel cheap and sordid as they furtively made sure they caught different buses back to Castlefield. And yet she couldn't quite bring herself to walk out on a husband who was clearly unstable, damaged by a war he'd never asked to be a part of except to want his wife and children to have the chance to grow up in a free world.

By August Lucy knew she had fallen pregnant. She was quite certain that Michael must be the father, though mainly perhaps because she wanted him to be. Tom had bothered her less and less lately so it seemed likely, but how could she be sure? How could she go to either her lover or her husband and say with any conviction or sense of joy that she bore his child? She decided to say nothing to either. After all, it might prove to be a false alarm. And the delay would at least give her time to think.

Delay, in fact, only made Lucy worry more. She felt herself shrink a little whenever she felt Tom's eyes upon her, almost as if he knew what she was thinking, what was happening inside her body.

Afraid she might start to show, she took to wearing a corset whenever she was at home with Tom or out and about where people would see her, pulling the pink laces in quite tight. Only when she was with Michael did she leave it off, half hoping he would notice the slight thickening of her waistline and then she might at last find the courage to tell him of her suspicions.

It shamed and troubled her to discover how indecisive and weak she was becoming, as if she'd forgotten who she was and had lost all faith in herself. Why didn't she just come out with it all? Tell Michael she was pregnant with his child. Tell Tom she was leaving him. Tell Polly . . . Oh, dear God. She couldn't.

What she dreaded most was what her mother would say. Not that Polly would have noticed anyway, she was too caught up in her own problems. Perhaps she didn't even care, Lucy thought, uncharitable in her misery.

While little Matt struggled to shake off a summer cold, Benny grew increasingly harassed trying to cope with a fractious baby all night while maintaining a full day's work at the shop. Despite his own concerns, even he realised Lucy wasn't herself when he again asked if she'd mind baby Matt for an afternoon, and she sadly refused.

'Where's that bright rebel of a sister I once had?' he teased. 'I know you're missing Belinda. I am too, for Christ's sake, but life goes on. We can't stop in bed and grieve forever, much as we might want to.' He had to pause here to compose himself before continuing, 'Couldn't you have the babby now and then, Luce? I feel awful putting on good old Doris all the time.'

'It's not that. It's — it's Tom. He doesn't like me working. Thinks I have enough to do.'

'Ask him at least,' Benny urged. 'Use your feminine charms.' And Lucy merely looked at him and knew, deep in her heart, that the longer she put off confronting Tom about anything, the less likely she was ever to find the courage.

In the first week of September she went to see her mother at the warehouse. Polly showed her usual pleasure at seeing Lucy but barely paused in her labours of setting up a new loom with her mate Maisie Wright, except to ask if

Lucy wanted a job as a spool setter as she'd be needing another.

Lucy thanked her for the offer, wishing fervently she could accept but knowing Tom would never agree. Besides, if it was true there was a baby on the way, what would be the point? She felt desperate to talk about it, to share the agony of her suspicions with someone who cared, but Polly was too busy explaining the process to her to listen.

'See here, each square on the pattern sheet has been given a number relating to the particular shade of wool to be used, a total of two hundred and fifty-two for the pattern width. Then we set out the correct shade of bobbins on to this here spool table, in rows of colours which correspond to the pattern of squares. Clever, eh?'

'Mam, can I just have a word.'

' 'Course you can, m'cushla. Then these threads, see, will be wound in short lengths on to spools and then taken over to the loom for weaving into carpet. Isn't that grand? Ye'd learn it in no time,' Polly continued, oblivious of her daughter's distress. When Lucy didn't respond, she glanced up and perhaps noted for the first time her daughter's pale cheeks and pinched expression for Polly's shrewd gaze narrowed in that familiar way. 'I was forgetting Tom's views on women working. You'll have to take that husband of yours in hand. He's living in the past, so he is. The war has changed all that nonsense. Talk to him, Lucy. Getting a job would do you good, instead of being cooped up in the house all the day. It might put a bit of colour in yer cheeks. Explain that to him.'

'I've tried. The thing is – it isn't simply Tom. Actually I'm . . .'

'Aw, give me the right thread, for goodness' sake, Maisie. This job's difficult enough as it is.' Polly wiped the sweat off her brow. 'It's number thirty four not thirty seven. The pale blue. Keep yer mind on the job and not on your new chap,' she teased her friend. 'Sorry love, what were yer saying?'

'The problem is . . .'

'Aw, Maisie, will ye keep hold of it. Hadn't I just threaded it through the flippin' hole.'

Lucy suddenly yelled at Polly, '*You* talk to him! I can't. Matter of fact, nobody ever listens to a word I have to say for more than ten seconds at a time.' Whereupon she turned on her heel and stalked away, head in the air. Polly stopped threading wool to gaze after her daughter.

'And what can be eating her? Did she get out of bed the wrong side?' Polly shook her head in despair, pushing back a lock of hair with a tired hand before picking up the wool again and threading it through the correct slot. She longed to rush after Lucy, to ask her what was wrong, but this task couldn't wait. It was desperately important that they get the loom running. Knowing it was essential that the business prosper, she'd invested heavily in this third machine, stretching herself to the limit in order to meet the orders she'd got waiting. She wouldn't be so hard strapped for cash if so much wasn't tied up in dratted furniture that wasn't selling near fast enough for her liking. 'What a trial life is at times.'

'Aye, and then you die,' Maisie agreed.

Polly made it her business to keep up to scratch on everything that was going on in her family and, in spite of Charlie's frequent and wise advice not to interfere, could rarely resist doing so. She was always ready to take up the cudgels on their behalf and fight all comers. But now, for the first time ever, she listened to what he said and left well alone.

If Lucy had got herself into some sort of a muddle then she must, as both Minnie and Charlie insisted, get herself out of it. What could she do to help the daft eejit anyway? Benny had a battle of his own to fight and was waging it well. She admired him for the care he took of his son, and for the work he was putting into the business. Shouldn't she be the happiest woman in the whole world to have him here with her at last? Yet she felt swamped by worry.

Although some of their customers came into the new shop by chance while out and about in the street, most came via the credit club operated by Hubert. In many ways this was an advantage. It was a sure market, necessitating very little in the way of advertising. They were paid within thirty days for every sale, no matter how long it might take the customer to pay Hubert on a weekly basis. And if customers got behind in their payments, or did a moonlight flit, which was common enough in these parts, this would be dealt with by the ubiquitous Ron. Polly suffered no financial loss at all. And of course the profit margins were excellent. It was largely because of this side of the business that she was able to expand her carpet manufacturing quite so rapidly.

Because of these benefits, Polly was reluctant to complain to Hubert when she experienced difficulties, though inevitably some items moved less quickly than others while some wouldn't shift at all. Right at the start he'd assured her that he had other outlets in the city as well as in Rochdale, Stockport and Bolton, so could easily move goods on to there. Unfortunately, he consistently failed to do so and Polly became increasingly frustrated and finally infuriated by the delays.

'Ye'll have to tackle him about it,' she curtly told Benny one day, after counting sixteen unsold balloon-backed chairs. 'Nobody wants these Victorian monstrosities. Haven't I told him so a dozen times?'

'He's asked us to give them a proper chance.'

'And so we have. Far longer than any other shop would tolerate.' She smoothed a hand over the chair seats. 'Feel that leather. It's cracking already. Cheap, that's what they are, just like those dratted book cases which are coming apart at the seams. Tell him I'm still waiting for compensation on losses there too. No wonder we aren't selling these chairs. Manchester folk have too much sense than to buy outdated rubbish. See you get rid of them. If you don't talk to Hubert, I will.'

She could tell by the way Benny's mouth folded into a tight line that he didn't care for her tactics.

'Don't sulk, laddie. Business is business. Sale or return means exactly what it says – if they don't sell, you return them. Have 'em packed up this minute and Tom can drive them to Hubert's warehouse this very afternoon.'

The next morning on her way to work Polly called again at the shop and there the chairs still were, all lined up against the wall as if they were at a ball waiting for some Victorian misses to recline upon them. She felt a tide of hot-blooded Irish fury bubble through her veins as Benny patiently explained how Ron Clarke, in charge at the time Tom had called, had absolutely refused to unlock the stockroom doors so he'd been forced to bring the chairs back again.

'Something about the proper paperwork not being done.'

'Proper paperwork? Sure and won't I give the pair of them proper paperwork indeed.'

Benny wagged a placating hand. 'Mam, don't interfere. This is my part of the business, remember, and Hubert Clarke is my father-in-law – ex father-in-law. I'll deal with the matter.'

'See that you do,' Polly warned him tartly. Jesus, Mary and Joseph, if it wasn't one of her children creating havoc in her life, it was the other.

Chapter Twenty-two

Now that all the new looms had been delivered and set up to her satisfaction Polly spent a quiet morning in the office poring over the accounts, which were becoming a real source of concern. She wished now that she'd waited a bit longer before taking on a third loom, though the manufacturing side of her business was doing well. It was the retail part which troubled her.

Charlie was perking up, insisting on getting out and about more as the pain subsided a little and Polly was glad about that, but the responsibility of being the main bread-winner in the family still lay heavy upon her.

After a quick sandwich lunch, the first of several young girls answering her advertisement for spool setters began to arrive and she went to interview them. This took an hour of her valuable time and even when she'd set two girls on, neither of them much over thirteen since they'd just left school, Polly wished with all her heart that Lucy too would come in the business. She would have made more of the job than the pair put together. What an old stick-in-the-mud Tom was, to be sure. Should she have a word with him herself? she wondered.

But when she put this idea to Charlie he said, 'What as? His employer or his mother-in-law? Leave well alone or you'll make things worse for Lucy.'

Aw, but it was hard to do that, for hadn't she neglected the girl lately, fussing about her own affairs when all the time Lucy might need her? Something was wrong. Polly could sense it. What had Minnie said about Tom? Shifty indeed. Tch! But she did promise herself a private word with Lucy, the first opportunity she got.

The next morning Polly put one of the young girls with Maisie to learn about spool setting. The other she took over to Joyce, who checked faults in the newly woven carpets; created perhaps because the hessian hadn't been properly woven in, or gaps had been left where they shouldn't, or the warp had broken.

'Show her how to mark the faults, Joyce. If she cottons on to that in six or seven weeks and watches you carefully, I'll mebbe let her have a go at mending them. Work hard and ye'll be happy enough here, lass. Though the pay's terrible, isn't it, Joyce?'

'Crippling,' Joyce agreed, and took the young girl under her wing, grinning widely.

It was half-past seven by the time Polly got home.

Charlie was trying to read the paper and complaining his eyes weren't focusing properly. 'I think I need specs.'

'Ye've already got some. Put them on.'

'They don't work any more. I need new ones. New eyes too,' he cheerfully told her. Polly sighed, wondering if he'd given any thought to what they might eat. Her stomach felt as if it were full of razor blades, all sawing at each other, yet she felt too exhausted to do anything about it. 'No part of yer old body seems to work as it should according to you. I'd ask for a complete refit if I wasn't so fond of the old one.' And she kissed him on the nose.

'How's it gone at the warehouse today?' he enquired, setting down his newspaper and fetching a dish of hot pot from the stove.

The steaming aroma made her mouth water as he spooned it out. Polly mumbled a reply as she forked some hungrily into her mouth, the meat so tender he'd clearly had it in the oven for half the day. 'Ooh, bless ye, this is good. Unlucky in business but lucky in love, eh?'

Charlie chuckled. 'Shop not going too well then?'

'Don't ask.' It wasn't till she'd half emptied her plate and sated some of her hunger that Polly addressed the question properly. 'I'm going to see Hubert Clarke first thing tomorrer to tackle him about this furniture, whether our Benny likes it or not. A deal's a deal and if he promises sale or return, that's what I mean to have.'

*

383

Polly and Charlie spent all that evening going over the accounts yet again; bank statements, petty cash books, details of loan payments and profit ratios, and their worst fears were confirmed. If the business was to prosper and all payments to be met, drastic action was called for. But the next day Hubert Clarke proved to be as arrogant and unruffled as ever, setting out at once to pacify, urging Polly not to panic, to show faith and courage in the enterprise.

'It's not courage I lack, it's money,' she bluntly informed him, planting herself in his office as if she'd taken root there. 'If you don't stand by your promises, Councillor Clarke, then I'll be forced to take my business elsewhere.'

He smiled at her, moustache twitching, only the dark eyes beneath the ridge of bushy eyebrows giving any indication of his irritation. 'Nay, Polly lass. Don't get into a lather. It'll all come out in the wash as they say.' Chortling good-humouredly at his own silly joke.

Polly frowned. 'It'll have to come out somewhere. I'm not going on like this. Haven't I shown the patience of a saint, to be sure? Over twelve months I've had those chairs and only sold two. You promised me faithfully that ye'd tek 'em back yet still I'm waiting and still you're delivering more stuff each and every week. Incidentally, that sideboard Benny ordered the other week never arrived, and we'd a customer waiting.'

'I think you must be mistaken, lass. That lad of yours must've got in another muddle over his paperwork. Ron delivered it personally.' And he smiled benignly at her, his expression seeming to challenge her to deny it, which Polly certainly did.

'I don't think so. We're very particular with our invoicing and docketing. I've too much money tied up in stock and some of it must go.'

'Go?'

'To be sure, don't you deliver stuff whether we order it or not? We'll have furniture coming out of our ears, so we will. It's not good enough, Hubert.'

'There's no need to worry, lass,' he assured her, coming from behind his great desk to pat her shoulder dismissively. He went on to promise that Ron would persuade one or two of their better off customers to take the balloon chairs or, failing that, he'd mebbe agree to her returning half a dozen, say. When Polly insisted he should take the lot, due to the state of the leather seats, he instantly backtracked, saying he couldn't take defective goods, not at any price.

'But they were in that state when we got them,' Polly insisted, shocked by his attitude. 'And what about those bookcases? Like cardboard they are, coming apart at the joints.'

'Happen they've had careless handling in your shop,' Hubert gently scolded, as if she were a naughty schoolgirl. Polly felt a strong urge to smack his arrogant face but managed to curb her temper and leave without doing any such thing for all she banged the door rather louder than she should on her way out. Later, she gritted her teeth with frustration when she told Benny that the chairs would need to be reduced in price and sold off at whatever they could get for them.

'And next time you take a new delivery, check every single item. We take nothing that isn't perfect. Check your paperwork. Check everything.'

Benny resented being taken to task over paperwork which was, in his opinion, perfectly correct, so insisted that she was fussing, that there was little wrong with the chairs and he would sell them, given time and a bit of luck. 'You just have to fix the right price and find the right customer.'

'And not go bankrupt in the meantime,' she tartly informed him. This wasn't what she'd expected, not at all. Something smelled mighty fishy to her. Polly believed that trust was essential in any business partnership. It seemed to be sadly missing in this one and she'd have to keep an even closer eye on Hubert Clarke in future. Him and his bargain furniture.

Within two weeks she was knocking on his office door again complaining that she'd ordered a batch of kitchen tables and chairs that had never arrived, nor the sideboard they were still waiting for. Hubert called in Ron, who insisted he'd delivered them personally. 'If you don't know what stock you do have, Polly lass, how can you hope to succeed?'

She returned to Benny in a lather of embarrassment but despite searching the entire shop and stock rooms from top to bottom the consignment remained elusive, as did the paperwork.

'No invoice or delivery note,' Benny insisted, 'so how can they have been delivered?' And there was a copy of the orders, plain as day. Unfortunately it proved to be their word against Hubert's.

Polly next asked to return two dining-room suites. 'They're in good condition but everybody passes them by. Too expensive for our neck of the woods. You'd do better sending them Cheshire way. I'll have them brought round tomorrow, shall I?'

Hubert refused point blank to take the suites back and also denied ever having agreed to a sale or return arrangement in the first place. Polly gaped at him open-mouthed. 'Will ye say that again? I reckon me hearing has gone on the blink.'

'Whatever you take, you keep, Polly lass. I should've thought that was obvious. It's usual business practice after all. However, I'll be generous on this occasion, since it's you.' He rocked back and forth on his heels, as if considering the matter, then offered the now familiar pat. It was such a patronising gesture that in different circumstances she might very well have slapped his hand away. Just the way he called her *lass* all the time set her hackles rising. 'I tell you what I'll do for you, lass. I'll take back the two suites in question and swap them for four good sofas. How about that? Fair enough deal, wouldn't you say?' And somehow Polly found herself forced to agree.

'Your father-in-law changes his mind with the wind,' she told Benny as she strode through the shop half an hour later, blind with rage and only too ready to land one on anyone who happened to be handy. 'The divil take the man but I'll have his guts for garters if those sofas don't sell! I'll cancel the whole deal, so I will, but I'll not be put upon.'

The four sofas sold within two weeks and, mollified, Polly grudgingly agreed to allow Benny to take a further consignment, covered in a lovely blue velvet-like fabric this time. It wasn't till several days later that she found time to examine them closely. The fabric showed clear signs of mould.

'Jesus, Mary and Joseph! What has he sent us now?'

Benny, who admitted that he possibly hadn't checked them thoroughly enough when they were delivered, since he'd believed his mother to be making a fuss over nothing, said that he would deal with the matter himself this time. But even he returned from the fruitless visit, white-faced and angry. 'Hubert says there must be damp in our shop. The fault is ours, he says, and he'll not offer credit for faulty goods. We're stuck with them, Mam. No one will buy them.'

'How can they have got damp in this shop? We've had them no time at all. Drat the man, I've had enough. No one is going to get the better of me. Certainly not Hubert Clarke.'

Oblivious to the squalls of rain misting the air, Polly marched down Castle Street, past the old merchant's warehouse where a couple of barges were unloading at the shipping holes, across the iron foot bridge and on to Potato Wharf, with such a fierce look in her eye and such a determined spring in her step that people turned to watch as she passed by.

She found Hubert superintending the unloading of a shipment of wooden crates, no doubt containing more of his rubbish, she thought. 'I've had enough, so I have,' she announced, silver glints of fire sparking in her greeny-grey eyes. Several of the men engaged in the unloading paused momentarily to glance in shocked surprise in her direction. It was unheard of to stand up to Councillor Hubert Clarke in that way, let alone beard him in his den.

Hubert grabbed her elbow and propelled her towards his offices. 'We'll save this for a more private place, if you don't mind.' The minute the door was closed, Polly wrenched her arm free to face him with the kind of expression which proclaimed she would stand no more of his bullying. 'I'm sure I've nought to be ashamed of. Have you, Councillor?' she challenged him. 'Haven't I only come to tell ye that I'll be happy to supply your credit customers with quality goods. Unfortunately, yours are anything but, so I mean to find a different supplier, one who doesn't sell faulty merchandise, who delivers what we order and nothing more, and whose word is worth a good deal more than yours.'

It was several chilling seconds before Hubert deigned to respond. His face gave the impression that he'd like to throw her into the circular sluice that gushed in the canal just outside his window yet his voice, when he spoke, was studiedly quiet as he leaned closer in conspiratorial fashion. 'I've no wish to quibble nor deny you your rights, Polly lass, but aren't you in a rather delicate situation? Don't you owe me rather a lot of money, after all?' He smiled his beatific smile into her shocked face and calmly informed her that if she did try such a manoeuvre, he'd let it be known, in the appropriate quarters, that she wasn't to be trusted. 'So far as I can see, your credit rating as it stands now isn't good, lass, not good at all.' And he clicked his tongue, accompanied by a sad shake of his head.

She could taste the tobacco on his tainted breath. 'Jesus, Mary and Joseph, and isn't that only because you pile stock on me that I don't want and diddle me left, right and centre?'

'I'd take care what charges you mek about me, lass. Not unless you can mek 'em stick.' Hubert flexed his shoulders, took out his watch, studied it carefully and dropped it back in his waistcoat pocket. 'It's a changing world, Polly lass.' It was almost as if the watch itself had told him so. 'There's no room in it for sentiment. Pay up what you owe and you can use whichever supplier you please. Till then, you'd best tek care. You don't want no nasty whispers going the rounds questioning your credit standing, now do you? That wouldn't do your business any good at all.'

Polly was so furious, her feet scarcely touched the ground as she sped home but, undeterred, she did indeed set about finding a new supplier. She'd been in tighter corners in her life, she told herself crossly, and she sure as hell meant to get out of this one.

It proved more difficult than she'd expected but finally she succeeded in discovering a firm out Salford way who could provide her with good, non-utility furniture at a reasonable price.

'It won't be easy,' she told Benny who, not unnaturally, objected to this decision, 'but I mean to become independent again. It was a mistake to tie ourselves up so closely with Hubert. It'll be a struggle but if we pull our horns in a bit, we can soon pay off what we owe him and then we'll be free.'

They were seated in the front parlour of number 32, relaxing after a substantial Sunday lunch. While Charlie took his usual nap, Polly was happily dangling her grandson on her lap. Baby Matt had his mother's lovely cornflower blue eyes which had not darkened at all; coupled with his father's brown hair and sturdy build, he'd break hearts one day she was sure. Polly tickled the baby under his chin, making him erupt into giggles.

Benny was shaking his head. 'And what if he sends his credit custom elsewhere? How would we manage then? Take on another supplier if you must, Mam, but don't sack Hubert.'

Polly felt a measure of happiness despite her worries over the business, because her son had seemed more content of late, much more settled and mature. She touched the baby's nose with her own, making him gurgle with fresh laughter. 'Mebbe I'll look for a new credit trader an' all. Hubert Clarke isn't the only one.'

'No, but he's the one with power in this neck of the woods. Make no mistake about that.' Benny lifted his son from Polly, deciding it was time for his afternoon nap and perhaps too much excitement would prevent him from sleeping.

'You're a good father,' Polly told him fondly as he changed the child's nappy, preparatory to putting him down.

'Aye, that's because he's all I've got, which is why I want to have summat to leave him one day, don't I?' Benny warned as he stuck the nappy pin in place, taking care to keep one hand protectively against the baby's plump tummy. 'I'm not sure I trust Hubert any more than you do, but don't push him too far, that's all I'm saying. For now, at least, we need his business.'

Much as it might grieve her to admit it, the point was valid.

When Hubert heard of Polly's new supplier, he got out his fine Wolseley car and had Ron drive the mile or two to Salford to see him, just for a quiet word. The next day a van drove up in front of Benny's shop and the goods which had been so recently delivered were all collected up again and taken away. Polly was furious.

'If this is war, won't I be the one to win it?' she cried, pounding her clenched fists on a brand new mahogany table so that Benny had to grasp her hands before she marked it.

'Just remember we're in this together. He did Belinda few favours in the past.' And mother and son's glances locked in a grim promise of unity.

Polly was fortunate and found another supplier, in Ordsall this time, one who seemed only too eager to deliver a shipment of kitchen tables and chairs. Two weeks later he called at the shop on Deansgate personally and asked for them to be returned. Benny ranted and raved at the man but was told their credit rating had not come up to scratch, that the word had been put about that Polly was in hock to Councillor Clarke. Like it or not, they were stuck with Hubert and she'd have to accept that.

Desperate to find a solution, Polly went again to her bank manager to explain how well her carpet manufacturing was doing, for all it was new and with a long way to go before it did anything more than break even. But, more important, how the retail side of the business was draining away all her resources through overstocking she couldn't seem to control, poor quality furniture they couldn't sell, and an exclusive contract she had no way to get out of except with hard cash. 'He seems to think he can deliver what he likes and refuses to take the stuff back when it doesn't sell. I've called a halt to payments but he's turned nasty.' After some hours of tough negotiating, the manager agreed to lend her the sum she required, though not a penny more.

'There you are,' Polly announced with no small degree of triumph as she slapped the settlement cheque down on Hubert's polished desk. He barely glanced at it, made no move to pick it up, then smiling up at her said, 'And where's the interest?'

Polly stared at him, dumbfounded. 'Interest? What interest?'

'On the loan. You surely didn't imagine that I'd given you free rein on my money for nowt, did you?'

'You said the loan was interest-free.'

'Have you got that in writing?' And of course she hadn't. Hubert Clarke, Polly realised, had been very clever, very clever indeed, taking full advantage of their grief over Belinda and other personal problems which had distracted them. She snatched back her cheque and left his office before she did him actual physical violence.

*

Some few weeks later, Hubert was driving home in his Wolseley. The smell of coal dust was strong on the night air as he drove along Liverpool Road, but within the confines of his motor he inhaled with satisfaction the aroma of leather and a good cigar. He didn't usually indulge while he was driving but he was feeling particularly in need of solace this evening. He'd already spent an hour with Myra but that hadn't helped calm him as it usually did, his mind not on the task in hand, as it were. Perhaps he was growing a little bored with her. She didn't seem quite so welcoming as she used to, always asking him if Joanna was missing Belinda. Ridiculous woman.

Nor was he satisfied with the way his business affairs were progressing. Ron, seated beside him in the front passenger seat, had just informed him that Polly was now going round the Manchester hotels trying to win a contract to supply them with carpets. She was canny that one. Never missed a trick.

The Pride family should have buckled long since beneath the pressure he was applying. He'd made sure he sent them nowt but rubbish, as well as stuff that had failed to sell anywhere else, yet still the blasted woman hung on. Maybe she was making more brass out of her carpet manufacturing than he'd realised. If so, it'd happen be a good idea to put a few spokes in that wheel as well.

He rubbed the cigar between finger and thumb, enjoying

the expensive aroma as he turned various ideas over in his head, then clamped it between his teeth as he changed gear and negotiated the corner into Deansgate. The simplest were always the best.

'Could you get inside that warehouse of hers?'

Ron gave a snort of contempt. 'Oh, aye. I can get in anywhere, me.'

Hubert smiled. 'Funny thing about the weaving industry. It never learns, does it? Spends a fortune on fancy new looms, but no matter how well they weave, whether it be coats or carpets, they still mek a lot of waste. Makes you wonder, don't it, if the folk as runs these places know just how dangerous it is to leave oily waste lying about in a weaving shed? Or even in an old warehouse.'

Ron swivelled his head round to consider his father for a long moment in silence. Then his narrow lips split into what might be called a grin, making him look rather like a lizard after it had caught its dinner. 'Aye,' he said. 'Dangerous stuff, oily waste. Owt can happen to it.'

Chapter Twenty-three

The papers were full of the Royal wedding. They spoke of the Princess's beautiful ivory gown, her radiant loveliness, the rose petals which showered the bride and groom. They described the cheering crowds who crowded the route and waited at the gates of Broadlands to welcome them on honeymoon. Everyone in the whole country seemed to find something to cheer about so far as Lucy could see. She even caught some of the excitement herself for hadn't she too found romance and, given half a chance, could be as radiant as any royal princess for all she must meet her 'prince' in a seedy hotel instead of a palace?

Unfortunately Lucy's 'prince' didn't seem to agree with her. She'd never seen Michael so upset and no amount of seduction or teasing on her part would mollify him. On the night when all the country was celebrating with parties and fireworks they had their worst quarrel of all. His voice rose to such an alarming pitch that Lucy felt quite certain half the hotel must be listening to their squabble.

'You say that you love me, that you can hardly bear for Tom to touch you. Yet you stay with him, day after day, week after week. If you loved me half as much as you say, then you'd up and tell him so, straight out, ask for a divorce and leave him. Then we could be wed.'

'You know I'd leave him if I could, Michael. I do love you only . . .'

'Show me. Prove it.' Distress creased his face, making him, in that instant, look almost old. 'By next Thursday when you come, I'll expect you to have made it plain to him. I've said I'll wait for you, Lucy, but not forever. I've had enough. If I can't have you right and decent, then I don't want you at all.'

It nearly broke her heart to see him so upset and two huge tears squeezed out from beneath her lashes. 'You don't mean that.'

'I do mean it, Lucy. I've had enough of this hole and corner affair.' And she saw that he had.

'All right, I'll think about it. I promise.' She longed suddenly to tell him about the baby, might well have done so then had his next words not robbed her of the fragile remnants of her courage.

'This is the end, Lucy. It's time for you to choose. That's all I ask – him or me. Make your mind up one way or the other.'

*

When the day for their usual meeting came round, Lucy woke with fresh determination in her heart. All week the fever of excitement had been growing in her. Michael was right. They couldn't go on like this forever. She felt a new resolve to put her life in order once and for all. She would first of all tell Michael about the baby and then the pair of them would go to Tom and explain the whole situation. She couldn't think why they hadn't thought of this before. It would be so much easier to face him together. Of course if she'd ever properly explained to him about Tom's violent mood swings, then Michael might well have offered. Tom surely wouldn't attempt to bully her if Michael were there?

The two of them might have to go away, of course, somewhere other than Castlefield or even Manchester. But she no longer cared where she went so long as she had her children with her, and Michael. The decision had been made.

She put on her prettiest pink dress, the one cut on the cross which so enhanced the neatness of her figure. She was three and a half months gone and there was as yet little alteration to her slender waist or the firm flatness of her stomach despite her worries and fussing with a corset. For the first time since realising she was pregnant Lucy felt happy, which only added to the surge of excitement she always felt when she was going to meet Michael.

'Where are you going tonight, Mam?' Sarah Jane asked, coming into the bedroom as Lucy was getting ready, Sean trailing behind her, thumb in mouth.

'I'm off out with my friend Joan,' Lucy fibbed, not meeting her children's collective gaze through the mirror. She tapped Sean's hand and the thumb came out with a loud sucking noise.

'I thought she was called Sally?'

'I've more than one friend.' Lucy made a mental note to be more careful. She understood now why they said liars should have good memories.

Sarah Jane flung herself on to her parents' bed, chin propped in hand, and watched with interest as Lucy applied Hollywood red lipstick to her rosebud mouth. Sean scrambled up beside her, sliding his thumb back in, eyes wide. 'Do you ever see Michael?' Sarah Jane innocently enquired, a wistful expression on her pale face.

The lipstick slipped from Lucy's fingers, leaving a trail of crimson over the corner of her mouth. She began to scrub at it with a licked finger. 'And why would I?'

'He never comes to see us any more. I thought he was our friend.'

'He used to take me fishing,' Sean said, speaking around the thumb. Lucy again removed it and worried why he'd recently taken up this babyish habit. She tucked her children up in bed, read them the story of the Gingerbread Man, and then, acutely aware she was late, half ran downstairs. As usual Tom was in his chair by the fire, reading the sports pages. He made no move as she shrugged on her best brown coat and carefully pinned on an evidently new and very perky little scarlet hat.

'I'm off out then,' she said, kissing the air an inch above the top of his head. Tom neither moved nor spoke. Lucy took a step towards the door. She wanted to call and speak to Polly first and if she didn't hurry she'd miss the seven o'clock bus and then Michael would think she wasn't coming. 'I won't be late. It's the first house pictures we're going to. You'll mind the kids?' No response. 'Are you listening, you?' And when he still didn't respond, she turned and left the house.

Only then did Tom fold his paper and get up from his seat. He hovered in the shadow of the front door while he watched Lucy hurry up the street and go into her mother's house. She was barely in there more than a second or two before she was out again, half running this time, in the direction of the canal basin and maybe the warehouse. Tom collected his jacket and followed her, though maintaining a safe distance.

Lucy hurried down Pansy Street, scarlet hat askew, coat flying open in her haste to put her decision into effect. She skirted Potato Wharf, barely glancing at the rushing sluice, and clattered over the iron foot bridge on her way to Polly's warehouse near Knott's Mill. Ahead of her were the railway bridges and viaduct that spanned the canal basin, a section she loved during the day when she could watch the comings and goings of brightly painted barges and folk about their business. But now, with dusk falling, she kept up a brisk pace, the thunder of train wheels going over just at the moment she passed beneath seeming to rattle the teeth in her head.

'Spare a penny, luv, or an 'apenny'll do.' A voice from the shadows beneath the arches made her jump and she hurried on, drawing her coat close, starting to button it. The November night was cold and dank and she wished, not for the first time, that Polly spent more time at home and less at the warehouse. A drunk with a whiskery chin lurched out from behind a pillar so that by the time she reached Castle Street Lucy was running flat out, arriving at the side door of the warehouse, built into the filled-in arch, quite out of breath.

It was unlocked and she wrenched it open, the shadows seeming to leap out at her as she stepped inside. She heard a sound, a rustling, and halted in her tracks, staring about with eyes grown wide with fright. The entire warehouse was shrouded in darkness, the only light coming from her mother's office. She glanced back over her shoulder, thinking the noise must have come from outside, and quickly pulled the door shut behind her. The darkness became even more intense and the looms reared around her like black apparitions in the dusty shafts of moonlight that seeped in through semi-circular windows set high in the walls. Lucy shuddered, then took a step out into the void. As she hesitantly negotiated a room littered with obstacles at every step, the sound of her heels echoed hollowly on the wooden flooring. So loud were they in her ears that had there been any other sound, she would not have heard it.

Polly set down the wad of papers she'd been studying when Lucy entered the office and stood up, arms akimbo, to consider her daughter. Lucy saw at once that she was wearing her most disapproving frown, not at all what she'd hoped for.

'Saints preserve us, what is it now? I can see something terrible has happened by the look on yer face.'

It took no time at all for Lucy to pour out her guilty secret, for the burden of it had weighed heavy on her of late. In order to quench any expressions of joy or attempts at congratulations she quickly added that it was Michael who was the father and not Tom. Polly showed her disapproval only by a slight widening of her eyes.

'And what does Tom think of all this?'

'He doesn't know, and you mustn't tell him.'

'He needs to be told.'

'I know and I'll tell him myself, as soon as I've spoken to Michael. He doesn't know either.' Lucy let it all pour out then, all her disappointment in the marriage, her efforts to please Tom in the beginning, quickly stifled by his selfish and cold attitude towards her. Polly responded as Lucy would have expected, with exhortations for her to show more patience, to allow for the fact that this man had spent years as a POW so how could he be expected to behave normally? Guilt crept through Lucy, making her feel small and cheap. She could see that her mother was doing her best to hide her shock but Lucy could sense her disapproval in the stiff way Polly's head moved on her neck, the pursing of the lips and the way her hands were folded tightly together.

'You neglect your children because of this foolish passion with yer fancy man. Running wild they are. And have ye thought of the babby? Ye'd be making it into a bastard if you choose Michael as the father. And, to my way of thinking, that's what ye would be doing – choosing. For how can ye be sure?'

Lucy hung her head, saying nothing, for how could she deny the truth of this? What proof did she have either way?

'Shame on ye, lass, fer such wickedness. I'm disappointed in ye, so I am. Didn't I think ye'd show more sense and be kind to yer poor husband when he comes home to ye at last?' Somewhere in the depths of the building there came a scraping sound, as if a door or window had blown in on a draught. For an instant Lucy was aware of it and then forgot it in her distress.

Tears ran down her cheeks at her mother's lack of understanding. Nobody did understand, but then, how could she explain the misery of living with Tom – the long accusing silences, his volatile moods and almost dehumanising control over her which assumed that he alone was capable of making decisions, as if she was an idiot with no mind of her own. And then there was the callous way he used her body which made her shudder whenever she thought of it. How could she face the embarrassment of telling her own mother all of that?

'If ye take my advice, ye'll kiss goodbye to Michael Hopkins, however lovely a man he might be, for it wouldn't be right. Don't tell him about the babby. What good would it do, except to bring more pain. Ye've not been with Tom a year yet. Give him a proper chance. Wouldn't he just love the chance to be a dad, a proper one this time, there every day to watch the child grow up? Ye owe him that at least, do ye not?'

Lucy felt herself driven almost to the limits of her endurance. Why couldn't somebody be on her side, instead of always taking Tom's? It was perfectly clear Mam wasn't going to find it easy to accept a daughter who'd given up on her marriage. But then, having been fortunate in both her husbands, how could Polly ever hope to understand? To all outward appearances Tom was an impeccable and caring husband, always smartly turned out and mindful of his family. Only she, his wife, was aware of his darker side, of a simmering anger that nothing seemed to mellow, and how often he seemed to be poised on the brink of explosion.

Lucy pushed her face up close to Polly's. 'I owe him

nothing. You don't understand – Tom *lies*! All right, I've no proof, but I know he lies all the same. I've only his word that he was anywhere near a POW camp. Who knows where he really was or what he's been up to all those years? Half the war he was missing, and more than a year after it, and not a single word. Nothing but silence. Michael is good to me, he's kind and gentle, and I can hardly bear for Tom to touch me . . . It's no good.' Her voice broke on a great hiccuping sob. 'However long I stay with him, I'll never feel the way about him I should.'

She began to sob in earnest now and, seeing her great distress, Polly put her arms about Lucy, a tide of sympathy and love for her daughter breaking down the barriers of disapproval.

'Aw, m'cushla, don't I know what it is to be in love, to have no other thought in yer head?' This expression of sympathy might have brought forth more details about the dark side of her marriage, and Lucy's secret fears, were it not for the crackle of erupting flames as they shot through the open doors opposite, and the smell of dense smoke suddenly becoming alarmingly evident to them both.

Lucy arrived home in the early hours of the following morning in great distress. Tom was waiting in the kitchen with the kettle boiling though it was past two, just as if he'd expected her to come in at any minute, but then he'd probably been half out of his mind with worry over why she was out so late. It was a wonder he wasn't standing at the door with sleeves rolled up and fists at the ready, she thought. Instead, he was surprisingly kind to her when he heard about the fire, and as tears of shock rained down her smoke-blackened cheeks, Lucy told more than she had meant to.

It was Tom who helped her out of her soot-blackened clothes, washed her face and limbs and dressed her in a warmed nightgown, just as if she were Sarah Jane. Then he assisted her up the stairs to bed, all the while explaining he'd known all along about the coming baby. Hadn't he heard her throwing up in the sink each morning? He was glad, he told her. He'd always wanted another child. They stood at the top of the stairs and he told her how delighted he was of this chance to be a proper father at last. He made no mention of Michael Hopkins, and neither did she. His only reference to her evening out was to enquire mildly if she'd ever got to the pictures. Lucy dolefully shook her head, then put her hand to it for it throbbed horribly. 'Sally wouldn't mind. She'd go in and see it anyway.'

His fingers closed about her arm. 'I thought you were going with Joan. Forgotten your friend's name already?'

'No, no. Both – Sally and – Joan were hoping to go, but at the last minute Sally had to cry off,' Lucy hastily fabricated.

'So poor *Joan* would be on her own?'

'Yes, yes – that's right. Joan would be on her own. God, I'm tired.' She made to move towards the bedroom but he was still holding her arm.

'You'll have to go round tomorrow and explain.'

'Yes, I will. We'll talk then, shall we?'

'And no one else was expected to be there, at the pictures?'

'No, no one. Just the – three of us.'

It was as she turned to step thankfully into the bedroom and the oblivion of sleep that it happened. Tom's attitude suddenly changed. One moment he was stroking her arm and smiling sympathetically at her, the next he was spitting his fury directly into her face. '*You're a liar!* I don't believe a bloody *word!*' And then she was falling backwards, over and over, down the narrow stairs. She had time only to wrap her arms instinctively about herself to protect the coming child as her hips and knees bumped and jarred on every step.

Seconds later she lay at the bottom, shaken and crying, having cracked her head on the door post, and Tom was beside her, cradling her in his arms, murmuring words of remorse and sympathy, stroking her bleeding head and saying he'd never meant to hurt her. 'Something just comes over me, Lucy. I can't seem to help myself.' Then somehow her tears had dried and it was she who comforted him. But in that moment everything changed, a turning point had been reached in her mind.

She assured Tom that she realised it had been an accident, that he'd meant her no real harm. Nevertheless she insisted on spending the rest of that night in her children's bed on the grounds that her head was aching so badly she might disturb him with her restlessness. In truth, only the warmth of her children's loving bodies was able to ease the horror of the night's events. Once, during that endless night, she crept to the basin that stood on the chest of drawers and vomited into it, her one fear that the fall had in some way harmed the baby. She could only pray that it had not.

Exhausted as she was by the night's events, sleep deserted her the moment she lay down again. Tom was a consummate liar. She felt his behaviour tonight had proved that. He'd given every impression that he believed this was to be his child, with his soft words and caring gestures, yet his actions in deliberately thrusting her down the stairs proved he didn't believe this to be the case at all. Lucy was shaking with emotion, shivering with shock, yet not for a moment dare she venture downstairs for a cup of tea or a warm by the embers of the kitchen fire. She was too afraid. Eyes wide open, she lay staring into the darkness, her thoughts turning to Michael for the first time, like an angel of light in her head.

He would have been disappointed, of course, that she hadn't managed to get away but he'd understand, and soon it wouldn't matter for they'd be together always. Thinking of his love made the shock ebb slowly away and a warm sensation flow through her veins as she came to a decision. She realised now that she could never find the courage to tell Tom she was leaving him, not face to face. She saw that there was only one course open to her. Tomorrow, while he was at work, she'd pack her things, hers and the children's, and go to Michael. Then they would indeed run away together. Far, far away from Pansy Street and the gossips of Castlefield.

It seemed no more than a matter of moments before she was dragging herself out of bed, putting on fresh clothes; her husband already seated at the kitchen table by the time she reached it, waiting for his breakfast as he scanned the morning paper, just as if it were any normal day.

'There's nowt in about the fire,' he said, just as if she'd made it all up.

'It happened too late for them to print anything.' Lucy crossed to the sink to fill the kettle. Every muscle screamed with pain, even her bones ached as if she'd fought the fire herself instead of simply helping Polly carry out as much stock as they could before it took a proper hold, which was precious little as it had spread frighteningly fast. She knew she must be covered in bruises. 'It'll be in the *Evening News*. I'll go and see Mam this morning. She'll be in a terrible state.'

Lucy cooked kippers for Tom's breakfast, handed him his hat and coat, even let him kiss her cheek as usual when he left the house. He made no mention of the baby, or her 'accidental' fall down the stairs, and neither did she. Exhaustion dragged at her, fogging her mind so that she couldn't think properly, making her eyes feel like burned holes in her head.

When he'd gone she forced herself into action: hastily packed bags with clumsy fingers, stuffed clothes in anyhow, ironed or not, and instead of taking the children to school, walked and dragged and hustled them to the end of the street where she knocked on Minnie Hopkins's door. Michael, she knew, would be delighted to look after all three of them.

It was Minnie who opened the door, holding a hand-kerchief to her face. Lucy saw at once that she'd been crying. Her first thought was that Minnie had heard about the fire but then how could she, it surely wasn't generally known yet, and why would it make her cry? Nobody had been hurt. And then inside her a creeping fear swelled and began to fill her entire body.

'What is it? Where's Michael? Dear God, *no!*' And somehow it didn't surprise her in the least to see Minnie open her toothless mouth and wail that he had gone, vowing never to return.

They crowded into Minnie's kitchen and listened to her sad tale. 'He was all I had, tha knows. He weren't really me nephew at all. He were me son,' she confessed on a great gulping sob. 'Me mam and dad were ashamed of me fall from grace and were going to send me to an 'ome for wayward girls. So I up and run away. Never went back.'

'Oh, Minnie, I didn't know.' Lucy could hardly take in this story as she sat in a state of disbelief. It couldn't be true. He wouldn't go off and leave her. Yet she knew that he had. Hadn't he told her to choose? And last night, the very time when she was to give him her decision, she'd missed their date completely because of the fire. But he wouldn't know why she'd failed to turn up. He would believe that she'd made her choice, and that it wasn't him.

'Why should tha know?' Minnie was saying. 'Nobody's business but mine. Least said, soonest mended.'

'But how did you survive, a young girl on your own?' Lucy now found her sluggish mind racing, half of it listening to Minnie's tale, the rest of it desperately seeking a solution to her own dilemma.

'Oh, it were 'ard at first. I near starved. Lived rough for a year or two, but I weren't the only one in t'same pickle. I met other girls. We got by. Then I found a job working on the wharves here, packing, and Michael used to help me. He were only small like but he were a right little Trojan. Wife of my gaffer spotted him and told me it were no place to tek a child. She were the woman what owned this house. Come down in t'world she had but still had a bob or two. She set me on as housemaid and told me I could fetch him wi' me. I said he were me sister's child, though I never had no sister. Fer t'lad's sake it were better if I made out I were his aunt. Saves all that nasty name-calling. But he were t'best thing that ever happened to me.' Despite her tough words, Minnie's faded eyes again filled with tears which she quickly mopped with a large white handkerchief, blowing her nose vigorously.

'Oh, Minnie, I'm so sorry.'

'He said thee'd quarrelled last time tha were together, that thee refused to . . .' She ran out of words, of breath even, as choking sobs finally doused her self-control.

Filled with a new, deeper sense of shame and guilt for robbing this old woman of her one and only joy in life, Lucy ran to put her arms about her, but sensing the rigid shoulders, the unyielding spine, hurried instead to grab the kettle and began to issue orders, as if someone had been taken ill and they must all rally round to deal with the emergency.

'Sarah Jane, fetch the cups. Sean, get the biscuit barrel.' Something sweet for shock, wasn't that right? But it was only the children, bewildered and exchanging anxious glances, who dipped into it. At least the treat kept them quiet and happy while Lucy strove to think. Poor Minnie didn't even have the heart to suck one of her favourite pear drops.

She'd no idea where Michael might have gone. No, she didn't think it would be back to the RAF, because of the missing foot. 'They wouldn't have him, would they?' No, she didn't know the names of any of his friends outside Castlefield, or even Pansy Street for that matter. The rumours about him being a conchie had done their work. And she didn't expect him to go back to his old house either since it'd been flattened by a bomb. It was as they talked that the true reality of her situation hit Lucy and the tears slid down her own cheeks. Michael was gone, she knew not where. She was carrying his child, of that she was quite certain, and since she'd no intention of ever returning to her husband, she knew she must bear it alone, just as Minnie had done.

Chapter Twenty-four

Hubert was satisfied at last that events were swinging his way, he could feel the tide of his luck turning. His financial situation was growing stronger by the day, greatly assisted by having taken over a small but significant clothing manufacturer which thus far had stubbornly evaded making proper payments on a loan. Taking control of the company would make him a far greater profit in the long run, but then that had been his object from the start. Yet another case of someone else's grey cloud providing him with a silver lining. All most satisfactory. Some people collected works of art. Hubert preferred more substantial artefacts, like properties or businesses. And now, with his next victim already picked out, he lit a cigar and sat back in his smart leather chair with a wide smile to await the turn of events.

He was interrupted in his reverie by the strident clang of the door bell. Hubert waited, one ear cocked, for

Joanna to answer it as she always did. The door bell clanged again.

'Damnation. What's wrong with the woman?' True, losing Belinda had proved to be a severe blow to his wife and she hadn't been the same since. Never in the darned house for one thing, her excuse being that what was the point in making a fuss about meals and her garden and such when there were only the two of them? A state of affairs which now would never change.

He clamped the cigar between his teeth and strode to the door, flinging it open with a growled, 'Well?'

He was mildly surprised to find his son-in-law standing on the doorstep, a gurgling baby propped on one hip – like some gyppo who couldn't afford a pram, and despite the fact it must be well past the child's bedtime. Class, Hubert told himself, would always out.

'I've come to ask if you'd owt to do wi' that fire?' Benny bluntly announced. 'Because if you had, I'd like to know why, since it damages your grandson as much as anybody?'

Hubert was momentarily startled. By heck, but Ron had been quick off the mark for once. He hoped it had been a bad one. He covered his confusion by studying the child which seemed to be surprisingly well cared for, smartly dressed in a blue knitted jacket and balaclava. Joanna had dreamed of grandchildren, yet couldn't quite bring herself to accept Belinda had actually given her one. No more could he. It came to him in that moment that there was one obvious way he could curb his wife's restlessness and make her happy for once.

'Now then, Benny lad. As you say, why would I harm this little chap or the business he's to inherit? All I can do now I've lost Belinda is to ensure her son gets what would've been hers by right.' Hubert really had no wish to be harangued by this ruffian, whom he'd never liked. Nor had he any intention of allowing the Pride family to keep either their business or his grandson. Little Matthew's inheritance would come from quite a different source. He'd easily get custody of the child, for Joanna's sake, when the moment came. After he'd taken his revenge for what this rogue had done to Hubert's beloved daughter.

Time, it seemed, had warmed his memory of his relationship with Belinda and now he viewed it as a close one, spoiled only by Benny and not by his own machinations. He'd conveniently forgotten his part in her eviction from the shop; the very reason she'd given birth in a back street with no medical assistance until it was too late. The fault, in his mind, lay entirely with this no-good piece of dross who was cluttering up his doorstep.

Benny was still glowering, as if trying to decide whether to believe his father-in-law or not. 'If you had any hand in what went on last night, don't think I won't find out and do summat about it.'

''Oo dusta think thee is, to threaten me?' Hubert's carefully practised diction always deserted him under stress, revealing that, self-made man though he may be, underneath he was no more than a step removed from his lowly origins in Quay Street where his mother used to take in washing to earn an honest crust, her one ambition to get her only son a better life. And hadn't he clawed and cheated his way up the ladder of success, right to the bloody top, if only to prove she hadn't wasted her efforts? He certainly had no intention of being knocked off his perch by this bit of nowt. 'I'll thank you to take yer mucky boots off my doorstep. It's a pity, to my mind, that I ever let them stand on it at all. I should've knocked yer clock off the first time I clapped eyes on thee. Then my Belinda might've been alive today instead of . . .'

He got no further. Snapping to attention, Benny took a step forward to shake his fist furiously less than an inch from Hubert's nose. 'Damn you to hell, Hubert Clarke. Me mam's right. You *are* the lowest of the low, whether you set that fire or not.' In that one moment he was very much the soldier with a power he understood and wasn't above using. The ferocity of the action so startled Hubert that he instinctively flinched away while Matt, alarmed by the anger in his dad's voice, started to howl. 'Mek no mistake, our family sticks together. Take on one, you take on the lot.' Then, as the baby's screams rose to a higher pitch, Benny smoothed his son's head with a gentling hand, swung on his heel and marched away.

*

It took till the middle of the next day before the fire brigade was satisfied the blaze was completely out. When they'd finally gone, all Polly's pent-up fury erupted in a tide of hot temper. 'Will ye look at this? What the fire hasn't ruined, the water has,' she cried, arms outstretched, encompassing the awful scene. The new looms were a mass of charred blackened metal while almost every scrap of wool, every bobbin and shuttle, every yard of carefully woven carpet, was destroyed, for they'd managed to save little. Over the whole building hung a stinking pall of smoke. It looked as if the Luftwaffe had been over and dropped their last bomb. Polly stood in puddles of water and looked about her in desperation for someone to blame. Her eye fell upon poor Benny and she at once laid into him for not having removed the waste as he was supposed to do.

'We were lucky I happened to be there at the time, dealing with some bills,' she ranted. 'Otherwise, saints preserve us, the whole building would have come down. Have you no sense in that head of yours?'

She regretted the words almost as soon as they were out of her mouth. The accusation was unfair and they both knew it. Benny wasn't the only one responsible for clearing away the waste wool. He worked as hard as she did on the business, sometimes even harder for, apart from little Matt, it was his only solace. She knew that he was desperate to fill every moment of his day with work,

even if it meant carrying the baby about on his hip while
he did it. This was the only way, he'd admitted to her in
one unguarded moment, that when night came he could
lay his head on his pillow and sleep, instead of thinking
about Belinda till the pain swelled in his chest so that he
could scarce breathe.

Polly quickly apologised, putting her arms about his
great shoulders and hugging him, for wasn't he her lovely
boy? But the accusation left a sour taste in both their
mouths. To justify her anger and prove the seriousness of
their position, she showed him the parlous state of the
accounts. 'We're over-borrowed and overstocked and don't
I know whose fault that is. No matter what I do to try to
get out of this mess, Hubert Clarke sticks his oar in and
stops me.'

She could see by the thin white line about his tightly
compressed lips that Benny still couldn't make up his mind
whether to trust his father-in-law or not. 'It's true he's an
awkward old sod and he and Belinda didn't get on too well.
But he's lost her, for God's sake. All he wants now is to
help build a sound business to pass on to his only grandson. He told me so hissel.' Benny picked up a hunk of
scorched wool and crumbled it in his hand. 'Some her-
itage.'

Polly was about to express her doubts that Hubert was
capable of such a sentiment when a voice from the door
interrupted her thoughts. 'The boy's right. My grandson is

more important to me than you might think. But isn't all of this partly your own fault, Polly Pride, for buying them looms?'

'Aye,' she agreed, turning to face her accuser. 'And my fault too for getting involved with you, Hubert Clarke, in the first place. But, like the phoenix, we'll rise from the ashes, see if we don't.'

'What with? Thee's insured, are thee lass?'

'I am.'

'But will that be enough? Insurance folk can be a touch choosy how much they cough up in a case like this. By heck,' he said, walking about and poking at charred beams with the point of his stick, coughing when he caused a shower of sparks and soot to fall all about him. 'Proper pickle this, eh? I thought I'd come over and express my sympathy, as it were. But I can see that even when you've cleaned the mess up, you've to re-equip and restock. Cost a mint, that will. And then there's the lost business. Never rains but it pours, eh? 'Course, if there's any way I can help . . .' he offered, smoothing the dust from his fine worsted suit. 'Tha's only to say.'

'We'll manage, thank you.' Polly suffered Hubert's gloating presence for the longest half hour she could remember before he finally took his leave, coldly refusing his offer of the services of his odious son to help with the clearing up. Benny was for giving Ron a 'seeing to' but Polly managed to persuade her son against such a reckless act.

Hubert had no sooner gone than Lucy arrived, looking wan and slightly dishevelled, as no doubt they all were. Polly went to her at once and mother and daughter put their arms about each other, indulging in a quiet weep, but it was Lucy who was the first to rally.

'Come on, Mam. You tell us what to do and we'll do it. We can't be beaten by this.' She'd come to help clean up along with Polly's stalwart band of workers, all eager to do their bit. There'd be plenty of time later to think about her own problems. Minnie Hopkins was at the ready with her sweeping brush, even Uncle Nobby and Aunt Ida were there with buckets and mops – 'To swill out t'muck,' as they kept repeating. Polly could only smile with gratitude at this show of support.

Charlie too had come along to help, which caused her to huff and puff some more, telling her husband he wasn't fit enough to be out and about, let alone working in a burned out shell of a warehouse. But Charlie was adamant he was perfectly capable of helping to root through the mess and spot anything of value which might have survived.

They worked all day and the best they could salvage were a dozen or so bobbins of singed wool.

'At least it's a popular colour,' Maisie joked. 'Your favourite pink beige.'

Benny flung down the pile of spindles he'd just been sorting, not a decent one amongst them, and rubbed a tired hand over his face, blackening it even more. 'Let's go and have a jar. I reckon we all need it. Mebbe things won't look so bad then.'

But when the insurance assessor arrived the following day, his verdict was far from reassuring. The site had been examined by both the firemen and the police, he said, and without doubt arson was involved. Without actually accusing her point blank, the steely quality of his stare made it clear to Polly who he considered had set the match.

'Saints alive, you don't think . . . You can't imagine that I'd set light to me own warehouse?'

The inspector cleared his throat somewhat noisily. 'I understand you're suffering a slight financial embarrassment at present?' His expression was a mask of professional sympathy, as if inviting her to confess all.

'And who the hell has told you that?'

'It's generally bruited abroad that you've been chopping and changing suppliers, yet not settling outstanding bills. Your credit status at present, Mrs Pride, is, I believe, in a sorry state.'

'Stockton. Mrs Charlie Stockton. Polly Pride is the name I use for my business.'

'Ah, as you wish.' He managed a smile though it did not reach his eyes. 'Nevertheless, I am correct, am I not?'

Drat him, and drat the man who'd put her in this mess in the first place, but Polly could not deny it. By going about seeking new suppliers while still in debt to Hubert

Clarke, she'd made herself appear to be the guilty party.

The insurance company couldn't pay out, he explained, until after a more intensive investigation had taken place which might, he admitted, take months. The authorities still had a great deal of work on their hands assessing bomb damage and which houses could be made fit for occupation. Civilian fires were given somewhat lower priority. It was made plain to Polly that although they may not have sufficient evidence to prosecute, they were deeply suspicious and their doubts such that they could delay payment for as long as they wished. Certainly long enough to leave her business in ruins.

No matter how many hours Polly and Benny might pore over the accounts, which they did every night in the kitchen of number 32, Charlie putting in his twopennorth, nor how fervently she might plead her case with the bank manager, the truth of the matter was that Polly had more debts than she could handle, more stock than she could sell, and the only successful part of her operation, the manufacturing of carpets, was now defunct. Even her carpet cleaning and beating machines were gone, reduced to rubble in the fire. The result was indisputable. Pride Carpets was no more and all her workers were now without jobs.

'Yer mean, we're all on the cob 'n' coal?' Maisie asked.

Polly admitted that, yes, they would indeed have to collect the dole, if they couldn't find other work. 'But you'll all get yer jobs back, so you will, soon as I'm up and running again.' Didn't she know herself how hard it was to get work? Hadn't she suffered at first hand, back in the thirties, the indignity of unemployment? Not to mention the endless worry over where the next shilling was coming from to put in the gas meter.

'An 'ungry sow won't foller an empty bucket.' This from Joyce, ever blunt, revealing the doubt they all felt that Pride Carpets would ever rise again from the ashes.

'And what about us?' Charlie asked, when Polly expressed these concerns to him. 'Where will *we* find the next bob for the meter?' Which silenced her completely

So it was that when Hubert Clarke came round with his proposal, she was in no position to argue.

'Now then, Polly lass, tha might as well admit tha's done for,' he cheerfully informed her. 'But I'll not see thee go bankrupt,' he continued, smiling magnanimously, and going on to outline, in painstaking detail, how he would be willing to take over the company, generously agreeing to keep both herself and Benny on as employed managers, though admittedly the wages he could afford would be only fair to middling. 'There'll always be a place for you both in Clarke Enterprises.'

Polly felt not the slightest degree of gratitude and made no bones about telling him so, which caused him to smile all the more as he took out his pocket book and reminded her of the sum still outstanding.

'Take the blasted furniture back, why don't you? That'll

more than cover the debt, surely to God,' she said. But Hubert sadly shook his head, agreeing that he must of course take possession of her stock, but with the added interest, he explained, the furniture, even if some of it wasn't now second hand and faulty from standing in her damp shop, would barely touch a fraction of it. Besides, he very reasonably pointed out, what other choice did she have, since she couldn't afford to re-equip or restore the warehouse following the fire, nor any longer pay the rent on the shop premises?

He took over her business, lock, stock and balloon-backed chairs. Polly refused his paltry offer of a job, thereby leaving the building for the last time with nothing but her pride.

When the knock came at the door, instinct told Lucy who it would be.

'If that's our Michael . . .' Minnie cried, jumping up from the table where she'd been peeling potatoes.

Lucy pressed her gently down again. 'More likely Tom.' She was surprised that it had taken him this long to come round. The children had not been sent to school for three days and she'd been grateful for Minnie's offer of accommodation for them all until she'd made up her mind what she was to do. Much of that time Lucy had spent with Polly down at the warehouse where all she'd built up over the last two or three years seemed to be unravelling.

She too felt she was living on borrowed time, for any day now the truant officer would be sure to come round. But then, if the children went back to school, Tom could easily steal them, just to spite her. Perhaps he'd already been watching and waiting at the school gates. Her stomach churned at the thought, yet Lucy knew they couldn't hide from him forever.

'Tha doesn't have to see him,' Minnie told her.

'Best if I get it over with. Put things on a proper footing. I can't spend me life hiding in corners just because I've left me husband.' And Lucy marched to the door with head high and a determined spring in her step. Tom stood outside, as expected, hands in pockets, trilby hat pulled well down over his eyes as if he were Humphrey Bogart on a spying mission. Lucy experienced a frantic urge to laugh but managed to calm her hysteria and face him with some degree of control.

'I reckoned I'd find you here,' he said, a purr of satisfaction in his voice.

'I don't care what you say, Tom, I'm not coming home.' There, she thought, that would show him she could stand up for herself at least.

'You mun do as I say.'

She felt her cheeks grow red with annoyance. 'I will not.'

'Get yer coat on, yer comin' home with me.' He reached for her but she backed away, cringing from his touch.

'Never.'

Tom's lip curled into a sneer. It made him look even more like a stranger, one she couldn't believe she'd ever loved. 'So where's lover-boy then? Hiding under the stairs, is he? I know he's not been in to his work?'

If Lucy had been hot with anger before, now she felt herself go cold with a new fear. 'How do you know he's not been in to work? Have you been looking for him? Leave Michael alone, for God's sake, d'you hear? What he does, where he goes, is his affair, not yours. *Leave him be!*'

Tom only laughed, a sound that chilled her while Lucy fought to steady her breathing, keep a grip on her frayed nerves. 'I did my best to be a good wife to you and if you'd thought of me once during the days of your escape, just long enough to let me know you were alive that is, then I might well have been here waiting for you. It wasn't my fault I fell in love with Michael. That's what lonely women do during wartime when they think their husband is dead – they turn to someone else. And when you did come home, were you kind to me? No. Did you make love to me with any sign of gentleness? *No!* Did you ever consider my feelings for one minute – like whether I wanted to carry on working, for instance. *No, no, no!* Now Michael's gone and I've lost him all because of you.'

'Stop yer hysterics and get on home this minute. That's my child yer carrying and I don't want it harmed,' Tom calmly informed her, as if he had every right.

'I pray every day that it isn't yours. *Drat you, Tom*

Shackleton!' She became aware of Minnie standing beside her gently touching her arm, and that she must have been shouting, for neighbours in the street had stopped to listen and stare.

'That's enough, lass. Tha's med thee point. Go home, lad. Best leave her alone for now.' And Minnie drew the sobbing Lucy back into the house and shut the door.

But Tom did not go home. He strode along Pansy Street, knocked loudly on the door to number 32 and asked to see Polly. When she came, anxiety clouding her lovely eyes at sight of him, Tom burst into noisy tears. 'You'll never guess what she's gone and done now . . .'

Never having seen a grown man cry before, Polly was appalled. 'Aw, Tom, whatever is it? Ye poor lamb. Come in, lad, come in.' And she took her weeping son-in-law into the warm heart of her home.

Polly came round to number 179 hot foot, wishing her children would just get on and live a quiet, orderly life instead of being such a trial to her. Minnie, having made them a pot of tea, quietly withdrew. 'If it isn't one of ye, it's the other, so it is,' Polly accused Lucy. 'What's got into ye, leaving yer husband? Have you run mad? They'll carry you off to Prestwich, so they will.'

'I'm not staying with a brute of a man just to make life simpler for you,' Lucy quietly responded, her patience very nearly exhausted.

'Brute is he now, the poor soul? Ye've not shown near enough patience, nor given him time to settle after all he's . . .'

Lucy flapped a hand wildly in the air to stop her mother. 'Don't tell me again how much he's suffered. What about me? Don't you want to know how much *I've* suffered?' And she related how once Tom had slapped her, was frequently losing his temper, and finally had pushed her down the stairs. 'You don't know what it was like living with him,' Lucy said, tears brimming over despite her best efforts to prevent them.

Polly folded her arms and shook her head in disbelief. 'And doesn't Tom tell a different tale?' Her voice changed to her soft Irish brogue. 'It's sorry I am that it's come to this the pair of you, but didn't I warn you, m'cushla? No man will tolerate a cheating wife for long, war or no war, so is it any wonder if he loses his paddy now and then?' She reached out to take her daughter's hand but Lucy snatched it away before she even touched it.

'What's he been telling you?'

Polly sighed. 'He says you confessed about the babby and that he forgave you. More credit to him for his generosity for there's many wouldn't be so understanding. He says he asked you again and again to give up yer fancy man and ye refused, eventually throwing yourself down the stairs in a fit of hysteria.'

Lucy stared at her mother out of eyes grown black with

shock as the pupils dilated. 'So you believe every word he tells you but nothing I say? I'm just an hysterical adulterer, is that the way of it? Right, so we know where we stand, don't we?' She marched to the front door and pulled it open, clearly prepared to throw her own mother out in the street. 'I think you'd best go before you say something you might afterwards regret. We'll talk another time when we're both calmer.'

'Lucy love, I'm only thinking of you.' Polly held on to her daughter this time, determined to have her say, oblivious of how she'd been the unwitting victim of Tom's lies every bit as much as her daughter had. She warned Lucy of loneliness, of the difficulties of trying to bring up a family alone. Hadn't she gone through all of that herself until she'd been lucky enough to meet Charlie? In their exchange of heated words she came close to saying that it served Lucy right if Michael had indeed gone forever, for having played fast and loose with both the men in her life, hadn't she now lost the pair of them? And then she recognised the fierce flash of fury in her daughter's eyes and quietly took her leave.

Chapter Twenty-five

Minnie was waiting for Lucy in the kitchen with a pan of milk warming on the gas stove. She mixed cocoa and watched while Lucy drank every drop. 'Yer eyes look like two lumps of coal in a snow drift. So it's your turn to be up the spout, eh?' she said, stating the obvious. 'Is it our Michael's? Aye, reckoned it must be. Does he know?'

Lucy shook her head.

'Thought not. In't like our Michael to run from responsibility. Well, don't worry about that daft bugger of a husband of yours. He couldn't knock t'skin off a custard.'

Lucy wiped the tears from her face with the flat of her hand, starting to laugh despite the fact that her eyes were welling up with fresh tears all over again at the sympathy in the old woman's voice. 'What am I to do, Minnie?'

'We'll think o' summat, but not now, eh, chuck? Here, have a pear drop.' And she popped one in Lucy's mouth, making her smile. 'I'll be gone no more'n a twenty minutes or so but I must go and see your mam. She were upset too, tha knows, and she's got her hands full 'as Polly. Tha should stop sharpening swords on each other and start counting yer blessings. Will you come round yon wi' me, and apologise?' But when Lucy made no move, Minnie heaved a sigh. Pulling her old brown shawl over her head, she continued, 'Eeh, well, I'll go and have a bit of a natter. Cheer her up. She should know she has friends in her time of trouble.' Then, turning to the children, 'I'll fetch a bag or two of chips back wi' me, eh? How would that be? And a nice bit of haddock. But only if you two 'as washed behind yer ears and have got into yer jammies by the time I gets back.'

'Ooh, yes, yes!' cried the children, jumping up and down with excitement, then charged out, racing each other to the bathroom. They didn't have a bathroom at number 32, so this was still something of a treat.

Lucy followed them at a slower pace, going through the nightly ritual of scrubbing mucky knees with a stiff loofah, inspecting ears and brushing hair, in a somewhat distracted frame of mind.

She was filled with guilt over this latest quarrel between herself and Polly, but why couldn't Mam just leave well alone? Why did she always have to stick her oar in? Lucy was half listening with some trepidation for the sound of Minnie's returning footsteps, fearing a heavier tread on the stair. Surely Tom wouldn't be so stupid as to attempt to break into Minnie's house? Though so far as he was concerned it was Michael's, and if he thought she was here alone, might that not drive him to some reckless act?

Sean, sucking his thumb, asked, 'Where's me dad then? Is he coming to stop at Aunt Minnie's an' all?'

'No, love. We're having a bit of a holiday on us own for a change.' She removed the thumb. 'Come on, you can eat your chips in bed if you like. I'll read you a story till Minnie gets back.'

This proposal went down well but once installed in the brass bed, which sagged alarmingly in the middle, Sarah Jane peered over the high rail to consider the gloomy room with its heavy mahogany furniture and the shadows that lurked in corners and flickered across the high ceiling from the night light on the bedside table. It looked big enough to house an army. 'Have we to sleep here with you every night?' There wasn't even a jerry under the bed, she'd noticed, because of the bathroom next door. Sarah Jane didn't much fancy the idea of trekking across the landing if she needed to go during the night.

Lucy thought of all the empty bedrooms in the old house and spoke without thinking, as if unwilling to acknowledge that she'd made a decision. 'No, you don't, love. You can both choose a room of your own tomorrow afternoon when you get back from school. Nice small cosy ones. How would that be?'

'Ooh, *yes, yes!*' the children squealed with excitement,

bouncing up and down on the feather mattress with delight at this unexpected turn of events. Life seemed full of them at the moment.

If only everyone could be so easily pleased, Lucy thought, then stifling a sigh, cuddled her beloved children warmly beside her and began to read 'The Three Little Pigs' in hopes of a good night's sleep ahead. But the calm didn't last long. Soon they were all huffing and puffing and rolling about the bed in an ecstasy of giggling hysteria. After that Minnie arrived and was soon doling out chip butties which kept the children quiet for approximately five minutes before they were up and bouncing again on the old sagging bed. Lucy let them play while she and Minnie talked. Life would become serious enough for them soon.

The following morning Lucy took the children back to school at their usual time, making excuses to their teacher that they'd both had colds for all they were positively glowing with health and chattering twenty to the dozen about how they'd moved house and were to have new bedrooms, happen with their own bathroom. On the way back down Lower Byrom Street to Minnie's house, keeping a wary eye open for Tom at every corner, Lucy started to worry over how Minnie would react to a more permanent arrangement, and how she herself could pay for their keep. But before she could open her mouth to ask, Minnie said, 'I've had a word wi' Poll and it's all sorted.'

'What is?'

She set a mug of tea in front of Lucy. 'Eeh, we mek more pots of tea in this house than they do at Lyon's. You're to stop on 'ere.'

'But . . . what happens when the baby comes?'

'We'll cross that bridge when we get to it. See how we get on fost?'

Lucy was so grateful, she wept.

'Nay, don't start skriking, I'll not chuck thee out on t'street yet,' Minnie Hopkins said, thrusting a spanking clean handkerchief brusquely into her hand. 'Anyroad, I'd rattle round this place like a pea on a drum on me own.'

'You could always sell it,' Lucy suggested, wondering for the first time how Minnie came to be living in this grand house, all by herself. 'Buy something smaller.'

'Nay, I'm not allowed to do that. It in't mine, d'you see. But I've the right to live in it, me and Michael, fer the length of my lifetime. After that it goes back into the estate. My former employer was cast out too, by her family, so they get nowt till I'm gone. She left me enough bees 'n' honey to get by, so why not share a bit? Money's med round to go round, eh? That's my motto.' And the old woman actually winked, chortling with delight at the old joke, her toothless mouth a wide open chasm of pink gums.

Lucy gazed in wonder at her one-time employer who had turned into such a treasured friend. 'Minnie,' she said, respect and gratitude warm in her voice, 'what would I do without you?'

Minnie laughed again. 'Tha'd be buggered!'

Hubert was interrogating his son. Ron, however, denied all knowledge of the fire. He was, in fact, stunned by the turn of events, agreeing that although this had been their intention, he hadn't actually got round to making all the necessary arrangements, like laying his hands on a bit of petrol to get it going, for a start.

'Then who did?' Hubert asked, wondering if it could have been an accident after all. Not that he concerned himself too greatly over the matter. Accident or design the fire had served his purpose very nicely, causing Polly Pride to shut up shop and her business to fall neatly into his lap. So pleased with himself was he that he made a date with a young widow he'd met at the auction mart, taking her out for a meal as a special treat, though in a place far removed from the twitching curtains of Castlefield. Not because he was bothered about his wife's sensibilities, but because he really didn't care for any whiff of scandal to affect his business.

She proved to be particularly accommodating, so much so that Hubert didn't get home until the early hours. It was fortunate, he thought, that he and Joanna now occupied separate quarters. Far more convenient. He slipped quietly up the stairs to his own room without hearing a sound

from hers. It made him smile to think of her so innocently
asleep.

The next day he paid a visit to Colin Wilnshaw, his
accountant, who outlined the advantages of this new
acquisition. The debt would not now be paid, admittedly,
but having regained possession of the entire stock of furniture for which he'd paid a mere fraction of what he
charged Polly for it, he'd recoup some of his losses by
selling it himself, though he'd send the rubbish on to other
dealers, of course. It was a pity, the accountant pointed
out, that the looms and carpets had been completely
destroyed. Hubert was also irritated that he hadn't been
able to take over the name of the company, Pride Carpets,
but insisted he wasn't particularly interested in carpets *per
se* and had no use for the warehouse, though the big new
shop would come in handy. Besides which there were
other, more important reasons to be pleased at seeing the
end of the Pride family's business venture. 'They'll never
get it going again, not in a million years.'

Wilnshaw smoothed his chin in a thoughtful gesture
before offering his opinion that a little care should perhaps
be exercised before Hubert attempted to take over any
further enterprises in the near future. 'We can't have you
looking too successful. I mean, we've no wish to arouse
suspicion in bureaucratic quarters, such as the Tax Office
for instance. It might be awkward to arouse their interest
in your affairs.'

Hubert paid lip service to this excellent advice whilst privately keeping his options open. Opportunities, he'd discovered, came when you least expected them and often had to be snatched or lost forever. But he was still puzzled about that fire. If it was arson, why would Polly risk such a thing? She would surely know that it was bound to make her insurance policy void.

The answer was supplied to him a day or two later when he had yet another visitor, one who'd called regularly over recent months, costing Hubert a great deal of money as a result and now claiming credit for the entire shebang. Tom Shackleton calmly informed Hubert that he'd done him a favour in his scheming against the Pride family by bringing the matter to a swift conclusion. He asked for a final payoff, promising that would be the last Hubert heard from him.

'You didn't do it out of the goodness of your heart then?' he dryly remarked, to which Tom merely smiled. 'How do I know that'd be the end of it, if I did pay up?'

Tom shrugged. 'I've lost me wife and family, so why would I want to stop on in Castlefield? I've allus fancied moving on and mean to do so, soon as I've completed one other bit of business. All I need is the wherewithal.' He named a sum which made Hubert wince.

'You set a fire and ask me to pay for it? Don't push it, lad, I'm the one 'oo has to pick up the pieces and mek a go of it. Tha's got some hold over me, I'll admit that, but

440

don't take me for no fool. Anyroad, what other bit of business would this be then?'

'Nothing that need concern you. A domestic matter, you might say.' And again there was that smile which, charming as it might outwardly seem, appeared strangely disconnected from the rest of his face. 'I could allus throw in a bit more information by way of a bonus, so you know yer getting a good deal like,' Tom added.

Hubert's eyes narrowed. 'Meaning what exactly?'

For a moment he didn't speak, but when Hubert walked over to his safe, opened it and took out a metal box, he began to talk fast while his greedy eyes fixed on the crisp notes Hubert was counting. 'I were in Polly's house the other night. Took a shufty at a few papers she'd left lying around while she cooked me a good supper. Very trusting of me is my mother-in-law.'

Hubert was instantly alert as he flicked the notes with his thumb, inches from Tom's nose. 'She's just about used all her spare cash, as you know, from starting the carpet warehouse up again and going into manufacturing. The problems she had with you finished her.'

'I know all of that.' Hubert sounded irritated. 'Get on with it. Have you summat else or not?'

'Only that she took out a mortgage on her house in Pansy Street in order to fit out the shop and come in with you.'

'Normal business practice,' Hubert said, rubbing his

chin between finger and thumb. 'Cheap way of borrowing money. I've done the same myself.'

'And then there was the bank loan. Not huge, you understand, but enough to help tide her over when things got sticky and she found herself over-committed.'

Hubert smiled. 'You mean, when I overstocked her and introduced new rules of play.'

'I wouldn't know any of that but I saw a letter from her bank manager. He's not too happy now and is asking how she means to make the payments. She's got a bit behind, do y'see?' Tom's face was a picture of innocence. 'Not that I would repeat such sensitive information to anyone outside the family, you understand? But then, you are family, are you not? By marriage like.'

'Aye,' Hubert agreed, his tone quietly thoughtful as he counted the notes into the outstretched palm. 'Indeed I am.'

Polly was sitting on a bollard watching the barges load in the canal basin, when Lucy found her. She came to sit beside her on a nearby step and without even glancing up, Polly said, 'Hubert Clarke has won. I've to start all over again, m'cushla, from scratch.'

'I know, Minnie told me last night.' She half glanced back at her newfound friend, who was pretending to feed the pigeons with bits of bread crust, keeping a discreet distance.

'I've lost count of the number of times I've done that already. Remember when I sold every scrap of furniture we had in the house, just to buy second-hand carpet? Yer dad thought I'd run mad, so he did.'

'You were wonderful.'

'I'm not sure I've the energy to start again.'

Moved to tears, Lucy put her arms about her mother and held her close. For all their differences at times, Polly was still her mam and in that moment as they clung to each other they were as one, together again, all differences forgiven and forgotten. They smiled into each other's eyes, mopped up each other's tears, understanding without needing words.

Then Lucy said, ' 'Course you can start again. You can do owt, you. Always have been able to. Isn't that what I love most about you, the way you get up, dust yourself off and bounce right back?'

'Not this time. All me bounce has gone. He's finished me, for sure, sweetheart. Benny's dealing with the legalities of the lease this very minute, but we'll still be liable for the restoration of the warehouse, whether the insurance company pay up or not. It's over, Lucy.'

Keeping one arm about Polly's shoulders, which seemed much too frail and thin, Lucy watched the barge in the cut before her, the mate blowing on his hands this cold frosty morning, having had to put out his fire in the bow as regulations demanded while it slid under the warehouse for loading. How careful everyone had to be to avoid disaster, she thought, just as her lovely mam had always been with the oily waste. Why would it suddenly burst into flame?

'Has anyone discovered what started the fire?' she asked, but Polly shook her head. A tear splashed on to her arm and Lucy wiped it away with one finger. 'What about our Benny? I suppose he was no help either.'

'He's been marvellous so he has,' Polly was saying, and wondered if she really was nodding her head or whether it was just the tremors of shock which had shaken her body on and off for days now. 'I don't know what I would've done without him.'

To Lucy's sharp ears, Polly sounded defeated, as if every ounce of her once formidable energy had indeed evaporated and she had no resources left, which in truth Lucy didn't wonder at. Her own opinion of her brother was far less charitable. Hadn't Polly always spoiled him? 'If it hadn't been for Benny, Mam, you'd never have got involved with Hubert Clarke in the first place.'

'Aw, don't blame him. He's worked like a Trojan, so he has. Didn't he only want the best for his little family? Where's the crime in that?' True she would never have needed to borrow money from the bank to buy stock, nor been at the mercy of Hubert Clarke's unscrupulous business practices if her son hadn't asked her to go in with him. And she'd have been spared a great deal of worry. But what was done was done and couldn't be changed, so why fret over it?

Lucy pointed out that Benny had always shown a tendency to be careless. 'Look at the way he lost Big Flo,' she reminded Polly who, surprisingly, laughed as she hugged Lucy close.

'Nobody could control that old woman. What a character! Had a mind of her own and a will power second to none, so she did.'

'But . . .' Lucy caught the expression in Polly's eye and stopped, pursing her lips tightly together as she struggled not to argue that all of this must be Benny's fault; all because of his foolish dreams and the fantasies he used to spin to Belinda, not forgetting his stubborn determination to work for no one but himself. Instead, unwilling to upset the happy rapport she'd at last established with her mother, she grudgingly admitted, 'I suppose he has worked hard, just recently anyway, as well as looking after little Matt.'

'Hey up, t'lad's here now,' Minnie said and Benny came running up Castle Street as if he had a fire on his tail.

'It's the bailiffs,' he shouted. 'They're stripping the house clean.'

Polly was on her feet in a second, rigid with fear. 'Charlie!' she cried, her voice little more than a whisper. Benny grasped her arms, soothing, calming.

'It's all right, don't fret. He's next-door with our Matt.' Then he cast an anguished glance from her to Lucy and back again. 'But they're tekking everything, every stick of furniture we own, and they say they'll have to sell the house if we're to avoid bankruptcy. It's the only way to pay off the bank loan and what's still owed to Hubert.'

Polly didn't wait for any further explanations, she was off, heading in the direction of Pansy Street to save the remnants of her pride. But it was too late. By the time they arrived the last item of furniture was being loaded on to the back of a lorry which drew away, giving a cheeky blast on its horn. Polly might shake her fist at it but that didn't alter the facts. The house was stripped bare, furniture and ornaments gone, even carpets ripped up. Each and every room stood empty, just as if it had been scrubbed clean.

'Sorry, love,' said the bailiff. 'I'll have to ask thee to leave.'

'You can't do this!' Benny yelled, beside himself with fury. Baby Matt, being gently jostled in the arms of Doris-next-door who stood by silently weeping, stretched out his arms to his dad and set up a howl of anguish.

'By heck,' Minnie said, too shocked to find a more appropriate comment as the Pride family filed out again and stood on the street, watching in stunned silence as the man locked the door, pocketed the key and walked off with a sympathetic nod. All that was left was an untidy heap of clothes, a large carpet bag, a few books, papers and other personal possessions, scattered about the paving flags. One or two sympathetic neighbours were gathering them up and putting them into brown paper carrier bags.

'So here we are then,' said Polly at last. 'Right back where we started. With not a scrap to our name.'

Chapter Twenty-six

Charlie was the only one who could offer comfort. He sat next to his wife on the horse hair sofa alternately patting Polly's hand, stroking her shoulder or her hair, and sometimes drying her tears as they fell. 'It'll turn out all right, Poll,' he kept saying, without being able to offer any reason on earth why it should.

They sat in Minnie's front parlour amongst the aspidistra, the whatnots and the overbearing Victorian furniture, heavy curtains blocking out the sun and the measured sound of the grandfather clock loud in their ears. To Polly it seemed to be marking out the final moments of her youth. From now on she would be an old woman with no future left to her. No warehouse to go to each day, no money to her name, not even a home to call her own. Twenty years ago or less she would have rolled up her sleeves and started again without a second thought. With youth and energy, most of all belief in herself, she'd always felt she could achieve anything.

But where was all that now? Vanished in the pall of smoke that still hung over the embers of Pride Carpets.

'We're finished,' she said again, as if by repeating this fact she might drum the awful reality into her head.

Lucy glared across at Benny, sitting with his head in his hands in the far corner of the room. 'See what you've brought us to.'

'No, no,' Polly said, shaking her head. 'Don't start on at him, Lucy. Hasn't he only done what he thought best for us all? And for that little treasure.' She smiled softly at her grandson who was sitting on Minnie's rug chewing on a crust. Recognising his nanna's smile he grinned back at her, showing two white teeth, and offered her a bite. Polly pretended to take one and the baby chuckled, hiding the crust behind his back.

'What are you accusing me of anyroad?' Benny wanted to know. 'Of wanting to mek me way in t'world? Of being a man? Of trying to addle enough brass to bring up me son? I mean, you could go so far as to say if only I'd never met Belinda — 'cause that's what set it all off — but I for one don't wish that, not for a minute.'

'Aw, no, bless her sweet nature, me neither,' Polly said, putting a hand to her mouth to stop fresh tears. Minnie handed her a handkerchief which she took without a word or even realising who had given it to her.

Lucy, ashamed suddenly of where her accusations had

led, said, 'I'm sorry Benny. I never meant it that way. Belinda was my very best friend. We all loved her. I wish she were here now, alive and well.' Lucy took the handkerchief from Polly and blew her nose upon it as her own tears spilled over. 'Instead the poor love died in that dreadful way because a no-hoper like Percy Sympkin, your odious landlord, wouldn't give you time to pay the rent arrears.'

Polly was nodding sadly. 'Aye, for all our Benny had finally been accepted by Belinda's family and had hopes of a brighter future. A tragic irony, eh?'

It was as if a light had suddenly been switched on in Lucy's head. As if everything had become crystal clear. This was no fault of Benny's. None at all. This whole thing had been planned from the start, and the loss of Belinda, Hubert's own daughter, had been little more than an irritation to him, an inconvenience rather than a tragic loss, serving only to fuel his jealousy and greed still further.

'Mam,' she said, her voice dropping to a low pitch of wonder at this new realisation, 'you're right. This is none of our Benny's making.'

'I'm glad you see sense at last,' he said, still sounding aggrieved.

'None of it is. Hubert Clarke engineered all of it from the minute he discovered Mam had a profitable little business. Once he knew she owned Pride Carpets, he started to put the squeeze on so's he could get his hands on it.

What he didn't bargain for was Belinda standing by you. He knew she was used to an easy life and solid middle-class comforts. He expected her to come running home the minute money got tight, then he could put an end to the marriage and Mam's business in one fell swoop. After she died, he continued with his nasty little plan, out of revenge, but he'd have done it anyway.'

Shocked glances were exchanged all round.

'By heck, you're right,' Benny said. 'He wouldn't give me the time of day in the beginning, then suddenly, for no reason, his attitude changed.'

Lucy was nodding. 'That must've been when he realised he could do himself a good turn by fattening his own profits while he bled us dry.'

Benny's mouth had gone dry as ashes. 'And Belinda? Are yer saying it were Hubert Clarke 'oo had us turned out?'

Polly let out a gasp while Charlie said, 'Surely not?'

'Yes, I am. Belinda loved you too much to go running home, Benny. She'd been bullied by her father all her life and she meant to stand by you; protect the man she loved from the one who'd denied her love all her life. Sadly, she was the one who suffered most from his diabolical plan. I can't prove it but I reckon if you put the squeeze on Percy Sympkin, he'd squeal loud and clear that the eviction was not his idea.'

'Christ! Then Hubert was responsible for his own daughter's death?'

'Yes, I believe so.'

For several long moments there was no sound in the room but that of the clock ticking solemnly. Then from deep within its mechanism came a low tone that lifted to a steady whirring and finally counted out the hour in ten doleful notes. As the last echo died away it seemed to stir the occupants of the shadowy room back to life, though it was Lucy who best expressed their feelings.

'I reckon it's time we fought back for Belinda, don't you? Time for the last battle.'

Polly looked at her usually placid daughter, eyebrows raised in mild surprise. 'Is this my quiet little Lucy talking, who usually has no other thought in her head than what's on at the pictures or what colour lipstick she should wear?'

Lucy flushed, with embarrassment as much as annoyance since there was some truth in the accusation. 'One minute you complain I'm too rebellious, the next I'm too quiet. Whichever, I'm not stupid.'

The teasing smile faded. 'So yer serious about all of this?'

'I am indeed.'

Benny was on his feet, red-brown hair tousled from the constant tugging of his fingers, round face a mask of pain. 'Aye, our Luce is right. It's long past time we started to be a bit less *nice* – or fair. Time we were a bit sharper on the uptake like. And time we stuck together instead of falling out between ourselves.'

'Aye, the lad speaks sense,' Minnie chipped in, unable to keep quiet any longer for all it was family business. 'If you ask me, 'im as did this needs to be taught a lesson, hoist by his own petard as it were. And I reckon I know how.' All eyes were upon her, mesmerised, as she continued. 'Everyone has some sort of weakness, an Achilles heel or some such, a secret they'd much rather keep hidden. Even Councillor Hubert Clarke.'

Polly was staring at Minnie in surprise, coming slowly to life at this sign of new support. 'That's true.'

'Theer must be summat he dun't want folk to know.'

'Indeed there must.'

'Well then,' Minnie said, 'all we need do is find out what it is.'

Benny's persistence finally paid off and Percy Sympkin not only squealed but wept with regret by the time he'd done with him. Benny picked him up by his coat collar and hung him on a hook in his own front hall by which time he was only too ready to confess that it was Councillor Hubert Clarke who'd forced him to evict the young couple, adding the further information that it had also been Benny's father-in-law who'd made sure that, by pulling in a few favours owed him, Benny never got his allocation licence. Young Ron had drummed up the petition signed against him from all those owing Hubert money. They did it to buy themselves a bit more time, and who could blame them? By the time Benny had heard the end of this sorry tale, he was purple with rage and flexing so many formidable muscles that Percy was snivellingly keen to turn the tables on his former persecutor who now seemed chicken feed by comparison.

Benny unhooked him, stood him up straight and gently dusted down his rumpled suit. 'Get me summat on him, Percy lad. Owt. I don't care what it is. Choose 'ow, I mean to 'ave him. There must be summat as Councillor Clarke doesn't want bruited about?'

It took Percy no time at all to come back to Benny with the results of his enquiries. There was snow in the air, cold enough to freeze even the mucky waters when they met late one night by the old Roman fort down by the Rochdale canal, a place where a discussion could generally take place without fear of interruption, or not until the pubs loosed anyroad. The old stones had probably heard many more secrets than these two were about to spill.

The information came free and gratis, Percy hastily assured Benny. 'Glad to help lad. Your Belinda were a right little treasure. Lovely lass.'

'Get on with it, you smarmy toad,' Benny growled, and so eager was Percy to help, he barely drew breath for twenty long minutes. Apparently Councillor Hubert Clarke was up to his neck in black marketeering.

'He's involved in that much funny business, stuff he doesn't want the authorities to know about, I'm hard pressed to know where to begin,' Percy explained. It seemed Hubert bought goods strictly for cash with nothing in writing and sold on at one hundred per cent mark-up, sometimes twice that. 'Other stuff he hardly pays anything at all for. Them chairs he sold to Polly were a case in point. He got them for almost nowt as bankrupt stock and charged her the earth for them. He also has a nifty habit of invoicing a shop for stuff that never does get delivered, or so one of his van drivers says.'

Then it wasn't a case of their own careless paperwork; they really were defrauded of stock they'd paid for, Benny thought, his rage deepening.

'Sometimes he buys stock in what he calls a ring, where he bids at auction but only against dealers who've agreed to drop out, so nobody pays too much for an item. They sort it all out between them, who's having what, before the auction even starts. Sometimes its new, bankrupt stock, sometimes second-hand. He doesn't trouble too much what he buys so long as it's cheap and he can sell it on to some poor fool who pays through the nose for it.'

'Someone like us?'

'Aye,' Percy agreed. 'And the poor buggers who pay Ron shilling by shilling each and every week, knowing they'll never get to the end of their debt.'

There was a great deal more of this and by the time Percy was finished, Benny was spitting mad with fury. How could he have been such a gullible fool? His former land-lord tucked a grubby muffler about his neck and rubbed his hands together to aid circulation. 'I saw another friend o' thine t'other day – Michael Hopkins.'

'He's no friend of mine,' Benny growled, for he didn't in the least approve of Lucy's walking out on her husband, though he did sometimes feel a tug of conscience that he'd never mentioned that odd conversation he'd once had with Tom. He'd put it from his mind, deciding the man was a bit sick in the head and probably couldn't properly remember what he'd been doing these last years, or where he'd been. War did that to a bloke. Anyroad, Luce had no right to be gallivanting with her fancy man, not while she was still married to her husband. All the same he was curious to hear about Michael Hopkins, and listened to what Percy had to say.

As the two men went their separate ways with a nod and a hand shake, Benny was satisfied that it'd been a most useful half hour. He'd discovered more about his father-in-law than he'd ever have imagined possible. He'd also learned that Joanna was not half so loyal as Hubert imagined. She had indeed spent much of the war keeping the soldiers and sailors happy, but not simply by knitting balaclavas. He took this nugget of information directly to Polly and together with Lucy, Minnie and Charlie, held what might be termed a Council of War.

*

It was agreed that Lucy's task would be to discover more about the goings on of Joanna Clarke. 'If she has a few grudges of her own against Hubert,' Lucy said, 'she might be glad to help. Particularly when she learns what really happened to Belinda.'

Benny readily volunteered to keep an eye on Ron, smiling at Polly's caution to 'go easy on him'.

'Don't worry. There are other possibilities I need to follow up first,' he told her, which he wasn't yet ready to divulge to anyone.

As well as investigating ways of getting the business going again, they were all given their separate jobs.

Charlie, with less pain thanks to the new pills he was on, opted to hold the fort at Minnie's house, keep an eye on the children when necessary and provide meals for them all. This was where they were all now living since where else could they go? Polly said she was lucky to have such a good friend as Minnie who was prepared to take her family in when she hadn't a penny to pay for their keep. 'It wasn't as if we were ever particularly close, you and me,' she said, trying to find the right words to thank Minnie for her generosity. 'But don't you always manage to be there when one of us needs you? I do appreciate that, to be sure.'

'I thowt of leaving you out on t'street and giving you a bit o' brick to lay thee head on, but then I thought, happen not. Waste of a good Accrington brick,' chortled the old woman, her cackling laughter making her false teeth click louder than ever.

For all Minnie's generosity everyone knew it was going to be hard. With no business and therefore no income coming in, they would all need to find new jobs which, for Polly and Charlie in particular, wouldn't be easy. Being poor was bad enough when you were young; in middle age, Polly said, it didn't bear thinking about.

'What we need do is to scupper Hubert, then happen we'll manage to salvage summat from the mire,' Minnie kept reminding them.

It was to be Polly and Minnie who would set in motion the method by which they would achieve this seemingly impossible task and hopefully win back some of the money he'd so artfully stolen from them. They weren't sure of all the details and implications yet but the intention was to find a way to let him know that at some location, still to be agreed, there were goods for sale at a bargain price, strictly cash, no questions asked.

Minnie volunteered to act as decoy, since she was very nearly sure that he didn't know her well enough to recognise her. Even if he did, she argued, he'd no reason to suppose she was friendly with the family from Pride Carpets, but she doubted he'd ever paid much attention to an old woman who lived in a big old terraced house at the end of Pansy Street. 'He might recognise our Michael, if he saw us together, but he's not going to, is he?'

Lucy swallowed the lump which came instantly to her throat at mention of his name, turning her face away so no one would see the flicker of pain that crossed it. She'd had no word from Michael since he left. With each passing week her pregnancy was progressing and he didn't even know about it, let alone the fact that she had, at last, left her husband. Clasping her hands tightly together, she determined to hold fast to her strength and keep hoping that one day, perhaps tomorrow, he would come back for her.

In the meantime, perhaps her own marital problems would at least make it easier to prise some information out of Joanna Clarke. Lucy could certainly sympathise with the woman's need for a lover, for all she didn't care much for her choice. Frank Fenton was young enough to be her son, should in fact have been her son-in-law if Hubert had had his way. Lucy wondered if her husband had any idea about the reality of their friendship and rather doubted he did, since arrogant men such as Hubert Clarke rarely imagined their wives to be capable of asserting themselves, let alone having an affair, for all they subjected them to a miserable existence.

Joanna, however, looked far from miserable when she opened the door to Lucy. She was smiling and dressed in a pretty pink housecoat that had a ruffled collar and hem. She looked the perfect model of a housewife straight from the pages of *Woman*, except she probably wasn't eagerly waiting for her husband to come home. Lucy couldn't help glancing up the stairs behind her, as if half expecting to see lover-boy appear at the top of it.

'Mrs Clarke, I'm Lucy Shackleton, Benny's sister. I wonder if I could have a word?'

Joanna coolly responded that this wasn't possible and would have closed the door in her face had not Lucy managed to get in one more short sentence which included the all important words, 'I think I know why Belinda died.' The door stopped closing upon the instant.

She was shown into the conservatory which apparently was the warmest room in the house, kept heated all year round to nurture Hubert's carnations, which were his pride and joy. The lush greenery and sweet scents of the flowers were almost overpowering.

Joanna brought Lucy a sherry and then excused herself for a moment. She was back within ten minutes or so, dressed in a simple but clearly expensive scarlet wool dress which showed off her elegant figure to perfection; her face a carefully presented picture of cream foundation, powder and a matching bright red lipstick. As she drifted by, Lucy caught the scent of Californian Poppy, which was almost too cloying in the sickly sweet room. Joanna arranged herself delicately in a wicker chair and reached for her sherry. 'What do you have to say about my daughter? I hope you aren't here to make trouble or reopen old wounds, Mrs Shackleton. My family has suffered enough.'

'So's mine as it happens,' Lucy said, and launched straight into her tale, keeping strictly to the facts which she delivered as bluntly and smartly as she could. Then she sat back and waited with some trepidation for a reaction.

Joanna responded by saying, 'I know all of this. Frank discovered it for me.'

Lucy's mouth dropped open but she quickly closed it again, remembering to mind her manners as Polly had instructed her. 'You *know* that your husband was responsible for Belinda's death, and yet you have said nothing?'

'*Indirectly* responsible. He didn't personally kick her out on the streets. It was a mix-up, a mistake.'

'Oh, I see. It was meant to be my brother, was it? It would've been all right for him to be chucked out, I suppose. 'Course Benny wasn't pregnant, true, but you obviously had no qualms over making him homeless. But didn't either of you stop to think for one minute that Belinda might insist on staying on with him, through thick and thin as it were?'

And now Joanna did begin to look agitated, clasping and unclasping her hands, darting anxious glances anywhere rather than meet Lucy's accusing eyes. 'I do assure you that I knew nothing of this at the time, nothing. It was only after — after Belinda had died that I learned the truth of it. I wouldn't have wanted anything serious to happen to Benny, truly I wouldn't. *I just wanted Belinda to come home!*'

It was very much a cry from the heart yet Lucy felt nothing but contempt for the woman, and immense pity for her friend. Poor Belinda, no wonder she was eager to run straight into Benny's arms when he obviously worshipped the ground she walked on, no matter if he was a dreamer. She'd probably have done anything to escape her dreadful parents. Their utter selfishness left Lucy gasping, not to mention appreciating her own mam and Charlie a bit more.

'But she didn't come home, did she? Would never have done so.'

Joanna shook her head, a sad little gesture which should have been heartrending yet somehow left her beautiful face unmoved. 'No. Belinda always had a strong will, but then she got that from Hubert. Whatever he sets his heart on, he doesn't stop till he gets it.'

'We've discovered that much,' Lucy dryly commented, then as if to escape the claustrophobia of her situation got up and began to prowl about the conservatory, fingering leaves, smelling sickly sweet flowers which somehow reminded her of graveyards, so she sat down again. 'Did you never think to curb it, this determination of your husband's to have his own way in everything? Did you never try to put your daughter's happiness first?'

It was Joanna now who got up to stand with arms wrapped tightly about herself and gaze out through misted glass on to a dull grey winter's day, almost as if she were viewing a world she was no part of. She looked like an exotic flower held fast in a tropical paradise. 'There's something you should understand about me, Mrs Shackleton. I loved my daughter. If I was inadequate as a mother, she accepted that. We were never, how shall I put it, a particularly demonstrative family. She led her life and I led mine. We agreed to differ for much of the time. Occasionally I would attempt to . . .' here she paused, drew in a deep breath, '. . . yes, I shall say it, I attempted to civilise her, and curb her foolish rebellions.'

Lucy almost laughed out loud as she got up again and went to stand beside Joanna. 'That's rich, that is. You thought *Belinda* needed civilising? Not yourself or Hubert — just Belinda?'

'She tended to go to extremes, just to annoy us. Like joining the *army*, for goodness' sake. All on a reckless whim of rebellion to score a point over Hubert. I couldn't let her ruin her life out of stubbornness.'

'You don't think she might genuinely have wanted to go into the army? And really loved our Benny.'

Joanna looked confused, as if these thoughts had never truly occurred to her before. 'Sounds rather monstrous put so bluntly but, no, I never did consider that for a moment. I did everything I could to persuade her from marrying him.'

'Even though you were sleeping with the man your husband wanted for her?'

'Frank was no more than a mild amusement. I would've given him up for Belinda.'

'Generous of you.' Lucy had heard enough. If she stayed another minute listening to this selfish woman, she might spew up at her feet. She half turned to go but Joanna caught her arm.

'Never underestimate my husband, not for a moment. I may be weak and foolish but he's utterly ruthless when it comes to getting his own way, particularly in business matters. He trusts no one save for his accountant, Colin Wilnshaw, who makes sure he doesn't pay a penny more than he should in tax. Hubert's made a fortune because he's a man of considerable acumen and courage, always ahead of the market. You have to admire him for that, though it isn't the only reason I stay with him – for all I've threatened to leave him often enough when he's too blatant over his women friends.'

'Women friends?'

'Someone called Myra is the most recent mistress, from Slate Wharf, would you believe? Though she may be history now. Dear Hubert has learned to be more discreet over the years and we rub along rather well, in fact.' Lucy didn't wonder at it. Joanna's explanation of how she enjoyed the comforts her husband provided had unfortunately revealed nothing Lucy didn't already know. 'We've developed a way of life which suits us well,' she finished, smiling brightly, almost as if the loss of a daughter was merely an unfortunate consequence of a business undertaking gone wrong. Lucy felt physically sick.

'As for Frank Fenton, I'm afraid the poor boy became increasingly dependent upon me, particularly when Belinda refused to marry him, and then when she died . . . Well, I shall let him down lightly.' And the smile became less fixed, the beautiful mouth curling delightfully at the corners, like a woman with a secret. Lucy wondered if there was another candidate already waiting in the wings. Depressingly, Joanna Clarke gave no indication of considering herself a wife scorned, or one eagerly awaiting an opportunity to put the dagger in.

Lucy grabbed for the door handle, suddenly anxious to quit the suffocating heat of this rarefied existence. 'I won't waste any more of your time. There's clearly nothing I can tell you that you don't already know.' Yet despite, or perhaps because of her failure to learn anything herself from Joanna, Lucy paused at the door, the words almost bursting out of her. 'But I'll have you know that you can't play with folk's lives the way your husband does without creating havoc. Apart from ruining my mam's business and leaving her homeless and jobless with a sick husband to care for, there's no doubt in any of our minds that if Hubert hadn't interfered, Belinda would've been alive today. Benny would have got his allocation licence from the Board of Trade, tried and probably failed with his joinering, and then gone in with Mam, as he'd always wanted to do deep down. The only problems they ever had were those caused by your husband which, in my view, is disgusting. You'd think a father would want his daughter to be happy, even if it did cut across his own plans for her. And she at least would have been alive, well and happy.'

Joanna's beautiful face had become ashen, her lips thin and trembling. 'That's absolute nonsense! Hubert wasn't responsible for Belinda having a difficult birth. She might still have died, even if she'd had the baby inside the flat and not in a back street.'

Lucy almost sneered. 'You hang on to that thought, love. It might be the only comfort you have in a lonely old age.' And she escaped into the cold street to draw in a thankful gasp of coal-tainted fresh air which at least had the benefit of being honest muck, she thought, as she headed for home.

Chapter Twenty-seven

It was agreed that a casual meeting in the Queen's on Gartside Street was the best way to arouse Hubert's interest, since it wasn't a pub where Minnie was known, and the beer was good, not watered down in any way. Even so some doubt was expressed as to whether Minnie could carry it off, until they saw her dressed for the part.

She looked entirely different, which of course was the whole idea. Having delved into her old employer's trunks and boxes kept in the loft, Minnie had decked herself out in a grey sealskin coat that didn't smell too strongly of moth balls and a pair of well-polished court shoes made of finest Italian leather. A shiny black straw hat with a figured veil and a coiled velvet rose sat on top of her smartly rolled bangs and she sported matching gloves and a large black leather handbag. Instead of her usual thick lisle stockings, she wore a pair of purest pale silk which made her skinny legs look like sticks of coltsfoot rock.

The finishing touch was a fox stole which she clipped about her shoulders, the mouth of the stuffed animal opening to bite on its own tail.

'By heck. Yer a right bobby dazzler,' Benny chortled, impressed by the startling change in her.

'Aye, till I open me mouth,' Minnie ruefully admitted. 'Eeh, I'll go to th'end of our yard, I'll have a job on, carrying this off.'

'Just soften those broad vowels a bit,' Polly suggested with a grin. 'There's no harm in being a Lancashire lass, just sound like a richer one, that's all.'

'Aye, I mun try to hemulate the grand tones of my lady employer,' she said. 'How happy hi am to make your acquaintance.' Overdoing it to such an extent that they all fell about laughing. But the laughter quickly subsided for this was serious, if not dangerous, business. Minnie had every intention of taking Hubert for every penny she could.

They went carefully over the plan in fine detail, leaving nothing to chance, and finally decided that some trust would need to be established between them. Funded by Minnie's savings, Polly bought a consignment of three dozen pairs of leather gloves, fleecy lined, in tan, black and mustard pig skin. They cost seven shillings a pair wholesale to sell at eleven shillings and sixpence, but Minnie suggested they ask five bob, so as to prove their worth as suppliers. They'd make a loss, to be sure, but this part of the operation was viewed as an investment in future deals.

A brief note was sent to Hubert to the effect that if he came to the Queen's tomorrow night at eight he might hear of a bit of business to his advantage. In point of fact he was there ten minutes early and Minnie was the one to keep him waiting. Stricken with nerves, she proceeded into the snug and deposited a box containing a few samples of the gloves on the table in front of him. She was sure that he would notice her hands trembling as she untied the string to let him examine the contents. Minnie didn't even dare glance up to meet the glowering expression of suspicion she knew would be on his face. Nevertheless she could almost hear his brain ticking up profits when she told him the price she wanted for them, and what he could ask from his own customers. No doubt he would add a shilling a pair at least to her suggestion.

To her vast relief the deal was struck in less time than it took to shake a dog's tail as she later told her admiring band of fellow conspirators. Bolstered by success, Minnie was airily promising him she'd keep an eye open for other bargains for him in the future; that she rather thought she might have a very special consignment coming up soon. In the meantime, would he be interested in a dozen or so felt hats? He would, a deal was struck, and she promised to include them with the gloves. (Once she'd run round to Lewis's and bought them, of course.)

'He's sending a van round tomorrow evening sharp at

seven. You did manage to rent a bit of a warehouse, eh Pol?' Polly had, though only for the day, again with money loaned by Minnie. If the plan didn't work, she would be forever in her friend's debt.

Ron arrived on the dot to take possession of the goods and, as agreed, Minnie was there to greet him, still resplendent in her sealskin coat and shiny black straw. As soon as he handed over the cash, she proceeded to count it before handing over the parcels: 'So's he don't tek me for a fool,' as she later explained. Satisfied, she gave the nod for him to start loading the van with the boxes of hats and leather gloves, and within minutes he was slamming shut the doors and on his way. Then Minnie locked up, taking care to change back into her own clothes before scurrying back home to Pansy Street.

Questions were thrown at her thick and fast the minute she walked in the door of number 179. 'Did he fall for it? Was all the money there? Did Ron suspect anything?' Dim as he was he might just have recognised her but no, Minnie assured them, everything had gone smoothly.

'Right,' said Polly. 'Stage two.'

Over the next few weeks they bought and sold several more small consignments of goods to Hubert and he proclaimed himself well pleased. 'No wonder,' Minnie said. 'Robbing meself, I am.' Not once did he ask any questions about where she lived or how she'd come to hear of him.

Quietly, and without fuss, she built up an excellent working relationship with him, for all she expected at any moment for Hubert to guess who she really was and not the Violet Davenport she purported to be — a name so far removed from Minnie's own it made her quake to think of it, let alone use it.

They then decided to do nothing for a week or two, observing with interest as Hubert looked in at the pub on their regular night and seemed disappointed to find Minnie not there.

'Right,' said Polly. 'It's time.'

Discreet enquiries by Charlie among contacts he had in Liverpool led them to a supplier of wholesale jewellery, which they thought far enough from Castlefield to ensure complete secrecy. Polly then bought the finest man's watch she could find, one which had a Swiss movement and a good leather strap, together with a matching lady's model. She also purchased a beautiful double row of pearls, very reminiscent of the Queen's wedding gift to Princess Elizabeth. The pearls cost a good deal of money and everyone admired them with something like awe. 'If the greedy tyke's eyes don't light up when he spots these, we're sunk,' she admitted.

No one thought this likely. Hubert was ever on the look out for a new opportunity and Polly was sure he wouldn't be averse to moving a bit upmarket. There were plenty of women with money burning holes in their pockets, now the war was well and truly behind them and with the promise of affluence in the years ahead. The difficulties would come if he started asking how Minnie came by this jewellery in the first place, so a story had to be concocted and memorised by the old woman. Finally she was word perfect and vowing she'd already got him eating out of her hand. Soon she'd snap his head right off.

'Well, just make sure you keep your teeth in,' Lucy warned.

Tom was running out of patience. He'd waited day after day to get Lucy on her own but the only time he ever spotted her was out with Benny or her mam. They'd suddenly become bosom pals, much to his disgust. She hadn't even been collecting the childer from school, lazy tyke, but leaving it to Charlie to hobble up the street leaning on his stick, poor blighter.

One of these days, when he got tired of waiting, he might take a stroll up to the school himself, see if he could persuade the teacher to let him take the kids out early, before Charlie arrived. After all, they were his childer. That'd fetch her running smart enough, if he had the kids. Tom smiled to himself. He'd more power than she realised. He just hadn't chosen to exercise it yet. He was too interested in watching the activity that was going on, trying to work out what they were up to.

When he'd decided to come back to dear old Blighty,

he'd thought he'd be on easy street. He expected to fall back into a job, have a wife eager to do his bidding and children to play at his feet and make him a happy man. Instead there were no decent jobs to be had, save for working for peanuts for his mother-in-law which didn't appeal one bit. That was finished now, of course, but it was doubtful whether it would ever have got any better despite her big talk and ambitions. Serve her right to be brought down in the world a peg or two. He'd suffered, so why shouldn't they have a taste of it too? They'd had it easy long enough.

He was sitting in the Queen's on Gartside Street, since his credit was all used up at the Dog and Duck, enjoying a pint on the slate and wondering if he dare ask for another the same way or whether he should risk cash. He did have some money in his pocket but was reluctant to part with it. He was still pondering this vital matter when Hubert Clarke walked in. It wasn't often you saw him in here, so Tom watched with interest as the councillor bought himself a double whisky and found a quiet corner away from the darts players and the domino brigade. A matter of moments later a second person came in, one who excited some interest for all a respectful silence fell, for surely here was money all togged out in sealskin and shiny straw? The woman looked oddly familiar though he couldn't quite place her so Tom splashed out on another gill and, keeping well back in his own corner, continued to pay close attention, his interest sharpened when she calmly walked over, bold as you please and seated herself opposite Hubert.

The two appeared to be in deep conversation for several moments, the woman sipping occasionally at a sweet sherry Hubert had procured for her. Then she seemed to shake her head, clip a dreadful fox fur stole in place about her shoulders and, chin set in stubborn determination, walked from the pub. Tom was instantly torn. Should he follow her, see where she went and what she was up to? Or stay here and watch Hubert Clarke? It was all most tantalising.

The decision was made for him when Hubert himself got up and without a glance at those about him, briskly followed the woman. Just before the door swung to, Tom caught a glimpse of the pair of them standing talking on the pavement before turning and walking away together out of sight.

He downed his beer, slammed down the glass, snatched up his cap and followed. Something was going on and he meant to find out what it was.

Minnie led the way along the street with trepidation in her heart, still fearful of discovery. Hubert had been seriously interested in the watches, she could tell, particularly when she'd told him she had a hundred of each to offer, exactly the same. And she'd seen how his eyes had lit up at sight of the pearls. A sticky moment came when he balked at the price and interrogated her on the source of her supply. She'd turned huffy, saying she had to respect confidences as she was sure he understood. If he wasn't interested he needn't bother, there were plenty of others who were, and she'd walked out, wondering if she'd blown the whole enterprise. Now here he was, asking her not to be too hasty, to give him another chance. She could only suppose that because of those earlier successes, he was willing to trust her and deal again.

So here they were, concluding this piece of sensitive business standing outside some solicitor's house on the corner of Gartside Street. Seemed appropriate somehow.

'It's cash on the nail, you understand,' Minnie emphasised, looking him square in the eye so he knew she wasn't one to mess with. She also explained she'd prefer it if the goods were collected later in the evening. 'P'rhaps around nine tomorrow night?' She very nearly slipped up and pronounced the word 'neet'. It'd been Benny's idea to arrange a later collection. By that time there would be fewer people about and it would be darker and more difficult to see what was in the boxes if Ron decided to open one. Even so, it would be risky. This time Hubert would be getting nothing but rubbish for his brass. Minnie felt the strain beginning to tell on her and wouldn't she be glad when she could peel off her stockings and soak her sore feet in a bowl of salts? These fancy shoes were killing her.

'It shall be arranged,' Hubert agreed, and smiled his most charming smile which almost made her shudder, though she managed to respond in kind.

'Tomorrow at nine then? Your son will fetch the van to our warehouse, as before?'

Hubert agreed that he would. Minnie nodded. They shook hands on the deal and she departed, a sprightly spring in her step which gave the lie both to her sixty-four years and her aching feet.

It was a crisp cold night down by the canal the following evening, a strong smell of tar in the air and the sound of a ship's hooter echoing somewhere in the distance. Beneath the railway arches a match flared, briefly illuminating the man's face as he lit a cigarette. He made no attempt to move from his hiding place, which offered an unhindered view of the road leading to where he'd seen the woman go. Knowing it to be a cul-de-sac, he was quite certain he wouldn't miss anyone calling to see her, nor her own return trip home. He cupped the cigarette in his hand, to hide its telltale glow and settled down for a long wait.

At the end of the cul-de-sac, by the rented warehouse, Minnie waited, heart in her mouth, ears attuned for the sound of a van's engine. Somewhere deep in the shadows she knew Benny lay hidden, just in case there was trouble. He wouldn't show himself unless absolutely necessary but just knowing he was there gave her confidence. She still wore the sealskin coat but had opted for a more workaday hat in the shape of a black felt and dispensed with the fox fur stole as not quite appropriate for the occasion. What she dreaded most was Hubert himself turning up. Ron would no doubt take whatever she offered him without question but Hubert . . . She'd taken some precautions against that unwelcome scenario, but would they be enough?

Minnie sat plaiting her fingers, peering out from time to time into the darkness, lit only by a single light bulb over the warehouse door. Somewhere out in the ink-black night, she heard a sound which made her jump with nerves before realising it was merely the scrape of a barge against the canal wall as it slipped out into the canal.

''Asta heard owt yet?' she hissed into the darkness, worried that her poor hearing might have let her down, and was loudly shushed. Biting her lip, Minnie waited and waited. Nine o'clock came and went and still there was no sign. By quarter past she was wishing she'd brought those pills the doctor had given her for her blood pressure. By half-past she was feeling quite sick and ready to give up. He wasn't coming. He'd cottoned on to their little scheme. 'Eeh, heck, this is a rum do,' she moaned, half to herself. She was, in her own words, all of a-flunter by the time she made out the reassuring sound of a van reversing up the narrow alley to the warehouse door. It's black silhouette emerged slowly out of the night mists, halted, and then the driver's door was pushed open and a figure emerged, boots scraping on the slippery setts.

'Evening, Violet. Thought I'd do this trip meself.' The familiarity jolted her even as her heart sank with misgiving. It was Hubert himself, just as she'd feared. 'Come inside,' she bravely offered, and her voice sounded surprisingly calm, even cheerful. 'Take a nip to warm yourself while my men load up.' This was her main defence strategy, so as Minnie preceded him into the cavernous warehouse, she sent up a silent prayer that he would follow.

'I won't say no.'

What it was they talked of in the confines of that hired office she was never afterwards to recall, but it took two whiskies and a good deal of banter before there was a tap on the door and she was able to tell him that the van was ready.

'It's been a pleasure doing business with you,' Hubert told her, feeling benevolent as his stomach warmed to the spirits.

Minnie could hardly wait to get him out of the door but gave no sign of it as she smiled benignly up at him, nodding pleasantly. 'You have the cash?'

'Indeed. Indeed.' He handed her a large parcel which she ripped open. Heart pounding, she flicked the notes casually with her thumb.

'Aren't you going to count it?' She knew she should but that would take time and the notes all looked satisfyingly present and correct. Besides, instinct told her that if she showed no trust in him, he would respond in kind and insist on her opening up the boxes of pearls and watches Benny had just loaded on to the van. Instead she shoved the packet into the depths of her leather handbag.

'I'm sure you and I have no reason not to trust each other, Hubert,' she said, refilling his glass. 'Since we're aiming to do more business in the future.'

'I'll drink to that, and to more good profits.' Minnie was relieved to see him down this third tot in one, though how he would see to drive after so much lubrication she really couldn't imagine. Not that she cared if he ended up in the drink. The money was in her bag and tucked firmly under her arm. Still he lingered, gazing down upon her with a frown that could only be described as curious.

'How did you get into this business?' he enquired. 'Woman of your class, I mean.'

Thankful she hadn't consumed as much alcohol as he, which meant her brain could still register, Minnie told her well-rehearsed and heartrending tale of first losing a husband, who'd gone down with his ship, and then her entire family, including two sons, when a bomb flattened her house. 'So I must make my own way in the world, as most of us have to these days, Hubert,' she said with a rueful smile.

He shook his head sadly, making the usual remarks about the pointlessness of war – which sounded odd coming from one who'd made a small fortune from it.

'You're still an attractive woman, Violet. Let's drink to a new future for you, a new love in your life.' And again she was compelled to refill his glass though her heart was beating so loudly she was sure he must hear it. When this had gone the way of the first three and still he made no move but stood, swaying slightly, a vague smile upon his bewhiskered face, it was Minnie who pulled open the door, with just a hint of desperation in the gesture. 'I'll see you out,' she encouraged, but Hubert politely and punctiliously insisted he could find his own way.

'It's bitter out there. You don't want to catch your death, Violet.'

She continued smiling as he tipped his hat to her and took his leave. Then Minnie's shaking legs finally gave way and she sat down abruptly upon a handy orange box.

Benny was at her side within seconds and together they counted the money, relieved to find it was correct to the last shilling. Minnie prudently changed out of her 'disguise' and locked the door of the warehouse. A figure drew back into the shadows as she emerged from the end of the cul-de-sac, drawing her shawl over her head, with Benny half a step behind her. After no more than a brief glance about them, the pair walked away at speed beneath the bridge and, engrossed in their own excited whispers, neither noticed the soft sounds of footsteps fall into place behind them.

Polly was relieved when they both arrived back safe and sound, if slightly out of breath. The incriminating items of clothing were stowed away back in the loft, wrapped in newspaper and stuffed to the bottom of the chest from whence they had come, never again to see the light of day if Minnie had any say in the matter.

'And that's the last anyone will see of Violet Davenport,' she finished with no small sense of relief.

It had been a good night's work, they all agreed, and the bundle of notes felt satisfyingly thick in Polly's hands. 'Nowhere near enough to buy back everything we've lost but it will at least help to get the business going again, once I've paid back what I owe you, Minnie. I still have the name Pride Carpets, since I managed not to go bankrupt, and the cleaning contracts from the big hotels. They'll give their contracts back to us as soon as I get the machines up and running, I'm sure.' She heard Benny's groan and smilingly told him that, no, she didn't intend just to stick to carpet cleaning but it was a start, was it not?

Benny, buoyed up by the success of the night's scheming, pulled a cheeky face at her, saying he'd make sure that's all it was. But, as agreed, the very next morning he set out to visit every single hotel and boarding house in Manchester and district. It took him several days, and when he was done he returned with the promise of several orders for lengths of new carpet as well as repeat cleaning contracts.

He slapped the orders down on Minnie's kitchen table. 'You'd best keep that warehouse on, Mam. We're going to be busy.'

They all showed their surprise and due appreciation of Benny's efforts but Polly expressed reservations. 'If we start throwing money about, taking on premises, buying or hiring machines too soon, won't Hubert smell a rat? Won't he guess that it was us who stung him?'

'Does it matter?' Lucy wanted to know.

'It does, aye,' Minnie put in, feeling suddenly hot under the collar at what Hubert might do if he ever found out who'd set him up. 'He's not a man to cross, isn't our Hubert. Let's hang fire a bit, eh? Then happen you'd consider a new partner for Pride Carpets, Polly, when you do get going again.'

She frowned. 'Who?'

'Me. You don't have to pay me back. Think of it as an investment. As a matter of fact I could put in a bit more, match what you won off Hubert, pound for pound. I'm warm wi' brass, tha knows. I were left quite comfortable by my lady employer and it's built up over the years.'

Polly was smiling long before she'd finished talking. 'Welcome aboard,' she said, and would have hugged the old woman had Minnie not waved her off, claiming she didn't hold with such soft nonsense and offered Polly a pear drop instead.

*

The silence from Councillor Hubert Clarke was disturbing. Benny prowled high and low but no word reached him on the streets of Hubert having been stung for a lot of money for watches and jewellery that had turned out to be not half as good as he'd expected. He hadn't even found Ron. 'We've hit him in his pocket, where it hurts most, and he's that mad he's keeping the shame of it to hissel'. He must be livid that he didn't think to check every box before he left. But then, he never let us check stock in advance either, did he?'

Polly said, 'He rarely waited for us even to order it. Wouldn't he just land it on us without a by-your-leave and then refuse to take it back?'

'But we've only wounded him,' Benny moaned. 'He'll recover, drat him.'

This thought sobered them all, then Lucy remembered something. 'He doesn't like paying tax. Joanna Clarke told me so.'

Polly said, 'Nobody likes paying taxes, m'cushla.'

'No, but we pay them though, all the same. How do we know Hubert does? He pays cash for goods, with no invoices. So how can anyone prove what he's bought where, or from whom? Certainly not the tax people and Hubert isn't going to tell them, is he? Joanna said he had an accountant, a Colin Wilnshaw, and it was his task to make sure that Hubert paid as little tax as possible. He also has a woman friend, Myra somebody or other, who lives near . . .' Her mind went blank. 'Oh, lord, I can't remember.'

'Try. Think hard.' They were all keenly interested now, sitting on the edges of their seats. If Hubert was evading taxes, then they might have a stronger weapon over him than they'd ever dreamed possible.

'Slate Wharf.'

Chapter Twenty-eight

It took surprisingly little effort to persuade young Ron
that it was long past time for him to seek his fortune elsewhere. Benny marvelled at his own self-restraint as he
placed the rail ticket in Ron's grimy paw and personally
escorted him to Liverpool Road Station. The ticket was to
London, one way, and in a fit of generosity Benny gave
Ron a fiver to help him on his way.

He even extracted from him a telling amount of information on what he was responsible for, and what he wasn't.

It was amazing really how grateful the little weasel was
as Benny stood on the platform and watched him climb
aboard. Anyone would think he'd expected much worse
from his sister's widowed husband. He even managed a
cheery wave as the train shunted out of the station. Benny
went straight to the Gents to wash his hands the minute
the train had vanished in a cloud of blue smoke.

His next call was upon Myra who seemed only too

willing to allow him into her home, simply because she liked the look of him: big brawny sort of a chap, young, good-looking, and with masculinity oozing from every pore was the way she'd describe him. Benny couldn't help but smile at her teasing. No wonder Hubert had found her fascinating. She was still attractive and alluring for all she was well over the hill in Benny's opinion. She coyly informed him that he was exactly the sort of feller she wouldn't mind seeing a bit more of, and despite their thirty-year age difference, she wasn't joking.

The cramped parlour into which he was shown, with its shaded pink lamps, cherub statuettes and *chaise-longue* draped in some sort of animal fur, made him feel slightly nauseous. Benny accepted the drink she offered him but left it untouched on a marble-topped table.

He wondered how to set about the task, whether to be upfront and honest or side-track the issue by asking her about friends in high places, hoping to find out something that way. In the event she forestalled him by seeming to guess what it was he required.

'You're Belinda's chap, aren't you?' she asked, bright blue eyes moist with sympathy. 'She were a lovely lass. Not appreciated by that queer family of hers but, though we never met, I liked and admired her.'

Benny felt a lump come to his throat and it took several moments before he could respond. He still ached for his wife. There wasn't a moment in his day when he didn't miss her. Sometimes the pain was so bad he thought he'd go mad. At other times, he was aware of her presence and it comforted him.

'I loved her very much,' he told Myra. 'I'd've done owt to save her.'

'I dare say you would, lad. I told Hubert no good would come of trying to evict the pair of you, but would he listen?' Myra snorted her disgust then sipped at a violent green liqueur. 'Always thought he knew best, did our Hubert. I've seen him only once or twice since she — since you lost your lovely lass, but it weren't the same. I couldn't feel for a man who was so hard on his daughter. I've three children of me own, so I know what I'm talking about. There's nothing more precious.' She stood up and swept an armful of photographs from the mantelpiece to show Benny. He dutifully admired her son, her two daughters and several grandchildren, a family in whom she showed a proper pride.

'You're not still with him then?'

'By heck, no. Heartless old sod! I hope he gets what he deserves.' It was all plain sailing after that. Myra gave him facts and figures, dates, companies Hubert had deliberately made insolvent, even the combination of the safe where he kept the ill-gotten gains the tax man didn't know of, and which was in his study at Potato Wharf. Myra knew all of this because Hubert was apparently loquacious in his cups. And plainly indiscreet.

'Some pillow talk that must have been,' Benny laughed as he later related this tale to the others.

Minnie's eyes gleamed while Lucy simply remarked, 'We've got him.'

It was the more practical Polly who said, 'Fetch pen and paper, Minnie. We've a letter to write. We'll address it "To whom it may concern" and begin "With reference to the business affairs of Councillor Hubert Clarke . . ."'

Tom arrived at the school early, as he'd promised himself that he would. The children's teacher was uncertain at first about letting them go but when he pointed out that they both had a dental appointment, she relented. Attention to hygiene had always been one of Miss Bell's hobby horses and, really, the school dental service left a great deal to be desired. She applauded Mr Shackleton for his care, but then hadn't he suffered himself in the war so was it any wonder he wished to spare his children the agony of the school dentist?

Sean was so excited when he saw his dad that he didn't notice his sister's more reticent attitude. 'Have you come to take us back to Minnie's?' she asked in her quiet little voice, so like Lucy's own.

'No, yer mam's asked me to fetch you home wi' me. She's already there, mekking yer tea.'

'Sausages?' Sean wanted to know, bouncing up and down. 'Are we having sausages?' But Sarah Jane still felt unsure and began to back away, saying she'd left her lunch box in her desk. She felt a sudden urge to see that someone in authority, even Miss Bell, her teacher whom she didn't usually care for much at all, knew she wasn't really going to a dentist at all, or even to Minnie Hopkins's house for that matter, but back home with her dad. It somehow seemed terribly important.

'Don't be so daft,' Tom said, taking a firm hold of her arm. 'You won't need it.'

'I will. To put me lunch in ready for tomorrer.'

'We can find you another box,' he insisted, and maintained his grip on both children, as he marched them out of the school yard and through a maze of streets in the direction of Liverpool Road.

Hubert moved restlessly about his beloved conservatory, pinching out carnations in an effort to calm himself. He couldn't recall ever feeling more angry in his entire life. The heat of his fury blurred his vision and left him gasping for breath. Reaching into the pocket of his waistcoat, he took out one of his pills, the tightness in his chest having worsened for some days now, ever since he'd carried all those dratted boxes out of the van. From time to time he rubbed his arms which were aching badly, wishing he'd made Ron do the job, then he'd have someone other than himself to blame. But the boy seemed to have vanished off the face of the earth. Hubert hoped he was out collecting money. They'd need every penny after what he'd lost the other night.

He knew when he'd been had, and he knew by whom. Trouble was, he couldn't prove it.

When he'd opened the boxes of watches the following morning, rather late admittedly, due to his thick head, he'd stared in disbelief at the rusting, misshapen bits of metal that passed for watches and for which he'd paid well over the odds in the mistaken belief he was buying top-notch merchandise. As for the pearls . . . Wear them in a rain shower and he suspected they'd instantly lose their sheen and turn back into the cheap paste they undoubtedly were. They might actually dissolve.

No doubt about it, he'd been done good and proper. Polly Pride and her contemptible family had taken their revenge.

The moment he'd realised, he'd stormed back into the house, red in the face and raging against injustice, shouting for Ron and vowing he'd see the whole lot of them at the bottom of the cut sooner than let them get away with it. Joanna had been so alarmed by the noise he was making she'd come running from the kitchen, insisting he tell her what was wrong, and Hubert had blurted out the whole sorry tale.

But had she shown him the proper sympathy he deserved? Had she heck-as-like. She'd put back her head and laughed. It had been the most unladylike sound to come out of her mouth in a long while, not to mention the most disrespectful.

Now, several days later, and still with no sign of their stupid son, she stood with her arms folded and informed him she was taking a leaf out of Polly's book, and Benny's, by starting again. 'You remember Benny? He was married to our daughter once. Lovely boy, had we but realised it. Bit of a rough diamond but he'll go far, I'm sure. I can tell that he's already making good progress, despite a few unexpected setbacks at the start.' Her blue eyes, so like Belinda's, were sparkling with delight as if entranced by her own wit.

'What in damnation are you talking about, woman?' And Hubert demanded to know where his breakfast was as he'd telephone calls to make, business matters to arrange, a counterattack to plan. Joanna was in a mood over summat he could tell, though what exactly he couldn't imagine, but she brought him a pot of coffee and a round of toast, as he'd known she would.

'You going out?' he enquired, without much curiosity as he fleetingly scanned her attire of smart green coat and hat which he didn't recall having seen before. But then, what his wife did with her time was largely irrelevant to him.

'Sorry, darling, but you'll have to get your own breakfast in future. I'm off. I'll send someone round for my luggage later. Oh, I almost forgot, this morning's post.' And she handed him a large brown envelope which he scarcely glanced at as she floated a kiss upon his brow.

'Luggage? What luggage? Off where?' And as she swept out through the door he could have sworn she said she was running off with Colin Wilnshaw, but that couldn't be right, could it? Colin was his accountant and absolutely essential to the security of Hubert's affairs.

It was then that the telephone rang. Hubert snatched it up and listened in silence to the voice at the other end for some minutes before slamming down the receiver and at once starting to dial. 'Get me Wilnshaw,' he barked at the unfortunate secretary who answered.

'I'm afraid he isn't in, sir,' she replied in a quavering voice which, to his horror, sounded close to tears, for she had instantly recognised Councillor Clarke's unmistakable tones. 'He appears to have gone.'

'*Gone?* Gone *where?* What are you prattling on about, woman?'

'He's left his wife and family, left the firm, taken everything and g-gone. Vanished. There's not a thing of value left in the safe.' And now she did burst into noisy blubbering tears but Hubert was no longer listening. He was tearing open the brown envelope which bore an official stamp, and roaring with rage at its contents before charging out of the house.

The man turned up his coat collar so that it almost met the brim of his trilby hat. Keeping as inconspicuous as possible beside the lamp post, he smiled to himself as he watched the Wolseley roar into the yard and skid to a halt. He'd already seen the two officials go inside and guessed it meant they didn't bring glad tidings of great joy for the occupant of this particular warehouse on Potato Wharf.

The family had done well. Their plan, whatever it might have been, seemed to be working. Hubert Clarke, he suspected, was about to get his just desserts, and not before time. He'd never seen Clarke in such a rage as when he'd stumbled out of the car, slamming the door far harder than usual and storming into his warehouse.

As the man turned to leave, still smiling and longing to know the full details which his observations, no matter how painstaking, had failed fully to ascertain, he saw another figure emerge from a nearby alley. Tom Shackleton. The last piece of the jigsaw. He'd know him anywhere. And with him were Sarah Jane and Sean. More worryingly, both the children looked bewildered and Sean as if he'd been crying. As Tom hustled them towards the canal basin and across the foot bridge, the man slipped quietly out after them.

It was while Lucy was sitting in Minnie's front parlour, wondering why Charlie hadn't appeared with the children yet, that the door knocker rattled. This couldn't be them. They'd charge straight in. Who could it be? Not Lily Gantry with more bad news, she hoped. She really wasn't up to that old troublemaker, not today with all this business over Hubert going on.

Polly had sent the letter days ago, since when she and Benny had lurked beneath the railway arches, keeping a watch on Potato Wharf in case the inspectors came. Lucy felt sick with nervousness. Hubert Clarke, as Minnie so frequently reminded them, wasn't an easy man to cross. But as she went down the lobby, Lucy glimpsed a uniform through the glass of the vestibule door. She opened it to find not one but two very official-looking soldiers in full dress uniform. They looked exceedingly smart with their brass buttons, chevrons glowing white, and red caps on their heads.

On seeing her they both saluted, then one stepped forward and handed her a paper. It identified them as Military Police, though Lucy had already guessed as much.

'Would you know the whereabouts of one Private Tom Shackleton? We understand he used to live in this street, ma'am, and, according to our information, has unexpectedly returned home. We very much wish to question him. Looks as though he's been AWOL.'

'AWOL?'

'Absent without leave, ma'am. He's a deserter.' The man's voice was unemotional, official.

Somehow Lucy managed to step back from the door. 'There must be some mistake. I think you'd best come in.'

As they followed her into the small front parlour, Lucy

found she was shaking. She would have liked to have sat down but it didn't seem quite the thing to do, so she stood facing them, feeling confused and helpless, while the two MPs proceeded to explain they'd been given information that Tom had been hiding in Spain for some years.

'Spain? Don't you mean Italy? He was in Germany for a long time, as a prisoner-of-war,' she corrected, though with no real conviction in her voice.

'Sorry to contradict, ma'am, but according to our source, he left Italy long before the war ended.' And they went on to question her, asking for details of where Tom might be now.

Before she had time to gather her wits the door burst open and Charlie came hobbling along the passage. Lucy could guess by his expression what had happened, even before he got a word out to tell her. He was beside himself with worry and by the time he'd told his tale about the missing children there wasn't a stain of colour in Lucy's ashen face. 'I must go to him. Get them back.' She was halfway to the door when one of the MPs stopped her.

'If he's got his back to the wall, he could prove dangerous.'

'They're my kids. And Tom is my husband.'

'And our prisoner. Besides, I wouldn't be too sure about that. According to our information, he married a young woman out there, a Spanish *señorita.*'

Lucy felt her whole face grow stiff with shock.

'Married? How can he have married? He already is married, to me.' She felt bewildered, unable to take in what was happening.

The MPs dropped their official stance and for the first time looked shame-faced, apologising for bringing her such bad news. 'We have to take him in for questioning, love. Sorry.'

Lucy drew in a deep, steadying breath, realising they were only trying to do their job. 'He won't hurt the children, or me, if I go to him. Maybe I can persuade him to give himself up. Let me try. It'll surely make it better for you, and him too, I should think.'

The MPs conferred but finally agreed to let her try on the grounds that it would indeed go better for Tom at the Court Martial if he surrendered of his own free will.

'Thank you.'

'But we'll be outside. Watching,' they said. 'Give us a shout and we'll be there in a jiffy.'

Lucy saw Sean first. He was sitting on a chair by the fire sucking his thumb. She could see no sign of Tom. When the little boy spotted her through the back window he had the sense not to jump from his seat, simply removed the thumb and grinned at her, then nudged Sarah Jane with his foot. Lucy saw her daughter was curled up on the rug and her heart leapt to her throat. Had she been hurt? Why was she lying like that? But Sarah Jane sat up and stretched, rubbing her eyes, making it clear she'd only been asleep. Lucy put her finger to her lips to urge them both to keep quiet as she let herself in through the back door. Within seconds her children were in her arms and she was asking them if they were all right.

'Didn't I tell you Mam would be home soon?' Sean said, not understanding.

Sarah Jane seemed more aware of what was really happening. She half glanced over her shoulder, then grasping her mother's arm, thrust her towards the back door. 'Let's go to Minnie's. Quick, before . . .'

'Before what, Sarah Jane? You weren't thinking of going anywhere without me, were you?' A voice from the lobby door stopped them all in their tracks. Lucy spun about to face Tom and gasped when she saw him. In his hand was a gun, the German Luger she'd once caught a glimpse of in his drawer and dismissed as a product of her vivid imagination. Now here she was, looking down the barrel of it. Time seemed to slow, to stretch endlessly as a sense of utter disbelief swamped her. This surely couldn't be happening?

'Tom? What are you doing?' Her voice sounded calmer than she felt. 'Why don't you put that thing down. You wouldn't want to hurt Sean or Sarah Jane, now would you?'

'I'm aiming it at you, Lucy, not the children. Can't you tell?'

She moved her lips, stiff with fear, into what must be a

parody of a smile. 'Yes, 'course I do. I do see that I've hurt you, Tom.'

'Yes, you've hurt me. You're the guilty party. Not these innocent children. Isn't that right?' And when she didn't immediately answer, he repeated the question, only louder. '*Isn't that right?*' Making them all jump and Sean at last realise all was not well with his dad. He started to cry.

'Hush, sweetheart, it's all right. Yes, if you say so, Tom. But let me send the children out, so we can talk this thing . . .' She got no further as he suddenly yelled at her to be quiet.

'*Don't tell me what to do!* I'm in charge here. I'm the one with the blasted weapon. Can't you see it?' He was shaking the gun now, waving it about in front of her face, and Sean stared at it, wide-eyed with horror.

'Don't you 'urt my mam,' the little boy bravely shouted, and Lucy hushed him again, anxious he shouldn't irritate Tom into some reckless act. This was the last thing she'd expected. Yet Lucy realised now that she should have been alert to the possibility. She'd underestimated Tom for too long. She should have protected her children better.

'Let Sean go. He's just a baby. Let him go. Sarah Jane too.'

'And have them fetch help? Think I'm stupid? Once you have the children back, you'll run off with that fancy man of yours. I know what you're up to, Lucy. I've seen all the toing and froing. Knew summat were up. I've been watching. Seen him hanging about by the wharf.'

'Who? Michael?' Hope leapt in her but Tom only laughed.

'That got you going, eh?' And it quickly died again. She tried desperately to make her brain work, to think, to plan, to decide what she ought to do. Should she tell him about the MPs waiting outside for her signal? If she shouted, could they break in before he fired the gun? Or should she keep on talking and smiling and hoping for the best? While she was still desperately trying to make up her mind, Tom stretched out his hand and, flicking a finger, said, 'Come here, son. Come and stand by me.' And before she could make a move to stop him, Sean had done so, apparently mesmerised by the chill command in his father's voice. Tom grasped the boy and held him close to his side, oblivious to his noisy crying. Lucy thought, Dear lord, surely they can hear him outside? Why didn't someone help her?

Now Tom was beckoning to Sarah Jane, ordering her to come to him quickly before he lost his temper good and proper.

Swallowing her fear, Lucy took a tight hold of Sarah Jane's hand and pushed her behind her own back. 'No, you're not having her.' And lifting her chin she braved the furious anger that twisted Tom's face into something utterly unrecognisable. 'Listen to me, Tom. I'm not going anywhere.'

'You will, though. Everyone leaves me. Francesca left me for her old lover, just as you're doing.'

Lucy froze. So that was her name. It didn't seem the moment to accuse him of bigamy. 'It's not true, Tom. I haven't seen Michael in – oh, I don't know – ages. Not since before the fire, in fact.'

'I don't believe you,' he barked at her. 'You *lie, lie, lie* all the time, just to serve your own evil purposes.'

This seemed rich, coming from the smoothest liar of all, but Lucy had the good sense not to say so. 'Don't shout, Tom, please. You're frightening the children. Anyroad, it'll do no good, love,' she gently urged him, using her most cajoling tones. She let go of Sarah Jane's hand. Pushed her further away. Took a step closer to Tom. 'It's all over. Give me the gun before you hurt our lovely kids. You know you'd be heartbroken if you did anything to harm them.'

'It's *you* I mean to harm.'

'No, I don't think so, Tom. You've had a bad war, I accept that. Now it's all over. They've come for you. The MPs, I mean. It'll be much easier if you give yourself up. Don't make it any worse.' She held her breath, wondering if she'd done the right thing to warn him as he stared at her in silence, and Lucy could have sworn there were tears as well as panic in his eyes. A flicker of hope rose in her breast, quickly quenched by his next words.

'The fighting at Salerno was a mess,' he told her, his

voice scathing, filled with brash arrogance as if entirely unconcerned by the fact that the truth of his inauspicious war career had at last been revealed. 'A combination of mud and military bungling. I wasn't hanging around just to get shot or die of disease. I escaped through Greece, across North Africa and have been living all nice and cosy in Spain ever since. Then Francesca left me, stupid bitch. Went back to Diego. Not that I really cared, you understand. I was getting bored with her in any case.' Spoken with a touch of his old bravado. 'So I decided to come home to you, Lucy. That you were worth the risk of coming back here.'

'You mean, you couldn't think of anywhere else to go?' she responded, the first hint of bitterness in her tone. Tom was quick to respond.

'No, it's true. I did miss you. But I only intended stopping around long enough to persuade you to come somewhere fresh, start a new life some place. America mebbe. Or Australia. Except you were hooked up with this Hopkins chap.'

'I'm sorry,' Lucy said, though she wasn't at all.

'Now I suppose bloody Benny's grassed on me?'

'Benny? What does he know about any of this?'

'Only what I told him. And he promised to keep his bleedin' mouth shut.'

Lucy decided to pursue this matter later and again held out her hand. 'Please, it's over now. Give me the gun.' It was almost there, almost within her grasp, when there was a loud crack. Then every door seemed to burst open at once and the room was suddenly filled with people, Benny and Michael coming from one direction at the back and the MPs from the front. It was several long moments of pandemonium before Lucy realised that the gun had been fired.

A pair of handcuffs was being slipped on to her unprotesting husband's wrists. Words were spoken, informing him of his rights and where he would be taken. Tom was shouting, 'I'll get you for this! Shooting yer bleedin' mouth off.'

'You're wrong,' the MP informed him. 'It wasn't your brother-in-law. It was someone else who says you set fire to a warehouse, thereby adding arson to the charges you face. We'll be investigating the matter fully, of course.' The two policemen were obviously enjoying themselves.

Tom paled and, switching his attack, said, 'Bloody Hubert Clarke! After all I've done for him. I'll kill him.'

'I don't think so, Private. You'll be tucked away somewhere very safe for quite a long while.'

It was only when Tom was safely shackled that an ashen-faced Benny asked if anyone was going to spare a thought for him. The bullet had nicked his shoulder. One of the MPs gave it a cursory glance and assured him he'd live. When Benny groaned in pain, the policeman laughed and began to strap it up with a scarf, packing it with a tea towel

Lucy brought and promising to drop him off at the hospital on their way back to base.

'Actually it was me. I was the one who shopped you,' Michael said, and smiled with satisfaction as Tom made a lurch towards him, quickly intercepted by the two MPs. 'Benny and I met up some weeks ago and he told me about your lies. Then, when he confirmed that Ron was innocent of arson, we guessed you were responsible for that too. I thought it about time you settled the debt you owe to society, and to Lucy. Soon as I was sure Hubert Clarke was in the bag, I brought in the military.'

Lucy was glaring at her brother. 'You knew Tom lied?'

'Don't be angry, Lucy. He did say summat about Spain once but I felt I shouldn't get involved, because of you and Michael. But then after the fire I saw things a bit different. I'm really sorry, truly I am. You were right all along. Tom Shackleton is bad news and I shouldn't have made any promises to him. That's why I had to come dashing to yer rescue, Luce, like the bleedin' cavalry.'

Her eyes filled with a rush of tears. 'You great soft lump! I could batter your daft brains in, if only you had any.' And putting her arms about Benny's broad shoulders she hugged him, causing him to yowl in protest as she accidentally pressed against his injured shoulder.

'Went all through the war without being wounded and here I am, having pot-shots taken at me in Civvy Street. Don't that tek the biscuit?'

After they'd gone Lucy had to sit down, for her legs had given way at last. She'd wasted all those years waiting for Tom, all that loyalty and sympathy, all that agonising and believing herself still beholden to him; being patient and not wishing to deprive him of his children and a good future with them. She'd thought she was the guilty one, believed so much of what he told her despite her reservations.

And all the time he was a deserter. Not only that, but a bigamist as well.

She put her head in her hands and started to cry. 'Oh, Michael, you were right, I should have left him ages ago. I love you so much, and Tom has told me nothing but lies from start to finish.' And she launched into a flurry of apologies and explanations.

Michael interrupted her. 'Say that again?'

'Tom has . . .'

'No, the other bit, about loving me?'

Lucy looked up and smiled at him, a smile so radiant it lit up her entire face. 'I love you. I love you. *I love you!* There, is that enough?' She could hear the two children giggling, Sean with his hand clapped over his mouth, a picture of glee.

'No, it isn't,' Michael said. 'I want you to say it every day for the rest of our lives together.'

She beamed at him, then kissed him softly on each cheek and after that full on the lips. 'We are going to be together then – for the rest of our lives?'

'I reckon so. Just as soon as that military court has finished with Tom Shackleton, we'll take him to another. Right?'

'It'll be a pleasure. Then I'll say it every day to this little one too, shall I? Our child.'

'Oh, my love.' And his arms came about her and Sarah Jane was wriggling between them, Sean jumping and scrambling into Michael's arms, determined not to be left out of the loving.

'We'll have to take the new baby to see the fireworks,' Sean yelled. Sarah Jane was shouting too in her excitement. 'You promised us, Michael. You did. You did.'

'Well then. I always keep my promises, don't I? It's a date.' And then they were all laughing and hugging, Michael with his arms full of love, for nothing and no one would ever separate them again.